There's only one

MARTINA COLE

IT'S IN THE BLOOD

MARTINA COLE

WITH JACQUI ROSE

LOYALTY

H

HEADLINE

First published in 2023 by
HEADLINE PUBLISHING GROUP

First published in paperback in 2024 by
HEADLINE PUBLISHING GROUP

1

Cataloguing in Publication Data is available from the British Library

ISBN 978 1 4722 4949 4

Offset in 10.44/13.92pt ITC Galliard Std by Jouve (UK), Milton Keynes

Printed and bound in Great Britain by Clays Ltd, Elcograf S.p.A.

Headline's policy is to use papers that are natural, renewable and recyclable
products and made from wood grown in well-managed forests and other
controlled sources. The logging and manufacturing processes are expected
to conform to the environmental regulations of the country of origin.

HEADLINE PUBLISHING GROUP
An Hachette UK Company
Carmelite House
50 Victoria Embankment
London
EC4Y 0DZ

www.headline.co.uk
www.hachette.co.uk

To my latest grandchild – baby David.
Welcome to the family.

Prologue

2007
June

Without the shedding of blood, there is no forgiveness.

Hebrews 9: 22

The screaming coming from down the corridor made Dara Tailor feel physically sick. It was one of the few things she couldn't handle. It brought back too many memories. Not that Dara didn't feel like screaming herself, but she was genuinely afraid that once she started, she might never stop.

She was struggling to stay calm. It surprised her that even after all these years, and after everything she'd been through, she was still capable of feeling fear. God, she hated that. She saw it as a sign of weakness, even if she'd learnt how to hide it well.

Dara looked towards the rusting metal bars across the window. She massaged the back of her neck, the screaming continuing to pierce the air. She'd hoped the couple of lines of coke her brief had given her might've relieved some of the tension. If anything, it had made it worse. How the fuck had it all come down to this? Jesus, how did she get herself into this mess?

Absent-mindedly, she rubbed the tiny scar on her chin from all those years ago. It was a constant reminder that some things could never be forgotten.

Watching the rain trickle down the thickened panes of glass, she swore quietly. She had grown up staring at views like this. Views blocked by bars, behind locked doors. This should really feel like home to her, but instead it petrified her. The last time she'd felt this scared was when she'd been a kid. Dara pushed that thought away. She didn't want to go there. Not today.

Feeling a headache growing behind her eyes, she got up and began to pace. She must have been here most of the morning, and now the waiting was beginning to rattle her.

Taking a deep breath to steady her nerves, Dara caught a glimpse of herself in the mirror. Jesus, she looked a mess. Her hair, usually styled in an immaculate honey-blonde bob, now looked dull with a mass of dark roots starting to show through. She hadn't noticed the lines around her green eyes until now. Everything about her looked worn out. It didn't help that the mirror was made of plastic, giving a distorted reflection of herself. But then, what fucking difference did it make?

'You ready?'

A short, stocky man, dressed in a uniform that was both too big around his waist and too tight around his thighs, stood by the door jangling the ring of keys hanging from his belt.

She answered coldly, 'Why the fuck wouldn't I be?'

He winked at her. 'Oh, I don't know, I mean, if I were in your shoes, sweetheart, I wouldn't be too eager. But then again, it's not me who's up to my eyeballs in shit, is it?'

Dara knew his game, fuckers like him got a buzz out of goading people, but she wasn't going to give him the pleasure. She winked back, making him wait, adjusting the sleeves of her blouse under her jacket before finally following him along the windowless corridor.

Her shoes clicking on the stone floor created an empty echo, and Dara's heart began to race. She suddenly felt cold. She focused on nothing but the back of the man's shiny bald head, concentrating on the rolls of neck fat spilling out over his off-white collar.

At the foot of the wooden stairs, Dara realised she was beginning to shake. But there was no way she was going to let those bastards see how she felt inside.

Dara was determined never to show the way she was *really* feeling. So if they thought she was nothing but a hard-faced cow, then that was all right with her.

Pausing, and holding on to the polished banister for support, she glanced to her side. 'I don't suppose you've got a hip flask hidden in that jacket of yours, have you, mate? I could do with a swig of the hard stuff right now.'

'No, and if I had, I wouldn't give it to scum like you,' he sneered.

Dara stared into his small, piggy black eyes. What a wanker.

Her stare moved up the wooden stairs towards the bright light. This was it. Her stomach churned. Fuck. She closed her eyes. She clenched her fists. Christ, she'd been through worse, much worse. As a kid, she'd made a vow that nothing was going to break her, and she wasn't about to let that happen now, no matter what.

She just had to remember *why* she was doing this. She exhaled slowly, and began to walk up the stairs, deliberately grinding her heel into the man's right foot as she passed him. '*Arsehole.*'

As she reached the top step, Dara could hear the gasp from onlookers in the public gallery. She didn't move. Panic rose up in her. Her eyes roamed the rows of seats. Hostile faces stared back.

'Over here.' She felt her arm being tugged.

'Wait, please.' Her voice was barely a whisper.

Dara continued to look up to the gallery. Where the fuck was she? She'd *promised* she'd be here. Her breath hitched and just as Dara thought she was going to be overwhelmed by panic, she saw her. Sitting at the end of the middle row.

Grace Perry.

Immediately, Dara let out an audible sigh. She swallowed. The tension in her shoulders relaxed. She could do this.

Moving into the dock, she smiled at Grace.

The clerk cleared his throat, stood up from his plastic chair, and began to address her. 'Ms Dara Tailor, you have been charged with a count of murder, contrary to common law. You have also been charged with . . .'

Dara's attention slid away from the clerk's droning voice, and she gave another small smile to Gracie, as she'd always called her. Her and Gracie. They'd had so many dreams together. At one time they'd been inseparable.

A sudden wave of sadness passed through Dara. How could it have got to this? Though maybe this was payback for everything she'd ever done in her life. Her day of reckoning.

'. . . Ms Tailor, I asked you, *how* do you plead?' The clerk's voice broke into Dara's thoughts.

From the dock, she saw the colour drain from Gracie's face. Her wide, frightened stare reminded Dara of the first time they'd met.

'Ms Tailor, you *must* answer. What is your plea?' The judge was staring at her with disdain from underneath his grey bushy eyebrows.

As Dara opened her mouth to speak, memories from all those years ago came flooding into her mind . . .

Book One

1983
Thursday

Hell is empty
And all the devils are here.

William Shakespeare, *The Tempest*,
Act I, Scene ii

Chapter One

As soon as she saw the state of her mum this morning, Dara knew she'd have to bunk off school today. She pulled on a pair of slightly damp jeans and an old grey jumper from the overflowing laundry basket, then grabbed her bag and ran out of the flat. Now, taking a look at the December snow falling, her whole body was trembling, and she couldn't stop her teeth from chattering. She wished she'd put on her coat.

Dara jammed her hands into her pockets, trying to keep her fingers warm. As she wove her way through the busy streets, the sound of traffic was a constant hum. She couldn't remember the last time she'd been anywhere quiet. She was surrounded by noise and chaos. She'd give anything to go on holiday to one of those places in the glossy magazines. Though the likelihood of that ever happening was zilch; the furthest she'd ever been was Brent Cross.

Looking around, she broke into a jog, ignoring the icy pavements. It would take longer to get to the shops today because of an incident at the pub on the Black Prince Road. Her next-door neighbour had been delighted to tell her that the landlord had attacked his wife with a carving knife. Dara guessed he'd finally found out she'd been screwing the Polish guy who lived opposite.

She had to go the long way round, through the estate, being

careful to avoid all the smackheads. She'd already been robbed twice in the last few months.

The last time had been on her birthday. Not that she'd had any money to give them. So they'd forced her to take her baby sister, Rosie, out of the tatty Silver Cross pram social services had given them. Then they'd scarpered with it.

Rosie had screamed her head off. And when they'd got home, her mum had given Dara a battering, and kicked her out for the night. She'd ended up spending her thirteenth birthday alone, curled up in the bin stores, under the block of flats.

Dara knew what everyone on the estate thought of her family. It was no secret that her mum was quite happy to pull her knickers down for the price of a double vodka. The constant flow of punters, plus the noise and arguments coming from their cramped, dirty flat every single night, made everyone in their block hate them. And in turn, Dara hated her mum with a passion.

She wished she could wake up one morning and find her mum had dropped down dead. Just like that. Being Catholic, she always ended up confessing to Father O'Brien. Though if there was one thing her bitch of a mother had taught her, it was that she wanted more in life than the shit she'd been handed.

A black cab sped past, interrupting Dara's thoughts as it showered her with spray from a large puddle of slush. '*Wanker!*' she shouted as she attempted to wipe mud off her top.

Stifling a yawn, Dara hurried along the street. She was knackered. She'd been up all night trying to comfort Rosie, who was not only teething but also running a temperature. And she needed to get back to her as soon as possible. Dara hadn't liked leaving her crying in her cot, but what other choice did she have? The weather was too shit to bring her out, and her mum had been too busy giving some old geezer a blow job in the front room.

Dara strolled into the store on the corner of Kennington Road and Lollard Street. Culture Club was playing on the radio. It was warm inside and she was relieved to get out of the slushy snow.

Feeling her wet sweater stick to her skin, she looked around. The shop was empty and her heart dropped when she saw a skinny security guard with bad skin, watching her like a fucking hawk. Dara had been hoping to see Roger, one of her mum's ex-boyfriends, who lived on the other side of the estate. He spent his entire shift with his eyes down in the *Racing Post*.

Dara started to browse the aisles, trying to look as casual as possible. Through the rows of tinned spaghetti hoops she caught the man watching her. She pretended to be interested in a packet of rice. Why couldn't he just piss off?

By the time the next song had finished playing, she felt like she'd read every single food label in the store. Biting her nails nervously, she scraped the chipped pink varnish off with her front teeth. She really had to get back.

It was already 2.30 p.m. and her mum was as regular as clockwork when it came to wanting her gear. When she needed to score, she became a complete bitch: violent and unpredictable. And even at thirteen, Dara felt it was her job to protect her younger brothers and sisters.

She stared down at her dirty trainers. The snow had seeped through the holes in the soles, and now her toes felt painfully cold. Refusing to cry, Dara felt her hatred towards her mum rise up in her. Everything went on drugs. Every penny her mum earnt went to feed her expensive habit, and if she didn't have enough for a bag, she'd sell anything she could lay her hands on. The few times her mum *was* flush from turning extra tricks, she'd spend it down at the Red Lion, talking shit over a bottle of vodka, rather than buying the things they all needed. Like food.

11

Dara glanced over to the guard again. He was like a dog with a bone, following her up and down the aisles. She moved towards the display of confectionary as a young black couple walked into the shop, chatting away loudly. She noticed the guard's attention turn towards them.

She picked up a packet of Spangles and slipped them into her pocket. She looked behind her, where the guard was busy stalking the couple up and down the alcohol aisle.

Grabbing her chance, Dara snatched a tin of formula milk along with a box of Calpol off the shelf. She shoved them into her bag and headed towards the exit. Keeping her gaze down low, she turned back and pocketed a couple of packets of chocolate buttons. Treats were in short supply in their household.

Striding towards the door, she licked her lips nervously. She didn't want to be caught again for shoplifting. She hated having to steal, but she had no choice. They got milk tokens from the welfare, which were worth a few quid, but her mum either sold them to the neighbours for half price to get cash for gear, or she'd exchange them for cigarettes and cans of lager from the off-licence on the corner.

Rosie often went without. She was too young to drink normal milk, so the bottles Dara nicked off the doorsteps in Ravensdon Street were no good for her.

'Where do you think you're going, you little thief!'

A hand grabbed Dara's shoulder and spun her around roughly.

She stared at the guard's face. Close up, his cheeks were dotted with yellow pus-filled spots. His bad breath made her recoil.

'Get your fucking hands off me, mate.'

'Not until you show me what you've got in that bag of yours.'

She glared into his dark, narrow eyes. 'Piss off, that's my personal property.'

'Then if that's the case, you won't mind showing me, will you? I know your sort,' he sneered at her.

'I said get your fucking hands off me, you cunt.' Panicking as he began to drag her down the aisle, Dara tried to twist out of his grip.

'Oh, no you don't, missy.' He gripped her even harder, wrapping his arm around her chest to pull her along.

'Get off me!' Dara screamed. She bit down on his wrist, sinking her teeth into his skin, drawing blood.

'You stupid little bitch!' He let go and slapped Dara hard across her face.

She staggered back, falling into the display of cornflakes. Her cheek throbbed and she scrambled up, grabbing her bag from the floor. As she ran, she aimed a kick at the glass bottles of pop on the bottom shelf, smashing them into the aisle, in the hope of slowing him down.

She darted for the door, but the guard had other ideas and he tugged her hair, trying to pull her back.

She was too quick for him to get a proper hold. 'Fuck off!' she yelled as she charged out on to Kennington Road, running down the street. At the corner of Black Prince Road, she paused and glanced over her shoulder. Her heart immediately dropped.

The guard was right behind her.

Chapter Two

Frank Baker shivered and wrapped his scarf around his neck. He had on three M&S vests, an oiled wool jumper his wife, Judy, had bought him last Christmas, and a thick green anorak, but he was still fucking freezing. He never used to feel the cold, but now, at the age of fifty-two, it penetrated his very bones. His hands felt like blocks of ice.

Frank knew that operating a JCB excavator wasn't everyone's idea of fun, but it suited him down to the ground. Judy always put it down to *boys and their toys*. But it was the solitude Frank liked.

He was left alone with his thoughts. Thoughts that his Judy would never understand. Thoughts that it was best to keep to himself.

It still irked Frank, what had happened. Some silly bitch he thought he could trust had opened her mouth. When he'd shown Melanie the photographs, she'd pretended she liked them. They'd sat drinking a glass of red together in front of his gas fire, and he'd opened up to her. Telling her things he'd never shared with anyone else. It had excited him, and they'd ended up having rough sex on the kitchen floor.

He really thought he'd found someone who understood him. Yet within a few hours of her leaving his house, the police had turned up. Frank had been dragged out in front of his neighbours, in only his thin pyjamas, another thing he couldn't forgive.

Melanie had been the prosecution's star witness, and Frank had found himself serving six months for possession of indecent images. As sentences went, it could've been worse, but Frank had hated HMP Gartree with a passion. The place had been filthy, full of men who didn't own the most basic fucking manners.

When word had got round about what he'd been up to, his life wasn't worth living. It took two savage beatings and several broken bones before the screws decided to move him into solitary for his own safety.

The only silver lining was he'd met Dennis. Frank had found a kindred spirit in him. Dennis had opened his eyes to things he couldn't have imagined. Even now, when he thought about them, he had to make sure he was on his own because of the way they made him feel.

After being released from Gartree, Frank had packed up and moved down south. The further away from Leicester, the better. He'd got himself a job on a construction site and met his Judy, who'd been working behind the desk of the local Co-op. Within a year they'd got engaged, married, and had two miscarriages. Frank had held her hand throughout, and dabbed her eyes when she'd stayed up all night crying. Twenty years later, he was still there for her. For richer, for poorer, in sickness and in health. Sharing everything . . . well, almost.

Frank smiled to himself. Judy had only ever known him as Frank. He'd never been keen on his old name, Sidney. He'd got used to Frank. It suited him. Gave him a fresh start and a new history. And his dear, sweet Judy was none the wiser.

He gazed out of the cabin window, seeing his breath in the freezing air. The ground was as hard as iron, making it difficult to excavate. Although most of the site had already been stripped of everything. The two old Victorian houses with their high walls had been knocked down. The ivy had been dug out. Even the rats had gone. And Frank felt a sense of satisfaction. Pride almost.

The snow was heavy now and the single wiper was struggling to make any difference. If it carried on like this, he'd have to call it a day. He'd be pleased to get home to a nice hot bath and a cup of tea. The wind blowing off the River Thames made it feel like he was sitting on an iceberg.

As usual, Judy had packed a flask of tomato soup to help him get through the day. Judy, the perfect wife. Caring, loyal, attentive. Happy to overlook that minor indiscretion last year and give him an alibi. Without question.

Frank rotated the shift lever. The digger shuddered forward, and the grab bucket scraped at the earth. Expertly moving the boom around, Frank emptied the soil on the large mound by the boundary line. He was about to reverse and pick up some more soil—

'*Fuck me!*' Frank slammed on the brake and turned off the engine as Jimmy clambered on to the pile of earth in front of him. 'What the fuck are you doing, you dozy cunt? Get out of the way. Have you got a fucking death wish, or something?' Frank hammered his fist on the window.

He'd been doing Judy a favour, bringing her nephew to work with him. Her sister had put the pressure on. Mandy was an interfering cow, and Frank loathed her.

In his opinion, Jimmy was nothing more than a waste of fucking space. The lad was pretty much unemployable because he was a lazy bastard. But Judy adored her younger sister, so pleasing Mandy meant pleasing Judy. And Frank wasn't stupid. He never knew when he might need another favour from his wife.

Lifting up his flat cap, Frank scratched the patch of psoriasis on his scalp. He watched Jimmy stumble and slip on the mound of earth, like riding a giant wave.

Frank rolled his eyes, losing patience. He wrenched the cabin door open in frustration as Jimmy sprinted towards the digger, holding something in his hands.

'Uncle Frank, Uncle Frank!'

He wasn't in the mood for whatever shit Jimmy had to say. 'What the fuck are you playing at? You could have got yourself killed.'

'I've found something, Uncle Frank!' Jimmy panted the words out.

Frank stared at him, remaining silent for a moment. Jimmy was tall and lanky, wearing a red checked lumber jacket several sizes too big for his frame. He had a thick head of shocking-red hair and was so pale he looked positively ill. Probably because he spent most of his time holed up in his room with his nerdy metal-detecting friends, smoking too much weed. He was pathetic. One of life's losers. Frank didn't like company at the best of times, and he certainly didn't like Jimmy's. He decided there and then not to bring Jimmy to work with him tomorrow.

Frank frowned. Another thing he didn't like was guessing games. 'What the fuck are you talking about? Found what?'

Jimmy held up what he'd been carrying. 'It's a bone . . . Look, Uncle Frank.'

Frank had forgotten to bring his glasses with him. He squinted for a moment, then shrugged. 'Animals. It happens all the time when you start digging down into the ground.'

Jimmy shook his head. 'Nah, I don't think so, it's too big . . . and there's more over there. Come and take a look.'

Reluctantly clambering out of the cab, Frank felt the shock wave of sciatica in his leg, and winced, kneading his buttocks. Mumbling to himself, he shoved his frozen hands in his anorak pockets, then hobbled across the length of the site, following Jimmy.

17

'Right here.' Jimmy dropped to his knees and frantically started scraping at the loose soil. 'See. *Look!* And ain't it small, Uncle Frank?'

Frank stared at what Jimmy had pulled up. Even without his glasses it was clear what it was.

'Maybe I should call the police, Uncle Frank?'

'No, no, leave this to me. I'll go and phone them.'

Jimmy's eyes were wide with excitement. 'What are you going to tell them?'

Frank pulled his battered tin of Golden Virginia out of his pocket and began to make a roll-up. 'The truth, of course . . . that we've found human remains, and we think they belong to a child.'

Chapter Three

Alan Carver loved himself. He stared in the mirror, straightened his paisley tie and winked at his reflection. Oh yes, he approved of what he saw. He was a physically big man who liked to preen himself to the point of vanity. His Italian blood gave his skin a healthy glow. He still owned a good head of hair, and Alan even liked the fact it was greying. He thought it made him look distinguished. Important. He wasn't a man to be fucked with.

As for women, well, he'd never had any problems in that department. By the end of any given night, Alan could get the knickers off most of them. Married or single. The way he saw it, the ones who resisted were losing out on a quality piece of dick.

A daily run kept him trim, plus the occasional few rounds in the ring at the Thomas A Becket gym in Bermondsey. As a young man Alan had watched boxing legend Henry Cooper train there, and seen Muhammad Ali and Joe Frazier pop in occasionally for sparring sessions. Alan had envied them all. He'd coveted their lifestyle, the adoration, the money. He'd wanted that power. Because power, to Alan, was more of a turn-on than a long, hard fuck.

Satisfied with his appearance, he walked the length of his private office and snorted two fat lines of cocaine off his new mahogany desk.

He pinched the end of his nose, feeling the burn on the inside of his nostrils. It cut at the back of his throat, and he swallowed, tasting the bitterness of it. Fuck, it was good. It gave him the edge he needed.

Feeling the coke rushing through his bloodstream, Alan stared out of the large window at the snow driving down on to the river. His office was on the top floor of County Hall, the headquarters of the GLC. The building stood defiantly on the South Bank of the River Thames, with a perfect view of the Houses of Parliament. A place where he had aspirations to be. He had made it this far, so why not go for the fucking top?

Thinking about the possibilities gave Alan another rush of pleasure. He shoved his hand down his trousers, pulling out his already erect penis, and with one hand leaning on the window, he began to masturbate vigorously, spreading his legs wide and keeping his eyes locked on Parliament. The real power was in politics.

It was over prematurely as, with a loud groan, Alan climaxed. He wiped the window with a tissue, before throwing it in the bin. Then he zipped up his trousers, shrugged on his suit jacket, and picked up the pile of papers on his desk.

He walked out of his office and strolled down the long hallway. He was only ten minutes late, although that was deliberate. Alan had always liked to keep everyone waiting, no matter who they were: Livingstone, Thatcher, Foot, the Queen Mother, he didn't care. They might be at the top of their game, but he didn't play second fucking fiddle to anyone.

He'd come a long way since the backstreets of Stockwell. Though they weren't memories Alan liked to dwell on. His father had been a miserable cunt who'd spent most of his waking hours with his face buried in a pint of beer. His mum, who'd come from Italy and stayed in London when she'd met his dad, clearly regretted marrying and longed to go back to Italy. She'd taken to her bed one day and never really got up again.

His childhood had been sad and dull. The terraced house they'd lived in was cold and silent. His parents were like strangers to him, and they aspired to nothing. Alan despised them for that fact. He hadn't looked back when he'd left home at sixteen to make his own way in life.

When word had got to him that his mother had died, he'd sent a wreath of lilies and a sympathy card, but hadn't bothered going to the funeral. And on the day his father had been buried, he went for a massage in Soho.

Alan flung open the double doors, and strode into the Council Chamber at the heart of County Hall. This was his arena, and each time he entered he got a fucking hard-on. He smirked as he saw the other members of his team sit up straight.

'Apologies for the late arrival,' Alan boomed, enjoying the sound of his own voice echoing around the chamber. Throwing down his papers on the table, he looked at the sea of faces. He liked the fact that his reputation preceded him, and it was a fucking formidable one at that. He didn't suffer fools lightly, in fact, he didn't suffer fools at all.

He'd been in the town planning department at the GLC for the past few years, and never in his life had he known such a bunch of fucking pricks. Looking around, he decided that by the end of the year, none of them would have jobs. He needed people who had balls of fucking steel, who'd stand up to the bitch of a prime minister who seemed intent on destroying the country. Thatcher needed to be brought down a peg or two. Make that three.

Alan sniffed loudly, tasting the remnants of the coke at the back of his throat. With his customary arrogance he launched into the speech his assistant had written for him.

'The rejuvenation projects in the city are something I am proud of. I think it's fair to say, London is not only the envy of Britain, but of Europe. We are doing more, investing more, caring more, than any other city, but that doesn't mean we should ever be complacent. Unlike the Conservative Party, who have their own agenda, this is not about us, this is about the people out there.'

Alan pointed dramatically to the window, savouring the murmur of agreement. 'Every family, every person, every child, deserves decent housing, a decent quality of living. We are—'

The double wooden doors to Alan's left creaked noisily open. All eyes turned towards the sound.

Reenie, his loyal and discreet secretary, stood in the doorway, looking uncomfortable. Alan glared. Stupid bitch, her timing couldn't have been any worse. He'd had them hanging on his every word. What the fuck did she want?

Reenie nervously patted her mop of blonde hair as she looked at him shyly with her piercing-blue eyes. Her figure had seen one too many cream doughnuts from the canteen, but Alan reckoned she'd been a decent enough fuck. At the time, it had seemed like the perfect way to conduct a job interview. Not so much the casting couch, more the political one.

Reenie gave him a small wave, which only irritated Alan more.

'*What?*' he mouthed to her silently.

Reenie tottered in her high heels down the stairs to the main floor of the chamber.

'Excuse me, sir . . .' She gave a nervous smile. 'I'm so sorry to disturb you.'

Alan leant into her ear, whispering, very aware of the silence in the room. 'It's a bit fucking late now, Reenie. Are you taking the piss?'

'Sorry, no, I—'

'This better be good,' he snapped, interrupting her.

'I realise this isn't ideal timing, sir, but there's a telephone call for you.'

Still with his face near her ear, and almost overpowered by the smell of her lavender perfume, Alan growled, 'And it couldn't have fucking waited?'

'He insisted it was urgent.'

'Who did? What the fuck are you talking about, woman? Spit it out.'

'Frank Baker, sir. I told him you were in a conference, but he wouldn't have it. He insisted. He started shouting down the phone . . . He needs to speak to you urgently. He says he's found something you'll want to hear about . . .'

Chapter Four

Jason and Jake Wakeman strolled into the Rose and Crown as if they owned the place. The Wakeman twins had been coming here for years, and before them, it had been their father and grandfather who'd frequented the pub.

For as far back as anyone could remember, the Wakeman family had been a tight, organised crime syndicate. A few years ago, the twins had branched out on their own. Soon their reputation was harder and more fearsome than any of the previous generations. An air of menace followed them like a bad stench.

The mere sight of Jason and Jake walking into the pub made the other punters sit up. Most of the regulars were faces, past and present, with their own histories of brutal violence. A ripple of unease spread. No one wanted the brothers' attention on them.

Jason nodded a greeting as he strode towards the bar. Nothing much had changed about the whole place since he was a kid. The same wood-panelled walls were adorned with photographs of Victorian London. The floorboards were always highly polished, and the open fireplace stood opposite a bar lined with hand-painted ceramic casks and craft beer pumps. It was somewhere the Wakeman twins didn't need to watch their backs.

'Now what can I get you, darlings? Your usual?' Dolly Daniels winked at them.

She had worked behind the bar for the past twenty years, and had known the boys since they were small, but she was still wary of them, especially Jason. There was something unhinged about him. He was a nasty, sadistic bastard who'd taken to violence as a duck takes to water. He was thirsty for it.

Dolly forced a smile and stared into Jason's dark green eyes, thinking how cold and empty they were. A dead man would have more emotion in his eyes than Jason did.

'I'll have my usual, thanks, Doll.' Jason grinned back at her.

Being twins, though not identical, they were as handsome as each other, and they knew it. But it was only Jason who was arrogant about his chiselled, magazine-cover good looks.

Jake sported a long scar down his right cheek. An injury which Dolly knew had cut deep for many reasons.

Leaning on the bar, Jason looked around. He ran his fingers through his thick black hair, making a mental note of who was in the boozer. Only regular punters entered the Rose and Crown. It was where conversations were had, away from the Old Bill, and where deals and money exchanged hands. Any new faces were unwelcome and viewed with suspicion.

Jason addressed everyone. 'All right, gentlemen. What's people drinking then?' Always a flash bastard, he slammed down a wad of notes on the bar. 'I tell you what, why don't you get another round in for everyone, Dolly, and have one for yourself, yeah?'

'Thanks, Jason, I will.' Dolly looked over at Jake and smiled warmly at him. He was so different from his twin brother. 'What can I get you, Jake?'

'Orange juice, please, Doll.'

Dolly laughed, the wrinkles around her mouth deepening. 'You still off the sauce?'

Without warning, Jason spun round and scowled at her. 'This

isn't fucking Prime Minister's Questions. In case you hadn't noticed, Parliament's over the river, darlin'. So if my brother wants a fucking orange juice, then that's what you give him. Now do yourself a favour: shut the fuck up, and do what you're paid to do.'

'Leave it, Jase,' a man's voice cajoled. 'Dolly doesn't mean anything by it, do you, Doll?'

'Todd, it's fine. No harm done, hey.' Dolly's voice wavered, as did her smile. She stood motionless behind the long wooden bar.

The pub went quiet. The punters placed their drinks nervously on the tables, watching what was unravelling.

Jason very slowly turned around to stare at Todd, a face from Soho the twins had done business with several times. The man was a complete muppet.

The smile on Jason's face didn't meet his eyes. 'What the fuck did you say to me, T?'

The pub was completely silent now, save for the sound of the fire crackling and the wail of a distant alarm. Todd stayed silent.

'Dolly, what did he say?' Jason kept his eyes on Todd, whose face was rapidly draining of colour.

Like everyone in the Rose and Crown, Dolly knew when to keep her mouth shut. 'I . . . I . . . I didn't hear, Jase, I'm sorry.'

Snarling, Jason clicked his fingers and pointed at her, but didn't say anything. He sauntered towards Todd, and tilted his head to one side. 'I'm going to ask you again, what did you say to me, you cunt?'

Todd looked around for support. 'You know me, Jase, I just opened my mouth without thinking. I didn't mean nothing by it. I was only saying.'

Jason screamed, sending chills down everyone who was there. '*Only saying?*'

Fear was etched across Todd's face, and beads of sweat sat on his forehead. He cricked his bull neck from side to side. 'Jase, come on mate.'

'Mate?' Jason laughed manically. 'Am I hearing right? You and me are apparently friends now. Well, that's fucking news to me, *mate*.' Incensed, he lunged forward and dragged Todd by the hair, forcing him to his knees in front of the open fire. Holding and twisting a clump of hair in one hand, Jason grabbed the iron poker, slamming the sharp end into Todd's teeth and shattering them. Todd's mouth swelled to twice its size as blood poured everywhere.

Todd yelled in agony when Jason smashed the other end of the poker into his nose. There was a loud, sickening crunch of bone splintering, mixed with Todd's screams. Red-faced, Jason walked towards the bar. He turned back round, took a run up, and kicked Todd in the side of the head with his foot.

Todd slumped forward. He lay unmoving, while Jason continued to put the boot in, frenzied and panting.

'Now do you want to tell me to *leave it*, hey, Todd?' Noticing a splash of blood on his expensive suit, Jason opened his arms in frustration. 'For fuck's sake,' he hissed. 'Now look what you've done, you fucking cunt, do you know how expensive this whistle was?'

'Enough! That's enough!' Jake roared, dragging his brother away. 'What is fucking wrong with you, Jase? Jesus Christ.'

'The cunt had it coming.' Jason nonchalantly slicked back his hair.

Exasperated, Jake shook his head and glanced down at Todd before gesturing over to another punter. 'Get him out of here, Ricky, will you? Take him to Doc's and send the bill to me, okay? Just keep him away from the hospital.'

Ricky shrugged. 'Of course, that goes without saying.'

Jake sighed and pulled a handkerchief from his pocket, flipped it open, and gave it to Jason. 'For fuck's sake, Jase, why do you always have to take it too far! Have you never heard of having a quiet drink?'

Wiping the spittle off his face, Jason stared at his brother intently. 'How many fucking times do I have to tell you? It's all about respect. I can't let him talk to me like I'm some sort of muggy cunt . . .' Without finishing his sentence, Jason looked at the expensive watch on his wrist. His expression darkened as he stalked around the bar and reached across to the cream phone hooked on the wall. 'You don't mind, do you, Doll?'

No one refused the brothers anything, not if they knew what was best for them. There was only one answer. 'Of course I don't. Help yourself, Jase.'

After only a few seconds, without bothering with any niceties, he growled viciously into the handset. 'Is she fucking there?' There was a short pause as Jason listened to the person on the other end. A moment later, he slammed the phone down and marched back around the bar, heading for the door.

'Jase, hold up!' Jake called after him, knowing exactly where he was going. Calmly, Jake strolled towards his twin, noting the tension and the pulse in his jaw. 'Don't forget our meeting with Carver later, we need to sort stuff out. And the Albanians are getting a bit jumpy . . .'

Jason sniffed, and spoke with contempt. 'You're a big boy now, Jake, I'm sure you can deal with it on your own if I'm late.' He reached for the door handle.

'Jase?' Once again, Jake stalled him.

'What? What the fuck are you chewing my ear off now for?'

'Go easy. Just go easy, okay?'

The minute Jason had left, there was a sigh of relief all round.

Looks were exchanged, and the hum of chatter resumed where it had left off.

'You need to put your brother on a leash, and tell him to calm down. He's getting worse.' Dolly touched Jake's arm gently.

Shrugging, Jake picked up the orange juice she had poured, and swirled it around in the glass. 'Doll, when I want your opinion on my brother, I'll ask for it.'

'Come on, Jake, you can see what he's like. Todd didn't deserve that.'

Jake smiled at Dolly. 'You can't help yourself, can you?'

'You have too much loyalty, you know that?'

He knocked the orange juice back, crunched down on a piece of ice, then pulled a ten-pound note out of his jacket, slapping it down on the bar. He moved to go.

'Jake?' Dolly's expression was troubled.

He didn't want to deal with this now, but he listened anyway.

'We both know where he's gone. And you do know, Jake, that one day he'll probably end up killing her, don't you?'

Chapter Five

'Grace, where are you? We're going to be late, sweetheart.'

Twelve-year-old Grace Perry stood in her newly decorated pink-and-cream bedroom in a small terraced house in Stockwell Park. She rolled her eyes. Her mum had been shouting up the stairs for the past ten minutes, and rather than hurrying her up, it was only slowing her down. She couldn't decide what to wear, and her mum's constant nagging was making it worse.

She was feeling anxious, something that happened a lot to her these days. She never used to feel like this. Only since her dad had died, last year. Grace missed him so much, and it made her sad. That part she understood, but what she didn't understand was why, only a few weeks after his funeral, she'd started spending hours every single day washing her hands. She'd tried to stop, but she couldn't, and it exhausted her. It also hurt.

Her small hands were constantly chapped or bleeding. Her mum would slather them in Sudocrem each night, wrapping them in bandages to make sure the ointment didn't go on the bedsheets. Grace had also taken to repeatedly checking that all the doors and windows were locked in the house.

'Grace, Grace, come on! For goodness' sake, we'll miss the show if you don't hurry up. What are you even doing up there? And turn that music down, please.'

Grace didn't bother answering. She looked around the room. She wished she knew why she had to put everything in order, and why everything had to have its place, and be just right. Even now, when she was trying to get ready and go out, she found herself having to fold and unfold her clothes before she could get dressed.

It had crossed her mind that something was very wrong with her, but she didn't know what.

She'd lost all her friends because of the way she was. Not that she'd had many in the first place, but this had made things twice as bad. Grace knew exactly what other kids thought of her. All they saw was a strange-looking girl with a splodge of red curly hair, a freak who wore braces, and needed thick-rimmed glasses to see the blackboard. Most days, they told her as much in the playground. Grace had decided they were probably right; she was weird.

'*Grace!*'

'I'm coming, Mum!' She sighed and reluctantly pulled on her blue jumper and acid wash denim skirt. Then, after taking a quick glance around to make sure everything in her room was where it should be, Grace walked out on to the landing.

The whole house was covered in framed family photographs, reminding her how happy life had been. She hated seeing them now, and sometimes when she walked past them she squeezed her eyes almost shut so she wouldn't have to look at them.

'Well, about time too, slowcoach.' Looking flustered, her mum met her at the bottom of the stairs. 'I thought you'd fallen down the bleeding plughole . . . Oh, you look so lovely, Grace.'

'Thanks.' She didn't feel it, and she didn't believe it, but she wasn't going to tell her mum that, she'd only get upset.

'So, are you all ready now, sweetheart?' Her mum paused and tilted her head to stare at Grace. 'Are you okay? You do know you can talk to me about anything, don't you?'

Grace bit down on her thumbnail and nodded.

Her mum clasped her hands together. 'Are you excited? What does it feel like to bunk off school with your old mum?' She winked at Grace, and cheerfully put on the fur coat she'd bought second-hand from a stall in East Street Market.

In the small entrance hall, Grace shrugged, trying to muster up more excitement for her mum. 'Kind of excited, I guess.'

The Eurythmics were playing at the Hammersmith Odeon that evening. Grace hadn't wanted to go, and she'd thought about pretending to be ill. But she'd felt guilty. Since her dad had died, her mum had been really sad as well.

'So, come on then, or we'll miss it. And make sure you wrap up well. Put a scarf on under that coat, Grace, it's bloody freezing. It's started snowing again.'

Grace dragged her beige duffle coat off the hook. She gave her mum a small smile, and walked out of the house, her head bowed, leaving her mum to lock up.

Maria Perry sighed and took one last look at herself in the hall mirror. Good looks on either side of the family were in short supply, though kindness was in abundance. She hurriedly closed the front door and slipped the keys in her pocket.

She followed Grace down the road and pulled out a packet of John Player Special from her bag. Grace hated her smoking. The poor girl had watched her father die slowly of lung cancer, and although she'd begged her mum to give up, Maria found she couldn't. The truth was, she enjoyed it. It helped with her nerves, and seemed to take the edge off life's stresses. Especially since Artie's death. She'd loved him with every inch of herself, and God, she missed him terribly.

'Honey, wait for me.' Stepping out of the way of a young girl running down the street, Maria called after Grace, took a deep drag from her cigarette, and sighed again as they headed towards Kennington Road to catch the bus.

Grace was their only child, and they'd spoilt her, wrapped her up in cotton wool, though that was more Artie than her, to be fair. From the very first moment he'd cradled his baby daughter in his arms, he'd doted on her. He'd acted as if Grace was a china doll, and as a result she'd grown up a fragile little girl. A worrier, like Artie. Life didn't seem to fit her daughter like it did other kids.

Throwing her cigarette butt in the gutter, Maria checked her watch. They'd be late if they didn't get a move on. She hurried to catch up with her daughter, and slipped her hand in hers.

Grace took her mum's hand, but immediately her heart began to race. In front of her, she saw a group of her classmates standing by the bus shelter. She thought they'd be in school. She really wished they hadn't seen her taking hold of her mum's hand, although a part of her also wished she didn't care what they thought.

'Mum, can we cross over?' Grace pulled her mum roughly towards the road.

Her mum stared at her, then slowly moved her focus to the group of girls standing by the bus stop. 'What have I told you? You are beautiful and clever, Grace Perry, and whatever those bunch of nasty kids say, you are *not* to care. You hold your head up high, all right?'

'Mum, please,' Grace muttered, dreading what was about to happen.

'All right, Grace, how are you doing?' Hannah, who was the ringleader, yelled over. A cruel smile played at the corners of her mouth. 'I see you've got dressed up in your best gear. Where did you get that from, the bottom of a skip? *Tramp*.'

The others laughed.

Mortified, Grace wished the ground would open and swallow her up. 'Mum, let's just go the other way, *please*.'

'They can't keep doing this to you, Grace, and expect to get away with it. I'm going to tell them exactly what I think.'

'Mum, no, just leave it.' Grace looked up to the grey sky, feeling the sleet on her face. Why did her mum always have to prove a point? This was worse than anything she could have imagined.

Ignoring her pleas, her mum marched across to where the group were standing and began to tell them off. Grace would never be able to live this down. Life at school was just going to get worse.

The next moment, Grace watched in horror as Hannah pushed her mum against the wall of the betting shop, before running off laughing with the others.

'*Mum!*' Crying, humiliated and angry, Grace ran up to her. 'Why couldn't you just have left it? All you've gone and done is made it ten times worse.'

Her mum calmly brushed down her coat. 'I'm sorry, but they have to be told, they can't go about being rude . . .' She reached out and stroked Grace's cheek, wiping the tears away. 'Look, don't let them spoil this outing for us. Why don't we go and have a gr—'

'Mum?' Grace frowned as her mum suddenly stopped talking. Her face began to drop to one side. 'Mum? Mum, what's happening? Mum, tell me what's happening. *Mum!*'

Grace screamed as her mum dropped to her knees, falling forward and smashing her face on the pavement. Blood poured from her broken nose.

'Mum! Mum! Mum! *Mum*, wake up, Mum!' Terrified, Grace began to shake. She lifted her mum's head up, but she saw that her eyes had rolled upwards, showing the whites.

Loyalty

Grace had never been so frightened in her life before. She screamed again, louder and louder, but her cries were drowned out by the busy traffic on Kennington Road.

'Help me, help me, someone, please . . . please don't let her die, please, please, please, don't let my mum die . . .'

Chapter Six

Dara was sure she'd finally managed to lose the guard. It had taken some doing, weaving through the large council estate and the back alleyways. The last time she looked, he hadn't been following her. *Wanker!*

Dara thought it was probably best if she didn't go straight home. The last thing she needed was for the guard to know where she lived. She really didn't need any more shit on her doorstep. The council had already threatened to evict her mum again.

She wandered past the chippy, feeling the warmth from the deep-fat fryers. After only a few minutes, the waft of fish and chips was too much for her. She was starving, and the smell only added to her hunger pangs.

It was a shame her mum's mate Shirl had stopped working there. She often gave Dara a large bag of chips for free, with lashings of salt and vinegar. Sometimes she threw in a bit of cod or saveloy for Dara to share with the others. But Shirl had got caught robbing the till, sticking pound notes down her knickers, and was given six months in Holloway, so that was the end of any free meals.

Dara clambered over the broken wooden fence at the back of the estate, where the kids often sniffed glue. Her top snagged as she jumped down on to the path. She picked her way through the discarded needles from the smackheads, conscious of a large hole in the bottom of her trainers.

Somewhere in the distance Dara heard the sound of sirens. There was always something happening in Kennington Road. Only a couple of days ago, there'd been a robbery at the jewellery shop opposite the all-night laundry, and the Old Bill had been crawling everywhere. Her mum had yelled at them out the window, effing and blinding, then passed out on the couch.

Dara's mum was nothing but an embarrassment. Every place they'd been evicted from, it was always because of her. She got into fights with the neighbours, and made so much noise playing music or having screaming rows with her punters or pimps, the council eventually moved them on. Dara refused to cry about it, and angrily she wiped the tears away.

She wrapped her arms tightly around her tiny waist. She was so hungry it hurt. It happened often, though she was more bothered about her siblings than herself. To listen to them crying because they didn't have a meal, haunted Dara.

A light snow was beginning to fall again, and the snowflakes landed on Dara's face as she waded through a pile of litter. A large brown rat squealed and scrambled across her path. She barely gave it a glance. The whole estate was a shithole, and right now she had bigger things to worry about.

The nearer she got to home, the more worried she was about Rosie. And what state her mum would be in.

Her heart was pounding as she raced up the concrete stairs of her block, two at a time. The corridor stank of piss and vomit. She jumped over a puddle of sick and made her way to the battered front door of their flat.

Taking a deep breath, Dara put the key in the door and let

herself in. There was no noise coming from any of the rooms. Her mum must have scored some gear, which was a relief.

She dropped her bag on the floor and noticed a fresh leak, with water dripping from the hall ceiling. The inside of the flat was really no better than the outside. She never brought any friends home. The shame would kill her. She'd once been to a mate's house up near the Elephant and Castle: everything had been tidy, smelling fresh, gleaming. There were sandwiches and crisps spread out on a fancy sunflower tablecloth. It was then that Dara realised what a pigsty her family lived in.

The brown patterned wallpaper had yellow nicotine stains running up it. The plaster on the ceiling was peeling, exposing wires and black mould. Most of the rooms had bare floorboards, though there was a smelly, crusted green carpet in the bathroom.

All the furniture came from a local charity, except the sofa, which smelt like the previous tenant had died on it. The bedrooms were no better. The bed Dara shared with two of her siblings had a grubby, soiled mattress on it, and one corner was propped up with a pile of old porn magazines.

Her dream was to get a little terraced house with her own front door, so she'd never have to step over some drunk who'd passed out and was lying in their own vomit. And a garden – a bit of green that wasn't covered in dog shit – would be nice, and enough food for her and her siblings, so they'd never be hungry again.

'Dar, Dar . . . Dar . . .' Two-year-old Ned came running up to her. His nappy was hanging off his bum, weighed down by urine.

She gave him a big hug.

'Dara. You been so long,' four-year-old Tammy whined.

'I know, and I'm sorry. A stupid git was following me. But I got rid of the bastard, so it's fine.' She winked and giggled. 'Where's

Mum?' Dara added, hoping there hadn't been any trouble while she'd been away. 'Is she out?'

'No, she's in there.' Tammy pointed to her mum's room.

'Okay, let me just go and check on Rosie, and afterwards I'll see what I can find in my pockets.'

The little ones squealed excitedly, clapping their hands, and doing a jig on the spot.

Dara put her head around the door. Rosie was asleep in the broken cot her mum had smashed up a while back in a drunken rage. Dara had managed to fix it by tying the rails together with a pair of old socks.

She listened to Rosie snuffling loudly as she clung on to her grubby blanket. She must have cried herself to sleep, but at least she'd wake up to some milk. That was something, Dara supposed. Though she wished she could give her more.

Closing the door quietly, she popped her head into the next room. Her mum was bang out of it, which Dara was grateful for. She spotted the drug paraphernalia on the floor, as well as the empty bottle of vodka thrown into the corner next to a used condom. Dara kicked it under the bed and checked her mum hadn't choked on her own vomit. She nudged her in her chest, and a groan told Dara she was asleep.

She pulled a face as she rolled her mum on to her side. Her arms were scarred with track marks and bruises. She'd taken up injecting heroin in the past year, rather than smoking it. It had made her mum's behaviour even more violent and cruel. Stupid cow.

Dara picked up a towel from the floor, and threw it over her mum's naked body. When her mum was so out of it, she often ended up soiling herself. And she didn't want the others to see that if they didn't have to.

Dara fleetingly wondered what other kids their age were doing right now. Normal stuff: riding bikes, dancing along to songs on the radio, experimenting with make-up, doing their homework, sitting down to tea. Sighing, she gave her mum one last look before turning away and firmly shutting the door.

One by one, her siblings all came out of their bedrooms. Dara knew they felt safer when she was around. There were seven of them altogether, including herself, with as many dads. Most of the time, none of them went to school, and social services didn't seem to care. They popped around occasionally to check on them, but never did anything.

Not that she minded. The social workers were nothing but interfering old cows, wanting to know *everything* that was going on in the house. The way they questioned her, they were more like the Old Bill than social workers. Of course, she never told them anything. She always sat there tight-lipped.

Opening her bag, Dara sat cross-legged on the floor in the hall-way. She brought out the packet of Spangles she'd stolen, and gave them to Tommy, who was the shyest of them all. He was also the one who was constantly picked on by her mum. He'd just turned seven and for some reason, since he was born, he was always the first in line for their mum's wrath.

She ruffled Tommy's unruly, curly brown hair, trying to ignore the shiner he'd got last week from her mum's new boyfriend. She tickled his tummy. 'Share them with Rory, okay.'

Tommy's face lit up and he nodded. 'Thanks, Dar, you're the best.' Then he put his arm around his twin brother's shoulders. Rory hardly ever spoke. They looked at Dara with so much love. They were always so grateful for the smallest things, and she promised herself that, one day, she'd give them the world.

'And as for you lot . . .' Dara pulled the chocolate buttons out from her pocket for the younger ones. 'Hold out your hands.'

Giggling, they did as they were told. Her gaze flitted between her siblings. They might have fuck-all, but at least they had each other. It was the one thing that stopped her running away. She'd never leave them. They were her life.

Dara laughed as they sucked on the chocolate noisily. 'You want another one?'

They shouted in unison. 'Yes, pl—'

The hammering on the door drowned them out. Fear rushed through Dara, and she froze for a moment.

'*Open the door, it's the police.*'

Dara's heart began to race. She grabbed hold of the twins and dragged them into her room, before running back to get the others.

The letterbox flipped open.

A pair of watchful eyes glared at her. 'Open up, Dara, we know you're in there. I can see you . . . Come on, Dara . . . We know what happened in the shop. We just want to talk to you. Your social worker's here as well . . . *Dara?*'

'Dara, is your mum in?' Helen Johnson, the family's social worker spoke to her gently through the battered letterbox. 'Dara, I need to speak to your mum, you know the rules, if you don't open the door we'll have to force it, and we—'

Dara kicked the letterbox closed, and ran into her bedroom. She looked around in desperation and tried to push the wardrobe across the door. Her siblings began to cry. Rosie was woken up by the loud noise, and started to scream.

Dara lifted the baby up from her soiled cot mattress, listening to the constant hammering on the front door. Clinging on to Rosie, she shrieked at the top of her voice, 'Leave us alone. We're fine. So you can all just *fuck off*!'

The next moment, Dara heard the front door come crashing in.

41

Chapter Seven

Frank Baker was fucking fuming. He could feel the rage rushing through him. He'd walked along the Albert Embankment, but every phone box had been destroyed, no doubt by the little bastards who lived in the estate over the river. Eventually, he'd found one on the Lambeth Palace Road, but it'd taken him a good fifteen minutes. And he'd been holding for the past ten. He was so cold, it felt like his bollocks had frozen.

Waiting for Alan Carver at the best of times pissed him off, but right now, he'd be happy to swing for the cunt. He couldn't stand the man. Not only was he a vain cunt, he was a jumped-up arrogant bastard who'd got lucky. If he wasn't careful, someone would end up putting him permanently in his place.

Hearing the pips, Frank pressed another ten-pence piece into the slot. If Alan took much fucking longer, he'd run out of money, and the snotty secretary wasn't likely to help. She'd been a complete and utter cunt, refusing point-blank to accept a reverse phone call before instructing him to hold the line.

'*For fuck's sake.*' Seeing Jimmy waving to him, Frank cursed out loud. Could the afternoon get any worse? He watched his nephew cross over the icy road, heading straight for the phone box.

Hardly able to contain his annoyance, Frank opened the heavy door of the phone box with his foot, craning his neck around to speak to Jimmy. 'Have you been following me? I thought I told you to piss off home?'

Jimmy, seemingly unconcerned by the way Frank snapped at him, shrugged. 'I was just wondering what the police said, Uncle Frank?'

Frank gave him a tight smile. He didn't need the likes of Jimmy trying to interfere. 'I don't know yet, I'm holding for them now. The best thing you can do, is go home. I'll come and tell you what they say later.'

Jimmy paused for a moment, then nodded.

'Oh and, Jimmy, keep your mouth shut about this. Don't go blabbing to your mum. We—' Frank abruptly stopped what he was saying on hearing a loud, familiar voice at the end of the line.

'Hello, Frank, it's Alan. Like I said to Reenie, this better be fucking good. I've already told you not to call me if you don't have to.'

Irritated, he waved Jimmy away, and closed the phone box door.

'I think this is something you'll want to hear, Alan. I think you've got a bit of a problem.'

In his office, Alan leant back in the thick, cream leather chair he'd got last week on expenses. One of the many perks of the job. His feet were up on the mahogany desk as he listened intently to Frank telling him about what he'd found. He couldn't actually believe what he was hearing. This was not what he needed.

'Have you called the police?'

'No, of course not. What do you take me for, a fucking mug?'

That was exactly what Alan took Frank for. He mulled over the information before saying, 'And it's definitely human?'

'Absolutely. Looks like it's a kid's . . . but maybe . . . well, maybe that's something you knew already.'

Alan whipped his feet off the desk. He hissed down the phone and jabbed his finger into the air, punctuating each and every word. 'What the fuck are you trying to insinuate? Who the fuck do you think you're talking to? Why would I know anything about it?' He took a deep breath and smoothed back his Brylcreemed hair. 'Did anyone else see you?'

There was a long pause.

'My nephew . . . I said he could help out, you see, his mother is my wife's—'

'I didn't ask you for your fucking family tree.' Alan cut him off angrily.

'It's fine. I've told him not to say anything.'

Alan sighed and pinched the bridge of his nose, feeling the start of a headache behind his eyes. He opened his top drawer and pulled out a small wrap of cocaine. Emptying it out on his desk, he absent-mindedly watched a tugboat on the Thames as he snarled, 'You better hope it's fucking fine, Frank, or you're going to wish that you never woke up this morning . . . Look, I have to run this past someone, and I've got a meeting to attend. Call me back in two or three hours, but in the meantime stay at the site.'

'Are you serious? It's freezing here.'

'Stop being a fucking pussy, Frank. Don't make me come down there . . .'

And with those words, Alan slammed the phone down.

Hunched up, and with his hands jammed into his pockets, Frank stomped back towards the site. It crossed his mind he'd made a mistake telling Alan. He didn't want the devil to be brought to his front door. If the police somehow *did* get involved and started asking questions, they'd soon find out his real identity. That would be a fucking disaster. No way was he going to have his life imploded by Alan fucking Carver.

Bringing out his tin of tobacco, and immediately feeling the wind bite at his fingers, Frank wondered if he should give Dennis a call. He'd met Alan through Dennis. If anyone could put that cunt Alan in his place, it was Dennis Hargreaves, and with that thought, he turned back to make another call.

Chapter Eight

Samantha Wakeman had a lot on her mind. Deep in thought, she hurried out of Vauxhall Station, barging straight into a short, grizzled old man who was shaking a tin cup.

'You're eager, Sam, how's tricks?' He grinned widely, showing off gums where teeth once were. 'Spare a few pennies, darlin'?'

'Sorry, Kit . . .' Samantha shook her head. She was breathless; her anxiety settled in her chest like a stone. 'I'll catch you tomorrow.'

His straggly eyebrows knitted together as he frowned. 'Everything all right, darlin'? You look a bit flushed?'

'Yes . . . yes, everything's good, thanks. Work's been really busy.' Samantha walked backwards as she edged away from further conversation. 'Anyway, I've got to dash.' She was late, and as much as she usually enjoyed a quick natter with Kit, she really didn't have time to stop and chat.

'Okay, well, you take care of yourself, Sam, won't you?' He waved goodbye.

A surge of tears rose up in her at Kit's kindness. She blinked them away and broke into a jog.

Being late was never a good thing, but being late *today* was nothing short of a disaster. The weight in Samantha's chest threatened to crush her. Why the hell had she been so bloody stupid? If only she'd made her excuses and left the meeting early, instead of sitting in the stuffy room, letting the time get away from her.

Knowing she hadn't got anything in the fridge for supper, she'd dashed into the Co-op on her way to the station. But then there was a queue at the ticket barrier, and she'd missed her train. Samantha had burst into tears as she'd watched it disappear into the tunnel, knowing that those few extra seconds at the ticket barrier had put her back fifty minutes. She was in big trouble.

Samantha was sweating profusely, despite the biting wind. She undid the top button on her red wool overcoat with one hand, and clutched her shopping bags in the other, wincing as the thin handles cut into her palm. She rushed across the main road, being careful not to slip on the icy surface, and headed quickly for Langley Lane.

Samantha had lived in the two-bedroom property for almost ten years now. Her father, Ron, a gentle mountain of a man, had earnt his money getting up at 5 a.m. every day to bake bread to sell down Brick Lane. And although Samantha's parents had been estranged since she was little, he'd still left the house in his will to her and her mum.

For the first couple of years after he'd died, Samantha had set about refurbishing the place, buying new furniture as well as carpets and curtains. She'd taken on extra shifts in her new job, in addition to working any spare weekends at the local cab station.

It'd been tough, but it'd been worth it. After living in a tiny high-rise flat near the Elephant and Castle, she'd relished coming back to her beautiful home after a long day. But then everything had changed, everything had become messed up, and now it felt less like home, and more like a prison.

If someone had told her eight years ago that this was how her life was going to be, she would've laughed. Though there was certainly no laughing now.

She rushed down the path, getting her keys out of her pocket before she'd even reached the front door, and let herself in. Dumping the shopping bags in the hallway, Samantha called out. 'I'm back. *Hello!*'

There was no reply.

Still rushing, she shrugged off her coat and checked her hair in the hall mirror. Using the red band she kept on her wrist, Samantha tied her long, wavy chestnut hair up into a ponytail. She'd only just turned thirty-one but the first grey hairs were pushing their way through.

She felt constantly tired these days, as well as constantly anxious. Though there was no point in complaining about it. She knew that. Not that she had anyone to confide in any more. And anyway, she wouldn't dare.

Taking a red lipstick out of her bag, Samantha hurriedly applied it with a shaking hand. Remembering her blusher was upstairs, she pinched her cheeks instead to get some colour into them. It wasn't great, but that would have to do. She needed to get supper started. She'd wasted enough time already, and she didn't want to make a bad situation even worse.

Stepping back, Samantha did a quick once-over in the mirror. Noticing a small mark on her skirt, she spat on her fingertips and frantically wiped it off. It was a joke. When had she ever cared about a stain? Wiping marks off her clothes, worrying about how she looked, wasn't who she was. Then again, she didn't really know who she was any more. She didn't recognise herself, and she certainly didn't like what she'd become. God, how she wished things could be different.

'Sam? Sam? Sammy? Is that you, love?'

'Yeah, I'll be with you in a minute, Mum.' She picked up the shopping bags and moved through to the pristine kitchen, placing them on the counter.

'Sam!'

'Give me a sec.' She kept the mild frustration from her voice. Sighing, she opened the cupboard above the sink and grabbed a glass along with the bottle of red wine she always kept in there. She poured herself a large drink, knocked it back it one gulp, rinsed the glass quickly, and put it neatly on the draining board.

The alcohol was a welcoming hit in her bloodstream, and for a moment Samantha stared through the plastic window blinds at nothing in particular. Blinking rapidly, she snapped to attention. She blew out her cheeks and put the bottle of wine back.

She hurried through to the dining room, which had been converted into her mother's bedroom, and painted on a large smile.

'Hello, Mum.' Kissing her on the top of her head, Samantha got a waft of Pears soap.

'Oh, Sammy, I was worried. I wasn't sure where you'd got to.'

Phyllis Parish sat in her favourite green chair, with a packet of twenty Peter Stuyvesant cigarettes on one side of her and a full-to-bursting stainless-steel ashtray on the other. She was surrounded by china ornaments and figurines she'd collected over the years, crammed together on every available surface. The brown house phone sat on her lap like a pet cat.

She gazed anxiously at her daughter. 'Is everything all right, Sam, you're not usually this late. I wish you'd called me.' Her eyes moved to the small clock above the hearth.

'Everything's fine, Mum, I missed the train, that's all. I'll get you a cup of tea, shall I?' Samantha smiled again.

Her mum had been housebound for the past five years. Her chronic arthritis made it difficult for her to walk, and as a result she relied on Samantha for most things, including taking her to the bingo on Wednesday nights.

'Did you get me those peaches in syrup, love? Me bowels are playing up again and I can't stand those prunes you got last time.'

'I did . . . I'll go and get that cuppa for you, but I need to put the supper on first.'

As Samantha turned to go, her mum grabbed her hand. 'Sammy, love, try not to cause any trouble, will you? Not like the other day. I just wonder why you can't learn to keep your mou—'

'Don't say it, Mum.' Samantha interrupted her and snatched her hand away. 'You know, sometimes I can't believe the bloody stuff you come out with. It would be nice if for once, just for once, Mum, you were on my side.'

Phyllis screwed up her face. Her yellowing false teeth were too big for her mouth. 'Stop being childish. It's not a question of sides, darlin'. I want the best for you, and sometimes the best is keeping quiet and knowing your place.'

Samantha marched back into the kitchen. She closed her eyes for a moment, and took another couple of steadying breaths. Why did her mum constantly make her feel like everything was her fault? It not only pissed her off, but it really hurt. She loved her mum dearly, but Jesus, she was a difficult woman.

Shaking with anger, Samantha walked back across to the cupboard, grabbing the bottle of wine she'd almost finished. It helped take the sting out of life. It had been a shitty day, and she had a feeling it was going to get worse.

She switched on the small pink radio cassette player sitting on the window ledge. Radio 1 was playing Spandau Ballet's 'True'. Sam stood listening to Tony Hadley's honey-toned voice floating over the airwaves.

God, what she wouldn't give to walk out of the front door and just keep on walking. It was one of her secret fantasies: get on a train and disappear. Go where no one could find her. Scotland,

Ireland, France. She really didn't care where it was, as long as it was anywhere but here.

Samantha poured herself an even larger drink than before. She was on call tonight, and yes, she shouldn't be drinking, of course she knew that, but right now, it felt like it was the only way to get through the rest of the day.

'Where the fuck have you been?'

The hairs on the back of Samantha's neck stood up. Without looking towards the kitchen door, she gently placed the glass in the sink and switched off the radio.

Clenching her fists into balls to try to stop her hands from shaking, she turned around.

'Hello, Jason. It's good to see you.' She masked her fear with a smile, at the same time as her heart started to race.

Jason Wakeman glared at her, thinking, as he always did, how beautiful his wife was. Not that it was going to stop him. He straightened up. Brushed down his designer suit with his hand. Rolled his shoulders. Cocked his head. Pushed his tongue from inside one cheek to the other. Enjoyed making her wait, savouring the fear already sharpening her features.

A bitter laugh left him and he loosened his tie. 'I never fucking asked for a *hello*. I asked, where the fuck have you been? And if you know what's good for you, Sam, you better start giving me answers *right now* . . .'

Chapter Nine

It wasn't often that Alan Carver was rattled. But the phone call from Frank wasn't good news. Human remains. And a kid's. Fuck, fuck, *fuck*.

Alan lunged forward in his chair and swept the pile of documents off his desk. The cup of tea Reenie had brought in earlier was sent crashing to the floor, spraying shards of Wedgwood's finest bone china everywhere.

What the fuck was he supposed to do? He knew he had to make a few phone calls, but he needed time to think through how to manage the situation. The last thing he wanted was for it to blow up in his face. On top of this shit, he had to attend a public meeting of the licensing committee tonight. And afterwards, he was meant to be seeing the Wakeman twins.

The sooner he could dump those two pricks, the better. Fuck knows what he was going to tell them. They weren't going to be happy with what he had to say. No, he'd just have to stall them until he knew *exactly* what was going on with the building site. Jason was a loose cannon, and yes, he was a South London boy, but Alan didn't fancy getting on the wrong side of him. If he didn't tread carefully, it could easily turn into a nightmare. He hadn't come this far only for it to be fucked up by some dead kid who was nothing to do with him.

He rubbed his chest, massaging his sternum with his middle finger. Dealing with this shit was going to give him a heart attack.

As Alan's heart continued to thump faster and faster, he unlocked his top desk drawer, rummaging in it. He was sure he had some Valium somewhere. Feeling right to the back, his fingers hit the plastic pill pot and grazed a stash of photos hidden underneath.

He managed a small smile. If the heat got too much, if it all went tits up, and the spotlight started to shine on him, well, Alan wouldn't hesitate to use them. When people in the public eye did bad shit, especially *illegal* bad shit, they'd do anything to prevent that information getting into the wrong hands.

At the sound of a timid knock on the door Alan briskly shut and locked the drawer. He sat up straight in his chair, exuding an air of importance. Clearing his throat, he called commandingly, '*Come in.*'

Reenie craned her neck around the door, giving Alan an apologetic smile.

Alan popped the lid of the bottle of Valium. 'What the fuck do you want?' Shaking out a couple of pills into his palm, he threw them into his mouth, and looked around for a glass of water. 'Forget it,' he muttered, and swallowed them down.

Reenie hesitated as she took in the state of the office. Her stare came to rest on the debris of papers and broken china spread across the floor. 'Oh my goodness, shall I clear that up for you, sir?'

Her fussing and softly spoken voice were starting to irritate the fuck out of him.

Alan shook his head. 'The cleaners can sort it out. Leave it.' It was too much fucking effort to be amenable. 'Look, why don't you go home?' he snapped. 'I've got a few phone calls to make.' He glanced at the time, clicking his fingers impatiently. 'Go on.

Off you go. Shoo. Oh, and Reenie, don't forget to pick up my dry-cleaning in the morning, darlin'.'

Without saying anything, she nodded and hurried away.

Alan picked up the phone and punched in a number. It rang a couple of times before it was answered by a haughty-sounding woman. Alan knew the type and pictured her sour face. It struck him that a good long fuck was what she needed. A hard cock, in Alan's opinion, could make the most uptight of bitches relax. His ten inches of prime penis was guaranteed to raise a smile on the most miserable cow's face.

'I'd like to speak to Chief Superintendent Lewis. It's Alan Carver.'

'Oh hello, Mr Carver. I'm afraid he's not in his office, sir.'

Alan heard the disdain in her voice. He didn't have to put up with this shit. 'Then you need to find him, and tell him I need to speak to him urgently. Pronto.'

'I'm sorry sir, but—'

'Listen, darlin', I've just told you I need to speak to your boss urgently. So if you want to hold on to your job, I suggest you go and find him. Fucking fast.'

After a few seconds of silence, she replied curtly, 'Of course, sir, I'll see what I can do . . .'

Ten minutes later, Alan was still impatiently rapping his fingers on the desk. The snarky bitch was trying to get one over on him. Sitting in the office, doing her nails, with no intention of going to find her boss, while he sat here waiting like a cunt.

His bollocks were on the line, he couldn't hang on any longer. The public meeting would be starting shortly. He'd just have to speak to the chief superintendent later. For the second time that afternoon, Alan slammed down the phone.

Alan grabbed his coat and swiped up his car keys from his desk. He'd go to the public meeting and once it was finished, he'd sneak out the back to avoid the Wakemans. It wouldn't be the smartest move to speak to them before he'd talked to a couple of other people first. He needed to know exactly what he – no, what *they* were up against. Not giving Jason the answers he wanted was like poking a crazed pit bull with a stick.

As he headed out of his office, Alan was already making a plan of action in his head. With renewed determination, he strode down the corridor. He didn't notice a figure emerge from the shadows and slip into his office.

Chapter Ten

Jake Wakeman was sitting in the Beehive, a tiny bar in Millbank, nursing the glass of whiskey he'd ordered over an hour ago.

He was supposed to be going to the public meeting with Jason, then on to discuss plans with Alan, before meeting the Albanians back at the Rose and Crown. He needed to make a move, but he didn't have the remotest interest in going anywhere. Dolly's words had messed with his head: *one day he'll probably end up killing her.* Why the fuck did Dolly have to go and say that? He wasn't Jason's keeper.

Maybe he should learn not to give two fucks, but what Dolly had said, well, he couldn't just brush it off. His brother was capable of anything, and Samantha certainly didn't deserve the crap Jase dished out. It was true, his brother *was* getting worse. But he didn't need Doll to tell him that Jase was becoming a liability. Jesus, he knew that, although he'd never admit it to anyone.

It was another reason why he had to stay off the booze. Things were getting more difficult with the Albanians, and business was shifting, so he had to be on his A-game. The street wars around drugs – around Es and coke – were getting out of hand. Yes, they still had their fingers in a lot of dirty pies, but they also had Alan Carver. He was a prize fucking arsehole, but what he brought to the table meant they could slowly step back from dealing solely in drugs.

London was booming, the eighties were bringing new opportunities, and property redevelopment was the new cocaine. That's where the real money was, if they could hold on to their set-up with Alan. But now that Jason had invited the Albanians in on this latest deal, to generate more money, it was a big fucking *if.*

God knows, he'd warned Jase. He'd told him not to deal with them. Dren Bala and Zef Kasa, who ran the gig, were the biggest fucking crooks he knew. They were ruthless meatheads, not to mention untrustworthy bastards, but Jason had gone in with them regardless. Un-fucking-surprising. Jase didn't listen to anyone. Not in business, not in his personal life. *Shit.*

If Jason had been anyone else, Jake would've got rid of him a long time ago. Put a bullet in his head, and now he'd be feeding the fishes at the bottom of the Thames. But he owed Jason, *big time.* In spite of everything, they were brothers, twins, blood, and they stuck together, whether he liked it or not.

Sometimes, loyalty didn't taste so fucking great.

Jake looked around. The whole atmosphere was chilled: candles were dotted around on the tables, and the juke box was pumping out the Isley Brothers' 'Between the Sheets'.

Turning back to his drink, Jake swirled the amber liquid around the glass, smelling its aroma. Fuck, he was tempted. Why did he do this to himself? It was the third time he'd come here this week, the third time he'd ordered the best whiskey in the place just to stare at it.

This was a place no one he knew came to. Here, Jake didn't have to watch his back, or keep up a front. But it was more than that. This place connected him to his past, before . . .

Jake quickly stopped that thought. He pushed the glass away. Booze was his poison. He liked it, or rather it liked him. The problem was, Jake had never been able to order one, or even two, then go home. It was all or nothing. And when it was all, he'd been fucking crazy.

Until one day things had got out of control. *Fuck*. He closed his eyes for a moment. The images of that day flashed through his head. He could still smell the blood.

Snapping his eyes open again, Jake distracted himself by pulling a packet of Marlboro Red 25's from his pocket, tapping one out and lighting it with the candle on the bar. He drew on it deeply, taking the smoke right down into his lungs.

'Now you're a face for sore eyes.' The owner, who also worked behind the bar, sashayed up to Jake, her generous hips rolling from side to side. She cackled throatily as she stared at him with watery blue eyes heavily rimmed with black eyeliner. 'But I can't have you in my bar with that look on your boat race. Fuck me, Jake, you look as if you've been told your dick's falling off!' She roared at her own joke. Her large, fleshy breasts jiggled in her low-cut satin top as she rescued a stray lock of hair from her towering, dyed-blonde beehive.

'Sorry, Deana, I'm heading off anyway.'

He turned to go, but she moved around the bar and grabbed him by his hand. 'Hey, Jake, you know I'm only joking, right? You know you're welcome to stay here, rain or shine, as long as you want.'

'I know, but I really should be somewhere else.'

'Is everything all right, babe?' She looked at the untouched glass of whiskey. 'You know you can talk to me, love. It won't go any further.'

Jake didn't feel like going into it. The truth was, he wouldn't know what to say, where to start.

He leant over the bar and kissed her gently on her cheek. 'Thanks, Deana. I appreciate it, but I'm okay. I'll catch you later.'

'Come on, Jake, tell me what's going on.'

He stared at her. He'd known Deana for a long time. She'd been a brass down in Soho. That's where he'd met her. In fact, at just turned fifteen, he'd lost his virginity to her. She was twenty years older than him, but he'd given her some old bullshit about being sixteen – he'd certainly looked it – so she'd taken his money and popped his cherry. And it had been such a good session, he'd gone back every Friday to the small walk-up in Berwick Street. She'd been a good teacher, and by the time the year was up, not only was Jake proficient in the art of pleasing a woman, but they'd somehow become firm friends.

After a few years they'd lost touch. Truth was, Jake never thought he'd see her again. Then three years ago, he'd been sitting in a café in Camden Lock, doing a deal with some arsehole who was trying to give him grief. And that's when he'd heard it. Her cackle. He'd recognised it straight away. There was no mistaking it. And when he'd turned around, there she was. Those big blue eyes, twinkling at him.

She'd been smart, stashing all her money away, not working for any pimps, and she'd kept clean by some small miracle. It had allowed her to save enough to take over the lease on the bar, and get her out of the game completely.

Jake gave one last look at the whiskey now, then took a deep breath, stubbed out his cigarette, and winked at Deana. 'Listen, there's nothing to tell.'

Arms folded, she blocked his way. 'No. Not until you tell me what's going on.'

It was pointless arguing with Deana, she was like a frigging ferret when she got her teeth into something. He couldn't help but smile. 'Just the usual shit with my brother.' It was partly true.

'When isn't there? Does he know that you come here?'

Jake shook his head. 'Probably better that way. You know Jase . . . and he's never had a soft spot for you.'

'He's never had a soft spot for anyone that takes your attention. You're a part of him, and he thinks he owns you.' Her concern was genuine.

Jake brushed it off. 'Anyway.' He gave her one of his dazzling smiles. 'Me coming here behind his back means I can have you all to myself.'

Deana, clearly unimpressed, reached over to the untouched glass of whiskey and downed it herself. She winked back at him. 'Silly to waste it, eh?' She laughed again, but then her expression turned serious. 'You still seeing that girl of yours?'

'Which one?' He grinned, but it was forced.

'You know which one. You don't bleedin' fool me, Jake Wakeman. I know there's a heart in there. You didn't answer my question. You still seeing her?'

Good-humouredly, Jake shook his head. 'Commitment is a mug's game. I like women as much as the next man, but I prefer my freedom. So to answer your question, Deana, no, I ain't seeing anyone . . . satisfied?'

She stared at him again and scraped at the wax dribbling down the glazed candle holder. 'Why don't I believe that?'

Walking towards the door, he shrugged and blew her a kiss.

'Mind how you go,' she hollered after him. 'But Jake, if you are still seeing her, please be careful. It's a dangerous game you're playing.'

Jake didn't bother turning around. He pulled up the collar of his expensive beige wool coat and walked out.

Chapter Eleven

The hammering on Dara's bedroom door was relentless. 'Just piss off, we don't need you!'

Her siblings had picked up on her fear, and were all screaming and crying. Her mother still lay bang out of it next door, oblivious to what was going on. It was hard to think straight, and the panic was rising inside her.

'Come on, Dara, let us in,' one of the coppers ordered. 'Otherwise we're going to break this door down too. I'm sure you don't want that.'

Shaking, she held Rosie tightly in her arms, jigging her up and down. 'What I don't want is you lot coming into our house. I've told you already, *piss off!*' Dara's heart was pounding erratically. She rushed across to the window, desperately trying to open it.

The bloody thing was always sticking. Dirt clogged the gaps in the frame, and trying to prise it open, as well as holding on to Rosie, made it even harder than normal.

Nervously, Dara kept her eyes on the bedroom door. The broken wardrobe pushed across it was beginning to move, inch by inch, and it wouldn't be long until the police made their way in. Why couldn't they leave them alone? So she'd taken a few things from the shop, what was the big deal? It was hardly the crime of the century.

'Dara, it's Helen. Open up, don't make this harder than it already is. We only want to help you.' Her cow of a social worker spoke smoothly through the door.

'Fuck off, you bitch.'

'Dara, *please*. There's no need to be like that . . . Let's try to sort this out.'

Dara screamed at the top of her voice. 'I've already told you, *leave-us-a-fucking-lone!*' Her voice cut through the air.

'Dar, are they going to take us? Dar?' Tommy ran up to her, pulling on her top. His eyes were filled with terror.

Bouncing Rosie on one hip, she shook her head. 'No, no they ain't. I promise I'll never let them, you hear me?'

She noticed the dark patch on the front of his trousers. He'd wet himself through sheer fright. Deep hatred for her mother, for her social worker, for the coppers, for that wanker in the shop who'd grassed on her, burn looked through her. She'd make sure they all fucking paid for doing this to her brother, to all of them.

She turned back to the window again, and banged the latch with her palm, desperate to force it open.

At the same time as the window started to ease, there was a loud crash. The wardrobe tumbled over on to its side. The next moment, the door was flung open.

Dara saw the look of disgust in the policeman's eyes as he entered the room. Sniffing the air, he pulled a face. It stank. She knew it did. There was the pungent smell of urine and shit from Rosie's nappy, mixed with the damp odour that permeated the whole flat. Dirty laundry was piled in the corner. She was never able to get on top of it, even though she tried so hard.

All she wanted was to give her brothers and sisters a decent home. She didn't want this lot bothering her.

As more uniformed policemen stormed in along with Helen,

Dara's siblings ran over to her. The tallest of the police officers managed to grab Ned and Kirsty.

'Don't you touch them!' Dara screamed. 'Don't you fucking touch them! Tam, come here, quickly.'

Tammy tried to reach Dara, but she was held back by another officer. She let out a long wail and struggled to escape, reaching out her arms for her sister. 'Dar! I want Dar!'

'You're hurting her, can't you see you're bloody hurting her!' Dara's words tumbled out. She was beside herself with anger. 'You're nothing but a bunch of fucking bastards.'

'Hello, Dara.' Helen, their social worker, stood calmly by the doorway. She was a small Caribbean woman with a strong Jamaican accent. Her long black weave was growing out and sat lopsided on her head. She raised her voice over the crying children, but there was still warmth in her tone. 'Dara, we know what happened in the shop, and we've seen your mum lying next door, she's not in any fit state to look after you or your brothers and sisters right now.'

Dara wiped Rosie's running nose with her sleeve. 'But I can! *I can!* I can look after them. They're fine with me.'

'Here's what's going to happen now,' Helen continued. 'I'll explain it, in case there's anything you want to—'

'Just go away, you're frightening them.' Dara stared defiantly at Helen.

The social worker gestured with her head to the officers. They picked up the terrified children and marched out.

'Stop! Where are you taking them! Where are you taking them?' Fear rushed through Dara. 'You can't take them. They're all I've got . . . They're all I've got. Put them fucking down! Put them down . . . Please, please, I'll do better. I'll do better. I'll try to look after them better. I swear I will.'

'Dara, it's not your job to do better. It's your mum's, and if she

63

can't look after you, then you know how it works, you'll have to come into our care. So why don't you hand over Rosie, we'll look after her, and Tommy can come over here with us.'

Dara clung on to Rosie as tightly as Tommy clung on to her. She shook her head. 'No, you're not taking her. She's not yours, and he isn't going anywhere with you either.'

'Dara, listen to me, I think—'

Helen stopped what she was saying as Rory, Tommy's twin who'd been standing in the corner unnoticed, suddenly spoke up. It was a whisper, but everyone turned to look at him.

'Tommy . . . Tommy, I'm scared.' He was trembling and clinging on to an old blanket, like a baby seeking comfort.

'Ror. Ror, it's okay.' Tommy rushed over to his twin, wrapping his arms around him. The moment he left Dara's side, the police grabbed him as well, dragging both boys outside.

'*Dar! Dar!* Help, Dar!' Tommy's screams faded as the officer tugged him out.

'It's better if they go and wait downstairs, we can talk properly now.' Helen stared at Dara and reached out her arms. 'I know how much you love Rosie, I know how much you love all of them, but you need to hand her over to us, then we can get you both cleaned up and make sure you have some supper inside you. When was the last time you ate?'

Dara moved towards the open window. 'That's none of your business.'

'Dara, please give Rosie to me. Let's get this sorted out.' Helen smiled placatingly.

'No, you're not having her. I told you.' Blinking rapidly, Dara half-clambered through the open window. She sat astride the ledge, clutching tightly on to Rosie. 'If you don't go, I'll jump. You come near us, I'll jump.'

'Dara! Dara! Don't be stupid. Don't do that. Come down.' The panic in Helen's voice cut through her words.

Dara saw the exchange of looks between the two policemen who were still left in the room. 'What? I'm stupid now, am I?'

'No . . . no, no, I didn't mean it like that. I'm sorry.'

Tears rolled down Dara's face. 'Yeah, but you still said it, that's what you think, ain't it? That's what you all think of me.'

'No, it's not. Not at all. I think you've done brilliantly, Dara. Looking after your brothers and sisters isn't easy for someone your age. You've done so well.'

'Don't fucking patronise me.' Dara's breathing was tight, and she couldn't stop the heaving sobs racking her body. She glanced down, and saw three other police officers standing by a line of panda cars.

Dara buried her head in Rosie's hair. It smelt of the lice shampoo she'd used on her. 'Please just go away, I'm begging you.'

Helen took a step forward but the moment she did, Dara shuffled her weight further on the ledge. 'Dara, I know this isn't easy for you, but right now I can't let you stay here, but that doesn't mean you can't be with Rosie.'

They were the first words Dara was interested in hearing, and she perked up. 'Can I?'

Helen nodded. 'Yes, of course.'

'What about the others, though? We need to stay together.'

'I know you do, and this is going to be only temporary – maybe for a night or two – until your mum wakes up and feels a bit better. There's no reason why you can't be with your siblings. We're not going to separate you. We wouldn't do that . . . trust me.'

Dara peeked at the drop below. They were up on the third floor, and it was a long way down.

Yet again, Helen reached out her arms for Rosie, who was

red-faced from screaming. 'Dara, let me take her, she doesn't look very well.'

Dara nodded in despair. 'She's got a temperature. That's why I took the Calpol from the shop. It's the only reason I did it.'

'I know, Dara. I know how much you look after them,' Helen reassured her, holding Dara's stare.

The atmosphere was tense. Dara didn't know whether to trust Helen or not. They were all the same. Teachers, the Old Bill, social workers, none of them really cared.

She looked at the officers standing by the door, then back at Helen, who was smiling warmly at her. 'And we can stay together?'

'Yes, Dara, absolutely.'

Slowly, Dara pulled her leg back in and reluctantly handed Rosie to Helen. The instant the baby was out of her arms, Helen's smile disappeared. She motioned sternly to the police officers and moved towards the door with Rosie.

'Wait, where are you taking her?'

Helen continued to walk away, ignoring Dara.

'What are you doing, where are you going? You lied to me, you bitch . . . Wait, she needs her bear, she needs her teddy bear!' Dara shouted after them.

The bear she'd stolen from Mothercare lay on the floor. As she picked it up and started to follow Helen, the two officers slammed her against the wall, trying to handcuff her.

Dara yelped. Her arm was twisted behind her, and a knee was driven into her back. 'Get off me, you're hurting me!'

The officer released his grip slightly, turning Dara around by the shoulder. 'Right then, young lady, we need to get you out of here. Are you going to be sensible?'

Dara nodded. Then, without warning, she kneed him in his balls. Seizing her chance, she darted out of the door and charged down the stairs, taking the other policeman by surprise. In the distance she saw Tommy and the others being dragged along, like criminals, towards the waiting police cars.

'Tommy! Kirsty!' Panicked, she shouted out their names. Her heart hammered even faster as she saw Tammy banging on one of the car windows as she was driven away.

'Dara!' Tommy spotted her. 'Dara, you promised, you promised they wouldn't take me.'

He was pushed into the car and Dara sprinted faster, trying to get to him. 'Wait, no, wait. I promised him, I promised him I'd keep him safe . . . Please. No, please, please . . . *no*. I need to say goodbye . . . *Wait!*'

The police car sped away and Dara dropped to her knees, howling like a wounded animal. A hand grabbed the back of her neck, and she was pushed forward on to the hard ground. Her head smashed against the floor and she felt her chin split open. Blood splattered everywhere. The physical pain came as a welcome relief for Dara, but as she felt the policeman's boot stamping on her back, holding her down, she cried uncontrollably. 'Let me say goodbye, just let me say goodbye . . .'

Chapter Twelve

Jason Wakeman stood staring at Samantha in the small, pretty kitchen in Langley Lane, waiting for an answer. He wasn't going anywhere until he was satisfied she wasn't lying. There was no way he was going to let her mug him off, and if it took until tomorrow to get the truth out of her, well, Jason was more than happy to wait.

'Where the fuck have you been, Sam? It's not a hard question to answer, darlin'. Come on, spit it out.' He smirked, tapping his watch. 'I've got a meeting to go to, and if I'm late, I'll be blaming you.'

Samantha struggled to get her words out. 'I . . . I . . . I . . . I . . .'

Incensed, Jason rammed his face into hers and screamed. 'What's with all the bloody stuttering, Sam? Never knew I was married to porky fucking pig.'

'Sorry . . . sorry.' She cleared her throat. 'Sorry.' Her mouth had suddenly become dry, and she licked her lips. 'I've been here, Jase. I've been talking to Mum.'

He took one step back and nodded slowly. 'Is that right, babe?'

'Yeah, yeah, I was talking to her, and she—'

Jason's hand shot up and grabbed her chin, squeezing it hard. 'How many times have I told you not to fucking lie to me?'

'I'm not. I've been here, I swear.' Samantha's chest rose up and down rapidly.

Jason's green eyes were piercing. 'Well, that's funny, cos I called your mum earlier, and she told me you weren't in. Didn't she tell you?'

He dropped his grip and Samantha gave the tiniest shake of her head. Speaking in a whisper, she watched the vein throbbing in Jason's neck. 'No, no she didn't.'

'Okay, so I'm going to ask you again, and let me tell you, darlin', I'm beginning to lose my patience: *where the fuck have you been?* And this time, babe, you better give me the right fucking answer.' Jason suddenly frowned. He tilted his head to the side and narrowed his eyes. 'Have you been drinking?'

'No . . . I mean, yes, but only a glass when I got in. It's been a stressful day, Jase.' As Samantha stared into Jason's eyes, she knew she needed to try to calm him down. 'It's no big deal.'

'I'll be the judge of that . . . Carry on.'

'The meeting overran . . . I was working today. I've put my schedule on the wall like you wanted me to.' She pointed nervously to the cork board by the fridge. 'Then I went to pick up some food for us. I thought I could cook something nice. I got a bit of steak.' She looked over at the bags of shopping. 'I missed the train though . . . I'm sorry, Jase.'

'So you missed the train?'

'Yeah.' She sounded breathless, when she wanted to sound confident.

Jason stabbed his finger against her temple. He snarled, 'Are you fucking stupid. Is there nothing in that pretty little head of yours? Who the fuck misses a train?' He shook his head, staring at her in disgust. He sniffed her breath again. 'You're nothing but a fucking lush, ain't you, babe? Look at the state of you. You're a mess. Maybe if you hadn't been knocking it back, perhaps you wouldn't have missed the train.'

Samantha backed away, banging her heels against the skirting board. 'For God's sake, Jase, I only had a drink when I got back.' The alcohol had given her a touch of confidence, and they both heard the flash of anger in her words.

Jason's face flushed red, and his eyes darkened. He ran his tongue over his bottom lip. A smirk danced at the corner of his lips. 'You're some cheeky bitch, you know that?'

Somewhere in the street Michael Jackson's 'Thriller' was being played loudly, with a deep bass. The photograph of Jason and Samantha's wedding day on the kitchen wall jumped in time with the beat. Jason grabbed her head and banged it against the wall. It thudded against the brick with a loud crack. 'I'd watch your fucking mouth if I was you, darlin'.'

Pain rushed through Samantha, but she held Jason's glare defiantly. This was nothing new. This was exactly what her mum had been talking about: keep her mouth shut and smooth things over. But she knew she was going to get battered no matter what. And quite frankly she was fucking sick of it. She was sick of him laying his hands on her whenever he liked – and he liked it a lot.

'You never change, do you, Jase? You never get tired of this shit, do you?'

She saw the punch coming and managed to turn her head, avoiding the full force, but not before his knuckle had caught her tooth. He dragged her across the room by her hair and pushed her against the table. The small fruit bowl smashed on to the kitchen tiles.

'*Sammy? Sam, is everything all right?*' Phyllis called out over the blare of her television, turned up to the highest volume.

'Everything's fine, Phyllis, it's only me,' Jason yelled out chirpily.

'Oh, Jase, come on in and see me.'

'I will, but I'm just having a little word with Sam, darlin'.'

Jason yanked Samantha by the hair, pulling and dragging her

across the kitchen towards the sink, where he forcibly dunked her head into the washing-up bowl full of water.

He held her head down with his hand. And as she fought for breath, Jason screamed at her. 'I've fucking buried men for being less frigging lippy than you!'

Desperately, Samantha tried to grab hold of his hand. She clawed at his leg. Her lungs felt like they were about to explode.

'You ain't fit to be a wife, you know that, Sam? YOU'RE A MESS. Why the fuck I married you, I don't know.'

He pulled her head out of the washing-up bowl, and immediately Samantha took a giant gulp of air.

'Is this how it's always going to be, Sam? Me coming around to see you, and you being a feisty cow?'

Wheezing and coughing, Samantha shook her head. 'No . . . no, I'm sorry, Jase.'

He snarled at her. 'No, you ain't.' He pushed her head back under the water before quickly lifting it up again, holding her inches away from him. His eyes darkened, and he began to breathe harder. He let go of her hair and moved his hand down her body, leaning forwards and grabbing her face again, though this time he jammed his tongue into her mouth.

Samantha felt his erection. She tried to pull away, turning her head to the side. 'Jase, don't, please.'

The minute she'd said it, Samantha regretted it.

'Who the fuck are you telling *don't*? What's the matter, Sam, you found someone else? Is that it? Is that why you were late coming home because you've been putting it around? Is my wife a fucking slag, now? You been sucking dick elsewhere?'

Samantha's eyes fixed on the patterned wallpaper. Her body went rigid. 'No, no, of course not, Jase, it's just that Mum's next door.'

'Your mum's always next fucking door, and anyway, she's got that telly on so loud she wouldn't hear a stampede of fucking elephants charging through the house.'

Jason's face was now inches away from Samantha's, and he pushed her legs apart with his knees. His hand continued to roughly explore her body. 'Why do you always wind me up, Sam? It's like you're baiting me, darlin'. It's like you want this. Is that what it's about, you want it rough, babe?' His breathing was short and shallow now, and he roughly pulled up her blouse, grabbing her breasts.

Samantha had stopped screaming years ago. She stayed silent and closed her eyes as Jason dropped his hand from her breasts and moved it down to hitch up her skirt. With one swift movement, Jason tore her knickers off. She felt his penis enter her as he grabbed her around her throat with one hand.

Jason panted out his words, thrusting deeper and harder as he continued to choke her. 'If I find out you've been cheating on me, Sam, I'll kill you, and I'll make sure I do it slow and painfully, you understand me? I said, *DO YOU FUCKING UNDERSTAND?*'

'Yes . . . yes.' Tears welled up as Jason relaxed his grip slightly. 'Yes,' she croaked.

'Yes, what?'

'Yes, Jason. I understand.'

Still inside her, he paused and looked at her, and with his hand still on her neck, he kissed her slowly, then ground his teeth into her bottom lip, drawing blood.

She yelped, and pulled her face away, feeling the blood run down her chin. He clutched on to her ponytail. She wasn't going to show him it hurt.

'You're my wife, and if you ever try leaving, or I hear about you with some other geezer, it'll be your biggest mistake.' He rested his head against her shoulder and moaned in excitement. He squeezed Samantha's neck harder, until she gasped for air. 'Because I'll snap this pretty little neck of yours.' At which point, Jason began to climax.

Tucking his penis back into his trousers, he stood and looked at Samantha. Without warning, he drew his fist back and punched her in the stomach. She crumpled to the floor, spluttering.

'Next time, Sam, be where you say you're going to be . . . Oh, and tell your mum that I'm sorry I couldn't stay, I've got a meeting to go to, but I'll see her soon.'

He bent down, kissed his wife tenderly on the cheek, and strolled out of the house whistling.

Even though she heard the front door shut, Samantha lay motionless on the floor for several minutes. She stared up at the ceiling, watching the car headlights from the street outside flash across it. Nothing much went through her head. She felt numb.

She became aware of the phone ringing, and forced herself to her feet. She pulled down her skirt and hobbled through to the hallway. Was this how her life was always going to be? Every time Jason did this, she swore it was going to be the last time, but here she was still. And she hated herself for it.

Wrapping her arm across her stomach, she picked up the phone with her free hand, taking a deep breath to make sure she sounded cheerful. These days, she was good at putting on a front. 'Hello . . . Yes, this is Samantha . . .' She paused to listen and quickly wrote down some details on the small pad next to the phone. 'No, that's fine, no problem, I'll be there as soon as I can.'

Placing the phone down, Samantha walked back into the kitchen. She grabbed the hand towel from the side, rubbed her hair and wiped away the blood. She was sore, and she could do with a nice, long hot bath, but she needed to go out. She glanced at the time. Best to get changed and catch the bus, rather than walk. The sooner she got there, the sooner she could get back.

She opened the freezer, yanked the ice tray out, and made a small compress using a shirt from the top of the ironing pile. Her lip was burning, and she placed the ice on her mouth, wincing at the pain.

'Sammy?' her mum called. The television was turned down briefly. 'Sammy, where's Jase? Has he gone? He said he was going to come through and see me . . . Sam? *Sam!*'

Without saying a word, Samantha slowly climbed the stairs. Halfway up, she held on to the wall and began to sob. There was nothing she could do, was there?

Even though she hadn't wanted to admit it, she'd known from the beginning that she was making a big mistake. Jason had arrived at the church an hour late, coked out of his head. Specs of blood marred the white rose in his lapel buttonhole, and he'd clearly been in a fight. After the ceremony, like a cliché, he'd shagged one of the bridesmaids in the cloakroom.

Instead of setting off together on the honeymoon they'd planned in Cornwall, Samantha had gone home alone after the speeches. The next morning, she'd woken up to her mum's voice, calling for her bedpan to be changed.

Jason had woken up with two hookers he'd picked up, after a night spent boozing and smoking crack in Honey's, the Soho club he and Jake had shares in.

Still, that was just the way it was; she'd made her bed and now she had to lie in it. Even if they didn't live together, she was Jason's wife, and that meant for better or for worse. He could do whatever he liked, short of killing her. Though Samantha had no doubt, that was only a matter of time.

Chapter Thirteen

By the time Jake strode into the school yard on White Hart Road, it had already gone six o'clock. The floodlights dotted around the playground gave him a good look at who was here. There were a dozen or so people in a huddle by the fence. More than he'd expected on a freezing evening. A few of them he recognised. He gave the others a steely glare, which was enough for them to lower their gaze.

He'd hoped that Jason would already be here. Where the fuck was he? Not that he couldn't handle this on his own. As jobs went, this was a piece of piss. Wanting to see Jason was about putting his mind at ease, in case . . . well, in case he'd done anything fucking stupid.

Massaging his temples, Jake tried to push the image of a nice, long glass of whiskey out of his head. It felt like he could almost taste it, the burn of that first drop at the back of his throat, followed by the warm glow as it hit his stomach. It was such a pull.

Cricking his neck from side to side, Jake took a deep breath. He'd been trying to knock the booze on the head for the past few years, though this was the longest he'd been sober. Five months. And fuck knows, it felt like a lifetime.

'Jake . . . Jake . . .'

It was Jason. Finally.

Whistling, Jason strutted towards Jake with a large grin on his face. 'All right, bruv.' He winked, putting his arm around Jake's shoulder.

'What time do you fucking call this?' Jake shrugged off Jason's arm. He stared at him hard. 'Have you been sniffing?'

Jason rolled his eyes, looking Jason up and down. 'Fuck me, we really are the fun police tonight, ain't we? What you need to do, little brother, is get laid, or have a drink, one or the other.'

'I might be your little brother by all of one minute, but it feels like there's only one adult around here,' Jake snapped. 'And it's not you.'

Jason laughed. 'You see, that's what I'm talking about . . . You need to release some of that fucking tension. I'm off to the club tonight to get some decent pussy. You should join me – in fact, I *insist* on it.'

Jake shook his head. Jason straight was hard enough to handle, but Jason on coke made him too unpredictable to read. Still, at least he was here.

Catching a glimpse of Jason's right hand, Jake frowned. He grabbed hold of it and lifted it up, staring at his knuckles. They were raised and red, and a small, fresh graze was sliced across the skin.

'What the fuck have you been doing?'

There was a hint of droll humour to Jason's voice as he answered. 'I had a run-in with the wall.'

Letting go of his brother's hand, Jake stepped away. 'Sometimes . . .'

'Sometimes, what?'

Feeling a blast of icy wind, Jake pulled up the collar of his coat as high as it would go. He leant into his brother's face, smelling the hint of his woody aftershave, as he lowered his voice. 'You . . . did you have to go and do that?'

The very notion of his brother laying his hands on a woman turned his stomach. He'd seen their dad beat the living daylights out of their mother, until one day, when the twins were a few months short of turning fourteen, she'd had enough and sliced up her own wrists before throwing herself into Prescott Wharf. When they'd dragged up her body, her face had been half eaten by the fishes. The day they'd found her was the first time he'd felt real hatred. It wasn't just his mother who was dead to him, but also his father.

Jake watched the grin on Jason's face start to fade. 'Jog on, Jake, all right.' His eyes darkened. 'You know how it is, from time to time, we all need to be reminded of our place, don't you think?'

Jake spoke fiercely, keeping his voice low. 'You know Samantha didn't deserve that, you're out of line.'

Breathing heavily, Jason screwed up his face in anger. 'What I do, Jakey, with *my* missus, is *my* business, not yours. Make sure you remember that.'

Jake wasn't going to rise to it. He laughed bitterly. 'If you're looking for a fight, Jase, you aren't going to get one here. So drop me out.' He finished the sentence with a nod and walked away.

This wasn't the time, or the place, to have it out with Jase, especially not when his brother was fucked up on coke. But if he was honest with himself, working with Jason was becoming increasingly difficult. Hopefully, once this deal with Alan was completely signed off – which should be any day now – he'd be able to rethink his situation. There was no doubt that if Jase got even a sniff of him wanting out, planning to go it alone, there'd be fucking hell to pay. Jase would see it as a betrayal. No one left Jason. Unless they were six feet under.

Jake walked towards the school entrance, where people were beginning to file in. He smiled his widest smile and greeted them with a pleasant 'Good evening'. Jason stood on the opposite side of the entrance, wrapped up in a long, dark coat, looking like a mean fucking bastard.

Recognising one of the people in the line, Jake gestured to him with his head. The man looked ill at ease, but hurried across to where Jake was standing.

Jason stepped across to join them. 'Good to see you, Councillor Watkins. You all right, mate?' He grinned cheekily.

'Jason . . . Jake.' It was a tight reply from Watkins.

God knows, the man looked like he was about to crap himself. Anyone dealing with the Wakeman twins knew to watch their back.

Jake straightened the lapels on the councillor's coat, enjoying the man's discomfort. 'I take it I can still rely on you this evening, Councillor?'

Watkins narrowed his eyes. 'I don't think you're leaving me much choice, do you, Jake?'

Jake frowned. Instead of taking offence at Watkins' tone, he dismissed it and smiled. 'Come on, what are you trying to say? Of course you've got a choice, mate. But it's all about how you use that choice, ain't it?'

Watkins moved his gaze between the brothers. 'You two are pieces of shit, you know that.'

Jake roared with laughter. He had to give it to Watkins, he had some front, and begrudgingly, he respected that. 'That's what I like to hear, Councillor, fighting talk.'

Jake banged him hard on the back, letting him go into the school.

'*Jake!*' From across the other side of the playground, his name was being called.

The man waved to the brothers. He was over six foot tall, dressed in an expensive Savile Row coat, his velvet pork pie hat covered in light snow. He wandered casually over to the brothers, with confidence oozing from him.

'Fuck me, it's nippy this evening, boys.' Bouncing his shoulders up and down in an attempt to get warm, he shook Jason's hand, then Jake's. 'Everything all right here?'

Jake shrugged. Like so many people he had to deal with, Ray Hicks was a prime fucking arsehole. Still, when it came to earning money, Jake wasn't all that choosey who he dealt with. And Ray was rolling in the stuff.

Since the government had made betting shops legal, Ray had earnt a small fucking fortune. Most of South London was littered with shops with Ray's name above them. Though some of the councils, along with the residents, were none too happy about having them on every corner.

Jake could remember when gambling moved from backstreet rooms to legal shops. The Wakeman family had run a lot of the illegal gambling places in South London, reaching almost as far as Norbury. They'd made a healthy living out of it. From when they were knee-high, the twins had been taken along with their dad and his firm, learning the ropes. They'd watched from the side as the Wakeman gang had battered people senseless who couldn't come good with their bets. They'd timed it right, nipping out of the back to avoid the police raids, as well as paying off the bent coppers of course. That was a given. Twenty years or so on, nothing much had changed on that score.

'Yeah, everything is going as planned.' Jake eventually answered Ray, but said nothing else.

For now, it suited the twins to be acquainted with him. Ray was happy for them to wash their dirty money through his shops, and in return, with a nod from Alan, they helped Ray out with any problems that came up for him.

Acutely aware that the silence from Jake was him being dismissed, Ray wandered into the school.

Jason moved to follow him, flicking his half-smoked cigarette into the base of the Christmas tree standing in the entrance. He paused, and looked over his shoulder at Jake.

'And Jakey, if you *ever* mention Samantha again to me, you and I are going to fall out big time. Understand?'

Jake watched Jason stroll into the hall. He dabbed his forehead dry of the light snow. Oh, he understood all right. He fucking got it.

Loyalty or not, if Jase carried on like this, he'd have no choice but to put his brother firmly back in *his* place. Sooner, rather than later.

Chapter Fourteen

Grace couldn't stop crying. She stared at the machines and monitors surrounding the hospital bed. 'Mum? Mum, *please* wake up . . . Mum.' There was nothing.

Eyes closed, her mum lay on the bed, hooked up to a ventilator. There was a tube in her mouth, as well as other various long tubes coming out of her arms, attached to plastic bottles that were drip-feeding her.

Grace curled up her nose at the strong smell of iodine in the air. None of it felt real. One moment they were off to see the Eurythmics in concert, the next her mum was lying here in St Thomas' Hospital. The screech of the ambulance sirens kept playing over and over in her head.

They'd told her that her mum had an aneurysm. Whatever that meant. She'd been too afraid to ask. Grace just wanted her mum to wake up. Why couldn't she open her eyes and tell her everything was going to be all right?

'Mummy, *please* . . . Mummy, can you hear me?' Grace touched her mum's hand. She was amazed how warm it was. 'Try to wake up, Mummy.' She willed her mum, then found herself begging her. 'Please, please, please just try. Try to open your eyes, *please.*' She stood back for a moment, hoping for some sort of miracle to happen. That's what they'd learnt about recently in school, hadn't they? Christmas miracles.

Somewhere between the Kennington Road and being brought with her mum to St Thomas', she'd lost her glasses. But even for Grace, who was short-sighted, it wasn't hard to see how badly bruised her mum's face was from where she'd fallen and smashed it on the pavement.

Tears welled in Grace's already sore, puffy eyes. Her headache was getting worse, and a crushing pain drove down from the top of her skull. She rubbed her chest, trying to catch gulps of air. It felt like something heavy was sitting on her, making it hard to breathe, and her throat seemed to be closing, blocking her airways. Frantically, Grace scratched at her neck, but no matter how much she tried, she couldn't get her breath. Her heart raced faster, and her breathing became more rapid.

'Hello, Grace . . . Grace?' The door of the single-bedded room opened. 'Oh my goodness, are you all right?'

A woman Grace had never seen before hurried over to her, dropping the folder and bag she'd brought in.

'I can't breathe . . . I can't breathe.'

'It's okay, Grace. I'm here now . . . try not to panic. Take slow, deep breaths.'

Grace nodded and did as she was told. Listening to the woman's soothing voice went a long way towards helping her to calm down. From underneath her thick curly fringe, Grace sneaked a proper look at her.

The woman had warm green eyes, her long chestnut hair was tied in a ponytail, and her face was so pretty, Grace thought it could be on the cover of a glossy magazine. Though as pretty as she was, Grace couldn't help noticing how swollen and red her lip looked.

'I'm Samantha, but you can call me Sam if you like. It's good to meet you, Grace.' The woman smiled, despite her bruised lip. 'I'm going to be your social worker, just while your mum's ill. So if there's anything you want to ask me—'

'Is she going to die?' Grace cut in straight away, her voice trembling.

Samantha crouched down, staring up at Grace.

'Look at me, Grace,' she said, and took hold of her hand. 'Everyone's working really hard to keep your mum stable, but while they're looking after her, someone needs to look after *you*, don't they?'

'Can I stay here with my mum?'

Samantha squeezed Grace's hand. 'I'm afraid not, Grace, because we want to make sure that you have a nice bed to sleep in tonight.' She paused, and smiled briefly again, clearly still nursing the cut on her lip. 'Why don't we get you changed, Grace? I brought you some clothes.'

There was blood all over Grace's skirt and top, probably from clinging on to her mum when the paramedics arrived. She hadn't wanted to let go, and it'd been difficult to prise her off.

'Hello, Grace.' A heavyset man with eyes too close to the bridge of his nose, and a long angular face, topped off with a grey, wiry beard, shuffled into the room. A large pipe stuck out of the breast pocket of his old, rubbed tweed suit. He looked at Samantha, and nodded to her.

'This is Mr Miller.' Samantha introduced him to Grace, but didn't explain why he was here.

There was no attempt at a smile as he spoke to Grace.

'So, I'm sure Ms Wakeman . . . er, Samantha, has explained that as your mum can't look after you for the foreseeable future, you'll be taken into our care. Hopefully, we'll have transport later tonight to take you to Holly Brookes, and—'

'She can't go there,' Samantha interrupted. 'She's got a god-mother who lives in Newcastle, I'm going to get in contact with her. Hopefully, she can take Grace.'

Mr Miller wiped his tongue along his lips, licking away the spittle in the corner of his mouth, and glared at Samantha with disdain. 'That's not your decision.'

Grace didn't understand. The social worker was so pretty, and she had a lovely smile. Why didn't Mr Miller like her?

'I think, given the circumstances, Holly Brookes isn't suitable for Grace. Let me try to find some emergency accommodation for her tonight. Sending her there isn't right.'

Mr Miller's dead grey eyes stared coldly at Samantha and his face was devoid of all emotion. For a fleeting moment, Grace thought he was going to slap the social worker. The broken veins on his cheek, looking like tiny thread worms under his skin, reddened. He moved to go.

'Wait.' Samantha reached out a hand. 'Please, I'm—'

'This isn't up for discussion, *Ms Wakeman*. Emergency accommodation is in short supply, and clearly this is going to be a long-term placement.'

Samantha appeared to be fighting back tears. 'You know what that place is bloody well like.' She spoke through gritted teeth, as if not wanting Grace to hear. 'Yet you'll still send her there . . . How can you sleep at night?'

'Very well, actually.' He stepped closer to Samantha, until he was almost in her face. 'Now excuse me, I need to make that phone call.'

Mr Miller turned on his heel and marched out. Samantha's gaze followed him.

The moment Mr Miller was out of sight, Samantha ran to her handbag, and hurriedly fished out a pen. Tearing a corner off the hospital notes lying on the side, she quickly scrawled something down, then glanced over her shoulder, before turning back to look at Grace.

She held out a piece of paper. 'Grace . . .' Samantha stared at her. 'What I'm going to say is *very* important. You need to keep this number safe. Hide it. But if you ever need me, call the number. It's my home number, but you must *not* tell anyone that I gave it to you. Do you understand me?'

The look in Samantha's eyes made Grace fearful. The last time she'd seen anyone look like that was when her mum had woken her up in the middle of the night to let her know that her dad had passed.

Samantha crouched in front of Grace. 'I'm going to try my hardest to get in touch with your godmother, but in the meantime, promise me, you'll keep this safe.'

Grace's eyes slowly moved from where Samantha was kneeling, to the spot behind her, where Mr Miller – who neither of them had noticed coming back in – now stood.

'Secrets and lies, secrets and lies, Ms Wakeman? Well now, that will never do, will it?'

It was a moment before Samantha moved, and Grace wondered why she was shaking. With her fist tightly clenched around the piece of paper, Samantha eventually stood back up and turned to face Mr Miller.

He smiled at her cloyingly. 'I think I'll take that, don't you?' He wrapped his hand over Samantha's, and Grace knew he was squeezing her hand hard, as the whites of his knuckles showed.

Samantha was forced to drop the paper. It floated to the floor, though neither she nor Mr Miller made a move for it.

'Be a good girl and pick that up for me, will you, Grace?'

As Grace handed him the paper, he looked at it, then she

watched him lean in, until he was almost nose to nose with Samantha, before whispering into her ear.

Breathing heavily, Samantha gave a small nod. She turned to Grace, who realised she was trying not to cry. 'I'm so sorry, sweetheart.'

Samantha rushed out of the room without looking back.

Grace turned her attention to Mr Miller, who bent down towards her. She shrank back, recoiling from his stale breath and the strong odour of pipe tobacco.

He stroked her face.

It should have been a kind gesture, but there was something about it Grace didn't like.

'Right then, Grace, I've spoken to transport, and they can take you to Holly Brookes within the next couple of hours.' He winked at her, and a smirk played on his lips, as if he was relishing the prospect. 'Now then, are you ready for your new home?'

Chapter Fifteen

The drive from Abingdon Street to Piccadilly Circus wasn't far. Ten minutes, if the roads remained clear. As luck would have it, despite the snow, they were tonight. Undetected, the Rolls Royce purred to a stop in the shadows of Coventry Street, far enough away from the statue of Eros not to be seen, yet near enough for the passenger to watch the Dilly boys – rent boys – parade themselves on the meat rack.

Boys as young as eleven congregated, peddling for trade on the steps of the bronze winged archer, poised with his bow. On cold evenings like this one, they'd often take themselves off to sit in the window of the Wimpy Bar, or sell themselves down in the men's toilets, which was a violent twenty-four-hour scene.

Dennis Hargreaves sat in the luxury and warmth of the back seat of his Rolls, just watching and admiring their youth. Looking passed the few hunched figures rushing towards the tube station, Dennis surveyed the row of possibilities. He found himself catching his breath. Yes, that one would be perfect. He smiled, savouring the feeling. What did Frank once say he called this moment? Ah yes, the hunter and his prey.

'That one . . . that one, there at the end.' Tapping the back of his driver's seat, Dennis pointed. The arthritis in his finger caused it to be crooked and bent. 'You know which one I mean?'

'Of course.'

As his driver got out and made his way across to the Wimpy Bar, Dennis settled back down into his seat. It occurred to him that it was an unnecessary question to ask. Geoffrey had been with him long enough to know his tastes. Perhaps next time, he'd play a game and wouldn't choose for himself, instead he'd leave it up to Geoffrey to decide. Even better, to make it more fun, he'd put a bet on it. If Geoffrey could pick out the one he'd select, he'd keep his job; if he couldn't, he'd lose it. Though the more Dennis thought about that, the more he decided it was a rather dull consequence. Dennis was a man who liked high-stakes thrills. The better option would be: if Geoffrey couldn't pick the right one out, he'd force him to spend a few hours with Frank and his friends with their *very* particular tastes.

The idea of watching Geoffrey go through the same as the hitchhiker from a few months ago caused Dennis to become semierect, and his laugh exploded as images of the blood raced through his head.

Catching a glimpse of himself in the driver's mirror, Dennis slicked back his freshly cut silver hair. He needed to tell the barber not to take so much off the sides next time. It was the small things that upset Dennis.

Continuing to enjoy the warmth, Dennis observed two policemen strolling towards the car. He waited until the smaller of the two – a young officer with a moon face and a flurry of freckles – knocked on the blacked-out window.

In no hurry, Dennis pressed the button of the electric window. It swung down smoothly.

'Excuse me, sir, can I ask you what you're doing here, you know you're not . . .'

The officer stopped and suddenly changed tack as Dennis moved into the light.

'Sorry, sir, I didn't realise it was you.'

Dennis smiled, tucking his silk cravat further into his navy cashmere coat. 'That's all right. How are you?'

'Good, sir, though I'm not liking this cold.'

'How's the family?'

'Very well, thank you, and my wife appreciated the flowers you sent her. She's on the mend now . . .'

PC Gilbert was a low-level bobby, harmless enough for Dennis's purposes. He listened to him chattering away tediously, until Geoffrey finally reappeared, with the young boy Dennis had selected in tow.

When the boy got into the car next to Dennis, Gilbert continued to talk, although he did shift his gaze and nod, more to himself than to anyone else.

'Anyway,' Dennis smiled. 'We need to be making a move.' He took his wallet out of the inner pocket of his handmade suit, and pulled out two crisp fifty-pound notes. Rolling one up, Dennis reached through the window to Gilbert. 'Why don't you get your good wife something for Christmas, and maybe treat yourself for once?'

Gilbert, as usual, couldn't move fast enough to snatch the note out of his hand. 'I will, thank you, sir.'

Dennis cleared his throat noisily and beckoned the other policeman over. He'd not had many dealings with him, nor could he recall the man's name. Still, no matter.

There was only a slight moment of hesitation. Predictably, the policeman stepped forward.

'Good to meet you.' Dennis smiled.

'And you, sir.' And with those simple words, he took the proffered note, slipping it quickly into his pocket.

Dennis hid his smirk as he watched the officers stroll away, each contemplating what they were going to spend this easy money on.

Rolling the window back up, Dennis finally turned to the boy. He was even more perfect close up. He was small, slightly emaciated, with pale blue eyes and an impish innocence that made him look angelic. In his hand he held *The Beano* comic. His fingers were filthy, the nails embedded with dirt, which gave a clue as to how long he'd been on the streets. If Dennis were to guess, which he prided himself on being pretty good at, he'd say the boy was anywhere between twelve and fourteen.

Without saying anything, Dennis opened the cream leather armrest separating them. He pulled out a sandwich his housekeeper had made, and handed it to the boy. It was the best beef and horseradish. Which seemed rather a waste, given what the evening would hold. Another dark smile twitched at the corner of Dennis's mouth as he stifled his laughter.

The drive seemed to be taking longer than usual, though Dennis wondered if that was simply his own impatience. It had been too long since he'd done this. He watched the streets rush past, turning only once to speak.

'Are you warm enough?' Without waiting for an answer from the boy, Dennis turned the dial up in the middle of the walnut partition.

His gaze roamed across the slushy streets of London as the Rolls Royce picked up speed.

Cutting through Aldgate, Dennis gave way to temptation and allowed himself to take another peek at his catch. The boy seemed more relaxed now. That was always good. It helped. However, the night was still young.

Heading towards Mile End, they sped through the grime of East London until they hit the Leyton Road and turned down several smaller streets to a large, sprawling, run-down housing estate. The car, going unnoticed in the darkness of the winter's evening, pulled up smoothly by a row of metal bins.

Dennis's door was opened by Geoffrey. He stepped out, immediately feeling the cold in his bones. Walking round to the other side, he let the boy out himself.

'Geoffrey, give him your coat, it's chilly.' The thin top the child was wearing was no protection from the weather.

With a look of reluctance, Geoffrey took off his coat and gave it to Dennis.

Dennis gently placed the coat over the boy's shoulders. 'That's better, isn't it? Don't want you to get cold.'

A grateful smile spread across the boy's face. And Dennis was surprised at how wrong he'd been. Actually, at this angle, it was clear the child was no more than ten.

'You stay here.' Dennis exchanged a look with Geoffrey as he spoke to him. 'And our young guest can come with me.'

Guiding the boy through the estate, Dennis walked up the stairs and along the open stone corridor, coming to a stop by a front door with peeling red paint.

Looking around first, Dennis knocked. Three times. Then a pause. Then a further five knocks. The door to the flat was opened by a dirty-faced man who sported a coarse three-day shadow.

'I've brought our visitor.' Dennis grinned and sauntered into the flat with the boy. 'Graham, why don't you bring him a drink.'

Graham, a father of three young children, shared Frank's tastes – and had received similar convictions. He smirked and went through to the grimy kitchen to pour a large glass of red wine.

Within moments, he returned and handed it to the boy,

watching eagerly as he drank it down. 'Cheers to our new recruit.' Graham giggled and his grin was almost toothless; the remaining teeth were yellow and blackened, following years of neglect. Despite the cool temperature in the flat, he was sweating excessively with excitement.

Dennis looked at the boy. 'You won't need this.' He took the coat from his shoulders. 'Ready?' He swung open the door to the side of him.

The front room fell silent.

The boy turned to run, but Dennis held him back, placing his finger on his mouth. '*Sshhhh*, it's going to be fine.'

He watched the changing expression on the boy's face; from bewilderment to fear. Then Dennis saw the men gathered in a circle, like a waiting pack of dogs.

Dennis couldn't help but take a deep breath and smile again. There was always something special about a chicken run. Feeling himself stir, Dennis gently pushed the boy into the room.

'An early Christmas present for you all, gentlemen . . .'

Chapter Sixteen

Nodding to the assembled group of councillors in the school hall, Jake ambled to the back, to where the handful of residents were sitting. What the hell was the delay? These things bored the fuck out of him. He only hoped it was over quickly. Plus, it was almost as chilly in the hall as it was outside. He could see his breath, mixing with the cigarette smoke.

The chairman finally cleared his throat and convened the meeting. He put out his cigar in the metal ash tray on the small desk in front of him, before addressing the room.

'As we're all aware, this is a meeting of the licensing committee, though before we examine the application, apologies for their absence have been received from Councillor Bob Davies, Councillor John Stokes, Councillor Tim Jonathan. Those present today are councillors . . .'

Jake allowed his thoughts to wander as he gazed around at the players. Ray sat opposite him, looking tense. He was an ugly fucker, no doubt about it. The unfortunate size of his front teeth made it look like he'd been inbred with a fucking beaver.

Then there was Alan, over in the far corner, preoccupied by his own thoughts. He was different from anyone Jake had ever known. His oxygen was power *not* money. Power, allied to ego, was his driving force. The more favours owed to him by businessmen like

Ray, the closer he came to his goal of making it into parliament. Westminster was within touching distance.

But Jake knew the cunt didn't stand a chance of reaching his goal, not without help from the Wakeman twins. He and his brother had given him a leg-up to where he was now. Alan fucking Carver would be nothing without them. And if he didn't jump when they told him to on this latest deal, Jake would personally remind him where his loyalties lay.

Jake watched Alan sitting on his own in the hall. His usual arrogant demeanour had been replaced by the look of a worried man. What was going on with him? Jake and Jase had a lot riding on the latest deal, besides the vast sums of money they'd put into it. The truth of the matter was, the Albanians were crazy fuckers, and if this all went wrong, he and Jase would be dead men walking.

Yawning, Jake glanced towards his brother. He couldn't help smiling as he watched Jason grin maniacally at Alan and playfully draw his finger across his throat. Alan reddened and quickly turned away. For all his talk, the man was an out-and-out pussy.

At last, the chairman got to what Jake and his brother had come for.

'Representations from interested parties have been lodged and filed, objecting to the application for the premises at number 56 White Hart Road to be turned into a licensed betting shop. As there are no amendments to the original application from Councillor Davies, and taking into consideration the concerns expressed by many local residents, we'll now vote on the application. Can I ask you to raise your hand if you're *against* . . .'

A mutter of voices went around the hall before all eyes rested on the Wakemans. Three councillors raised their hands. Alan discreetly gestured with his eyes towards them. Jake acknowledged the signal and quietly moved around the hall to where the councillors were sitting. Two hands were hastily lowered: Councillor Watkins remained firm, his hand defiantly raised.

Jake banged on the leg of the councillor's chair with his foot, then dropped a pen on the ground by Watkins' feet. Kneeling to pick it up, he turned his head and muttered out of the corner of his mouth, 'Not the smartest of moves, Terence.' It was too quiet for anyone else to hear.

Terence Watkins' gaze moved over towards Jason, who stood with a dark expression on his face. The councillor's face drained of colour, and he slowly lowered his hand.

Jake winked, picked up his pen, and wandered over to the nearest chair, ready to keep an eye on the rest of the proceedings.

'Those in favour of the licence being granted, raise your hands.'

The assembled councillors raised their hands with great enthusiasm, though the look of fear in some eyes said quite the opposite.

'Those who want to abstain.'

No one moved, and a moment later, the chairman nodded, looking relieved as he announced, 'The decision of the committee is unanimous . . . The licence is granted.'

The tension in the air broke. As the people stood up to leave, the sound of scraping chairs filled the hall. Ray sauntered over, shaking Jake's hand again. 'Appreciate that, Jake. Were there any problems?'

'No, not really, most of them had already been paid a visit last week. But you know us, we like to see a job through.'

Ray nodded to the people filing out, looking to all intents and purposes like a benefactor who'd done good for their local community. 'Well, like I said to Alan yesterday, I'm grateful for you guys doing what you do. Otherwise those cunts in the council start playing hard ball with me. Bunch of fucking hypocrites, most of them come in and have a flutter on the gee-gees. Why don't you and your brother pop round for a drink next week, we could—'

'Sorry, mate, I have to catch Alan.' Jake cut Ray short, leaving him mid-sentence.

He pushed through the small crowd, but by the time he'd got outside, there was no sign of Carver anywhere. He saw Jason marching Councillor Watkins briskly across the school yard.

'Jase, Jase, hold up.' He broke into a jog.

Jason was hurrying towards his car. Three other vehicles, filled with a dozen or so of their henchmen, were parked nearby. Jase rarely went anywhere without a small entourage these days. The coke was making him more paranoid, which ultimately made him more dangerous.

Jason opened the back door of his car, gesturing with his head for Watkins to get in. 'You coming, bruv?'

Jake shook his head. 'What the fuck are you doing? We're supposed to be meeting Alan, and then Zef and his fucking cronies.'

Jason looked around, giving an exaggerated shrug. 'Don't see them.' He grinned. 'Besides, I need to give Terence here a tour of the docks, and have a little word with him, don't I, Councillor Watkins?' Jason leant into the car and clapped Watkins on his cheeks. 'It'll be nice to have a little chat . . . You sure you won't come, Jake?'

Jake shook his head.

Jason slammed the door on Watkins and walked around to the driver's door. 'Last chance, Jakey. It'll be fun.'

Without bothering to reply, Jake stepped away from the car. He gestured to one of the henchmen sitting in the car behind, who was smoking a joint out of the open back window. 'Make sure Jase doesn't go over the top, okay? Otherwise I'll be holding you responsible, all right, Gus?'

Most people who went for a little drive with Jason ended up finding out, too late, that the journey was a one-way trip. But no doubt Jason would just take Watkins to one of the old warehouses on the waterfront, to put the fear of God into him and remind him of who really ran the area around here.

Watkins, like harder men before him, would literally piss himself from sheer fright, before being dropped backed off at his house, untouched. And it would do the job. Watkins would think twice before trying to go up against the Wakeman twins again.

Shrugging his collar up, Jake wandered back along the street. He was about to cross over at Tavy Close when, from the corner of his eye, he saw Alan speeding away in his Jaguar.

'Alan! *Alan!* Alan, wait up!'

He yelled after him, trying to wave him down, but the car disappeared from sight, turning the corner at speed.

'*For fuck's sake.*'

Jake stood staring at the empty road. Alan was up to something, quite what, he didn't know. But finding out was only a matter of time.

Chapter Seventeen

'Move out of the way, you stupid cunt.' Alan banged furiously on his car window at the elderly gentleman who was crossing prematurely at the junction of Kennington Road. 'Go on then, what are you waiting for? Move, you fat fuck. Can't you see it's my right of way, mate?' As Alan's blood pressure soared, and with patience having never been his strong point, he swerved aggressively, doing a sharp right.

His thoughts were preoccupied with the Wakemans. He'd seen Jake waving to him in the rear-view mirror, but there was no way he was about to stop and chat. All through the meeting Jason had been looking at him as if he wanted to rip his head off. And it occurred to Alan, not for the first time, that the balance of power had shifted too much for his liking. Granted, the Wakemans had certainly had their uses in the past, but those two pricks had got way above their fucking station.

Sighing loudly, Alan indicated left. He had a sneaking suspicion he wouldn't be able to get rid of them that easily. They went back a long way. That was part of the problem. And they both knew where the bodies were buried.

Halfway down Black Prince Road, Alan slowed and parked by one of the broken street lamps. He'd wound himself up enough to give himself a headache. Stretching towards the glove compartment, he flicked it open and pulled out a half-smoked joint.

He lit it, drawing the smoke deep into his lungs, and continued to smoke until he felt calmer. Whoever said it was easier at the top, didn't know his fucking life.

Alan clambered out of the driver's seat and looked around, making sure he locked up the Jag properly. The little fuckers from the estate would have a field day with it. Sticking his hands in his pockets, the sub-zero temperature only added to Alan's foul mood.

He knew this area well, and he quickly headed through the estate towards Vauxhall Walk. He had a feeling that Jason's wife, Samantha, lived not far from here. She was a proper sort. A great pair of tits, and a trim, tight figure. He'd give her the fuck of her life, lucky bitch. He imagined his cock going into her mouth.

'Hey, mate, have you got any money?' A stooped figure stepped in front of him. Alan ignored her and continued to hurry towards the Embankment, watching his footing so as not to step in any dog shit.

'Well, how about a blow job, mate? Fiver.'

Irritated, Alan spoke over his shoulder. 'I'd rather stick my dick down the fucking khazi, it's probably cleaner, darlin'.' Stupid whore.

He veered across Pedlar's Park and, taking the short cut, made his way down a narrow path behind the buildings lining the Albert Embankment. He hurried past the long row of railway arches, the tracks above him leading in and out of Waterloo Station.

Alan slowed down by the last archway and felt a vibration around his waist. He opened his coat and glanced down at the pager on his belt. He recognised the number: it was Chief Superintendent Lewis getting back to him. He'd have to call him back later, he wasn't about to start tramping around looking for a phone box now.

A few hundred yards further on, he strode into an open space directly opposite the Thames. Where the fuck was Frank? He'd specifically told him to stay on site. In the dark, he could see the lights bouncing off the river. It was a spectacular view. No matter how small this piece of land was, it was certainly a prime spot. A prime spot he regretted selling off.

But what option had he had? The Wakemans had put pressure on him and eventually, thinking it would be a golden handshake for the pair – meaning he could finally get rid of them, once and for all – he'd gone ahead and sold it off.

They'd got it for a song, compared to what it was worth. Like all the other times before, Alan had paid off enough councillors to make sure the deal went through, with no awkward questions asked. Job done. And it would all have been fine, if it wasn't for this latest discovery.

'I thought I fucking told you to stay here?' Alan caught sight of Frank lolloping towards him.

'I did, I haven't moved. I've turned into a pissing ice statue. It's freezing.'

'Shut the fuck up.' Alan wasn't interested in Frank's complaints. He'd only employed the man because Dennis had insisted. And the one thing you didn't do, was say no to Dennis Hargreaves.

Alan surveyed the plot of land. This was a big headache. More than a big headache, it was a fucking nightmare.

'And do you think there are more?' Alan asked, turning back to Frank.

'More what?'

'What the fuck do you think I mean?' Even though there was no one else about, Alan still lowered his voice. 'More remains.'

Frank flicked his cap up and stared around the site. 'Might be . . . I couldn't say.'

Alan felt the tension gripping his body. He had a nasty feeling that Frank was enjoying witnessing his discomfort. 'You couldn't say, or you won't fucking say?'

Frank leant in towards Alan, his huge stomach touching him. Alan could smell his rancid breath.

'I don't know, Al, it might be just that one kid, or it might be more.'

'Jesus Christ . . . and don't fucking call me Al.'

Alan fell silent. He had to think what to do. Fuck. The building they'd knocked down had been a children's home, Fitzwilliam's. Whatever the fuck had gone on here, Alan didn't want to know. The problem was, if there *were* more remains, it would become harder to hush things up. The spotlight would fall on *him*, exposing the deals he'd been making, including this one. The trail would eventually lead to the Wakemans. And Jason. Shit fucking creek was an understatement.

'Dennis wants you to cover this over.'

Alan glared at him. 'What? You've spoken to Dennis?'

'Yeah, I called him after I spoke to you, and he's not very happy. He wants you to cover it up. He wants you to pull out of the deal with whoever is developing the site, and cover this whole piece of land with concrete.' Frank smiled. 'Maybe you could make a kiddies' playground out of it, *Al*.'

Alan was sorely tempted to knock the cunt out. But instead, he thought back to the agitated phone call he'd received from Dennis after he'd sold the land. He'd been given instructions to inform not only Dennis himself, but Chief Superintendent Lewis as well, if there were any problems.

He hadn't taken much notice at the time, but in hindsight, it was odd that Dennis had insisted that Frank and a couple of other men should work on clearing the site once contracts had exchanged hands, and before the sale was formally completed. He hadn't ever quite worked out their relationship, or how Dennis and Frank knew each other, but he'd never been overly concerned, and had just gone along with it.

And as for the Wakemans, well, they hadn't been too bothered about what happened on site. Why should they? They weren't interested in getting their hands dirty. The only part that had concerned them was how long it was all taking to complete the paperwork. But now it was all starting to slowly make sense.

'So, can I tell Dennis that it's all going to be sorted? That you're going to tell whoever you sold it to, the deal is off now.' Frank interrupted his thoughts.

Alan rubbed his chest, wishing he'd brought some more Valium along with him. How the fuck could he cover this plot of land over with concrete? He couldn't exactly give the money back to the Wakemans. He'd already spent it on bribes and backhanders to ensure the sale went through. Plus filling a few extra pies he had his fingers in. It was no longer his, he didn't have it, and he had no access to get that sort of money either.

Earlier, he'd been planning to get rid of Jason and Jake, but this fucking cock-up made that impossible. They were supposed to be signing off the contract for the land tomorrow, and that didn't look like it was going to happen. So what the hell was he going to tell them?

Alan had never experienced true, cold fear, until now. With Dennis on one side, and the deal he'd made with the Wakeman brothers on the other. There was no other way of putting it. He was fucked.

Chapter Eighteen

Samantha couldn't sleep. Sick of staring at the ceiling, she sat up and switched on the pink night lamp on the bedside locker. The girl, Grace, was playing on her mind. There'd been a vulnerability to her. Of course, every kid that went through the system was vulnerable, but most of them, apart from the very youngest ones, were streetwise enough to know what was going on. Not that any kid would be streetwise enough to survive Holly Brookes. And once again, a chill gripped her.

She looked at the new digital alarm clock she'd bought last week from Rumbelows. It was three thirty. She might as well get up and make herself a drink, rather than just lying here worrying. It wouldn't do her any good.

She grabbed her cream dressing gown from the end of her bed, slipped it on and wandered quietly down the stairs. The last thing she wanted was to wake her mum. She'd had enough of Phyllis's demands for one night.

Halfway down the stairs, Samantha paused, thinking she heard a noise.

'*Hello?* Jase? Jase, is that you?' She frowned.

There was no reply. It was probably nothing.

As she headed into the kitchen, a hand suddenly covered her

mouth. Instinctively, she began to fight. But she was no match for the intruder.

'*Sshhh*. It's only me.'

All fight left her, and Samantha felt the grip on her mouth loosen.

She spun around.

'What the hell are you doing?' Tightening the belt of her dressing gown, she stared at Jake.

'I didn't want to wake Phyllis.'

'So, you thought you'd scare the shit out of me instead?'

Jake shrugged. He stared at Samantha's swollen lip, and once again anger swelled in him. 'Sorry, but I wanted to see if you were all right.'

Samantha bristled and moved across to the kettle, flicking the switch down hard. She looked through the gap in the blinds, looking out on to the deserted street, feeling more than uncomfortable that Jake was here.

'Sam?' He touched her shoulder, turning her around to face him. His green eyes bored into hers. It was like staring at Jason, which always unnerved her. 'Are you hurt?'

'Why are you even here? Jake, do me a favour and go.' Trembling, she turned away again, willing the kettle to finish boiling. She caught her breath as she felt his body pressing up against her back, and felt his breath against the side of her face. For a moment she closed her eyes. 'You shouldn't be here, Jake.'

'Shouldn't I?' he whispered.

She shook her head. Breathing him in. 'No, you need to go.'

'What if I don't want to?'

Holding herself rigid, she shook her head. 'Jake, just go. Jason could—'

'Jason's with his whores. He's at the club.'

Finally, Samantha turned around, her vision blurred by tears. '*Please*, I'm asking you.'

He touched her face gently, caressing it, and she leant into his cupped hand. Then, angry more at herself than at Jake, Samantha moved away.

'What the fuck are you doing, Jake?'

'Samantha?' Her mum hollered from next door. '*Sam?*'

'Oh, great.' She rolled her eyes at Jake. 'Yes, Mum, sorry.' She called to Phyllis. 'I couldn't sleep, so I'm making myself a cuppa.'

'Oh, lovely, you can make me a brew too then.'

Sighing, Samantha barged Jake out of the way to grab a mug from the cupboard. 'Thanks very much, now I've got to deal with her.'

Jake blocked her way. 'Sam, talk to me.'

Her eyes met his. 'This is crazy, Jake. If Jason turns up unannounced, I don't even want to think about what will happen.' Her voice was resolute. 'And I'm tired, I've had a really bad day and I don't want to do this.'

'Sam, is someone there with you?' Phyllis shouted from her room.

'No, Mum, of course not, it's the radio.' Samantha shouted through to Phyllis, at the same time as pulling Jake into the hallway.

Jake pleaded. 'Sam, please, I needed to see you, I was worried, and to tell you the truth, I can't stop thinking about you.'

'Since when, Jake? Is that before or after you chose your brother instead of me?'

'Sam, where's my bleeding tea?' Her mother sounded aggrieved.

She closed her eyes, and yelled, 'It's fucking coming, okay!' Then she slammed the door so as not to hear any more from Phyllis.

'How many times do I have to tell you? It wasn't like that.'

There was a hint of frustration in Jake's tone, and Samantha matched it with her own bitterness. 'Really, Jake? Because the way I remember it, that's exactly how it was.'

'And you seem to be forgetting, you jumped into his bed pretty quickly afterwards.'

The slap to Jake's face took him by surprise.

'Get out.'

Jake rubbed his cheek. It hadn't hurt, maybe bruised his ego a little bit, but he deserved it. 'I'm sorry, I shouldn't have said that.'

Samantha was unrepentant. 'No, you shouldn't have . . . and anyway, what the hell are we doing still talking about it? It's in the past. Let's leave it there.'

'But what if I don't want it to be in the past . . . I fucked up. I fucked up big time, I know I—'

'Stop. Just stop it.' Samantha interrupted him. 'How dare you come around here whenever you like and do this to me . . .' She paused. 'I want you to leave.'

'Only if you tell me that you don't feel anything for me any more.' As Jake spoke, he moved closer to her again.

Samantha caught her breath. Being this near to him made her remember what it had felt like when they'd been together. His touch on her skin. But she knew what would happen if Jason even got a sniff of Jake coming around. And she wouldn't be responsible for that. No matter how much she wanted him. She wouldn't have his blood on her hands.

She stared at him intently. 'I don't feel anything, Jake . . . Do you understand that? You and I were a mistake . . . one which happened a long time ago . . . and I don't feel anything at all for you.'

A flash of hurt crossed his face. Without saying another word, he walked away, slamming out of the front door.

In the kitchen the kettle finished boiling, just as Phyllis – who sat up in her bed in the front room – was working out that it wasn't actually the radio she'd been hearing at all, but Jake Wakeman's voice.

Book Two

1983
Friday

Silence in the face of evil is itself evil.

Dietrich Bonhoeffer

Chapter Nineteen

The drive from London to the Sussex countryside in the early morning was a blur for Grace. The only thing on her mind right now was her mum. And with each mile they drove, Grace was aware that she was being taken further and further away from her.

From underneath her fringe, she looked warily at her chaperone. The woman hadn't said a word to her. She was sitting in the front seat, filling up the car with smoke.

Grace peeked nervously at the girl sitting next to her. They'd both got into the car at the same time, at the side entrance of St Thomas' Hospital. She hadn't said anything to her either. Through most of the journey she'd been dozing, on and off.

Seeing the girl frowning at her, Grace quickly turned the other way.

Whatever it was they'd given her, Dara decided it must be strong. The last thing she properly remembered was being taken to St Thomas' to have her chin stitched up. She was vaguely aware of getting into the car they were in now, and having to sit next to the strange girl who hadn't said a word. Through most of the journey she'd been crying.

The tablets were beginning to wear off, but they'd made her feel good, and Dara hadn't thought about anything at all. She'd been in a void. It felt like she'd been floating. For a short time it had made her forget about what had happened. Even better, for a short time it had made Dara forget who she was.

Yawning, Dara glanced out of the window as the car sped along the lanes. She'd never been out of London. It felt strange to be surrounded by fields instead of estates. And earlier she'd seen an actual real-life cow standing by a hedgerow. Her first thought was how much her brothers and sisters would have loved to see that, but she'd quickly shut that down. Hopefully, she'd soon be reunited with them.

The car slowed down and drove through a pair of large wrought-iron gates. Dara pressed her face against the cold glass. The place was lovely. Individual cottages were dotted through the grounds, and she spotted a treehouse over by the woods. Even the gardens looked immaculate. It took a good minute or so to get to the large house where the car finally pulled up to a stop.

Getting out, Dara followed the chaperone and the silent girl through the stone entrance to a large hall with high ceilings and a sweeping staircase in the middle of it.

'Wait here.' The woman disappeared down a corridor.

Dara began to take in her surroundings. It was the smell that got to her. She had been taken into care before, but had always been placed in foster homes with a family.

'*Oi!*' From the top of the stairs three girls walked down towards them. They glared at Dara.

'What the fuck are you looking at?' Dara growled at them, glaring back. She wasn't a bitch by nature, but she knew that these places were dog eat dog, and if she didn't stand up for herself from the start, they'd see her as a target.

It did the trick and they turned away, focusing their attention on the girl she'd shared the car with. Dara watched as the girl put her head down.

'Cat got your tongue?' The ringleader, a short girl with a shocking case of acne, grinned at her friend.

'I doubt it,' the friend replied, goading the silent newcomer. 'Even the cat would be afraid to go anywhere near that ugly bitch. Hey, we're speaking to you . . . Ain't you heard it's rude to ignore people?' She poked the girl hard in her chest. 'I'm talking to you.'

'Yeah, well, maybe she don't want to talk to you, have you ever thought of that?' Dara stepped in.

The girls looked between themselves.

'This isn't anything to do with you, so fuck off,' the short girl said.

A large smile spread across Dara's face. One thing she hated was bullies. She'd been surrounded by them all her life. If it wasn't her mum, it was her mum's boyfriends and pimps knocking her about – or worse still, knocking her brothers and sisters about. So there was absolutely no way she was going to let these bitches push the girl around.

'It *is* to do with me, because she's my mate, okay? And if you want me to fuck off, then you'll have to make me.' With her hands on her hips, Dara stood defiantly.

Once again the girls looked at each other, before backing away towards the corridor. They pointed at her as they went. 'You've made a big mistake, bitch.'

'Whatever!' Dara called after them as they went out of sight.

Making enemies on the first day wasn't the best way to start in a new place. And Dara had a feeling that it wouldn't be the last she heard from them.

'I'm Grace.' The girl spoke to her quietly, and she began to cry again.

'I'm Dara.'

'Thank you, Dara. For what you did just now . . .'

*

Grace's words tailed off. She was afraid she was going to be sick. She swallowed hard, but no matter how much she tried to stop herself from crying, she couldn't.

She wiped the snot away from her nose with her sleeve. She pulled at her jumper, the itchy wool was irritating her. She hated the clothes Samantha had given her. The polo-neck top was all scratchy and the red pleated skirt didn't quite fit properly, and neither did the tights.

Everything about what was happening was horrible, and with that thought Grace gave in to another bout of tears.

Dara shrugged. 'No problem.'

She sighed. She didn't want any hangers-on. Surviving in these places was hard enough already. But there was something about this tiny girl that reminded her of Tammy and Kirsty. A stabbing pain shot through Dara as she thought again about her siblings.

'Grace. It's a nice name . . . Gracie. I'm going to call you Gracie.' Dara could see that this girl needed her, and she felt a deep sadness, though there was something that told Dara that maybe she needed Gracie too. She smiled at her, and although Dara didn't know it quite yet, it would be the beginning of a lifelong friendship.

Their chaperone reappeared, shouting and gesturing for them to follow.

'Come on, come with me . . . Hurry up, we haven't got all day . . . Now!'

They did as they were told, hurrying after her along the corridor.

Dara shivered as she read the plaque nailed to the wall: *Suffer little children to come unto me.*

Chapter Twenty

Judy Baker hadn't slept well. She'd been worrying about her Frank as she sat in her kitchen in the house she'd shared with him in Newburn Street, Lambeth, for the past twenty years.

She'd been slightly annoyed at first. He'd promised they could take a drive out to Eastgate Shopping Centre, over in Basildon. She'd wanted to mooch around Marks and Spencer's, maybe even Dorothy Perkins. Pick up some nice bits and pieces. Then she'd been planning on going over to her sister's, to show it off. The one thing Judy loved more than shopping was boasting about it, especially to Mandy.

The shopping trips also fulfilled Judy's overwhelming need to walk around the baby stores. She loved the touch and feel of the tiny clothes in Mothercare. The prams, the high chairs, the sterilisers. Only last week she'd bought another bottle warmer, along with three Tommee Tippee teats to add to her vast collection.

Over the years Judy had stuffed a corner of the attic full of bibs, cardigans, Babygros, changing mats, even a stroller – and somewhere at the back of the wardrobe in the guest bedroom were packets of unopened nappies.

How she'd longed to be woken up in the night by the cries of a child who needed her. It was a physical ache. All she'd ever wanted to do was to be wife and a mother. So she couldn't understand why each time she'd fallen pregnant, within a few months of her jubilation, came the bleeding, the loss, and the mourning for the baby she'd already named and fallen in love with.

Unlike all those skanky bitches, the single mums over on the estate in Black Prince Road, Judy was convinced she would have made a fantastic mum. And Frank, for all his faults, would have made a wonderful dad. Then a few years ago, she'd gone through the change, and all she was left with from her womanhood were the hot flushes and more weight around her middle than a fucking pot-bellied pig.

Judy felt robbed. Cheated. Life had bloody well stripped her of the prize of being a mother, and the bitterness ran deep. She had to contend with the pitying looks people gave her after asking if she had children. The humiliation of admitting she didn't, leaving her red with shame and wanting to claw their eyes out.

So now, along with her secret hoards, Frank was her world. Yes, she had her sister and her nephew, Jimmy, who was a sandwich short of a picnic. But Frank was different, she lived and breathed him. So when Frank hadn't arrived home by seven o'clock last night, Judy had been beside herself with worry. All sorts of things had gone through her head: he'd had a heart attack, a stroke, been knocked down by a Routemaster on the Kennington Road, or . . . or he'd been arrested.

The idea of that had scared Judy so much she'd had trouble breathing. She'd spent the night staring out of the window and making cups of tea she didn't bother drinking. But as the hours had passed, it was the only conclusion Judy could come to, since she knew she wasn't the only one who had a secret hoard, was she?

She still remembered the day, some time ago, when she'd been searching for the tea towels she could have sworn she'd bought the previous year from Woolworths. That's when she'd found them. The photographs.

They had shocked her. It had taken Judy all day to get up from the edge of the bed she'd sat on. And it was sunset before she'd moved to the bathroom to be sick.

Then, five minutes after carefully wiping off the vomit from her avocado toilet seat, she'd packed her bags. But when Judy had reached her freshly painted garden gate, she'd turned back and put her things neatly away, before Frank had come home. *She* hadn't done anything wrong, so why the hell should *she* suffer for what other people did?

She had a nice life, a three-up three-down on the right side of Lambeth, a far cry from the squalor where she'd been brought up. No, Judy wasn't prepared to give it all up just because her husband had certain tastes. Besides, at least it wasn't another woman. That would be something *entirely* different. There was no bleeding way she'd put up with that.

Sacrificing her own happiness wouldn't change anything. It wouldn't stop her Frank from feeling the way he did. She couldn't blame him; her Frank had needs, certain needs which she couldn't satisfy, just like her mum had said her dad had needs, when he used to come into her room at night.

Taking the crotched tea cosy off the teapot, Judy poured herself a cuppa. Frank had called half an hour ago, letting her know he was safe, which meant not only could she relax, but he should be here any minute now.

Judy switched on the radio. 'Time After Time' was playing, and for a moment she just stood and listened to Cyndi Lauper's voice. Then she got up and rinsed the last of the dishes under the hot water, before flicking on the kettle to make Frank a Nescafé. She'd add an extra splash of Carnation Milk, the way he liked it.

Frank always looked after her so well. Judy knew she was one of the luckiest women alive to have Frank as her husband.

'Judy . . . Judy.' Frank bellowed from the hallway, masking the sound of the front door being closed. Relieved to be home, he walked into the kitchen and winked at Judy, throwing an envelope on the table.

She pulled it towards her and eyed it up, seeing all the twenty-pound notes. Dennis made sure he was paid well for the jobs he did.

Frank took the cup of coffee gratefully. It had turned into an all-nighter on site.

'That cunt, he thinks he's the dog's bollocks. But I'm telling you, one day Alan's going to fuck up badly, and I can smell that day's coming soon. Can you believe he made me stay there all night? It would've been warmer to sleep in a fucking freezer.'

'Come and sit down, darlin', and tell me all about it.' She pulled out a chair, and hurried round to sit opposite him, listening intently.

Frank recounted the story. Everything, from Jimmy's discovery, to exactly what they'd found, and back around to how Alan Carver had treated him like dirt.

'So why were there human remains, do you think?'

Frank was good at lying. Almost as good as Judy was at knowing when she was being lied to.

'I have no idea,' he said, looking vacant.

'And you don't think Jimmy will talk?' Judy said, frowning.

Frank shrugged, and they finished their drinks in silence.

Although Frank smiled at Judy as he placed his cup back on the table, the idea of Jimmy keeping his mouth shut, especially over something so serious, worried him. The stupid fucker had never been able to hold on to anything, let alone a bleeding secret. Though right now, Frank decided to keep that observation to himself. He wanted to think about it some more before he worked out what to do.

'I missed you, pumpkin.' Judy leant towards him, putting on a baby voice, which always got on Frank's nerves.

He held his breath and allowed her to undo his belt before she roughly stuck her hand through the zipper of his trousers, trying to pull out his reluctant penis. It felt like she was fishing a tea bag out of the caddy.

'Ouch.'

Hurt crossed Judy's face. 'You don't like it?'

Gritting his teeth, he pinched her cheeks gently. 'Of course I do, what makes you think that?'

Judy blushed with delight.

Frank's stomach turned as she opened her thunderous legs, exposing a mass of pubic hair even Christopher Columbus would get lost in. If it made her happy, then he'd go along with it, but Christ, he'd rather stick his fingers into an electric socket than into her wet pussy. Over the years he'd learnt not to pull a face as his fingers entered her. And while she moaned, Frank distracted himself by wondering if she'd put last night's supper in the fridge.

When it was over, he smiled at her, and she smiled back just as warmly.

He was a lucky man to always have her by his side. She would do anything for him. Anything at all. Nothing and no one would get in the way of her loyalty to him.

Chapter Twenty-One

Jason had his penis so far down Kitty's throat, it fleetingly crossed his mind that the dopey cunt had silently choked to death. The lack of pleasure he was getting from having his dick sucked by her, she might as well be a fucking corpse.

'Oi, stop a minute, darlin', will ya?' Pushing himself up on his elbows, he looked down at Kitty. Like all the whores who worked for him, Kitty's feelings meant nothing to him, and he continued to snarl at her. 'I said *stop*, fucking hell, if you're that fucking hungry go and get a kebab from Big Tony's.'

Rolling to the side, Jason leant over, dipped his finger into the pile of coke on the small walnut table next to the bed, and rubbed the coke on his gums. He hadn't slept, he hadn't come, he hadn't done anything apart from think about Samantha. Jesus Christ, she wound him up.

He couldn't get his head around it. Why did he fucking care? Because let's have it straight, in the beginning Samantha had been a disposable fuck, something to amuse him. Though somehow she'd known how to get right under his skin. The way she looked at him with her big fucking doe eyes, as if she was taking the piss. As if she thought that somehow *he* was below her. But it was also that look that said, *she didn't like him*, and that hadn't ever changed. If anything, it'd got worse.

That thought came to an abrupt end as Jason turned his head towards the closed door. 'Did you hear that?'

He kicked Kitty off the bed. Wiping her saliva off his swollen penis, Jason swiped up his T-shirt and trousers from the floor.

Pushing out her bottom lip and rubbing her nose along the back of her hand, Kitty shrugged. She *had* heard something coming from the club downstairs, but she wasn't going to tell him. Miserable bastard.

Innocently she stared at her pink chipped nail varnish and shook her head. 'Nah, I can't hear nothing.'

'For fuck's sake.' Jason's mouth hardened. He muttered under his breath and quickly got dressed.

He was sure he'd heard a crash. Where the fuck were his men? Whenever he stayed at the club, he always made sure there were at least three or four of them around. Though last time he'd laid eyes on any of them, they'd been on the top floor, fucked out of their faces, surrounded by a bunch of naked hookers.

Marching out of the bedroom with its gold-leaf wallpaper and expensive antique furniture, he staggered down the wooden stairs. He kept meaning to get them carpeted. He squeezed past the crates of beer and bottles of knock-off Lambrusco, stacked too high in the corridor, before hurrying through the kitchens.

He rushed through the black padded double doors, which took him to the main area of the club. But by the time Jason realised that he needed to go and round up his men, it was too late. The hard punch to the side of his head sent him spinning towards the bar.

A few of the hookers still hanging around the club screamed. Jason instinctively grabbed one of the wine bottles from the counter, swung it round and smashed it against the bar. With the jagged end, he lunged towards his assailant, slicing deep into the cheek and exposing layers of flesh. Still not finished, Jason twisted the bottle, pushing it right through into the man's mouth, leaving a gaping hole.

Blood poured everywhere and Jason dived behind the bar just as a small, fat man holding a cosh obstructed his way. The man moved to grab Jason, but he wasn't quick enough. Jason slammed his elbow straight into the man's nose before pulling him into a headlock.

'Who the fuck sent you? I said, *who fucking sent you?*'

There was no answer forthcoming.

'So you want to play it like that, do you?'

Jason rammed his fingers into the man's eyes. There was a loud shriek, along with the squelch of flesh. Jason pulled out the gun he always kept in the ice maker, and pointed it.

'I'll ask you again, who the fuck sent you? Go on then, mate, I'm waiting.' Panting, Jason paused for a moment, watching the man holding his hands over his eyes. 'You don't need your fucking eyes to answer, you cunt . . . No?' Jason moved his arm down and aimed the gun at the man's kneecaps. 'Well, maybe I'll help you remember the names, shall I?' And without the slightest hesitation, he pulled the trigger.

The man writhed on the floor in agony, and Jason stamped on his head. 'Who the fuck sent—'

'Jase, dear oh dear, what's the poor guy ever done to you?'

Jason watched Zef and Dren walk slowly down the entrance stairs and across the club towards him. They wore matching sheepskin coats. Expensive ones. They had enough gold jewellery hanging off them to look like they were part of the Brink's-Mat robbery, and they drove around in flashy red Bentleys. But they still looked like cunts in Jason's opinion. Two big, ugly bastards, muscular ones, especially Zef, who was rumoured to inject steroids into his thick, squat neck. They were two walking brick shithouses.

Zef and Dren enjoyed the danger they brought along with them. Every act of violence was performed with a smile, which unnerved a lot of people. But not Jason.

He allowed his gaze to dart around the club. Several large disco balls hung from the ceiling. Mirrors decorated the black and red velvet-clad walls – making the cavernous room look even larger than it already was – but the whole place was a fucking mess. The tables and chairs dotted around the edges of the dance floor had been turned upside down, and the private VIP area looked like a bull had gone on a rampage. His hookers were huddled against the bar, looking shell-shocked.

Bringing his stare back to the Albanians, and ignoring the two men in agony on the floor, Jason glared. 'Look what your fucking meatheads have done to my club. What the fuck are you playing at?'

Zef winked at Dren as he spoke. 'Me? What the fuck am *I* playing at? Now there's a question.'

There was only the lightest accent detectable in the way Zef spoke. His links to Albania went no further than Bethnal Green. 'So let me get this right, you want to know what I'm playing at, Jase, yet *you're* the one who made us look like cunts?'

Jason placed the gun down on the bar and walked around to the other side. He poured himself a glass of whiskey, knocked it back and slammed down the glass. 'What the fuck are you talking about?'

'Last night. Me and Dren were down in the Rose and Crown, sitting around like fucking muppets, and I could've sworn you were supposed to be meeting us there.'

Genuinely puzzled, Jason shrugged. 'My brother, I thought he was showing up.'

Zef chewed on the cigar he'd just pulled out from his pocket.

He lit it and took a deep drag, pulling the smoke right down into his lungs before answering. 'So it's your brother's fault, is it?'

'I never said that. What I mean is, there's obviously been a mis-communication, and for that, I'm sorry. But don't think you can come into my club and humiliate me like this.'

A wide smirk appeared on Zef's face. His cheeks creased in amusement and his dark eyes gazed intently at Jason. A small vein pulsated on one temple.

Jason didn't like the way things were going. 'I ain't some pussy, Zef, and I don't like you coming on to my turf, and looking at me like I'm some piece of shit.'

Dren strode round to where Jason was standing. His expression was changing by the second, but he kept his tone even as he played with the large, jagged knife in his hand. 'Is that right, Jase?'

Jason was not going to be intimidated. 'Yeah, it is.'

The two men were roughly the same height, both standing above six foot two.

'The thing is, I really, *really* hope for your sake, Jase, you ain't stupid enough to mess us about. We've put a lot of money into this deal, and we've got a lot riding on it.'

Before Jason had a chance to reply, a noise off to one side made them all turn towards the entrance stairs.

Jake ambled down them. He hadn't slept well, and already felt like shit. But whatever it was he was walking into, it wasn't going to help his mood. What the fuck? He gazed around. It was a blood bath. His brother was covered in claret. There were two geezers looking a mess on the floor. And then there was the nightmare of Zef and Dren, looking like two fucking Rottweilers. What the hell had his brother done now?

'What the fuck are you two doing here?' Jake came to a halt in front of Zef. He glanced at his watch. It was still only eight thirty in the morning, give or take. 'It's a bit early for cunts, isn't it?'

'Now that's not very nice.' Zef smiled widely, letting out a mouthful of cigar smoke at the same time. 'I'd expect better manners from my business partner.'

Jake laughed and chewed on his lip, though his eyes were devoid of expression. 'Stop being a muggy cunt, Zef, and just tell me what's going on. I take it it was you that made this mess?'

Zef's face darkened. He rubbed his stubbled chin with his pudgy fingers. A large diamond ring was squeezed on to each one.

'Like I told your brother, not only is it fucking rude, but it makes me edgy, to be stood up on the night before our deal is supposed to be going through.'

Jake had to admit, Zef had a point. He should've turned up, or at least got a message to them. Instead, he'd completely fucked them off to go and see Samantha. He didn't even want to think about the reasons behind that. As usual, his visit had messed him up. But putting all that aside, nothing justified Zef and Dren doing this.

'How the fuck are we supposed to work together if the minute things don't run smoothly, you come in like thugs?'

Zef was silent for a moment. His gaze followed his injured henchmen being helped out of the club. 'We wouldn't have to, if we knew what was happening. If you leave me in the dark, I have no other choice.'

Jake listened, but he knew this was the excuse the Albanians had been looking for to throw their weight around. It was supposed to be an equal partnership, but there was nothing equal about this shit.

'The final contract will be signed off today, and then it's all ours.' Jake kept his voice quiet. 'So you didn't have to come down and do all this shit.'

'Good, I just hope you're being straight with me, Jakey boy. There better not be any problems.'

The image of Alan's Jaguar speeding away flashed through Jake's mind. He still hadn't been able to talk to the cunt. He hoped Alan wasn't holding out on him. 'No, no problems at all, mate.'

Dren was still twirling the knife around in his hand. 'Good, that's what I like to hear. You wouldn't want to fuck us over.'

'Yeah, okay, mate, you don't have to repeat yourself, you've said your piece.' Jason was beyond irritated. 'You've proved your point. Now fuck off.'

Dren tilted his head to one side. His eyes moved towards the hookers leaning up against the bar looking stoned. He grabbed hold of a young woman, shoving his fist into her hair. She barely had time to register what was happening to her before he drew his knife swiftly across her throat. '*This* is proving a point . . . Now I expect to hear from you by the end of the day.' He held on to her hair tightly as the blood bubbled out of her throat. Then he threw her down like a discarded rag doll, turned and walked out.

With a grin, Zef nodded to the brothers, tapped the ash of his cigar over the woman's lifeless body, and followed Dren out.

Once they'd gone, Jake stared at Jason.

'Fucking cunts. Look at this place! This will take forever to get cleaned up,' Jason ranted.

'Is that it?' Jake demanded. Is that all you fucking care about?' He pointed. 'She's dead, mate, and we let the people *you* decided to go into business with come into *our* club and do that to her.' He pushed Jason hard in the chest. 'How do you think it makes us look, if those two cunts can do what they like, and we're letting them get away with it? All because of some poxy deal you made. I swear I could fucking kill you right now, Jase.'

He took a deep breath to try to calm himself down. It didn't work.

'I told you. I told you not to have anything to do with that lot, but you couldn't fucking help yourself, could you?'

'Leave it out, Jake, you sound like a fucking whiny girl.' Jason shoved his brother back.

'No, *you* need to leave it out, Jase. And you need to get in touch with Alan *now*. Because if something goes wrong, not only am I going to hold you responsible, but there's going to be a fuck of a lot of bloodshed.'

Chapter Twenty-Two

'You can have the top bunk if you like because I won't be here for long.' Grace pulled at the loose thread on the waistband of her jumper.

She was trying to stop herself from getting upset *again*. She heard the wobble in her voice, and felt her legs trembling, just like they had when the girls at school had bullied her. She quickly gulped down big mouthfuls of air, hoping to keep calm. It helped, but it didn't stop her tummy from hurting. Grace was cross with herself that she couldn't stop crying, especially as she'd made her eyes sore, and the tip of her nose red from where she'd been wiping it against her sleeve. And given herself the worst headache ever.

The two girls had only arrived a short while ago, but Grace already knew there was nothing she liked about this place. The dormitory was cold, and she couldn't imagine it ever getting warm, even in the heat of summer. Their bunk bed was next to the window, and she could feel the draught and hear the panes of glass rattling in the wind, as if someone was trying to get in. The ceiling was so high, even if she stood on her tiptoes on the top bunk, she wouldn't be close to touching it. There was a large decorative ceiling rose above her, with a chunk of plaster missing from it, and an ugly chandelier hung from it with somebody's sock caught on one of the bulbs.

She breathed out heavily, seeing her breath in the cold air, and glanced at Dara, wondering if her own eyes looked so sad. It was Friday today, which meant by Monday she'd be home, wouldn't she? Grace was sure of it. Even if her mum wasn't well enough to look after her, that lady she'd met in the hospital was getting in touch with her godmother, and then she'd be able to leave this horrible place, with its horrible smell.

Grace was determined to do two things: she'd squeeze her eyes really tightly together, and pretend she was back in her room, just like she used to pretend her dad was still alive and sitting on the park bench next to her. And she was going to be brave. That's what her mum always said to her when she got scared, *be brave, Grace, be strong, be fearless.* But the moment the words came into Grace's head, the picture of her mum lying in the hospital bed flashed through her mind, and her tears welled up again.

Dara leant against the ladder of the bunkbed, ignoring the obscene graffiti carved all over it, and frowned. She could tell Gracie was trying *so* hard not to cry. Just like Tommy always did when their mum clobbered him around the head or punched him so hard he'd vomit. God, she hated her mum. She remembered all her brother's beatings. Every slap, every kick, every blow.

Right then, Dara was also trying hard not to cry. She *really* needed to know what had happened to her brothers and sisters. She was getting worried now. No one had told her anything, and it wasn't right them being separated from each other. It had already been too long. They'd all be scared and asking for her. She knew they would.

They'd only ever really had each other, so they *couldn't* be apart, and her bitch of a social worker had known that. They needed her. If *she* wasn't there, who would look after Rosie when she woke up in the night, screaming that she didn't like strangers? And who would help Rory talk when he needed things but was too frightened to ask? No one else would give them all a bear hug and love them the way she did.

Dara swallowed back her tears. No way would she cry, especially not in front of Gracie. That would set Gracie off for sure. Dara knew how to stop herself from crying. She pressed down on the sharp nib of the pencil she had in her hand, digging it into the middle of her palm.

'Who told you that you wouldn't be here for long?' Dara attempted a smile as she forced the pencil deeper into her skin. She couldn't explain it, but it gave her relief. It was strange. It was the same kind of relief she'd got when her chin had been split open. It seemed to take the pain away from her head and put it somewhere else. 'How come you know that? Did they tell you?'

Grace shook her head. 'No, but I don't belong in a place like this.'

Without thinking, Dara snapped back, 'What, and I do?' She liked Gracie, she felt sorry for her – and she was pleased she'd told those bitches to fuck off – but she wasn't going to let Gracie look down her nose at her. She was sick of people doing that.

'Well, is it? Is that what you're saying, Gracie? You think I belong in this shithole?'

Grace hid behind her overgrown curly fringe. She looked uncomfortable, as if she hadn't meant it the way it sounded. 'No . . . yes, no . . . I mean, I don't know . . . Sorry.'

Despite herself, Dara couldn't help laughing. She raised her eyebrows in a comical frown. 'You need to watch what you're saying around here, you saw what those bitches were like earlier.'

'I don't care about them, because I'll be going home to my mummy soon.'

'Mummy?' Dara clambered up to the top bunk.

The thin frame creaked noisily. It had been used thousands of times before as both a climbing frame and something to jump off. Although the bed sheets were old, they seemed clean. They smelt clean. Dara barely remembered a time when her bed didn't have a weird smell, or stains on the sheets, or even some random punter of her mum's asleep on it.

From where she was sitting now, Dara could see the grounds, fringed by prickly bushes and hedgerows, and the woods which were also part of Holly Brookes. Tommy would love this. The only things they saw when they looked out of their flat were the over-flowing bins or the upstairs neighbour, who was always being done for shoplifting, lying in a pool of his own sick.

All the cottages and the main building of the home were red brick, with large windows. That miserable cow of a chaperone had said there were about twenty cottages with around fifteen to twenty kids in each. Apart from those three skanky bitches, they hadn't met any of the others yet.

Dara watched a group of kids in the distance, looking freezing as they trudged through a thin layer of snow on the ground, dressed only in white vests and navy shorts, and the girls in navy pleated skirts. It looked like they were being made to run around the grounds before breakfast. Like hell was anyone going to make her do that.

She dangled over the side of the bunk bed and stared down at Grace. 'That's another thing you've got to cut out, Gracie. You can't go around saying *mummy* in here. What did she do to you anyway? Was she a smackhead?'

Grace peered up at her. 'A what?'

'You know, a smackhead. Was she on the game as well? My mum was. Stupid fucking cow.' Dara wasn't quite sure why she was telling Grace all about her mum. She never gave anything away, and if someone did say something about her mum, they'd get a proper clump. But somehow Dara felt they were in this together.

Grace gave Dara's question a few minutes' thought, but she still looked blank. 'No, I don't know what a smackhead is.'

'How old are you?' Dara couldn't believe Grace was this naive.

'Twelve, well, I'll be thirteen soon.'

'And you *really* don't know what a smackhead is, or what being on the game is?'

Grace shook her head again.

'So you don't know what a blow job is then?'

'No, sorry.'

Dara smiled. 'No, that's good, Gracie. You're lucky.'

'Am I?'

'Yeah, you are . . . So then, why *are* you here?'

Grace thought about it as Dara climbed down from the top bunk and sat next to her. It entered Grace's mind that, however brief this friendship might be, it was probably the first time she'd had a friend since primary school. Grace took a *proper* look at Dara.

Her new friend was so skinny. Grace's mum – who'd been brought up by her Irish grandmother, and always liked to feed everyone up – would say Dara looked hungry. Then again, her mum claimed everyone looked hungry unless they were slightly rotund around the middle. But Dara really did look like she needed a plate of her mum's home-made shepherd's pie.

Dara also looked dirty. Her face. Her nails. Her clothes. Not that Grace minded, not that she cared what her new friend looked like at all. Even Dara's long mousey hair was matted, especially at the sides. Did no one help her comb it in the morning? There was one other thing Grace couldn't help but notice; she tried not to stare at Dara's head, and the things that were moving around in it. She hoped Dara wouldn't notice her moving back slightly as Dara's hair tumbled towards her.

She thought how sore the stitches on her friend's chin looked, then snatched her gaze away. Staring down at her own hands in her lap, she quietly began to tell Dara what happened.

From down the hall, a bell rang. The noise of kids charging along the corridors rose up through the floorboards, and the sound of feet running on the wooden stairs made its way into the dormitory.

A small man poked his head around the door. He had the build of a labourer who enjoyed his food. He wore glasses with thick lenses that made his eyes look like two black beads, and he stared at the girls with disdain. 'Come on, you two. Downstairs, *now*.'

'Have you got any news on my mummy—'

Dara poked Grace in the side.

Grace quickly realised what she'd said, and shrugged. 'I mean, my *mum*. Have you heard anything about my mum?'

'I don't know the first thing about her, or who she is, now hurry up.' The man disappeared back around the door as quickly as he'd appeared.

Dara gave Grace a sympathetic smile. 'Come on, it'll be fine. I'm sure you'll find out soon what's going on. Try not to worry.'

But even as her friend tried to reassure her, Grace couldn't help worrying. Things felt very wrong . . .

Chapter Twenty-Three

The smell of bleach invaded Dara's nose as they hurried down the stairs, managing to catch the back of the line of children filing into the dining room. The walls were painted green, the door a salmon pink, and the carpet was a kaleidoscope of stains and wavy lines where the vacuum cleaner had been.

'Ah, here are the new recruits . . . Welcome, welcome.'

They were greeted by a man in his fifties. His low-riding stomach pushed out of his shirt and hung over his belt. His hair was thinning, apart from the coarse tufts growing out of his ears. 'I'm Mr Barrows and I'm one of the house parents here.' He winked at Grace, then smirked when she shuffled closer to Dara.

As the other children sat down silently, he tapped the chair at the end of the long table. It was covered in a yellow-and-white-checked plastic tablecloth. He began to talk again, exposing a coating of white on his tongue and a rotten black tooth at the back of his mouth. 'I hope everyone will be showing the new girls how to behave, and telling them the rules . . .'

Dara was only half listening. She looked at the photos on the walls, reading the names underneath. She jumped as she felt hands grip her shoulders, hard enough to make her wince. She tried to wriggle out of the grip.

Barrows' face rubbed against her cheek as he leant forward.

'They're some of our patrons. Nice chaps. We're lucky to have them . . .'

He paused and smiled widely at her. Dara recoiled at the smell of his sticky breath.

'And if you're lucky,' Barrows continued, 'you might get to meet them. They sometimes come here, especially him . . .' He tapped one of the photographs, and she noticed the dirt underneath his long fingernail. 'You met Lord Dennis a few weeks ago, didn't you, Robbie?' He turned his attention to a young boy. The lad visibly paled; he was tiny and looked too small for the chair he was sitting in. His head was shaven. His eyes were hollow and sunken, and dark rings sat below them, like ink smudges.

'Yes.'

'Yes *what*?' Barrows snarled.

'Yes, sir.' Robbie flushed and quickly looked down.

Dara and Grace took a seat at the table.

'Ah, here's Cook,' Barrows announced as the door swung open. He beamed at the woman who entered.

Cook had a burning cigarette dangling from the corner of her mouth, and possessed arms thick enough to be fence posts. She clutched a large steel pan and ladle, and began to slop a thick brown liquid into the bowls in front of the children. It looked to Dara like a mix between semolina and porridge. There was a communal groan, but it was immediately silenced by the cold stare of Barrows.

'Right, everyone, I'll be back in a moment.' Barrows followed Cook out of the door.

Dara looked around, feeling unnerved. She frowned. Why hadn't they all broken into conversation, eager to have a laugh, or even wind each other up, while he was out of the room? Instead, every single one of the kids kept their gaze to themselves. The one eye contact she did make was with Grace. She gave her friend a reassuring look, receiving the tiniest of smiles back.

Ten minutes later, the heavy silence was still sitting in the air when Barrows returned. He prowled the room, staring at the bowed heads, then made a beeline for Robbie. He hit him hard on the top of his head with the rolled-up newspaper he was carrying. The blow made Robbie shrink further down into his chair.

'Are you going to tell me why you haven't eaten your breakfast yet? WELL, ARE YOU?' Barrow's lips were clenched in an unforgiving line. 'What is the rule?'

Robbie muttered something inaudible.

'You weren't so bloody silent when you were crying the other day, were you, hey, Robbie?' Barrows' eyes seemed to be popping out of his head in anger. 'Come on then, seeing as Robbie has suddenly forgotten how to talk, can anyone else tell me what the rule is . . . Brenda?' Giving her no choice, he clicked and pointed at a chubby Black girl who sat on the other side of the table from Dara. She had short messy plaits and a livid scar down one side of her face where her cheek had been burnt.

'You don't waste food, sir.'

'Exactly! Exactly!' Barrow's voice was jubilant. 'Well done, Brenda, at least someone knows . . . So, what are we going to do with you then, Robbie?'

Robbie's knuckles turned white as his hand tightened around the cup he was holding. He was trembling so much his tea spilt out on to the tablecloth.

'I think you better come with me, don't you?'

The other kids kept their heads bowed. None of them looked up when Barrows made a sudden movement. He cupped his hands roughly under Robbie's armpits, dragging him backwards off his chair. 'You know where you're going now, don't you?'

'Please don't take me to the outhouse, sir.' He sounded terrified.

'Shut up, you little sod. You should have bloody well thought about that before, shouldn't you?'

The door opened again, and another member of staff appeared. 'John, sorry to disturb you, we've got a little problem over at one of the other cottages. Would you mind assisting me?' The man spoke quickly to Barrows, completely ignoring Robbie being dragged across the room. It was as if the kid was invisible.

Barrows nodded, letting go of Robbie and leaving him in a heap on the floor.

Still no one moved and no one spoke, until Dara slowly scraped back her chair. She walked around to where Robbie was lying on the floor crying. 'Here, let me help you.' She reached out her hand to him.

He turned to look at her. A stream of snot ran out of one nostril, and he seemed surprised. 'No, you can't, you'll get into trouble if you do.'

'That won't be nothing new. Just take it . . . go on, take my hand. It's Robbie, ain't it?' She gave him a gentle smile.

Eventually he took hold of her hand, and she pulled him up on to his feet.

'I'm Dara, by the way. This is Grace.' She nodded towards her friend, who'd come to stand next to her. 'How long have you been here?' Dara frowned as she looked at him.

Robbie didn't look well. He was so pale, just like Rosie.

He shrugged his bony shoulders. 'Since I was a baby.'

'Well, I'm going home on Monday,' Grace said quickly.

Robbie glanced at her sadly, as if he knew something Dara and Grace didn't.

'Really?' he said, looking surprised. 'Most kids who come here never leave.'

137

Chapter Twenty-Four

'Those prunes didn't work either, Sam. Me bowels are so jammed, it's like the M25 at rush hour. You'll have to give me one of those suppositories.'

Samantha took a deep breath. She held tightly on to the lunch tray she was carrying, and closed her eyes for the briefest of moments, willing herself to find the strength for today. 'No problem, Mum, I'll do that later. I've got a phone call to make first.'

Samantha didn't care what her boss had said, she was going to try to get in touch with Grace's godmother. Grace had been her first thought when she woke up this morning, after she'd eventually got back to sleep. God, she was so angry that they hadn't waited. She'd been told they'd driven Grace to Holly Brookes with some other girl early this morning. The poor kid must be exhausted . . . and frightened.

She'd never actually been to Holly Brookes herself. Though she'd heard rumours about the place. How tough it was, and the way the kids were treated. It had been designed to resemble a holiday camp, but it sounded more like an army base.

There was a veil of secrecy around Holly Brookes, something which made Samantha really uncomfortable. A couple of years ago, she'd tried to find out more about the place from a few of her colleagues, but she'd been shut down immediately. Miller had even called her into his office to give her a dressing-down. For some reason, no one was willing to talk about Holly Brookes.

'Well, it comes to something when I'm at the bottom of my daughter's list, doesn't it? I didn't know your job was that special. I forgot you were the Queen's secretary.' Yesterday's letters lay abandoned on the mahogany telephone table next to her mother's bed. She reached out to grab one, waving it in the air at Samantha. 'Maybe this is from her, writing to tell me how important you are.'

'Mum, *please*. I've got a job to do. It's a quick phone call, it won't take long.'

'And neither will sticking something up my bum.' Phyllis pursed her lips.

'Why don't you have your lunch first?' Samantha placed the tray in front of her mum *very* gently, to stop herself from hurling it against the wall. 'There you go, Mum. Mashed potatoes, pork chops, and a spoonful of those mixed vegetables you like.'

Phyllis picked up her fork, and poked the chop. 'That gravy looks a bit lumpy. Did you use Bisto?'

'Yes, Mum, just how you like it.'

Phyllis frowned and looked at Samantha as if she'd placed a pile of raw, rotting meat on her lap. 'Where's the apple sauce?'

Samantha rubbed her temples, counting down from ten, before she answered. 'Sorry, I couldn't get any.'

'What?' Phyllis laughed scornfully. 'The whole of England has suddenly run out of bleeding apples, have they?'

'No, of course not.'

'Then why haven't I got any apple sauce? You know I like it.' Phyllis shoved her plate away from her. 'So what am I supposed to eat now?'

139

A lot of answers went through Samantha's mind, but with a great deal of effort, she simply smiled.

'I'm sure you can still enjoy it, Mum.'

Phyllis crossed her arms over her ample bosom. Her daughter was getting very complacent. It rankled no end that instead of being here most of the time, looking after her long-suffering mother, Samantha was swanning off to work, to look after some errant kids. All this talk about it being her vocation, well, that was the biggest joke she'd heard.

In Phyllis's view, charity started at home, but it felt like Samantha was looking after everyone else but her.

There was something different about her daughter's behaviour these days. She'd watched her change over the past year or so. Everything about Samantha offended her now, even her appearance was messy. She'd go so far as to call her daughter dowdy. Her hair hadn't seen a heated roller for a good while, and she couldn't be bothered with make-up most of the time. There was no question, she was a pretty thing. Phyllis liked to think her daughter took after her side of the family. But didn't Samantha realise, men wanted to come home for some comfort. She made no effort for Jason, no wonder he only stayed here once a week.

She only wanted what was best for her daughter. Granted, it wasn't ideal, but Jason raising his hand to her a few times was only him trying to knock some sense into her. Occasional bruises were the unspoken punctuation of marital vows. What was a man supposed to do when he didn't feel he was the master of his own house? Samantha was too quick with her comebacks. No husband wanted a mouthy mare for a wife.

Phyllis looked again at her pork chop and let out a long sigh.

'Well, maybe if you weren't so distracted, I might get some proper care out of you.'

'What's that supposed to mean?'

Phyllis stared at Samantha. She decided to keep that little titbit to herself. For now. No need to reveal that she knew Jake had come to visit her daughter last night.

Phyllis Parish had always liked to have something over on people, but especially on her daughter.

'Oh, nothing,' she said innocently.

Samantha grabbed the plate and whipped the checked tea towel over her shoulder. 'I'll make you a sandwich then, shall I?'

Her mother sniffed and grabbed a garibaldi biscuit from the plate on the nearby bookshelf. She stuffed it into her mouth. 'Doesn't look like I've got much choice. Oh, and Sam, maybe you should do something with your lip. Cover it up with a bit of powder, no one wants to see that. What goes on between man and wife should stay that way.'

'Funny that, seeing as you seem to know everything about my marriage.'

Samantha opened the door, but closed it again gently, without leaving the room. The relationship between her and her mum had never been an easy one, but it seemed to be at breaking point now. Or rather, *she* was at breaking point.

She rested her head against the door frame. 'Do you know how lonely it is for me, Mum? I'm really trying my best, but I speak to no one apart from you and the people at work. I go to bed on my own, I wake up on my own. I go nowhere. I look out of that bloody kitchen window every day, and it feels like I'm not part of what's going on out there. I'm only thirty-one but my life's ticking away. It's like I'm invisible, like I'm slowly dying here . . . *Mum?*'

Phyllis slurped her tea noisily. 'Well, I'll be dying if I have to wait for my potted meat sandwich much longer.'

That was it.

Samantha rushed into the kitchen, grabbed the half-finished loaf of Mother's Pride from the cupboard, slathered the potted meat thickly on to a couple of slices with the back of the nearest teaspoon. Then, without using a plate, she ran back through to her mum, and threw it on to her lap.

'Here you go, and try not to fucking choke on it!'

'Where are you going . . . Sam, *Sam?*' Phyllis was sitting in a thick cloud of cigarette smoke. She squinted up to look at the quartz starburst wall clock above the gas fire which was turned to high. 'Sam, you can't go out now.'

'Try me.' She marched away, grabbing her coat from the hook.

'*Sam . . . Sam.*'

Ignoring her mother, something she should've done a long time ago, Samantha hurried over to the freezer. She opened it, and pushed her hand to the back of the vegetable drawer. Jammed between a packet of ice-covered Brussels sprouts and some runner beans, was an empty tub of Wall's Cornish ice cream. It was where she kept her money hidden.

Everything she had, Jason either knew about or wanted to know about. Her wages went into his bank account. Not that he needed the money. It wasn't about that. It was about her having nothing. He controlled everything. He gave her a weekly amount for food, and she always had to produce the receipts and the change. He'd buy her clothes. Pay the bills, and give her mum money to go to the bingo.

So this was the only way she had anything for herself. The house had been left to her by her dad, but now she was married, it was Jason's. Apart from this couple of hundred pounds, she had nothing. She knew she was taking a risk, but whenever Jason did stay over – especially when he'd been drinking, or snorting coke – she'd collect the change, no matter how little, from his pocket. And when she was feeling really brave, some notes from his wallet. It had taken since the day she'd married him to save up this much. She only hoped that, one day, she'd have enough to walk out and disappear. Because if Jason ever found her . . .

'Samantha, where are you going?'

Samantha's thoughts came to an abrupt halt. She grabbed some money from the ice-cream tub, put the container back in its hiding place and closed the freezer.

'Out, Mum, I'm going out to clear my head. And maybe, just maybe, I might even get very, very drunk.'

And with that remark, Samantha grabbed her notebook and bag from the side, and walked out, slamming the front door loudly.

Chapter Twenty-Five

Alan Carver had known better Friday mornings than the one he was having now. To say it was the worst day of his life was probably not far from the truth. He backed away from the phone on his desk as it began to ring.

There was no doubt who was calling him . . . *again*. The Wakemans. He'd already had a series of threatening voicemails from them. Jason had relished describing in the greatest of detail what they were going to do to him if the deal hadn't been completed by the end of the day. And Alan was under no illusions. The Wakeman twins would certainly come good with their promise: he'd have a long, tortuous death.

At the moment, the prospect of signing off the deal – or coming up with a viable excuse – was fast disappearing. So Alan did what he'd always done when all else failed: he leant over the long, neat line of cocaine, and greedily snorted it up. Alan had been indulging his habit since leaving Frank in the early hours. Cutting up lines of coke on the polished wooden surface of his desk. Big, fat, long ones.

Holding his nostrils closed, he swallowed, tasting the bitter powder at the back of his throat. But instead of the usual rush of euphoria, a heightened sense of paranoia continued to build and flood through his veins. A self-comforting masturbation session might've been preferable, to ease his agitation. As the phone continued to ring, comfort was something Alan desperately needed right now.

The answer machine clicked in.

'Alan, it's Jase, mate . . . Where are you?'

Alan slid down the wall, crouching in the corner. It was pathetic – and God knows he was struggling to admit it to himself – but he was scared. Fucking terrified. And that wasn't only the coke talking.

'. . . Alan, come on, pick up . . . I know you're there. Hiding from us won't make this go away. You need to start talking. Tick fucking tock, Al. Today's the day, ain't it? But you seem to have gone AWOL. I really hope you're not ignoring us, because that would be very fucking silly of you. Very fucking silly. There are ways of dealing with cunts who decide to—'

Alan scrambled up and grabbed the answer machine, ripping it out of the socket and throwing it against the wall. 'Reenie . . . Reenie . . .' He rushed to his office door, poked his head out, and shouted down the corridor. 'Reenie! For fuck's sake, woman . . . Reenie!'

Moments later, Reenie hurried out of the small staff kitchen, frantically swallowing the last mouthful of the Battenberg cake she'd been enjoying, and dabbing at her mouth with a paper napkin.

'Didn't you hear me calling you?' Alan demanded, striding towards her.

'Mmm, sorry, sir . . . I . . . mmm, I . . .'

'Whatever you're about to say, Reenie, don't fucking say it,' Alan hissed. 'I'm not interested in the ins and outs of your petty little life, all right . . . I just want to make sure you don't put any more calls through to me for the rest of the day, do you understand?' His face was so close to hers, he could see the cake crumbs stuck in the greasy red lipstick smears at the corner of her mouth.

'Of course, sir, that's fine . . . Is everything all right? You look a bit peaky, perhaps you've picked up a c—'

'Yes, thank you for that, Doctor Quincy. Fucking hell, Reenie, you're my secretary, not my fucking doctor!'

'Sorry, sir, I was just worried and . . .' She pointed to her own nose and made a circular gesture. 'And you've got . . .' She trailed off discreetly

Realising what she was hinting at, Alan angrily wiped his nostrils clean of the coke with the back of his hand.

'Look, just . . . just . . .' He waved his hand. 'Just go and do some typing, or whatever it is I fucking pay you for.'

Alan stalked back into his office. He liked to think of himself as a smart man, and he was already busily editing out his own involvement in this mess.

He'd heard troubling talk through the grapevine: the Wakemans had done a deal with Zef and Dren, two fucking knuckleheads Alan had once had the misfortune of doing business with. If that was true, and it wasn't simply the criminal gossip mill in overdrive, it'd be a disaster. The Albanians knew how to pile the pressure on, and Dren in particular liked to personally collect his pound of flesh.

Alan's hands were shaking as he picked up the phone and dialled a number he'd memorised.

The call was answered straight away.

'Good morning, this is Lord Hargreaves' office, how can I help you?'

Cynthia Shaw was putting on her best telephone voice, but she didn't impress Alan. She could be announcing the daily discounts over the tannoy in the Presto supermarket on the Old Kent Road, for all he cared.

'Cynth, it's Alan Carver. Put me through to him, darlin'.'

'I'll just see if he's available, sir.'

Alan snorted another line while he waited to be put through.

'What do you want, Alan?' Dennis's gravelly, plummy voice boomed down the phone. 'I thought I told you only to use my direct line in exceptional circumstances.'

'We need to talk about—'

'Let me stop you right there. I don't need to talk to you at all. Didn't Frank pass on the message?'

Alan's mouth was sticky, and he wiped the strings of drying saliva from the corner of his lips. 'He did, but—'

'Then why the hell are you calling me? We've gone over this before. You only contact me when or *if* there's an emergency.'

In Alan's book, having his head caved in by the Wakemans constituted exactly that. 'There's a lot of pressure on me, right now, Dennis.'

'And how is that my problem?'

'The thing is, Dennis, I'm not sure if I can do what you asked me to.'

Alan pulled a face and moved the phone away from his ear as Dennis coughed in irritation.

'It really isn't hard. Quite simple, actually. Cover the site with concrete.'

Alan clutched the phone to his ear again and spoke firmly into the large green mouthpiece. 'I can't do that.'

There was a long silence.

'Hello? . . . *Hello?*' Alan was starting to panic.

In his own time, Dennis answered. 'Cover the site, Alan. That's all you have to do.' No swearing, no threats, just a softly spoken instruction. 'And don't call me again on this number. If you need to get in touch with me, call Lewis.'

Shit, he'd forgotten to call the chief superintendent.

147

'Or Frank,' Dennis continued. 'You can always call him.'

Alan knew that was never going to happen. The idea of discussing his business with someone like Frank Baker appalled him. He would rather stick his penis through a cheese grater.

'With respect, Dennis, that's impossible. The land is as good as sold.'

'Don't you *dare* tell me what's impossible. May I remind you, Alan, that I know certain things about you and your business dealings. Everything you've ever worked for, and everything you aspire to, can be made to disappear in a matter of moments. You might think you know a lot about me, but in order to bring me down, Alan, your reach has to extend far enough. And let me tell you, it doesn't even come close.'

A cold cocaine-fuelled sweat ran down Alan's back. There was so much he wanted to say, but for now, all he could do was sit back and take it.

'And now, please accept my apologies, but I have to go, I've got a meeting I'm already late for . . . But I'm sure I can rely on you to do what's needed.'

The phone went down.

'*Fuck.*' Alan jumped into action. Dennis thought he was untouchable, well he'd fucking show him. He'd show Dennis not only was his reach far enough, but when he got him, it'd be by the fucking throat.

He unlocked the top drawer of his desk and reached to the back, pushing the letters and other papers to one side . . . No, that didn't make sense. He rummaged through the drawer again, this time more carefully. What the fuck was going on? Alan's heart pounded, and white noise rang in his ear. Think. He had to think. Where the fuck had he put them? Fuck, fuck. Fuck.

He pulled the drawer out and emptied all the papers on to the floor. Then he hunkered down, going through everything dili-gently. They weren't here. How could they not be here? He was *certain* he'd seen them only yesterday, or was it the day before? Fuck, he couldn't remember. The coke, along with his panicking, was stopping him from thinking straight.

'Reenie! Reenie!' For the second time in less than half an hour, Alan rushed to the door, opened it, and bellowed, 'Reenie!'

There was no answer and no sign of her.

'REE-*NIE!*'

Alan was like a man possessed.

Finally, Reenie appeared. 'Sorry, sir, I was . . .' But remember-ing what he'd said earlier, she stopped and gave him a tight smile. 'It's fine, I'm sure you don't want to hear . . . So, how can I help you, sir?'

Perspiration sat like huge dewdrops on Alan's forehead. He blinked away the sweat trickling on to his lashes, then glanced furtively up and down the corridor.

'I can't find them.' He grabbed Reenie by the arm and pulled her into his office. 'Where are they?' he demanded, now up close and shouting into her face.

Reenie frowned. 'Where are what, sir? What can't you find?'

Almost overpowered by the smell of Reenie's hairspray, Alan stepped back and started to pick up all the papers he'd emptied out of the drawer, flinging an armful at her.

'The photos . . . The photographs I had. I need them.'

'I don't know what you're talking about, sir.'

Inflamed by the blank look on her face, Alan began to pace. His breathing was laboured, and he clutched hold of his chest. 'What part aren't you *fucking* understanding? I had some photographs in my drawer, and now I don't know where they are. Surely even you can grasp that concept?'

Reenie, as always, held her smile and her patience. What an absolute prick her boss was.

'Photographs of what, sir?' She stared at him from underneath her false eyelashes.

Alan glared back. He could hardly tell her what they were. They were supposed to be his contingency plan: photographs of Dennis in sick, compromising positions with boys young enough to be in primary school.

'Look, the point is, they were in my top drawer.'

'But I thought you kept that drawer locked, sir.'

'I do, I . . .' Alan pinched the bridge of his nose as his blood pressure soared and tiny lights flashed in front of his eyes. 'I always keep it locked, and that's why I'm asking you.'

'I'm sorry, sir, I can't help. If you told me what the photographs were, maybe I could look around and—'

'Forget it, just fucking forget it.' Alan bundled her out and slammed the door, leaning heavily on it.

He took a large lungful of air, and kneaded the middle of his chest with his thumb. He hoped to God the photographs were at home. Had he somehow forgotten he'd taken them there? He needed to stop Dennis putting pressure on him. Concreting over the site would be a disaster. It would be like taking the Wakemans' gun and putting a bullet into his own head.

If he could stall Dennis, even for a few days, then maybe, *somehow*, he could come up with a way of stopping the twins thinking of him as a dead man walking. For now, there was no Plan B. Unless the photos *were* back at home, he might as well start digging his own grave. What's more, if he didn't have them, who the fuck did?

Chapter Twenty-Six

Dara and Gracie's morning was turning into their worst day ever.

There was something about Holly Brookes that made Dara feel really uneasy. Being here gave her the same kind of knot in her stomach as she'd had on her thirteenth birthday when her mum had kicked her out for the night. She could tell that Barrows was a fucking piece of shit. She'd been around enough of her mum's punters to know what a scumbag looked and smelt like. She already knew he was a bully, she could see that in the way he'd treated Robbie. Bastard. Anyway, she hoped that she'd be out of here soon. No doubt it'd be another week or so before social services let her home.

Dara moved her chair slightly, so the sun beat down on her back, warming her up. Shafts of sunlight streamed through the windows of the sewing room. Holly Brookes was not only a children's home, there was also a sick bay on the grounds, an indoor swimming pool – which had just been completed and was going to have an official opening next week – a laundry house, and even a school. Dara and Grace were sitting around a table with half a dozen other kids, including Robbie. Unlike at breakfast, the kids were talking quietly to each other, which partly hid the tension that seemed to seep out of every brick at Holly Brookes.

She looked at Grace. Apparently, the girl had been cared for and loved for all of her life, and had never been away from her mum. This whole experience must be traumatic for her.

With a long sigh at the thought of it all, Dara muttered, 'Oh my God, how the fuck is anyone supposed to do this?' Exasperated, she dropped the needle and cotton she'd been holding on the table in front of her.

Gracie smiled, and it changed her face, ironing out the worry lines marking her forehead. 'You don't know how to sew?'

Dara raised her eyebrows at Grace and laughed. 'Do I look like I know how to sew? I can't even get this poxy piece of cotton through the hole. I don't know why they have to make it so pissing small.'

Grace enjoyed being with Dara. She'd never really known anyone like her before. The way she was, the way she spoke.

'Give it here,' she offered. 'I'll help you.' She took the needle and cotton from Dara, and stuck her tongue out in concentration, threading it easily. 'Here you go.'

'Thanks, doll.' Dara took it and pulled a face. 'But what am I supposed to do with it now?'

Grace blinked rapidly. '*Really*, no one's ever taught you how to sew? Not even your mum?'

Dara didn't know what planet Grace lived on, but it certainly wasn't the same one as hers. 'The only needlework my mum ever showed me, was how to shoot up.'

'What?' Grace looked a picture of puzzled innocence.

'Never mind.' Dara shook her head and smiled. 'But this ain't the eighteen hundreds, Gracie, people have sewing machines nowadays, so why would you need to learn?'

Grace had never really thought about it; she always did everything without question, so she couldn't actually answer that. The nearest she got to a response was saying, 'Everyone else here knows how to sew.'

'Yeah, well, it's weird . . .' Dara joined Grace in glancing around.

Barrows was over in the corner smoking a cigarette and thumbing through *Car Mechanics* magazine, with his feet up on the table next to his mug of tea. There were three large classroom tables, made up of smaller ones pushed together, with six or seven kids sitting around each. They were busy sewing the costumes for the Holly Brookes pantomime on Christmas Eve.

'I don't know why we have to bloody well help make the costumes anyway,' Dara muttered.

She was cold and hungry. And thinking about Tommy and her younger siblings being placed with strangers, well, it'd been making her feel sick all morning. Her head was throbbing as if it had a tight band around it, and it felt like it was going to explode.

Panic rose up in her again.

'Are you okay?' Grace touched her hand.

Dara gave a small, tight nod. She didn't know how to say what she was feeling. She'd never really been asked before. Only by various social workers, and they didn't really care what was going on with her. They were only ever trying to catch her out, waiting to see if she'd say the wrong thing, so when they'd asked, Dara had always said nothing.

'Yeah, I'm good . . . and thanks for asking, Gracie.' Dara meant it, she really did. But Grace's kindness still didn't stop her from waiting until Grace wasn't looking, before she jabbed the sewing needle cruelly into the top of her own thigh.

It hurt and Dara flinched, but it was exactly what she needed. Like a balloon deflating, the anxiety in her head slowly subsided and the urge to cry dissipated. Sewing might be a pointless waste of time, but Dara had found another use for the needle. She silently slipped it into her back pocket.

'You want a fucking photo or something?'

The three snarky bitches who'd picked on Grace when they first arrived were staring at Dara from across the classroom.

Dara rubbed her leg. She hadn't realised she'd been staring. 'Not of you, I fucking don't.' She stuck two fingers up.

The girls were quiet for a few seconds. 'You're asking for a smack.' The biggest of the trio sat upright. She had a heavy face with a jutting jawline and buck teeth.

'I'd like to see you try it. Offer's open any time.' Dara wasn't scared of them. They had nothing on her mum.

'Ignore them, no one likes them. That's Connie. She's the biggest bitch ever.' The Black girl with the scar on her cheek leant in towards her. 'I'm Brenda. I saw what you did to help Robbie at breakfast, that was brave.'

Dara didn't bother asking Brenda what she meant. 'I'm Dara,' she said.

Brenda's face was shiny, like it'd been glazed in cooking oil, and Dara wanted to ask her how she'd got that large, purple mark on her cheek.

'They're always trying to pick on everyone. Sometimes the house parents get them to do stuff too.'

'What do you mean?'

'Everything all right over there?' Barrows left his cigarette burning in the ashtray on his desk, and sauntered over to them.

'Yes, sir, sorry.' Brenda lowered her eyes and continued to sew the hem of the duck costume she was making.

As Barrows got nearer, Dara noticed Brenda's hands begin to shake. He walked up to them and stood behind Grace. His stomach pushed into her back.

'Look, it's snowing. It's pretty out there, like a Christmas card.' Barrows' voice was silky smooth. He pointed to the window, then squeezed Grace's shoulders gently and massaged them for a moment.

'I can't see.' Gracie sounded upset. 'I lost my glasses.'

'Well, that won't do, will it? I'm sure we can sort that out.' He looked at the hem of the costume she was sewing. 'You're doing a good job there.'

Grace turned her head, staring up at him, right into his nostrils. She could see thick, coarse hairs growing out of them. 'Have you heard anything about my mum? I think I'm supposed to be going back home on Monday, you see.'

'I haven't heard anything yet, but once we find out, you'll be the first to know. Promise. But for now, we're going to look after you. Is that all right?'

Grace nodded miserably.

'Hey, hey, hey . . . what are those tears for, missy? We can't have that, can we?' Barrows crouched down until he was at Grace's eye level, roughly elbowing Dara out of the way. He smiled, and wiped her tears away with his thumb. His watery eyes lit up. 'Why don't you come and see me in my office later?'

'She's fine. Just ignore her, she's being a cry baby,' Dara blurted out. Barrows' behaviour was making Dara feel uncomfortable. She didn't want him to have anything to do with her friend.

'Excuse me?' Barrows turned his attention to Dara, his smile dying quickly on his face. From the corner of her eye, Dara snatched a glimpse of Robbie shaking his head at her.

Barrows pushed his nose into Dara's face. 'Did . . . I . . . ask . . . for . . . your . . . opinion?' His words were punctuated and drawn out.

Dara's chest rose up and down rapidly.

He held on to a strand of her long fringe, running his fingers down it. 'I can see you're going to be a troublemaker, aren't you?' he whispered in her ear.

Dara kept quiet and didn't move. She could sense him challenging her, waiting for her to say something.

He glared directly into her eyes for a few minutes, then straightened up and walked back to his desk, muttering darkly to himself.

'Don't make him angry, Dara,' Brenda murmured to her. 'You don't know what he's like.'

A loud bell, like a fire alarm, abruptly went off. Barrow stubbed his cigarette out and left the classroom without saying anything. The moment he'd gone, the other kids scrambled out of their chairs and hurried across to the window.

'Oh my God, it's Barry . . . I can see him . . . Look.' Connie, who'd jostled her way to the front, spoke over her shoulder.

'Who's Barry?' Dara asked Brenda.

Grace shuffled her chair nearer, so she could hear what was being said.

The reply was so quiet and soft, Dara wondered how it passed through Brenda's lips.

'You hear that bell. That's to alert the other house parents that something's up.' Brenda squeezed Dara's arm nervously. 'Barry. He ran away last month. They found him yesterday. Maybe the police did, I dunno . . . but they've been waiting for him to arrive back.'

Dara thought seriously about what Brenda had just said, and wondered why the girl looked genuinely terrified. She gave a quick look at Grace who, by the look on her face, was picking up on Brenda's uneasiness.

'What's the bloody big deal about running away?' Dara asked. 'If I was here long enough, I'd do the same.'

Lots of kids on Dara's estate had done a bunk from home or

school, and after a few days they'd either come back on their own, or been brought back by the Old Bill. She couldn't see what the issue was. The only reason she hadn't run away herself was because she needed to look out for her siblings.

Brenda's eyes widened in disbelief. 'You don't get it, no one runs away from here. It's not allowed. Them's the rules.'

'Rules! Who cares about rules? What, you're telling me Robbie has never run away from here in his whole life? He said he's been here since he was a baby.'

'Yeah, he has. But he's never left the grounds.' Brenda looked across at Robbie. 'He'd probably be too scared. Holly Brookes is all he knows.'

'What? You're kidding me? He's just been shacked up here? That ain't right.' Dara shook her head. But when she thought more about it, she supposed it was no different from herself. Apart from the time she'd got on the wrong bus, she hadn't been further than Kennington. Until now.

The classroom door was flung open. A young boy – eleven or twelve years old – was dragged in. Dara guessed it was Barry. She watched as Barrows pulled him in by the scruff of his neck. The boy's feet skidded underneath him on the vinyl floor.

Behind them stood another adult Dara hadn't seen before.

'That's Mr Clemence . . . he works here,' Brenda whispered to Dara as the other kids hurried to sit down.

Clemence was tall and skinny. Chewing tobacco. His teeth were stained, dark red and brown. Dara's gaze travelled along the raised scar puckering the skin from the corner of his mouth right across his cheek. He was wearing a grubby cotton shirt and a pair of faded beige polyester flares. His shoulders were hunched over in front of him, as if he'd just shrugged off his jacket.

Barry looked positively tiny standing next to the two adults.

'A little reminder for you all.' Clemence's deep baritone voice didn't seem to suit his body.

Dara moved her eyes from left to right. She had no idea what was about to happen, everyone was so still. The whole class seemed to be holding their breath. Then, from underneath the table, Dara felt Brenda's hand grasp hers. Frowning, Dara turned to say something, but the fear in Brenda's eyes stopped her. Instead, she gave Brenda a small smile and took hold of Grace's hand as well.

The silence continued. The only sound Dara could hear was Barry's unsteady panting. As she stared at him, she realised there was a dribble of urine snaking down his trembling leg on to the floor. She looked around for a reaction from the rest of the class. There was none. No one laughed. Even the girls who'd been so mouthy earlier looked pale.

Dara felt Grace clutch her hand tighter, and she signalled back with a squeeze. From underneath the flat tweed cap he was wearing pulled down low over his face, Clemence's gaze caught hers.

Dara lowered her eyes.

'Listen up, everyone.' Barrows' voice was harsh.

Dara kept her eyes fixed on the chipped, grey table in front of her, and imagined the sneer on his face.

'If any of you are thinking of running away, Mr Clemence here is going to show you what happens. Let this be a lesson to you all . . . Over to you, Mr Clemence.'

Dara heard a rustle. Then a tiny whimper, which she knew had come from Barry. She heard something swishing through the air. A cane. Followed by a noise she would never forget, accompanied by a scream.

'Come on, everyone, count!' Barrows yelled above Barry's screaming.

'One . . . two . . . three . . . four . . . five.' The children chanted in unison.

'Louder!'

Dara saw Grace begin to rock back and forth on the chair next to her. 'Don't look, Gracie, don't look.'

No one was watching, yet the whole class was counting as the cane tore through the air, landing on Barry's small body, over and over again. Each strike sounded like a fire crackling. Logs on a flame; crackling and snapping, as if the fire was roaring.

Dara felt herself flinch with every strike.

Chapter Twenty-Seven

The first thing Judy Baker had done when she arrived at her sister's house was put the kettle on, and make herself a nice brew. The journey hadn't put her in the best of moods. Navigating three buses from her home in Lambeth wasn't her idea of fun. Added to which, she'd made the mistake of wearing one of her furs – a birthday present from Dennis last year – and somewhere between Bermondsey and the Isle of Dogs she'd leant on a piece of chewing gum, and now it was matted into the elbow of her best mink.

Judy didn't often visit Mandy on a Friday. Canning Town didn't appeal to her at the best of times. Fridays meant pushing and shoving her way through the throng of Rathbone Market to reach her sister's small, terraced house in Fox Road by the A13.

She'd left her Frank at home, telling him to get some rest after the night he'd had. Besides, this trip to her sister's wasn't purely for social reasons. Though, for now, Judy wanted to keep that to herself.

'You should have seen the skull, Auntie Judy, bloody hell, it was tiny, it was only this big . . .' Her nephew was almost jumping up and down on the spot in excitement. 'Uncle Frank thinks it was a kid's.'

Judy slipped her throbbing feet out of the black patent court shoes she'd picked up last week from Freeman, Hardy and Willis.

Her bunions had been stamped on more than a dozen times as she'd made her way through the market.

'Is that right?' she remarked drily.

'Yeah, and he said we shouldn't tell anyone.'

Judy glanced up for a moment before continuing to flick through the baby clothes section of the Littlewoods catalogue. 'And have you, Jimmy? Have you told anyone else?'

'No, well, just you and . . .' Jimmy trailed off.

Jimmy knew he shouldn't have said anything at all, and technically he hadn't, though that was only because the small group of mates he'd called had all been out. But tomorrow, when he saw them for their weekly jamming session, he'd be able to tell them . . . and *show* them.

Jimmy was bursting to share the secret he had. His mate Larry was a fly bastard, he'd never believe what Jimmy and his Uncle Frank had unearthed – not without some sort of proof. So when his uncle had gone to the phone box, well, that's when he'd decided to slip a piece of bone into his pocket.

They'd be so jealous. He could just imagine Larry's face when he got it out to show them. He even hoped it might get him a little bit further with Becky. So far he'd only managed a quick fingering in the toilets of the Wimpy Bar over on the Beckton Road. She'd only let him do that in the first place because she'd had an argument with Larry. Still, perhaps the discovery of the bone might change all that.

Whatever happened, he'd be the centre of the group's attention. He couldn't wait to recount the story, detail by detail, of how *he* had dug up a child's remains. Last night he hadn't slept – the spliff he'd smoked had done nothing to quell his excitement – and he doubted he would tonight either.

Jimmy had to really fight hard to suppress his giggles in front of his Auntie Judy.

'What's so funny, Jimmy?' Judy sighed. Her nephew had always been a few clowns short of a circus.

'Oh, nothing.'

Judy knew Jimmy was up to something. The stupid grin on his face was a complete giveaway. 'So you haven't said anything to anyone? You sure?'

'No. I swear. Cross my heart.'

'And hope to die?' Judy stared at him for a good few moments. She'd seen all she needed to.

Taking a last sip of her tea, Judy spat out the leaves from the bottom of the cup. 'Good, well, I better be off,' she announced.

Mandy shuffled through from the kitchen in an old pair of fluffy mules. They should've seen the inside of a bin a long time ago, but her sister wasn't given to throwing things away. Nor was she given to tidying. The whole place was a mess, as usual, and it had taken some doing to clear enough space for Judy to sit down in the front lounge. On top of that, there was the dreadful smell that permeated the house. Her sister loved fish, and regularly brought home fresh kippers for Jimmy to smoke in a contraption he'd rigged up in the backyard, before hanging them in the back bedroom to dry out.

'You're off already? Bloody hell, Judy, you've only just arrived.' Mandy sounded disappointed.

She was a large woman, tipping towards the unhealthy side of the scales. She had a pretty face, a permanent frown, and a mass of bleached-blonde hair hanging down like strands of dead grass across her face.

'It takes a while to get back, Mand, and I've still got to pop into the butcher's to get a couple of chops for Frank.'

'I don't know why you didn't get him to drive you over.' Mandy pursed her lips.

Judy knew her sister had never liked Frank; she only tolerated him for Judy's sake.

'I told you, he had a long night . . .' Judy stood up and gave her sister a hug. 'Right then, I'll see you next week.' She tucked her scarf into her fur coat, and wrinkled her nose; the mink stank of fish as well now. 'Shall I get Frank to come and pick you up? We can shoot over to the new C&A in Camberwell, get a few bits.'

'That would be lovely.' Mandy smiled, and went to follow Judy to the front door.

'Don't worry, Jimmy can see me out, darlin'. You finish up in the kitchen. I'll see you soon.' She nodded to her sister and walked through to the hallway with her nephew a few feet behind.

Turning towards him, Judy noticed some biscuit crumbs on his Pringle tank top, and she lovingly brushed them off. 'Now remember what I've told you. Don't say anything, will you?'

'I won't, Auntie Judy.'

'Good, and Jim . . .' An image of him running about as a young boy came into her mind. He'd been such a beautiful baby.

'Yes, Auntie Judy?'

For a moment Judy hesitated, but then she thought of her Frank. Her wonderful, wonderful Frank. She lowered her voice. Her sister could be a right busybody, though Mandy would never admit it.

'I've got a job for you, Jimmy. Well, Frank has. It's good money. *Very* good money. It'll buy you that expensive metal detector you wanted, *and* still leave you with a bit of change. You know the Bull and Bush on the Barking Road?'

Jimmy nodded.

'Well, meet Frank tonight at eight o'clock, by the phone box outside the pub. Don't be late, Jim, and keep your mouth shut about it.'

Jimmy's eyes lit up. 'Is this about the . . . you know, the . . .' He looked over his shoulder then mouthed '*remains*' in an exaggerated manner.

'Just wait and see, but I promise it'll be worth your while.'

She patted his cheek affectionately, then slowly turned and walked out.

Chapter Twenty-Eight

Outside Canning Town Station, Judy stared at the baby in its pram. The little mite was dirty. Filthy. His hair was matted, and she could see a thick layer of cradle cap on his crown. A crust of dried snot ringed his tiny nostrils, and Judy could smell the stench of poo and sick from where she was standing. It was clear his blankets hadn't seen a good scrub for a while, not like the pretty ones she had stored back at home. He would look lovely in them, especially the yellow ones she'd bought a couple of weeks ago from John Lewis.

Judy glanced at the mother chattering away in the phone box. She was wearing her dressing gown in place of a coat, tied with a length of string around the waist. A skanky scrubber like her had no right to have such a poppet of a baby. She didn't deserve him. And by the state of him, she didn't know how to look after him either. Or more likely, she just didn't care. It shouldn't be allowed. He wasn't even wrapped up properly. The poor little love must be freezing. And look, he didn't even have little mittens on his hands.

A light dusting of sleet began to fall. Judy continued to stare, picturing just how she'd dress him.

'What the fuck are you doing with my baby? You crazy bitch. Put him down.'

Judy blinked. The baby's mother was rushing towards her. And that's when she realised she was cradling the baby tightly against her body. She couldn't even remember picking him up.

'I *said*, put my baby down, you stupid fucking bitch. Are you insane? You want me to call the Old Bill?' The woman screamed at Judy and roughly grabbed the baby off her.

Judy said nothing. She calmly watched a lorry hurtling along the road. For a moment, the idea of pushing this screeching bitch into its path rushed through her head. At least then she'd be able to care for that poor baby. Feed him, bath him. Do all the things she'd been robbed of.

'You need to be locked up, you crazy cow. You're lucky I didn't put my fist down your fucking throat.' The woman bundled the baby into his pram, glaring at Judy. She pushed it away down the road before disappearing around the corner.

Judy simply smiled to herself.

She walked into the phone box and picked up the phone. The plastic mouthpiece had been burnt along the edges with a lighter, and it smelt strongly of cigarettes. After wiping the phone with her clean hankie, she punched in a number.

Hearing the beeps, and a woman's voice answering, Judy pushed a ten-pence piece into the slot. 'Oh hello, this is Judy . . . Judy Baker. I'm the wife of Frank . . . It's Cynthia, isn't it? I think we met once.'

'Yes, of course. I remember . . . How can I help?'

'I was just wondering if I could speak to Lord Dennis. Would you tell him it's important, please?'

'Of course. If you don't mind waiting a moment, I'll let him know.'

As Judy stood trying to keep warm, a gang of kids rode past on their bikes and banged loudly on the phone box. How she wished Frank was here with her. He'd give the little buggers what for! He made her feel safe, not to mention loved. She shivered inwardly at the thought of him sliding his hands down her body.

'Judy, my favourite woman.' Dennis's voice boomed down the phone.

She blushed and put on her best telephone voice. 'I'm so sorry to disturb you, but I really need to talk to you. It's a rather delicate matter, though. And before I say what I need to, if you don't mind – how shall I put this? – well, I'd rather you didn't say anything to Frank. I'm sorry to ask that.'

'Now look, there's no need to apologise, Judy. No need at all. I've told you, my door is always open to you, and you can come to me about anything.'

Judy positively beamed. She'd always admired Dennis and enjoyed the way he made her feel special.

'If you're free now, Judy, why don't you tell me where you are, and I'll send my driver to pick you up. How about I get my house-keeper to rustle up some of those delicious cream scones you like? But I must admit, my dear, I'm intrigued to find out what this is about. I can't imagine.'

She took a deep breath. 'It's about my nephew . . .'

Oh yes, Judy Baker would do anything for her Frank.

Chapter Twenty-Nine

It was well past lunchtime, and no sign of Jason. He was a late riser – no doubt shacked up with one of his hookers – but Samantha couldn't be too careful. She pulled the hood of her coat even closer around her face.

Since storming out of the house, she'd been wandering the backstreets of Lambeth, not really knowing where to go. She'd cut through a large estate off the Black Prince Road, which was strewn with rubbish and overrun by kids who should've been in school, roaming around in groups.

In the time it had taken her to drink the cup of hot chocolate she'd bought from the takeaway van on the corner of Old Paradise Street, she'd walked past a row of derelict terraced houses, watched a broken pram being pushed along by a girl – filled with kittens and empty milk bottles – and thought again about Grace.

She slowed her pace now, and began to walk over Lambeth Bridge. Halfway across, she stopped and looked down into the swirling River Thames, feeling the cold air coming off the river and the feather-light sleet landing on her hands, freezing her fingers. She closed her eyes, and the relief of being anywhere other than home rushed through her.

She stayed there for over an hour, just watching the river whirl by.

Although she knew what awaited her back at home, it was the freest she'd felt for a long while, despite the fact that she was still troubled by Grace. She still had the phone number for Grace's godmother in her handbag, so hopefully she'd find a phone box and get through. The sooner she got Grace away from Holly Brookes, the better.

Samantha continued over the bridge and along Millbank, until she came to a wine bar on the corner. She walked up the stone stairs and pulled the double doors open. A blast of heat hit her full in the face, and her shoulders relaxed at the sound of the soothing, soulful voice of Joe Cocker playing on the jukebox.

She made a beeline for the bar.

'A glass of red wine, please . . . and make it a large one.'

'Has it been one of those days already, love?'

With good humour, Samantha rolled her eyes. 'When isn't it one of those days?'

The barmaid smiled at Samantha. She'd seen it all before. 'That will be eighty-five pence, please, darlin'.' She poured the wine for Samantha, filling it way past the measuring line on the glass, and pushed the drink towards Samantha.

'Thank you . . . Oh, is your phone working?' Samantha nodded towards the payphone in the corner by the Ladies.

'Yeah, it should be. It only takes ten-pence pieces, though, and make sure you press the money in slowly.'

Taking the slip of paper out of her bag, and using the change the barmaid had given her, she dialled the number for Grace's godmother. It rang for a long time, before the answer machine kicked in with an ear-piercing *beep*. Samantha sighed and left a message.

'Hello, my name's Samantha Wakeman, I was wondering if you could give me call, please. It's about your goddaughter, Grace.

Nothing to worry about, and I'm not sure if anyone else has spoken to you, but I was hoping we could have a quick chat. My number is . . .' Samantha paused for a moment. She didn't want to give the office number; she wanted to make sure she spoke to the woman in private. She was already going against what Miller had said, so she needed to do this as discreetly as possible. 'It's 01 for London, then . . .'

Samantha gave her home number, then replaced the receiver and knocked back her glass of wine.

'Sam?'

She turned around.

'Jake.'

She'd known when she walked into the Beehive that this was where he came to drink on his own. *Without* Jason. Had she been hoping to bump into him? Yes. But until right now, she hadn't realised how much.

Taking a deep breath, Samantha looked Jake straight in the eye, and decided to just say it. 'I had to see you. Last night—'

'Who the fuck is this?'

The woman was all dyed-blonde hair, fake tan and boobs hanging out of a leopard-skin top. She stared at Samantha like a feral cat as she walked up to Jake, linking arms with him. 'You do know he's taken, darlin'?'

Humiliation engulfed Samantha. God, she was a fool. How could she have read the situation so wrong? She felt her cheeks burning. 'Oh, I'm so sorry . . . I didn't mean to . . . I'm just an old friend. Sorry. Shit, I shouldn't have come . . . Jake, I'm so sorry.'

She grabbed her bag and rushed for the door.

'Samantha, wait . . . wait up.'

Samantha heard Jake and the blonde arguing as she hurried out of the bar. Seeing a bus slowing at the corner, she ran for it, jumping on the back. As it drove off, she turned over her shoulder and saw Jake coming out of the bar, his figure receding in the distance as he looked up and down the street.

She sat down and closed her eyes, letting the embarrassment wash over her. That's what she got for being impulsive . . . no, for being bloody stupid.

It took forty minutes before Samantha was walking back down Langley Lane. She spent the whole bus journey regretting ever having stormed out of the house. Why couldn't she just accept that this was her life now? It would be so much easier. But there was something inside her that still continued to fight. Even if, one day, that fight could get her killed.

She put her key slowly in the front door.

'Hello, Sam . . . nice to see you, sweetheart.'

Samantha let her handbag slip slowly out of her hand and land with a thud on the floor in the hallway. She stared into Jason's face, chilled by his quiet voice and wide smile.

'Surprised to see me, are you, darlin'? Your mum called me. Said she was worried that she hadn't had her tea. Said she wasn't sure when you'd be back.' One side of his lip curled, and he took a slow step towards her. 'She also said, you were rude to her . . . So I thought, I need to come round.'

Samantha stared at him. She shook her head, and in that moment she was so, so tired of being scared.

'Why don't you just do what you came for then? Why don't we just get this over and done with, Jase?' Tears rolled down her face.

He slowly began to unbuckle his belt, wrapping it around his hand.

Samantha waited, ashen-faced and silent, as he walked up to her. He grabbed hold of her throat, slamming her against the wall.

The front door was abruptly flung open.

Jake stood on the doorstep. His expression froze as he looked first at Jason and then back at Samantha.

The silence held, ticking away between them.

Jason released his grip on Samantha's throat and stepped towards his brother.

'Now then, Jakey, are you going to tell me what the fuck you're doing coming to see my wife?'

Chapter Thirty

Dennis Hargreaves strolled around his office on Great Peter Street, admiring the plush, thick red tartan of the wall-to-wall carpets. Deep mahogany wooden panels lined the walls, from floor to ceiling. A large antique French chandelier hung in pride of place over the green chesterfield sofa. He turned to his hand-carved executive desk, placed strategically by the tall window to give a view of the Palace of Westminster. And also the boys' preparatory school.

The meeting between Judy and himself had been brief, although long enough for her to finish three cream scones and the pot of tea Cynthia had brought in. For all her roughness around the edges, he liked Judy. He'd even go so far as to say he admired her. The loyalty she showed to her husband – and therefore, in turn, to him – was certainly commendable. Not like that damn weasel Alan Carver.

Taking the last sip of his Earl Grey tea, Dennis lingered at his desk. He leant in and gently nudged the rook on the chessboard, his latest move in the ongoing game he had with one of his butlers.

He had to admit, he'd been disappointed in Alan recently. Dennis likened life to a chess game. People like Alan were his pawns, to be moved around the board as and when he needed them. Dennis always determined the strategy. In order to win,

Dennis knew there was always a move to be made; every decision had a consequence, and his pawns were only kept in play for as long as they were useful to him. If Alan wasn't careful, he'd find himself knocked off the board.

He pressed the intercom on his desk.

'Hello, sir.' Cynthia's voice came through the speaker.

'Ah, Cynthia, get Chief Superintendent Lewis on the phone, will you? I've got a little job for him.'

'Maybe that's enough?'

In a cold basement in Craig's Court, Charlie Archer stared at his boss. They'd been here for over an hour and nothing much had come of it. It was freezing, and right now he could think of better things to be doing than standing around watching a scene he'd witnessed hundreds of times before. His gaze followed the sweat running down his boss's shirtless back, beads of perspiration rolling along his knobbly spine.

'I'll fucking tell you when it's enough, Charlie.'

Charlie nodded and decided it wasn't worth his while to object. He knew what his boss was like.

He watched him take another run-up to the man hanging upside down, tied by his legs and dripping blood. His foot slammed into the man's jaw, dislocating it and slicing his cheek open with the tip of his metal-toed boot. Blood sprayed everywhere. On the walls, on the floor. Even a small splattering on the ceiling.

'Are you fucking going to talk now?'

The man swung from side to side, and it occurred to Charlie that even if the geezer did want to say something to his boss, it was unlikely he could. One eye was so swollen, Charlie doubted he could see out of it; in fact, it looked so damaged, he doubted he'd ever be able to see again. And as for his face, well, it was so battered, he looked like the victim of a road traffic accident.

The phone rang. Its shrill tone echoed around the basement.

'Get that, will you, Charlie?'

Without saying a word, Charlie threw his cigarette into the pool of blood trickling towards his feet. He nodded and walked across to the phone on the wall. He picked up the nicotine-stained receiver, listened for a moment, then held it out. 'It's for you.'

Wiping the blood off his hands, Chief Superintendent Lewis nodded and sauntered over, whistling.

'It's Dennis Hargreaves, he wants a word.'

Chapter Thirty-One

'What the fuck are you on about, Jase? Fuck's sake, do me a favour. I came to see *you*, not *Sam*. What's wrong with you, mate?'

Jake stood in the hallway of the house in Langley Lane, staring warily at his brother. He had to pick his words carefully.

Jason pissed off a lot of people; he was unpredictable, sometimes an out-and-out cunt, but at the end of the day, they were brothers. Was he really going to fuck that up because he couldn't stay away from Sam?

Jason had always been a violent womaniser. He didn't really give a fuck about Sam. All Jase had wanted to do was make his brother choose between him and Sam; Jake couldn't be allowed to have it all. And even though it had fucked him up to do it, Jake had proved his loyalty to Jason by dropping Sam. To show Jason that he would always be *his* priority, above and beyond anything and everyone else.

Beyond business, beyond money, beyond friendships, beyond women.

Jason had known how Jake felt about Sam. Until Sam, women had come and gone, names forgotten or not even asked. Jake realised he sounded like a cliché, but Sam was different. She'd got inside his head, and no matter how much he tried to hide it or deny it to Jason, his brother knew him too well. They were two sides of the same coin. Jason saw right through his bullshit denials.

Sam had been completely crushed when he'd told her, right out of the blue, it was over between them. He'd hated himself for doing it. Resented Jason for making him do it. And Sam had resented them both.

Jake's drinking had spiralled out of control, and when Jason swooped in on Sam she'd been at her most vulnerable. That had almost been too much for Jake. He'd stayed away, though he'd had no intention of staying away from Sam for good.

But then Jason went and marched Sam down the aisle.

And that was when Jake's resentment towards his brother started to grow.

Nobody needed to explain to him that seeing Sam behind Jason's back was bang out of order. He just told himself, he was only looking out for her. Someone needed to. It was no secret that Jason regularly knocked her about.

Or was this just an excuse to visit her? Maybe when it came down to it, he was as selfish as Jason. But he was genuinely torn between love and loyalty. Because, God knows, they weren't the same thing.

'You need to lay off the old oats and barley a bit, Jase.' Jake strolled further into the hallway.

Lying to his brother was the last thing he wanted to do, but he wasn't stupid enough to tell the truth.

He lit a cigarette and took a long drag. 'It's making you paranoid.'

'Is that right?'

Jason stared down at his fist and his bruised knuckles from the run-in at the club earlier. He had an urge to nut his brother, but he held his temper back.

He'd always known that Jake still had a thing for Sam, but he'd hoped his brother wouldn't be so fucking stupid as to continue to carry that torch. Jake had got soft with her a few years ago. He'd become slack with business because of her. His mind completely elsewhere. Jason could see it. The people they were doing business with could see it. And no one trusted or wanted to do business with some love-struck idiot who had his head so far up a pussy that he wasn't thinking straight. They'd had a reputation to uphold, and Jake had been going some way to fucking it up.

So he'd tested Jake. What brother wouldn't do that? He'd wanted to know where Jake's loyalty really lay. With him or with Sam. Jake had made the right choice, and to make sure Jake continued to make the right choice, Jason had made Sam his wife.

It had been easy. He'd consoled her when Jake had left, got her into bed, and down the aisle, all in a matter of months. Unlike Jake, he wasn't some soppy cunt, and love for a woman didn't even feature in his vocabulary. But that didn't stop Jason feeling the white-hot rage of jealously when anyone so much as looked at Sam.

Sam was now Jason's, which meant that Jake could concentrate on the important things: being the best businessman, the best enforcer, the best brother.

Jason just hoped that Jake wasn't playing him for a fucking fool.

'Yeah, too right it is. You need to wind your fucking neck in.'

Jake blew out smoke from the side of his mouth.

'You've been snorting that shit for almost twenty-four hours.'

Jason shrugged nonchalantly. 'And . . .?' He laughed scornfully. 'So come on then, if I'm being so fucking paranoid, why did you come to see me?'

For a moment, Jake stared at Jason. He glanced at Sam. He hated seeing the fear on her face, but what could he do? There was such a bitter taste in his mouth, the way Jason treated her. He'd seen the bruises, seen her change from happy-go-lucky to subdued and sad. How much of a hand had he played in that?

He shook his head, knowing that Jason was scrutinising his reactions.

'This shit with Zef and Dren has got me worried, Jase. We can't have it blowing up in our faces. They aren't messing about. I tried to call you, but you'd left already. We need to speak to Alan. Face to face. The clock's ticking, and I don't want that cunt turning us over. I was going up to see Bob in Vauxhall, so I thought I'd take a detour to see if you were here.' Jake shrugged. 'Happy now?'

Jason moved up close, took Jake's cigarette out of his mouth and took a drag on it.

He tilted his head. 'But I never come here on Fridays.'

Jake blinked rapidly. *Shit*. 'Yet here you are.'

He held Jason's stare.

Jason ground the cigarette into Phyllis's rubber plant. He kept his eyes on Jake's face . . . and that's when he saw it. The tiny pulse in Jake's jaw from where he was clenching and unclenching his teeth.

There was the giveaway. Every time Jake was bullshitting, that habit always gave him away. Lying bastard.

He pulled Jake towards him.

'Loyalty. Friendship. Brotherhood. Blood. You and me. It's all about trust, ain't it?' Then he grabbed the back of Jake's head, and he rested his forehead against his brother's. 'You know I love you, Jakey. You *are* me. And I'll do anything for you. But you're either loyal, or you ain't. There's no middle ground.'

Jake tried to pull away, but Jason's hold was too tight.

'I don't appreciate my loyalty being called into question, Jase.'

Jake's voice was low so Sam couldn't hear. 'I've always done what you've asked me to do. So don't talk to me about fucking loyalty.'

Jason continued to rest his forehead on his brother's. 'Someone pisses you off, I'll get you a gun. Someone hurts you, I'll break their fucking legs. And if you kill someone, I'll dig the hole to bury them, you know that, Jake. But just don't ever lie to me. Because I swear to God, even though it'll tear out my heart to do it, I'll fuck you up if you ever try to turn me over. If you want to survive in this world, Jakey, there's one thing you need to value above all else: loyalty.'

He pulled away and slapped Jake on the back of his neck. 'Now come on, let's go and sort that cunt Alan out . . . I'll meet you at the car. I'm just going to say goodbye to Phyllis.'

As Jason turned round, he clicked his fingers and pointed at Samantha. 'I'll speak to *you* later, okay? And then we can talk about where the fuck you were earlier.'

He pushed past her and strode into Phyllis's room.

'I'm going now, darlin'.' He gave her his best smile.

'Oh, that's a shame, Jase. I was looking forward to having a natter, Samantha doesn't bother talking to me most of the time.'

He placed five ten-pound notes on the arm of her chair and winked. 'Well, that won't do, will it? I'll have a little word with her, if you like.'

Phyllis put down her cup of tea on her tray, brushed off the cake crumbs from her cardigan, and grabbed hold of Jason's hand. She kissed his palm and in return he kissed her on the top of her head. 'You're a good boy, Jase. Sam doesn't know how lucky she is.'

'Phyllis . . .' Jason paused, aware that Samantha had walked into the kitchen. He lowered his voice. 'Be my eyes and ears, Phyllis, be my eyes and ears, darlin'.'

*

Phyllis nodded and watched Jason walk out of the room, leaving her sitting in her chair.

She waited a minute before quickly craning her neck around the back of the chair to see if her daughter was still hovering in the kitchen.

Certain Samantha was busy, Phyllis rummaged in the pocket of her cardigan – she'd knitted it last year through sheer boredom – and pulled out a cream handkerchief along with a piece of paper. She unfolded it carefully.

She stared at the phone message she'd taken about some child called Grace. From a Mrs Wilkins, who was apparently the kid's godmother.

She sniffed, as if offended by a bad smell, and checked over her shoulder once more before screwing the message up tightly. Then, with an air of self-righteousness, Phyllis dropped the scrunched-up paper into her tea, stirring it around and watching it disintegrate into a ball of mush.

She smiled to herself. That was more like it. How many times had she said it? Charity started at home, and Samantha needed to remember that.

Chapter Thirty-Two

'Alan . . . Alan, we know you're fucking in there. Open the door, mate. Or we're going to huff and puff, and blow your house down, you cunt.'

It was the dregs of the winter afternoon. Jason and Jake stood in the darkness outside the large, detached house in Dulwich village, confidently shouting and laughing in Alan's back garden.

Alan flattened himself against the bedroom wall, hiding in the shadows, and inched towards the window frame. He was furious at the intrusion – keeping up appearances with the neighbours mattered *so* damn much to him – but he was also terrified.

His heart hammered fiercely as he kneaded the middle of his chest. He was in a cold sweat. If the Wakemans had come to his house, they meant business. They'd been outside for the past twenty minutes, and it didn't look like they were going away any time soon.

Did they know he was in here? Maybe it was a mistake to have turned the lights off. He hoped to fuck they hadn't noticed. Before the brothers had arrived, he'd turned the whole house over, looking for the photos of Dennis and the young boys. He was just stepping outside to check in his garage, when he'd spotted their cars driving down the crescent like a fucking presidential cavalcade.

He was now a prisoner in his own fucking home. Bastards. *Cunts*. And to think he'd been the one to give those two pricks a chance.

Alan wasn't entirely sure what to do, so he waited for another fifteen minutes before peeking out of the window. Not fully convinced they'd gone, he tiptoed out of his room as silently as possible, and along the landing. At the end door, he stopped and listened again . . . Hearing nothing, he turned the wooden doorknob, wincing at the creaking sound, and stepped into his study.

At the bay window, Alan looked up and down the street. He closed his eyes, breathing out. Their cars had gone. Thank fuck for that. He waited another five minutes for luck, before deciding that a glass of whiskey was very much needed. As he reached the top of the stairs, his usual belligerence kicked in. He was fuming. How dare the Wakemans think they could come around here, to his home, and start threatening *him*. Well, he'd show them. He'd come up with a way to make them think twice before bothering him again.

Striding down the stairs towards the lounge, Alan continued muttering to himself.

'Hello, Alan.'

Alan froze.

Sitting in his favourite armchair, drinking his favourite whiskey, flicking a knife in and out of its case, was Jason. And a few feet behind him was Jake, along with some of their cronies.

Alan went dizzy with panic. His gaze darted around as Jason nodded towards the mess on the floor from all the drawers and books Alan had pulled out earlier.

'I think you need to invest in a cleaner, mate.' Jason winked.

'What the fuck do you want?'

Jason grinned at Jake. 'Is he having a laugh?' His smile dropped

183

as he weighed up whether or not he could be bothered to slap Alan right now, but on balance, he needed answers first. 'What I want, Al, is the contract in my hand.' He glanced at his Rolex. A gift from his father before everything had gone tits up. Jason had nothing but hatred for his dad; he wore the watch as a reminder of what happened when people turned him over, no matter who they were. 'Look at the time, Al. We warned you, mate. Remember? Tick fucking tock.'

Alan had to moisten his lips with his tongue before he was able to speak. 'There's been a delay. Nothing . . . nothing I can't sort out . . . I . . .' Still trying to get over the shock of finding the Wakemans in his front room, Alan scrambled for his words.

Jason's face was a picture of contempt.

'We don't deal in delays, mate.' Jake shrugged.

Alan had to start thinking on his feet. 'Yeah, yeah, I realise that. But there's been some rumblings, ain't there?' He looked between the brothers.

'What the fuck are you rabbiting on about?' Jason's patience was wearing thin.

'So . . . so some of my sources, ones I can trust, tell me there's a probe into land sales in London. Fucking journalists. They're doing an investigation for one of the broadsheets. I mean, it's a load of nosy bullshit if you ask me . . . a load of crap about the community's vison for the area, versus the developer's vision.'

Alan swallowed hard. He was impressed by the story he'd just come up with. As his conceit swelled, so too did his confidence. He even managed a smile.

'So you see, boys, that's why I've had to hold off. I thought it was best. Officially the land's still in the council's name, but once that final contract goes through – the contract we were supposed to sign today – well, it's going to be in your names then. One little dig around by those fucking journos, and your names will come up. Then questions will be asked, and they'll have a field day It'll be like Christmas has come all at once for them.'

'What the fuck has that got to do with anything?' Jason snapped.

'Come on, it's me you're talking to. You're already nearly as well known as the Richardsons or the Krays. A little bit of sniffing around, and those journalists might find out you've got connections to organised crime.'

Jake shook his head at Alan. Alan gestured with his arms to emphasise his point. 'So you see, me holding back with the contract and keeping your names well away from any journalists who are looking for a story, well, it makes sense. Like I say, you don't want questions being asked.'

Jason pointed the tip of the knife towards him. 'Questions being asked of *you*, Al, not of us. On paper we're totally legit, mate. It's you who's been a dodgy cunt, with all those land deals you've been doing. You and I both know you've been selling off bits of land for a while, to get favours.' Jason looked at his brother. 'This fucker's still got his eyes set on Number Ten. Ain't that right, Al?'

Both Jason and Jake burst into laughter.

'It'll be more like Court Number Ten when they catch up with you,' Jake quipped.

'You're the headline, mate, not us,' Jason added. 'So all this sounds like *your* problem, not ours. If people are asking questions, then it's simple, pay them off, like you always do. Maybe this is about you protecting your arse . . . You see, our business associates . . .'

Alan wouldn't call Zef and Dren business associates, they were fucking goons. He seethed inwardly as Jason continued to speak.

185

'. . . they've already had a word with us, Al. And let me tell you, they weren't happy bunnies, which means we're not happy.'

Jason took a sip of his whiskey.

It occurred to Alan that everything was the wrong way around. This was *his* house, *his* chair, *his* deal, yet Jason was lecturing *him* and drinking a bottle of his finest malt, which had cost him nearly a monkey. Not only that, these fuckers worked for him, yet they were trying to give him orders.

'I just need a little more time, Jase.'

'Hear that, Jake? This cunt wants more time.' Jason stared at Alan. 'You see, even if I wanted to give you more time, it's not only me I have to think about. What am I supposed to tell my associates? They've fronted some of the money too.'

'If you're talking about Zef and Dren, tell them what you like. At the end of the day, Jase, whether you believe it or not, I'm looking out for you.'

Jason picked his teeth with the knife he was holding, swinging his leg over the armrest. 'Now that . . . that I know is complete bullshit, because no one around here is going to believe you're looking out for us. The only person you've *ever* looked out for is yourself. So I'm afraid time's up, Al.'

They held each other's gaze for a while, until Alan broke it off. He turned around, but Jake stood in his way. There was nowhere for him to run

Alan took a step back. He clutched on to the sideboard for a moment before Jason got the first punch in, booting him in the stomach and doubling him over.

'Now then, Alan . . .' Jake grabbed Alan by his hair, pulling him upright by the roots of his recently trimmed barnet. He dragged him into the kitchen, followed by his henchmen.

'Sit down.' Jake threw Alan on to the chair with a hard thud.

'You're such a fucking muppet, you know that? From start to finish, you've been taking the piss, Al.'

'I ain't taking the piss.' Alan was desperate.

Yet the cold hard truth of the matter was Alan couldn't let the Wakemans have the land because of the child's remains Jimmy had found. That clearly had something to do with Dennis and his sick friends. And who knows what else was buried in that site along the Thames?

Jason laughed at Alan. 'How many times did we warn you? How can anyone be this fucking stupid? It was so easy. So fucking simple. All you had to do was not turn us over. None of this was necessary, mate.'

Alan watched Jason's expression harden as he leant forward and spoke more quietly to him. 'You see, if you'd come to us and explained what was happening, maybe then we could've done something about it. We could've had a word with the journalists sniffing around. Or we may have even been prepared to wait. But every time we asked you if everything was okay, you told us it was. Turns out you've been trying to hide stuff from us, Al. And the only reason people hide stuff, is because shit is going down.'

Alan's breathing was laboured and heavy. 'You work for me, remember?'

Jason clipped Alan around the back of his head. 'Wrong answer.' He grinned. 'Do yourself a favour, think before you open that fucking mouth of yours. Or you'll end up pissing me off *more* than you already have. Remember, I paid good money for that land, and this whole deal has just taken too long.' He took his knife and dragged it, blunt side down, along Alan's cheek.

Alan could feel himself starting to shake

'Don't worry, Al, I ain't going to kill you. Well, not today anyway, sentimental reasons really. You and me go back a long way, don't we? So I'm going to give you a chance, and today, I'll play nice.'

Jason nodded to Jake.

His brother walked up to Alan and put him in a tight head lock at the same time as Jason grabbed Alan's arm, slamming his hand on the kitchen table.

'Spread them.' Jason gave his order.

'What?' Alan spluttered, struggling to speak as Jake's muscular arm tightened around his throat.

'Spread them. Spread your fucking fingers, *now*,' Jason snarled

Alan instinctively clenched his fist into a ball.

Jason replied by putting the tip of the knife against Alan's throat, nicking his skin. A trickle of blood ran down the stubble on his neck, leaving a mark on Jake's sleeve.

'I *said*, spread them. Or perhaps you ain't hearing me right?' Jason moved the tip of the knife from his throat into the opening of Alan's ear, holding it there. 'You want me to clear out your ears for you? I can, if you like. I'll be able to get right in. Dig out all that crap in there.'

Terrified, Alan gave the tiniest shake of his head. His pupils had dilated to almost twice their normal size. Breathing heavily, he very slowly opened his fingers.

'That's better.' This from Jason, who was clearly revelling in Alan's fear. 'Ready, Al?'

'What . . . what the fuck are you going to do?'

'Hold on, mate, you're eager.' Jason laughed at the same time as bringing down his knife with force.

Blood and skin splattered everywhere, and Alan screamed as his little finger was cut cleanly off. His body went into spasms from shock as he saw what looked like a red river of blood pour out across the kitchen table and stream on to the black-and-white-tiled floor. He clutched his hand under his armpit, trying to stem both the pain and the blood as he rocked around in agony.

Jason walked casually across the room and picked up the severed finger.

'Maybe now, Al, you'll realise we're not kidding. You're lucky that wasn't your fucking dick. Next time, it will be. Get that contract to us by the end of the week. Or, bollock by bollock, I'll fucking chop you up.'

He sauntered back across to Alan and grabbed his mutilated hand, forcing it into the half-drunk glass of whiskey he'd brought through earlier. Alan screamed at the top of his lungs as the alcohol seared the open wound, burning like the fires of hell. The pain shot through him like a bitch.

'That's better, ain't it?' Jason was enjoying himself. 'We wouldn't want you getting an infection in that now, would we, Al?'

The brothers and their henchmen headed towards the hallway door.

Jason stopped, turned around and threw the cut-off finger at Alan. 'Here you go . . . You probably need that more than me, mate.'

An hour later, Alan managed to move from his chair to pick up the phone and make a call.

It rang a couple of times before it was answered.

'*Yes?*'

'Chief Superintendent Lewis, it's Alan Carver . . . I need your help, as soon as fucking possible . . .'

Chapter Thirty-Three

Grace was thinking about Samantha. Trying to make sense of things. She'd asked at least *five* grown-ups about her mum, and all of them, apart from Mr Barrows, had seemed uninterested. As the hours had ticked by, and nobody had answered her questions, her tummy had started to hurt more and more.

The last time Grace had been to the bathroom, she'd had diarrhoea. She'd sat on the toilet, racked with stomach pains, until Mr Clemence had walked into the girls' changing room looking for her. He'd shouted so loud she'd been terrified, almost too afraid to walk out of the cubicle. When she had, Clemence had grabbed her by her jumper, pulling her out of the toilets, and hadn't even let her wash her hands.

So despite her tummy still hurting, Grace was now too frightened to go to the toilet. She was having to hold it in, which was making her feel *really* unwell.

To distract herself from the discomfort, Grace was singing a song very quietly to herself, one her mum and dad had always sung to her at bedtime. She was all out of tears right now, but her eyes were still sore. In between the choruses, she sighed unhappily. She was feeling so poorly.

For the past couple of hours she'd been forced to sew sequins on to various costumes and watch as Mr Clemence and Mr Barrows directed rehearsals for the pantomime. They yelled out stage directions to some of the kids, while another teacher bashed out notes on the small out-of-tune piano in the corner.

The hall was packed with children from Holly Brookes. Grace thought the place looked less like a hall and more like a theatre. A large stage had been built at the front, with sweeping red curtains. They opened and closed, swishing along a bowed, rusting metal curtain rail, during scene changes. There were also stage wings, leading to the back corridors of the building where some of the older kids were painting scenery.

Everything was blurred, because she didn't have her glasses. And it had become stuffy and hot in the musty hall. But at least that was a welcome break for Grace from the biting cold.

'Why does everyone look so fucking miserable?'

Dara leant across Grace and whispered to Brenda. The girl seemed to have decided to tag along with them ever since the incident with Barry earlier.

'Wouldn't you be miserable?' Brenda whispered back.

Dara couldn't help staring at how tight and shiny the skin on the burnt side of her face was.

'No one wants to be in the pantomime. Barrows and Clemence choose who gets a part. Holly Brookes puts on a big Easter and Christmas show, as well as a summer fête, but no one wants to get chosen.'

'Why? I mean, who comes and watches it anyway?'

Dara thought about her own school. When they put on a play, the whole assembly hall was full of proud mums and dads. Her mum had never bothered showing up, much to Dara's relief. But here in Holly Brookes, no one had parents, did they? So Dara didn't see the point of it. Everyone was made to watch the rehearsals, so it wasn't like it was even a surprise for the kids. Barrows and Clemence were getting so worked up about it all. They'd done nothing but shout at everyone.

Brenda shrugged. 'I dunno why. I think it makes them look good, you know, makes Holly Brookes look good. They raise money for the school, cos they invite all the posh patrons. They all come along, and . . .' She trailed off, shaking her head.

Dara picked up that she suddenly seemed uncomfortable. She wasn't sure what was going on, but not for the first time that day, Brenda's unease made Dara feel tense.

'What are you humming?' Dara nudged Grace gently, wanting to think about something else. 'You've been singing that since we got in here.'

'Just something my mum taught me.' Grace looked shy.

'It's nice.' Dara smiled at her warmly.

Grace's cheeks flushed red.

'*What the fuck is wrong with you?*'

The bellow from Barrows wiped away Grace's smile, and made Dara jump. The hum of children's whispering in the hall abruptly ceased. All eyes turned to the stage. Barrows was hovering over a four-foot yellow duck. He ripped off the orange-beaked headpiece of the costume, to reveal Robbie. The boy was looking up at Barrows, cringing.

'Well? What's your line?'

'I . . . I don't know, sir.'

Barrows threw his arms up in the air. 'You don't know!' He shook his head, taking a half-smoked roll-up from behind his ear. He pointed it at Robbie, lit it and took a deep drag, before pointing it again at the boy. 'Why don't you fucking know? Everyone else here seems to know their lines, so what makes you so special? Think you can mess it all up for everyone else?' This time, Barrows poked Robbie in his chest. 'Hey?' He studied Robbie's face, then furiously looked around. 'Does anyone else know his line?'

A tall spotty kid put his hand up. 'Yes, sir, I do . . . *Which way to the beanstalk?*'

'That's right, Joseph. Which way to the *fucking* beanstalk. Do you hear that, Robbie? To the beanstalk. Not to the castle, not to the palace, but to the beanstalk where Mrs Hubbard is in the fucking cupboard, waiting for you.'

Dara wondered if Barrows was going to have a fit. His whole face, from his neck to his bald head, was red with blotches of rage, and even from the middle of the hall, Dara could see his eyes bulging in fury.

None of the children made a sound.

'You're an idiot, you know that, Robbie? You make stupid look clever.'

'He's out of order,' Dara whispered.

She went to make a move, but Brenda held on to her wrist.

'Don't . . . don't, you'll just make it worse for him. You won't be doing Robbie any favours. Leave it.'

'Leave it?' Dara wasn't going to do that. She'd never done that, and she wasn't about to start now. 'No, Brenda . . . I haven't been here long, but each time I see Barrows, he's bullying Robbie.'

'Seriously, Dara, leave it.' Brenda was ashen.

'Do what she says,' Gracie implored Dara, with a small smile. 'Brenda knows better than us.'

Dara looked at Robbie in the middle of the stage, then at Brenda, and gave her a nod, sitting back and hating herself for doing nothing.

'This time, Robbie, I'm going to take you to the woods!' Barrows screamed.

Everyone in the hall could see the spray of spittle from his mouth landing on Robbie's face.

'And you're going to be there for the *whole* night . . . That's right, Robbie, in the dark, all alone, which will give you plenty of time to think about your lines.'

The mention of the dark made Robbie step away from Barrows and shake his head, crying, 'No, no, please, sir.'

Barrows mocked him, imitating his voice. '*Oh no, sir, no . . .*' Then he smirked. 'Oh yes, Robbie, oh *fucking* yes. And let's hope, for your sake, the bogeyman isn't out there to get you.'

Brenda whispered to Dara and Grace. 'Robbie's petrified of the dark, that's why they do it, because they know how scared he'll be.'

'Where are they taking him?' Grace asked, her voice trembling.

'To the outhouse. There's a shed in the woods, they lock him in there.'

Dara's vision was blurred with tears. She could hardly see, though she was grateful for that, because it stopped her witnessing Robbie's fear as he was dragged offstage, screaming.

Chapter Thirty-Four

'That cunt Alan Carver called me, by the way.'

Chief Superintendent Lewis tugged on his large, expensive cigar. The end of it was wet and sodden. Not that he cared. Lewis, like so many of his associates, cared about very little, if anything at all.

Lewis could pinpoint the moment when he'd stopped caring about the world at large. It was when he was thirteen. On the day he'd been taken boxing for the first time by his father. Arthur Lewis, an amateur boxer himself, had taken his son to his gym on Blackstock Road, Finsbury Park, and had proudly shown him how to throw a punch.

Lewis had always admired and respected his father. He'd followed Arthur's instructions to the letter. Lewis's punch had landed square on the side of his father's head. Arthur had collapsed moments later with a bleed on the brain. Five hours later, he had been pronounced dead.

That was the moment when Lewis decided life was meaningless. What was the point of cherishing and loving anything, if eventually it was going to be taken away anyway? He could save himself the effort. Rather than feeling sad, he'd felt genuinely relieved that he'd learnt such a valuable lesson at a young age. There was no value to life.

This newfound philosophy had inspired him. So, regardless of his recent tragedy, Lewis had continued boxing, and over the years, he'd turned his slight teenage frame into the stocky build of a man who struggled to find shirts to fit his wide, muscular back. And he became strong enough to break the jaw of a mule with one punch.

Yawning, Lewis wiped his mouth, and pressed the power button on the car door. The window opened enough for him to tap the ash out.

He glanced at Dennis, at ease in his company. 'He was literally crying. How the mighty fall, eh?'

In the back seat of his Rolls Royce, Dennis barely bothered to turn his head towards Lewis. He shrugged and adjusted the collar of his tweed coat. 'What did he want?'

Lewis stared out of the window, watching the light pattering of sleet fall on the dirty pavement. 'What he always wants: to be wrapped up in fucking cotton wool. And for someone else to pick up the pieces . . . I didn't speak to him for long, but that was the gist of it. He's having a fit over this land deal he's got himself into. Prick.'

'Do you think he'll be able to sort it out without too much of a problem?' Dennis sounded weary.

Lewis rolled his eyes. 'Probably not, it sounds like he might need a bit of help from us.'

This time, Dennis did turn to Lewis. 'For God's sake, the man's a bloody idiot.' He shook his head, weighing up Alan's worth against the hassle he was causing. 'He's becoming more trouble than I need. This whole deal is turning into a disaster.'

Lewis nodded his head in agreement. 'I didn't have a long conversation with him, but I've already thought about how to get the ball rolling. Then we'll see how it plays out, shall we?'

Dennis didn't bother asking any more questions. He trusted Lewis to deal with the problem. That's what he paid him for.

'Do you know who it's with? The deal Alan's doing?'

'The Wakeman brothers,' Lewis answered matter-of-factly. 'From what I gather, they've been washing a lot of his dirty laundry for a while. They've been looking to get into property development for a while, so I suppose the land deal was perfect for them. Though I think the lines between what's legitimate and what isn't have got blurred somewhere along the way.'

Dennis chewed over this bit of information. He'd known there was a connection between Alan and the brothers. They were good at what they did. A couple of knuckleheads using their fists, but that was about it. He'd no idea Alan had gone into legal deals with them. It was ridiculous. That was like the organ grinder going into business with the monkey.

Dennis took a sip of his sherry, a tipple he always enjoyed in the car. 'Alan's greedy for power.' He let out a long, withering sigh. 'The man's almost pathological in his quest for it.'

Lewis continued puffing on his cigar. 'Just say the word, I can easily dispose of him for you. Nothing would give me greater pleasure.' He smiled widely. A genuine smile of delight at the idea of it.

Lewis had been called a bully for most of his life. But unlike a lot of bullies, he wasn't a coward. Far from it. He was a sadistic bastard, who took great pleasure in causing physical pain to his victims. He always had done.

Even before the boxing, Lewis had been drawn to violence. After his mother had died, Lewis's favourite pastime as a young child had been lying among the crisp, brown autumn leaves in the woods behind his house near Mill Hill. He'd watch the wild rabbits cautiously hop towards the pile of shredded cabbage he'd prepared. The rush of excitement never failed him as he waited for the right moment to reach for the rope trap, pulling it with a quick flick of his wrist, to tighten around the back legs of the innocent creature.

Seeing the fear in the rabbit's eyes was always the best part for Lewis. And in all his years, nothing had even got close to that sense of sadistic euphoria. Not sex. Not drugs. Not gambling. Nothing made Lewis feel the way he did when he saw fear and pain. Though when he got bored of the rabbits – as he later did with so many of his victims – he'd swing them against the trees, smashing their skull and body into a bloody pulp.

'Are you all right, Judy?' Dennis leant forward and touched her gently on the arm. 'We're forgetting about you there, you're so quiet.'

Judy finished a mouthful of the toffee fudge Dennis had brought for her, and patted her mouth delicately. She always liked to make a good impression. It was her attempt to distance herself from the poverty and chaos she'd grown up in.

'I'm fine, thank you, Dennis. Very happy just sitting here.'

Dennis smiled warmly and squeezed her shoulder. 'What would any of us do without you? I've said it before, and I'll go to my grave saying it, but Frank is a lucky man, isn't he, Lewis?'

'Absolutely.'

Judy basked in the warmth of the compliments. She checked the stainless-steel Timex watch Frank had given her a few birthdays ago. The elastic strap of the wristwatch nipped her skin, causing a constant rash, but she wouldn't dream of not wearing it. It made her feel close to him. It made her feel like Frank was by her side at all times, and that's the only thing that really mattered. Her Frank . . . and wanting a baby.

'I better go.' She looked between them and waited for the chauffeur to help her out of the car.

'Do you want me to come with you?' Lewis inquired gently.

'No, it's all right, I'll be fine,' she assured him.

The door of the Rolls was opened by Dennis's loyal and long-serving driver. Judy had never felt so important, and she nodded gratefully, pulling up the collar of her fur coat, before hobbling down the road.

It was dark and cold, and her bunions were still giving her problems from earlier. When she reached the corner and walked around it, she was immediately hit by a fierce wind.

'Auntie Judy! Auntie Judy!'

Standing in front of the Bull and Bush on the Barking Road, dressed in a navy-blue duffle coat, was Jimmy. He waved to Judy, and she tutted. He was hardly being discreet; the last thing she wanted was for him to be shouting her name around.

Annoyed, she gestured to him. 'Be quiet, Jimmy. Bloody hell, you're like a bleeding siren.'

Ignoring the scowl on her face, he ran over to her, bounding eagerly across the road.

'Where's Uncle Frank?' He was out of breath, and he grinned stupidly.

'He's waiting . . . Come on then. Hurry up. It's starting to sleet, and I'm going to get a chill. Last time I was caught out, I was in bed for a couple of days. It went right to my chest.'

Judy headed back to the car, with Jimmy following a few feet behind. He was chattering about the new metal detector he planned to buy with the money he was going to earn. By the time they'd turned the corner, he was already getting on her nerves.

'It's just over here, Jim. That one . . . over there.'

The moment he saw Dennis's Rolls Royce parked in the shadows, Jimmy whistled.

'Bloody hell, Auntie Judy, that's some motor.'

Ignoring Jimmy, Judy nodded to Dennis and Chief Superintendent Lewis in the back seat. The chauffer clambered out again to come around and open the passenger door.

Jimmy looked at Judy strangely. 'I thought you said Uncle Frank was here?'

She glanced over her shoulder. They'd parked in the shadows underneath a broken street light. She didn't want anyone catching sight of them.

'I didn't say he was in the bleeding car, Jim. I said he's waiting for you. I thought you'd like a trip in a Roller, I know how much you like fancy cars. And you'll be able to tell your mates. That girl you're sweet on, she'll be well impressed.'

Jimmy smirked at the thought of bragging to his mates. 'Yeah, I've always wanted a ride in one of these, you know I have.' He couldn't contain his excitement as he got into the leather front seat next to the driver. 'Do I look good, Auntie Judy?'

'Oh yeah, very good. To the manor born. Maybe one day, you'll buy one for yourself.' She gave a bored smile.

'Hello, Jimmy.' Dennis spoke pleasantly, tapping him on the shoulder. 'I've been looking forward to your company. We're going to take you on a nice drive, how do you fancy that?'

'Definitely.' Jimmy nodded enthusiastically. 'Is this about, you know . . . what me and Uncle Frank found?'

Dennis looked at Lewis then back at Jimmy. 'It could well be, Jimmy, it could well be.'

He looked at Judy. 'Thanks, Auntie Judy, you're the best.'

'No problem, Jim, no problem at all.'

She shut the door on him and as the Rolls Royce drove off, Judy watched the lights disappear into the distance. She'd say nothing to Frank about this. It was better that way. Though she was sure there'd come a day when Frank learnt the truth. He'd be ever so grateful to her.

And with that thought, Judy waved goodbye to her nephew for one last time.

Chapter Thirty-Five

It was late, though that didn't stop Dara being woken up by a small group of girls coming in from the next-door dormitory. She sat up in her bunk bed, letting her eyes adjust to the dark for a moment, before clambering down the ladder.

'What do you want?'

Connie pointed the torch at Dara. 'We've come for a word with your little mate. We just want a chat with her.' She nodded at Grace.

Dara motioned for Grace to get out of her bunk and stand close to her. She stared at the girls, really taking notice of what they looked like for the first time.

They were all dressed in the same ragged, thin cream night-gowns that were standard issue at Holly Brookes. They reminded Dara of the hospital robes she'd been put in after her mum's pimp had battered her unconscious one time. Even in the torchlight, Dara could see how dull and vacant their eyes were, as if all the life had been drained from them somehow. How long had they all been here? Dara didn't even want to guess. Maybe, like Robbie, they'd been here their whole life.

'You two need reminding how things work.'

Dara sighed. She could see, whether she wanted a fight or not, she was going to get one.

She squared up to them. 'You ain't going to stop, are you?'

Connie stared at Dara with complete disdain. She sneered. 'Why would we want to? You're a new girl around here, but you're walking around like you own the place, and your mate, she looks at us like she's smelling something nasty.'

Dara put her hands on her hips. 'If I were you, I'd fuck off. It's that simple. Or you might regret it.'

She glanced sideways at Grace. She sensed that Grace wanted the ground to open up. But Dara knew this was no time to be a chicken. The girls wouldn't simply get bored and go back to bed without any further trouble. She had to stand up to them.

Connie blinked rapidly, then burst into laughter. 'Are you joking? *Regret it?* You're the one who's going to regret it. Unfortunately for you, Barrows and Clemence have gone to the pub, so apart from Cook, who's as deaf as a stone, there's no one here. So you're fucked.'

'Is that supposed to scare me?' Dara raised her eyebrows. She was so used to fighting and standing up for her brothers and sisters, this confrontation with Connie felt natural.

Connie rolled her eyes at the other girls standing next to her. 'This bitch thinks she's something special. But look at the state of her. Look at her skanky hair, it's crawling with nits. Bug head.'

Connie laughed nastily, then without warning, she struck out at Grace. The kick to Grace's knee was hard and cruel. Her legs buckled and she dropped to the floor, letting out a squeal of pain.

Before Connie could kick Grace again, Dara brought back her fist and threw a punch, putting her full weight behind it. It caught Connie directly in the mouth, tearing her lip open and squirting blood everywhere. Connie yelled out, partly in surprise at how painful it was. Her face flushed red, her eyes widened with hatred,

203

and she lunged at Dara, taking an almighty swing at her head. The other girls formed a circle around them.

Dara had plenty of experience at ducking punches, and her survival instincts kicked in. She leapt forward and headbutted Connie, splitting one eyebrow open.

Enraged, Connie swung at Dara again. This time, it connected with Dara's nose. She felt the pain rush through her sinuses and into her face, but instead of it stopping her, it pushed Dara on. She jumped on Connie, and in a frenzy of anger began to batter her, grappling her arms as Connie grabbed handfuls of Dara's hair and tried to bite her face in return.

On the ground now, Dara felt her sides being kicked by the other girls.

'Dara! Dara!' In the background she heard Gracie's voice. 'Stop, Connie, stop! Leave her alone! *Dara!*'

Dara knew she had to get up if she was going to stand a chance. She couldn't lose this fight.

'You're hurting her, you're hurting her!' Grace continued to scream.

Summoning up one last push, Dara found the strength to dig her elbow into Connie's face. She felt Connie let go of her hair.

Dara staggered to her feet and looked at the other girls. They didn't seem so confident now. Although she would rather have left it, Dara knew she had to finish off this fight completely, if she was going to stop them from picking arguments. So she brought back her leg and gave one last final kick, indicating very clearly who was the winner.

With Connie still on the ground, Dara stood panting. She licked away the blood in the corner of her mouth before addressing everyone.

She pointed at the girls. 'This is a warning for all of you, you leave Gracie alone, understand? None of you touch her. Hear me? Any one of you bitches come near her again, I'll come for you. And next time, I ain't going to be so nice . . . now get out of our room.'

Grace watched them go. She couldn't quite find the words to say, but she did manage to mumble, 'Thank you. Thank you, Dar. I'll never forget what you've done for me. Just wait till I tell my mum.'

Dara tilted her head. 'You called me Dar.'

Grace nervously played with her hands. 'Sorry . . . sorry, *Dara*. I . . . I didn't mean to.'

'No, no it's fine. That's what . . .' Dara shrugged, feeling embarrassed at how pleased she felt. 'Well, that's what my brothers and sisters call me. It's good. I like it.'

They held each other's gaze and nodded at the same time. Their friendship was growing stronger with each passing moment.

'Let me clean that up for you.' Grace grabbed a tissue from the broken bed locker. 'Your nose looks sore.' She gently dabbed Dara's face.

Dara winced, though she didn't tell Gracie that the pain of Connie hitting her had felt good. Or rather, not *good*, but it had felt like a relief. She still let Grace wipe away the blood running from her nose, and she was grateful for Gracie's kindness.

'How's your knee?' Dara asked. 'You went down like a fucking lead balloon. I thought you were going to go through the floorboards.'

Grace smiled. Then she giggled. Then they both giggled.

'My knee's probably better than your eye. That will be a right shiner in the morning.'

Dara wasn't worried. 'War wounds . . . And at least they ain't going to bother you again.'

205

They were silent now, watching the sleet sticking to the window as the pearly moon shone down.

'Grace,' Dara whispered. 'Can you *really* see nits in my hair?' Her eyes were full of tears as humiliation washed over her.

Grace nodded. 'Yeah, but it's okay, Dara. I don't care.'

Dara thought about it for a moment. 'Cut my hair . . . cut them out for me, *please*.' She rushed to her bed, pushed up the mattress and grabbed the scissors she'd taken from the sewing room earlier. 'Cut it all off.'

'I can't, Dara.' Gracie was crying now. 'I don't want to do that to you.'

'Please, Gracie . . . for me.' Dara offered Grace the scissors.

Reluctantly, Grace nodded and took them. 'Are you sure?'

'Just do it.'

Grace began to cut Dara's hair, snipping away the long greasy strands full of nits and eggs. Snipping away the years of unkempt locks and neglect.

Ten minutes later, Dara stared in the battered mirror screwed to the wall, touching her head.

'Is it okay?' Grace asked, looking worried.

In truth, it wasn't as bad as it might have been.

Dara stared at her reflection, with her pixie haircut, and her slim features. 'I look weird. I look like I should be in the bleeding army.'

'No, you look lovely.'

Dara nodded. She might not be keen on the haircut, but one thing she was pleased about was that most of the nits had gone.

'You're a liar, Gracie, I look awful, but thank you for saying it . . . Look, you better go back to bed.'

'Why, where are you going?'

Dara didn't answer. Instead, she tiptoed across the room and prodded the girl in the bottom bunk opposite them. 'I need your torch.' She'd seen her earlier with one. 'Come on, hurry up.' Even though Dara hadn't been part of Holly Brookes for more than a moment, that still didn't stop her from taking charge.

The girl nodded and pulled out her torch from under her mattress.

'What's your name?' Dara asked.

The girl had seen the beating Dara had dished out to Connie. 'Louise,' she answered sullenly.

Dara pulled Louise gently up by her shoulders to a sitting position. 'How do I get to the outhouse?'

'What? You're fucking crazy.'

Dara scowled. 'I didn't ask you for your opinion . . . Come on, show me.' She half pulled Louise out of bed and across to the window. It was freezing in the dormitory and goosebumps ran up and down her body.

'If they catch you . . .' Louise shrugged as if the sentence didn't need to be finished.

'Well, they won't. Connie said they were all at the pub.'

'They are, but they'll be back soon.'

Dara didn't want to think about that. 'Just show me.'

'See those oak trees over there?' Louise pointed out of the window. 'If you go past them and carry on through the woods, there's a stream, go over that, and you'll see the outhouse. You can't miss it.'

'How do I get out?'

Louise shrugged again. 'The back door. The key's on the hook. They don't bother hiding it, because nobody's crazy enough to try to sneak out.'

'Are you going to see Robbie?' Grace's face was full of worry. She knew Dara was brave, but she clearly felt this was reckless.

207

'Yeah. I know it's stupid, cos I don't know him really, but I can't be tucked up in bed and do nothing when I know he's out there. I just want to make sure he's all right.'

'Can I come, Dar?' Grace asked.

Dara squeezed Grace's hand. 'No, you better stay here. I don't want you to get into trouble.' She pulled on her jumper and slipped her trainers on, feeling the floor through the large hole in one sole. Then she grabbed the rolled-up napkin she'd hidden behind the chest of drawers.

Before heading out of the dormitory, she stopped and rushed across to her bed. She pushed the pillow roughly under the sheets and bunched them around it, to make it look like the bed was occupied.

'I'll see you later.' Dara gave Gracie a hug.

'Be careful, Dar . . . *Please.*'

'Don't worry, I will be.'

Dara tiptoed out, her senses on full alert.

Though what she couldn't have heard – what none of them heard – was Mr Clemence coming in early from the pub.

Chapter Thirty-Six

The wooden stairs creaked so much, by the time she got halfway Dara decided it was too noisy to risk going any further, so she swung her leg over the banister and slid down it. She didn't want any of the other kids in the cottage to know what she was doing. She couldn't trust they wouldn't grass on her.

There was a strong, stagnant smell of boiled cabbage in the hallway, which made her feel sick, as well as the smell of shit coming from the downstairs toilets. She shone the torch ahead and ran along the stone corridor towards the back door. The key was hanging off the small hook, exactly where Louise had said she'd find it.

Dara looked over her shoulder before she unlocked the door. She took a deep breath, then opened the door before she changed her mind. The winter air hit her hard, and she caught her breath. It was freezing. Dara knew she needed to keep moving. She ran across the wide lawn towards the trees. Once she was completely clear of the cottages, and into the woods, she could slow down.

By the time she'd reached the oak trees, the wet sleet was getting heavy, turning to snow. Dara was panting heavily, about to go deeper into the words, when she suddenly stopped. Was that a noise? She was sure she'd just heard something. Her heart hammered. She moved into the shadows, just watching to see who it was.

A figure emerged.

Dara put her hand across the intruder's mouth and pulled them behind the tree.

'*Sshhhh*, Grace, it's me. What are you doing? I told you to go to bed.' She dropped her hand.

'I couldn't leave you to come out here on your own . . . Are you angry at me, Dar?'

Dara shook her head. Grace couldn't see very well, because she'd lost her glasses, and she was afraid of everything, it was almost like she was scared of her own shadow. Grace wasn't like any of the twelve-year-old kids Dara knew from her estate. They were all smoking and drinking, sniffing glue and getting into trouble with the Old Bill. But Grace, well, Grace just seemed innocent.

'No, of course not . . . it was really brave of you, Gracie.'

Grace looked shy. No one had ever said that about her. 'Really, Dar?'

'Yeah, really, it was . . . Now come on, let's not stand here. My feet are turning into blocks of ice.'

Now they were far enough away from the cottages, Dara switched on the torch and held Grace's hand to make sure she didn't trip over as they raced through the trees, running as hard as they could. At the stream they slowed to cross it. Dara jumped over first, scrambling up the small bank. She stopped and turned round to make sure Grace was all right.

They continued without talking, until Dara stopped again. She wiped the snow from her face, and pointed. 'I think I can see it.'

She shone the torch at it. The outhouse was made of rotten wood. The roof felting was all cracked and curled up at the sides, and Dara had no doubt it let in the rain and snow. The whole place looked like a shithole.

'Robbie?' Dara spoke his name quietly. Not hearing anything, she tried again, louder this time. 'Robbie, *Robbie*, it's me, Dar.'

She crept nearer to the shed. The snow was deeper here, and she felt it seep into her shoes. Still on alert, she took a quick look around, making sure Barrows or Clemence weren't prowling around. All she saw was the darkness under the trees.

'*Robbie*, are you there?'

Both Grace and Dara heard the groan at the same time. It made Dara's stomach feel like she had bellyache; that sound reminded her of her siblings, when they used to hide under the bed, terrified of her mum or whichever pimp she'd shacked up with.

Dara crouched down by the side of the outhouse, and pushed her fingers through the broken wooden slates. 'Hey, Robbie, it's me, Dar, and Gracie's here too.'

'Dara?' There was disbelief in his voice.

Hearing him speak made Dara smile. 'You okay?'

He pushed his frozen fingers through the broken gap in between the slats.

Dara grabbed hold of his tiny hand. She imagined she could feel the sadness in his fingers, telling her everything she needed to know in that brief contact.

'Now that you're here, Dar, I'm okay . . . I can't believe you came to see me . . . it ain't a trick, is it?'

Dara heard the fear flip into Robbie's words.

'A trick?'

'Yeah, you know, trying to get me into trouble.'

Dara glanced at Grace and saw her friend wipe her tears away.

'No, of course not. We wouldn't do that to you, would we, Gracie? We were worried about you . . . both of us were.'

Dara pressed her face nearer the side of the shed. Robbie's voice was so quiet she didn't want to miss a word he had to say. Then she remembered. The napkin. 'I brought you some food, it's only a dumpling from dinner, but it's all I could get, sorry.'

Robbie didn't say anything for a while, until Dara and Grace heard his broken sobs. Dara pushed the dumpling through the wooden slats for him.

'Thank you, Dar . . . thank you, Gracie.' He sounded weak.

'I'm so sorry, Robbie. I'm sorry they did this to you.' Gracie's voice cracked with emotion.

'You can't let them do this,' Dara said angrily. 'This is so fucking wrong . . . Why don't you just run away?'

'You saw what happened to Barry.' Robbie spoke in between mouthfuls of the dumpling. 'And I've never been anywhere, Dar. How will I know where to go? There's no one out there for me.'

'But at least it wouldn't be this, Robbie.' Grace agreed with Dara.

Through the trees Dara looked up at the full moon and wondered what her brothers and sisters were doing. She needed to get back to them as soon as she could. Even the idea of being back at the house with her mum would be better than being here.

She turned to Gracie, who was looking scared. It had taken a lot of courage to follow Dara into the woods.

'Sing him that song, Gracie. The one you were singing in the hall.'

Gracie flushed. 'Are you sure?'

'Yeah.' Dara leant towards the outhouse. 'You'd like that, wouldn't you, Robbie? Rosie always liked it when I sang.'

'Who's Rosie, Dar?' Robbie asked.

'My sister.' Dara fought back tears; they wouldn't do Robbie any good at all. She smiled and nodded at Grace.

Under the stars, in the freezing cold, they sat together on the cold stone by the outhouse. Dara's toes were numb in the cheap trainers she was wearing. Grace rested her head on Dara's shoulder. They were trying to be brave for each other, trying not to cry, and wondering what tomorrow would bring.

'*Lavender's blue, dilly, dilly, lavender's green, when I am King, dilly, dilly, you shall be Queen. Keep me—*'

'*Sshhhh.*' Dara froze. She could swear she'd just heard a scream. She stared out through the woods and saw something moving in the trees. Someone was there. More than one person. She let her gaze move around, and she saw a trail of footsteps in the snow. Large ones. *Men's* footprints.

'Wh-what's happening, Dar?' Robbie stuttered.

'I think someone's out there. There are people in the woods,' she whispered.

'Are they coming to get me?' Panic rose in his voice. 'Dar, don't let them get me, Dar, don't, *please*. Stop them, Dar, stop them.'

'It's okay, Robbie, it's okay.' Dara tried soothing him.

She looked again at the footprints. She frowned as she studied the prints some more . . . and relief swept over her. They were pointing in the other direction, heading away from the outhouse.

'Are they coming? Dar . . . *Stop them!*'

The fear Robbie's voice emitted was almost unbearable.

She rested her head against the wall of the outhouse. 'No, no, they're not, Robbie. They're not.'

Dara heard Robbie beginning to retch. It was a moment before he whispered, 'You better go. They'll skin you alive if they find you here . . . and they'll think I put you up to it.'

Dara hated the idea of leaving him, but she understood that it might make everything worse if they were caught.

Dara pushed the torch through the slats. 'So you don't get frightened of the dark.' She didn't care if Louise had a problem with it, she'd deal with her. 'I'll see you tomorrow, Robbie.'

'Bye, Robbie.' Grace took Dara's hand and squeezed it to show how proud she was of her friend.

Dara smiled at her. Then, as silently as they could, she and Gracie started running back to the cottage.

Dara locked the door, replaced the key, and took the stairs two at a time. Her feet were painful from the cold, and she was actually looking forward to getting into bed.

'You all right, Dar?' Grace asked, following closely behind, sounding anxious and exhausted.

Dara turned round to reassure her. 'Yes, I—'

Her hand was suddenly grabbed. She let out a startled yelp.

'Little boys shouldn't be in the girl's dormitory. Dirty fucker, what were you going to do? Have a feel?'

Mr Clemence glared at them from underneath his flat cap. He was standing by the doorway of the dormitory, swaying unsteadily, clearly the worse for drink. His clothes were covered in mud, as if he'd fallen in a pool of muddy water.

Dara tried to shake his grip off, but he was too strong. 'I ain't a boy, and this is my dorm.'

Looking puzzled, he stared at Dara's short hair, trying to focus on her.

'Dar.' Grace's voice was small.

'Gracie, go to bed.'

Dara matched Clemence's glare with her own.

'No, I can't leave you, Dar.'

'I said, *go back to the fucking dormitory . . . Now!*' Dara yelled at her friend, refusing to back down. She didn't want Grace anywhere near Clemence.

Grace hesitated, then did as she was told. She ran back to the dorm, leaving Dara standing on the landing, all alone with Clemence.

He was unsteady on his feet and stumbled back, losing his grip on her wrist. She tried to move past him, but he sidestepped and blocked the way.

'Where the fuck do you think you're going?' He spat out his words. A thick lump of phlegm shot out of his mouth and landed on his chin.

'Piss *off!*'

The first slap took Dara by surprise. It knocked her backwards against the banister, and for a fleeting moment she thought she was going to fall over the side.

Clemence wiped his sweaty hand on his trousers and stared at Dara with nothing but hatred. He lunged at her, dragging her down the stairs on her back, bumping her down each one so her spine knocked painfully against the sharp edges.

He pulled her along the corridor and threw her into a room she'd never been in before. She ran for the door, but he blocked her again. She fought as hard as she could, but Clemence pulled her into him, tearing her nightie. His laughter was deep and throaty as he wrapped his arms around her.

He stank of sweat and booze. His bad breath wafted into her face as he nuzzled her neck, and she felt the phlegm from his chin wiping off on her skin.

'Get off me, you bastard! Get off me!'

'Playing hard to get, are we?'

Clemence shoved her hard and Dara lost her balance, toppling on to the floor. She was crying now, and snot ran into her mouth. Her nose began to bleed again, and her face began throbbing from her earlier injuries after the fight with Connie.

'Little cock-tease, aren't you?' Clemence grabbed his crotch. 'You want to suck on that? You want that in your mouth?'

He straddled Dara, looking down at her. From where she was lying she could see his erection pushing against the material of his polyester trousers.

He roared with laughter again as she tried to crawl away.

'Fuck off!' she screamed.

Enraged, Clemence slapped her hard, knelt down, and flung his body on top of her. Touching her all over, pushing his hand up her gown. He fiddled with his zip, pulling his penis out.

Dara clawed at him, struggling to get out from under his weight, but she knew she was losing the battle.

'*Gary*, I think that's enough . . . *Gary*.' Barrows stood over them, holding a bottle of beer. His eyes were glazed and he looked none too steady on his feet, but he wasn't as drunk as Clemence. 'Gary, don't be stupid . . . leave it . . . for now.' Barrows smiled cruelly.

Dara had never thought she'd be so grateful to see him.

Clemence stood up and Barrows continued to stare at Dara, sprawled across the floor with her nightie ridden up to her waist, exposing her small mound of pubic hair.

'Maybe try closing your legs next time.' Barrows pointed with the bottle of beer. 'Now get up. And let's not talk about this again, shall we? Not if you want to ever get home.'

They left the room, and Dara listened to them laughing and joking as they headed down the corridor. She was alone and scared, huddled in the corner. Right then, she remembered what Robbie had said: *most kids who come here never leave*. She realised if she didn't escape Holly Brookes soon, she never would.

Chapter Thirty-Seven

Samantha sat on her doorstep staring up at the bright silvery moon. She warmed her hands on the steaming cup of tea she'd just made. She'd already finished off the wine, and had added a couple of bottles of red to her shopping list for tomorrow. If she was going to get through the weekend with only her mother for company, she needed some alcohol.

Samantha took a sip of her tea to warm herself up. She pulled a face, annoyed with herself for putting too much milk in it.

The night air was freezing, though at least she was sheltered from the snow under the cover of the porch. Being in the house with her mum had felt claustrophobic. Right now, she could hear her snoring from upstairs. Even the noise of her mother sleeping made Samantha want to head out and keep on walking.

She couldn't believe that her mum had called Jason, to let him know she'd gone out. It not only felt like a deep betrayal, but it also made her sad. It hurt that her relationship with her mother had got to the point where Phyllis would knowingly get her into trouble with Jason. The whole experience had rattled her more than she cared to admit.

'Hey, Sam, it's me.'

Samantha jumped. 'What is it with you and sneaking up on people?'

Jake stepped out of the shadows and walked down the length of the small garden path. She watched him. Jake and Jason were alike in so many ways, yet worlds apart in others.

He winked. 'You'll catch your death out here.'

'That might be welcome, right now.' She smiled at him as he came to sit down next to her. She could smell his aftershave. Paco Rabanne. It was the same as Jason wore, but Jake managed to make it smell good.

Comfortable with Sam, Jake took the cup from her hands, taking a sip. He handed it back to her. 'Too much milk . . .' He pulled a face. 'Look, I'm sorry about earlier. Has Jason been back?'

'No. Thank God. I could kill my mum.'

Jake nodded. When he'd dated Sam, Phyllis had been a living nightmare, but she seemed to have taken to Jason. He scraped at the ground with his finger. 'Promise me . . . promise me you'll call, if it gets too bad.' He pulled up the collar of his camel coat. 'Fucking hell, it's cold . . .' Then, looking serious, 'But you will, won't you? If it really gets too much, Sam.'

'What are you going to do, Jake? Jase is your brother. You're never going to go up against him, and I wouldn't want you to.'

'I'll worry about Jase. Just promise, all right?'

'No.' She took another sip of tea.

'Has anyone ever told you, you can be a stubborn cow when you want to be? It ain't up for discussion, Sam. You call me, all right? If it's today, tomorrow. In years to come. You just call, all right . . . I don't want you ending up—' Jake stopped. He shrugged and didn't bother finishing his sentence.

They both knew the word was *dead*.

They fell silent.

Eventually, Jake asked, 'You all right? I mean, of course you ain't.' He pulled out his packet of Benson & Hedges from his pocket, got one out, tapped the end and lit it, inhaling deeply. He raised his eyebrows when Samantha took it from his fingers, taking a drag herself.

She coughed. 'Now I remember why I don't smoke.'

'You never answered my question.'

Samantha let out a sigh. She watched her breath in the freezing air. 'I'm okay. Stuff on my mind . . . you know. There's this kid. Grace.' Samantha stared at Jake, then shook her head. 'Nothing, it's okay. It's just work, and I actually don't want to think about it.'

Cigarette in one hand, Jake turned her face towards him. His fingers gently touching the bruises on her mouth and around one eye.

Samantha stared at him. 'Have you ever thought about running away, Jake?'

'Do I look like I'm a kid?' Jake nudged her playfully. He held the cigarette in his mouth, the smoke making him squint, and took off his jacket, putting it over Sam's shoulders.

She continued to stare into his eyes and her heart beat faster. 'You know what I mean. Have you ever thought, *that's it*, and just wanted to get up and go, leave everything behind?'

Jake's gaze tracked the falling snow. 'Yeah, sometimes, but—' He stopped.

'But what?'

'But that would mean leaving you, and I've already done that once. I ain't going to do that again.' He stood up. 'Listen, I should get back to the club.'

She nodded, surprised at how disappointed she felt. Although Samantha knew he shouldn't stay around longer, it wasn't worth the risk . . . to either of them. 'Your jacket. Don't forget that.'

He took it from her, then bent down and kissed her on her

cheek. She put her hand over his and held it there as long as she could without crying.

'Take care, babe, I'll see you soon. And remember what I said, *you call me*, if you ever need me.'

Samantha watched Jake walk away.

Unseen, Phyllis opened the blind with the end of her walking stick, watching Jake stroll down Langley Lane.

It was duly noted.

Chapter Thirty-Eight

Mandy Williams decided the Old Bill were taking her for a complete and utter cunt.

She was frightened. It'd been two days since she'd seen her son, and she was beside herself with worry. She'd left it for almost forty-eight hours to report Jimmy missing, because she'd been afraid to voice her fears. It made it too real for her. But now, she and Judy were sitting in the reception area of Bow Street Police Station, waiting for someone to treat Jimmy's disappearance seriously.

'I don't give a fuck who's busy.' She pointed her chubby finger at the officer. 'I want to see someone *now*.'

'I'm sorry about my sister. She's just upset.' Judy gave a tight smile.

She glanced at Mandy. Her sister's hair was unbrushed and tangled. She was still in her yellow pyjamas, with a coat thrown over them, and wearing her filthy mule slippers, of course, which seemed to be permanently attached to Mandy's feet.

'Don't fucking apologise for me, Judy.' Mandy turned on her sister. 'Jimmy has vanished off the face of the earth, and nobody here seems to give a flying fuck. I've been waiting for nearly two hours, and I want to speak to the person in charge.'

Mandy folded her arms. Her large breasts hitched up high. She'd never been a fan of the Old Bill. She'd always thought they were a useless bunch of cunts, and now she was absolutely certain of it.

'What is it with you fucking people? Anything could've happened to him.'

The officer glared at Mandy. His skin was sallow and grey after years of night shifts, and it sagged loosely below his jawline. He'd been on duty since yesterday evening, and the last thing he needed was to deal with some stupid, loud-mouthed cow, who was no doubt making a crisis out of nothing.

'Madam, if you insist on using that sort of language, I'm going to have to ask you to leave.'

'You can ask me out on a bleeding date, for all I care. The answer will still be no. I ain't going anywhere.'

Standing next to her sister, Judy's stomach rumbled. She'd had to leave her poached eggs on toast after Mandy came knocking on the front door and shrieking that Jimmy was missing. Thankfully, Frank had already gone to work, so he was none the wiser. She'd been expecting Mandy to raise the alarm before – after all, Jimmy was her sister's world – and now it looked like they were in for a long wait. Mandy wasn't going to walk away without speaking to someone. Judy stifled a yawn.

'Come on, what are you waiting for? There must be some fucker around here that can see me?'

Mandy Williams was many things, and God knows there was no shortage of people prepared to bad-mouth her, but no one had ever accused Mandy of being a bad mother. 'Listen, arrest me if you want to, I don't care. Maybe then someone will listen.' She banged on the desk. 'But trust me, the sooner you get someone down here to talk to me, the quicker you'll see the back of me.'

Duty Officer Burling summoned up his most contemptuous stare. There was nothing worse than a hysterical woman. 'I'll try again.' He sniffed, and picked up the black phone on the desk in front of him.

'Everything all right here, ladies?'

Judy and Mandy turned at the sound of a man's voice.

Chief Superintendent Lewis stood smiling at them both. He exuded an undeniable air of authority, despite actually being the youngest person to ever hold his position. Something he had to thank Dennis for. Dennis, using his powerful influence, had seen to it that Lewis had risen quickly up the ranks.

He oversaw a large policing area this side of London. He wouldn't normally bother visiting the local police stations – that was the beauty of being in charge, he was answerable to nobody – but this morning, he'd had a call from Judy. She'd said they were on their way to Bow Street to report Jimmy missing. So he'd decided to make a *casual* visit to the station.

'Not really . . .' Mandy burst into tears, much to Judy's irritation. It took her sister a few minutes, and half a packet of Handy Andies, for her to calm down enough to speak.

'Why don't you come through with me?' Lewis looked across the reception desk at Burling. 'It's all right, Officer, I'll take it from here.'

'Are you sure, sir?'

'Absolutely. It's good for me to get back to grass roots occasionally . . . Oh, you couldn't bring some Earl Grey through, could you?' Lewis turned to the sisters. 'I'm Chief Superintendent Lewis, and you are . . .'

'Mandy, and this is my sister, Judy.'

'Good to meet you both.' He glanced between them.

As he stared at Judy, with her arm around her sister, Lewis had to admit he was impressed. She was acting like the concerned auntie. Giving no indication that, only the other day, she had joined him and Dennis in raising a glass of bubbly to toast their success at getting rid of the problem. 'Come through . . . Officer, I'll take them into Interview Room Three, if it's empty.'

The room Lewis took them into was stuffy, sparsely furnished and stank of piss. The walls were painted a glossy magnolia, and the tiny window had four thick, black bars across it.

'Take a seat, ladies.' Lewis gestured to the broken chairs with large stains on their padded, torn cloth seats.

Seated opposite them, behind the interview table, Lewis asked, 'So, how can I help?'

At that moment there was a knock on the door and a tray of tea was carried through by a small, dark-haired woman. Her appearance was old and haggard, and she placed the tea awkwardly in front of them all before shuffling out with a pronounced limp.

Mandy absent-mindedly started shredding the edge of the white polystyrene cup. She took a deep breath, tasting the whiskey at the back of her throat. She'd needed it this morning to get her through the rest of the day. She couldn't have come here on her own, and she looked gratefully at Judy.

Mandy began to recount her tale. 'My son's gone missing. The other day. I ain't heard from him, and his bed hasn't been slept in either. Jimmy's a good boy and he knows I'd worry, he wouldn't just go off without telling me. That's why I think something's happened to him.' She blew her nose loudly.

'And how old is your son?' Lewis tried not to sound bored.

He thought back to the moment when Jimmy's skull caved in. The scream and the fear had made him sound like a girl. Regardless, Lewis had enjoyed listening to his terror. They'd beaten him with a spade, though not before raping him, and he'd staggered around, the blood and saliva bubbling out of his mouth as his eye had popped out.

'He said something about meeting Frank the other evening.'

Lewis snapped out of his reverie. Trying to look attentive, he put his hands under his chin as if saying a prayer. For a split second, he almost forgot to ask, 'Who's Frank?'

'He's my husband.' Judy volunteered the information. She looked at her sister and passed her another tissue out of the packet.

Judy had specifically told Jimmy to keep his mouth shut. The more apparent it became that her nephew had been a bloody blabbermouth, the more comfortable she was with her decision to hand him over to Lewis and Dennis.

Still playing the part, Judy frowned at her sister. 'Frank? I think Jimmy must have been telling you stories, Mand. Frank and I have been tucked up early in bed all week, he's got a bit of a cold and he certainly wasn't planning on meeting Jim . . . Maybe he's seeing some girl, and didn't want you to know. Has he been secretive lately?'

Mandy took a moment to mull over what Judy had said. 'There is one girl he likes to hang around with. Becky. I don't think she's interested, but he's bleeding besotted with her.'

Judy feigned a large smile along with a deep sigh of relief. '*Well*, that must be what it is then.' She rubbed her sister on the back. 'See, he'll be fine, Mand, he's probably just got himself caught up with this girl . . . shacked up with her.'

Mandy looked at her sister miserably. 'You think so?'

'I know so. It'll be fine.'

'That could be it.' Lewis nodded.

As much as Mandy wanted to cling on to that hope, who was she kidding? No, she was certain something had happened to her precious son. 'But I know he would've told me. Jimmy and I, well, we're very close, and if he had a girlfriend I'd know about it.'

'In my experience, young men don't always tell their mothers everything,' Lewis said.

'I agree with the Chief Superintendent, Mand. I'm sure he's fine.'

'You don't have children, Judy,' Mandy snapped back. 'So how would you bleeding know?'

The truth of this fact cut Judy deeply, and a surge of hatred towards her sister, the like of which she'd never experienced before, welled up in her.

She held the comforting smile with difficulty. 'No, you're right, Mand, I haven't. But I loved Jimmy too.'

Mandy's panic was rising. 'Loved. Why the fuck did you say *loved*? You do think something has happened to him, don't you?'

Judy took Mandy's hand. 'I meant *love*. Don't read anything into it, Mand. It was a slip of the tongue. I should've said, I love Jimmy. You know I do, and I want him back home as much as you do, darlin'.'

'I'm sorry.' Mandy burst into tears. 'I'm so sorry.' She fell forward on to Judy's chest.

'I can see this is very distressing for you.' Lewis adopted a tone of reassurance. 'So what I can do is get the officer to fill out a missing person report. It's a bit early, but at least we can get some of the patrol cars to keep an eye out for him. Hopefully, though, he'll be home before you know it.'

Lewis began to get up, but the images of Jimmy being butchered ran through his mind, arousing him, and he sat back down again, waiting for his erection to subside.

'Is that it?' Mandy wiped her nose on her sleeve.

Confident he was able to stand up now, Lewis headed for the door, opening it for Mandy. 'For the time being, it is. But perhaps you can drop a photo in sometime, so we can get the officers on the lookout as soon as possible.'

'You think we'll find him?' Mandy was desperate.

'I'm sure of it.'

As Mandy walked ahead towards reception, behind her back Judy rolled her eyes at her sister.

Lewis winked.

They both knew Jimmy was long gone. And there was no prospect of ever finding him.

Chapter Thirty-Nine

The stolen photos from Alan's desk lay spread out across the dining-room table in a small house in Epping. Dennis and the young boys.

There was nothing to be done right now. Nothing that would make a difference anyway. There were too many bad apples in positions of power. Too many bad apples altogether. An old boys' network of protection. But the time would come. And when it did, it would be payback.

For now, it was a question of waiting. And then . . . well, then they'd all come tumbling down. One by one.

Reenie placed the photos back in the envelope, putting them away safely in the drawer. She stared at the sharp knife concealed there. She'd never forgotten her time in Holly Brookes as a teenager, and she never would. The nightmares lay in wait for her when she fell asleep.

Years ago, she'd tried to report what had happened to her and her sister at Holly Brookes. But no one had listened, no one had cared. She'd been treated like scum. And although she knew she could never change the past, never change what Dennis Hargreaves and his friends had done to her, there was one thing she *could* do.

Get revenge.

However long it took, Reenie was going to make sure she got sweet, sweet revenge.

Chapter Forty

Jason drove his penis hard into the woman on all fours, pumping in and out. He'd been trying to climax for the past few minutes, and he was getting bored now. Partly it was the cocaine that stopped him coming. But it was partly because his mind was on Alan Carver. It would have been easy enough to snuff out the bastard. Chop him up and feed him to the fishes. But if Alan was at the bottom of the Thames, how the fuck was it going to help with this land deal?

He'd contemplated getting rid of Zef and Dren, but that would have been like opening Pandora's fucking box. It would have made him and Jake a prime target for the other gangs. It would seem like *they'd* mugged the Albanians off. Taken money for a deal and then not come through with it. Though essentially, as things stood, that's exactly what they'd done.

Jason had heard through the grapevine that the other faces they regularly did business with were getting edgy, thinking that they were next in line to be screwed over by the Wakeman brothers. A fucking domino effect, courtesy of Alan.

He'd been staying away from the Rose and Crown, because he knew, when faces got edgy, they got dangerous. And no one wanted a bullet in the back of their head, did they? At least here in the club, he could vet who was coming in and out. He was having to watch his back all the time at the moment – something he hadn't done for many a year – and not just from the Albanians, but from every fucker the Wakemans had ever done business with, and who thought that they could take a pop.

'How long you going to take, Jase? I'm supposed to be picking my kid up from her gran's soon.' The hooker underneath Jason turned her head to look up at him, and let out a smelly burp from the omelette she'd bought at Fat Tony's.

Jason's dick went limp at the sight of the woman's scowling face. He sighed, then slapped her cheek hard.

She squealed loudly.

'Cheeky fucking cow. I pay your wages, Shelley, and don't you forget it. Because believe me, darlin', there's many a whore who'd love to work here. Understand?'

She nodded. His words had the desired effect. She turned away, and said nothing.

Angrily, Jason took a swipe at Kitty, the other brass, who was busy rimming his arsehole. He wasn't in the mood for any of it. The club was losing money. They'd ploughed too much into the land deal. Samantha was pissing him off. He was sure his brother was mugging him off. And the coke he was taking was altogether shit.

'I'll come back later, shall I?' Jake leant against the door, watching his brother clamber off Shelley. He'd been asleep in the next room.

'You want to join in?' Jason gestured. 'You might do better than me.'

If there was ever a time Jake wanted a drink, it was now. He shook his head at his brother and didn't bother saying anything. It wouldn't surprise Jake if Jason had shagged most of the whores in London. He was like a spoilt kid, insisting on getting everything he saw, before breaking it and discarding it.

Jake watched idly as Shelley pulled on her knickers and leg warmers, then slipped into her denim skirt. Chewing gum, she glanced at him and frowned. 'Can you smell smoke, Jakey?'

Before Jake had time to say anything, he felt the shock wave from a huge explosion downstairs. There was the sound of shattering glass, and plumes of thick black smoke billowed up the stairs.

Shelley and Kitty screamed in terror, grabbing the rest of their clothes.

'Shut the fuck up!' Jason yelled at them, scooping up his trousers and shirt from the floor and pulling them on. He grabbed the gun at the side of the bed, wrapped his top around his hand, and smashed his fist through the window. 'Jakey, come on . . . *Come on.*'

Jake shook his head. He pulled his sweater over his mouth to protect himself from the smoke.

Jason hoisted himself on to the fire escape with Shelley and Kitty. 'Jake, where the fuck are you going? *Jake . . .*'

Jake heard his brother call to him as he raced back down the stairs, battling the smoke. Fuck, there was debris and glass everywhere, though thankfully the fire hadn't started to take hold yet. He paused for a moment by the double swing doors leading into the kitchen, and tugged up his left trouser leg. He pulled out the small handgun he kept strapped to his ankle.

On high alert, Jake charged through the kitchen. It was intact, so there was no way this was a gas explosion. He'd bet everything on it being arson. A petrol bomb? He'd also bet everything on it being the work of the fucking Albanians.

He ran through the club, cursing his brother's choice of business associates. He'd warned Jase about them. This was a cut-throat game they were in, which was all the more reason to choose carefully who they went into business with.

He rushed out into Walker's Court, the small passageway fronting the club, and looked up and down. He was itching to get his hands on whichever little fucking toerag had got the brass neck to do this in the middle of Soho. It was deserted. *Shit*. He stood panting, and tucked his gun back into the holster on his ankle.

He needed to check on Jason, and turned to go back inside the club.

A sudden noise made Jake look round. A motor bike sped down the narrow walkway, heading directly towards him. *Fuck*. Jake threw himself against the window of the nearby pie and mash shop as the bike skidded to a halt in front of him. The motorcyclist flicked up the visor of his helmet, showing only his dark brown eyes.

Before Jake could do anything about it, the biker pulled out a gun from the inside pocket of his leather jacket and pointed it at him. They held each other's stare for a moment.

Jake's heart pounded. He wondered if this was how it ended.

The biker pulled back the trigger.

'This is from Zef and Dren . . .'

Chapter Forty-One

A week had passed, and Alan Carver thought he was in hell. Each morning for the past few days, he'd woken up certain he was on the verge of having a heart attack because of the sheer stress of it all. He was still in a *huge* amount of pain because of his little finger – or more accurately, the *lack* of his little finger.

Alan walked over to the window, opening the faded grey floral curtains. The sleet blew against the panes in an icy greeting. He stared at the view; he was in the middle of fucking nowhere. He'd told Reenie he needed to take a few days off, claiming a family emergency, but that was all he'd told her. Alan was shrewd enough to keep his own counsel. The truth of the matter was, he was in hiding.

It hadn't been his idea to get out of London as soon as possible. Lewis had insisted. With Dennis's agreement, that idiot Frank had driven him down to the hideout. The only problem was, nothing came without a shedload of fucking interest. The more they did for him – the more they helped him to get out of a scrape – the more he owed them. Until eventually they'd want his bollocks on a silver platter.

It wouldn't have been Alan's first choice to hide out in this shithole, freezing his nuts off. Holly Brookes children's home was hardly the Savoy. Thank God he'd remembered to bring a few grams of coke with him. To think that only a few weeks ago, he'd been on the up and up, poised to walk the corridors of power. And now he was having to share a bathroom with some guy called Barrows, a friend of Frank's, who seemed unable to perform the most basic hygienic act of flushing the toilet after he'd had a crap.

And so now, the day before Christmas Eve, he was stuck in a fucking staff cottage in Holly Brookes, surrounded by kids who looked like walking zombies. He'd vented to Lewis on the phone last night, and it seemed things might be starting to move. All being well, he'd be leaving here later today, after the opening of the new swimming pool, which had been paid for by generous benefactors, including Dennis.

Alan walked out of the bedroom, but not before he'd caught sight of himself in the mirror. For once, Alan wasn't impressed by what he saw. There were dark circles under his eyes. His stress was clearly showing.

In an even fouler mood, Alan marched out of the staff cottage. He scowled at a group of kids who were running towards the building where the indoor swimming pool was housed. 'Look where you're fucking going,' he snapped.

They shrank back, reminding Alan of frightened snails. Though there was one young girl among them, with her head almost shaved, who glared at him defiantly.

Little shit. Alan tutted.

Dara stared at the man in the posh suit who'd barged past them. She held his gaze until he turned away. *Prick.* She wasn't sure who he was, but she'd seen him around for the past few days. He seemed a proper dandy – looked like he had a few bob in his pocket – but that didn't stop Dara noticing he was a complete sniff head. When her mum had been on coke, she'd had the same look about her.

Dara knew you could dress things up all you liked, but you couldn't ever really hide them.

Shivering in the thin summer clothes they'd given her to wear, Dara ran along the path to catch up with Robbie, Brenda and Gracie. There was still no word yet of what was happening back home, and Gracie was becoming ever more subdued. Each day got harder for her to even get up out of bed.

'Come on, you lot, bloody hell, hurry up.' Barrows gestured to them. Wrapped up warmly in a brown sheepskin coat, he gave a clip around the ears to every child whose head he could reach. 'Make it snappy, and put a smile on your faces, this is supposed to be a celebration . . . Come on, smile, you miserable bastards. It's Christmas in a couple of days, you'll be scaring Santa off, and we wouldn't want that, would we? And then who'll eat his mince pie?' He roared with throaty laughter at his own joke.

Dara felt Robbie step closer to her.

'He always dresses up as Father Christmas. Him and Clemence,' Brenda whispered to Dara. She shuddered and pulled a face.

Barrows watched the children file past him into the building. Dara quickly dropped her eyes as she walked past Clemence and the other house parents. He hadn't spoken to her since the incident, for which she was intensely grateful. But she had a horrible feeling he wouldn't leave her alone for long.

As the children walked along the poolside, a medley of Donna Summer's music crackled out of the tall speakers fixed to the tile walls. There was a strong smell of chlorine, which had already started to irritate Dara's eyes. On top of which, the water looked freezing. There was nothing enticing about it at all. She only hoped they weren't going to make them all go swimming.

Dara sat down on one of the plastic chairs placed around the pool for the grand opening, settling herself between Brenda and

Gracie. She gazed up to the other end where that posh fella was standing next to a woman in a large fur coat, and a huge group of dignitaries – mainly men – were standing around hobnobbing with each other.

She recognised a lot of the patrons from their photographs on the wall in the dining room. They all were suited and booted, standing around chatting and smoking. There was one other person she recognised. She'd seen him on the telly. Dara recognised his face, for sure, but his shock of blond hair and the large cigar he was smoking, well, they were a definite giveaway.

Dara remembered how she'd once written to the show he presented. She hadn't asked for much at all, she'd just asked whether he could fix it for her brothers and sisters to have a happy day. Though looking at him now – the way he was laughing, the way he was looking around and staring at Connie and her friends – made Dara uneasy. She pushed away that thought and noticed the posh bloke glancing at her.

She discreetly stuck two fingers up at him.

Alan clocked the young girl giving him the V sign. No wonder these kids didn't have homes. They needed locking up. Bunch of animals.

'. . . isn't that right, Alan?'

Alan abruptly became aware that Dennis was speaking to him. 'Sorry, I didn't catch that.'

'I was just saying how much you needed us to get you out of the hole you'd dug yourself into.' He winked, and patted Alan firmly on the back. 'That's what friends are for, though, isn't that right? Loyalty among thieves.'

As always, Dennis was quietly smooth, and quietly dark. It struck Alan that everything Dennis said had a hidden meaning to it.

It was now his cue to grovel. 'Dennis, thank you for helping me out like this. I really appreciate what you're doing. Both of you.' Alan nodded to Lewis. He wasn't sure how he was managing to sound so fucking reasonable. Dennis had him over a barrel, and he knew it. They all did.

'Someone had to help you,' Frank chipped in. He was standing next to Judy and Lewis, and had clearly heard all about Alan's run-in with the Wakemans. 'How's your finger, by the way, Al?'

The others laughed along with Frank.

Humiliation rippled through Alan. But not just humiliation, *anger*. He could hardly get his breath. Frank was clearly enjoying his temporary fall from grace. Alan made a mental note, when the time was right, he'd do everything in his power to bring Frank down.

'At least it's sorted now, or it soon will be.' Dennis smiled at Lewis. 'You've got it all in hand, haven't you?'

'Absolutely. It's taken slightly longer than anticipated to get everything in place. But at least he's been able to lie low here while we arranged everything.' Lewis, like Frank, looked slightly disappointed that Alan wasn't going to be left to the sharks.

'So what's the moral of the story, Alan?' Amused, Dennis raised his eyebrows. 'Never do anything without consulting me, because next time, I might not be so understanding. *Comprende?*'

Alan battled not to direct a death stare at Dennis. He didn't need him speaking fucking Spanish to make him understand. Oh, he understood all right. The threat was loud and clear.

'Excuse me one moment.' Dennis gave his glass to Judy to hold. He walked up to the microphone and tapped on it, clearing his throat of phlegm before addressing the assembled gathering.

'Ladies and gentlemen. Thank you all for coming. As everyone knows, Holly Brookes is close to my heart. I've been lucky enough to be a patron here for over twenty-five years. It's a special place, and the opening of this wonderful facility wouldn't have been possible without all of you.' He turned and nodded to the group of adults behind him. 'The swimming pool will no doubt give hours of delight to so many children. Holly Brookes is a beacon of hope, and it's wonderful to give something back. And when better than at Christmastime?'

He looked over to where Dara, Gracie and all the other children were sitting. 'Tomorrow, I understand you've got a play in store for us. Well, I, for one, am very much looking forward to it. In the meantime, ladies and gentlemen . . .' He turned back to the adults. 'There's food and drink laid on. Do mingle, the children will love to talk to you. So without further ado . . .' He held aloft the scissors Clemence handed him. 'I officially declare the swimming pool open.' He cut the ribbon tied around the diving board, and a loud cheer rose up.

Under Barrows' instructions, the children stood up while the adults wandered over to chat to them. Dennis strolled up to Robbie.

'Hello, Robbie, we meet again.' He ruffled the boy's hair then glanced over his shoulder. 'Frank, I take it you're staying?'

Frank nodded.

'Alan, what about you?' Dennis inquired. 'Can I tempt you, before you go back to London?'

Alan shook his head, holding his bandaged hand. They were like a pack of hungry wolves, waiting for their feeding frenzy. 'No, not my thing.'

'Don't knock it until you try it. You might be surprised.' Dennis grinned, and this time he rubbed his hand along Robbie's shoulders.

'I don't think so,' Alan murmured.

He looked between Frank and Dennis. Peas in a fucking pod. He recalled how the two of them had met. Dennis had befriended Frank in prison. Not that Dennis had been an inmate. It was all part of Dennis's philanthropy. He was a prison friend and reformer, volunteering occasionally to visit those who didn't have anyone to visit them. And clearly Frank and Dennis had hit it off, finding things in common, things which didn't interest Alan. Not that Alan cared about morals. Power – not morals, not values, not feelings – was all that mattered to him.

'Suit yourself.' Dennis turned to Judy with a huge smile. 'Judy. My darling girl. Thank you for coming. I'm going to borrow your husband for a few hours, if that's all right with you? Business to discuss. So why don't I have my chauffeur take you and Alan home? And perhaps on the way, I'll get him to stop by Fortnum & Mason. As you know, I have an account there, and you're very welcome to use it. It's Christmas, and I know they do the most delightful hampers.'

He gave her a long hug and was gratified when Judy responded with a huge grin.

Judy had seen the posh Christmas hampers they did in magazines, and now she was going to be able to have one for herself. Just wait till she told Gloria, her neighbour, she'd be green with bloody envy.

Judy wasn't stupid. She knew the reason why Dennis was keen to get rid of her. But she was happy to play dumb. Although, she was pretty certain that both Dennis *and* Lewis were aware she'd guessed what their tastes were, a long time ago.

Frank was rather more naive when it came to realising how much his wife knew about him. After she'd come across his stash of hidden photographs, she'd made it her business to find out more about her husband's background. Oh yes, Judy certainly knew a lot more about Frank than she was letting on.

'Well, I'll see you later, everyone.' Judy gave a small wave, and stood on tiptoes to kiss Frank on the cheek before tottering off excitedly in her kitten heels.

Dara saw the woman in the large fur coat waddle out with the posh bloke. Turning away, she saw the other patrons taking some of the kids' hands and walking out with them. The man who'd made the speech was approaching Robbie with a hungry look on his face. Her stomach flipped over.

'Rob, Robbie.' She rushed up to him, pulling Grace by the hand. 'Hey, you coming?' Dara tried to pull him away.

'Dar.' Robbie's voice cracked, and his eyes pleaded with her.

'Can I help you, young lady?' The man was looking at her like she was something rotten stuck to the sole of his shoe.

Dara blurted out the first thought that came into her head. 'He needs to come with me, we have to finish off the costumes for the play, otherwise we'll be in trouble.'

She grabbed at Robbie again, pulling his arm, but a man she could have sworn was the Old Bill took her hand and prised it off. He bent down to her, his nose inches away. 'I'm sure they can spare him for now, he's going to show us around.'

They began to yank Robbie away, but Dara ran in front of them. 'Please, he has to come with me.'

The men exchanged a look. 'No, he's going to come with us,' the Old Bill said. 'We need him to assist us with our inquiries.'

The men roared with laughter at the joke.

Gracie tugged Dara's hand, looking puzzled. But Dara understood only too well, and it took everything she had not to be sick.

She watched them take Robbie away, hating them, but hating herself more for once again being unable to do anything to help. She dug her fingernails into her palms, so hard they began to bleed. Even at her young age, she swore that, one day, in years to come, she would find them, and they'd get what was coming to them.

Chapter Forty-Two

It was Christmas Eve and the dining room was quiet. Every single child sitting around that dining table knew what had happened last night. Some, like Connie, were feeling their own trauma. Others, like Dara and Gracie, were grateful it hadn't been them, and this time they hadn't been chosen. But they'd all heard the noises floating through the corridors, which had kept them awake most of the night.

Grace sat next to Dara, the taste of the lumpy porridge in her mouth making her feel sick. She was exhausted, she hadn't slept, she'd kept hearing screams; even now, it was like she could still hear them. The one time she had fallen asleep, she'd woken up and found she'd wet the bed. The last time she'd done that was when her dad had died. But she'd felt too embarrassed to tell anyone, even Dara, she just hoped it would dry and wouldn't smell too much.

She was about to turn to Dara when she heard the sound of the door being opened. She looked towards it, hoping to see her mum walk through the door and save her from this place. Or at least her godmother. Or even that nice woman, Samantha, who'd tried to give Gracie her phone number. It was only now that Gracie realised why.

Her heart beat faster as she stared at the door. Who was on the other side? Fear gripped her. It was like a constant companion, walking alongside her, waiting for something terrible to happen.

The door opened and Grace realised she'd been holding her breath. She let out a long sigh. It was Barrows and Miller. Hope soared again: maybe Miller would help her.

Then she saw Robbie behind the two men, and she gripped Dara's hand under the table.

Dara watched Robbie limp in. His face was etched with deep lines of pain as he struggled to walk the few paces from the door to the table. From where she was sitting, Dara could see his trousers were slightly stained on his bottom, and she realised it was blood.

Barrows and Miller stood to one side, smoking. They were dressed in almost identical clothing: off-white shirts, crooked ties, and wide camel flares. They looked like they'd come back from a party; in a way, Dara supposed they had. She'd heard the drunken laughter all night. She'd huddled in her bed, dreading the moment when they came into her room. But they hadn't. As she looked at Barrows and Miller now, it occurred to Dara there was no one here to help them. No one at all. They had to look out for each other.

'Hurry up and sit down, Robbie. Oh, and don't forget, everyone, we've got the Christmas pantomime dress rehearsal later.' An involuntarily sigh escaped from the assembled children, but it was cut short by Barrows' stare. 'Is there a problem here?'

'No, sir.' They all answered in unison and quickly put their heads down.

'There better not be, because I'm not having anyone fuck up their lines . . . Hear that, Robbie? I said, *hear that*, Robbie?'

Robbie acknowledged Barrows with the tiniest of nods.

'Right.' Barrows winked at Miller, took a deep drag of his

cigarette, and headed for the door. He directed a glare at Robbie as he walked out, and laughed. 'Oh, and eat your bloody breakfast.'

Dara continued to watch Robbie. Struggling, and clearly in pain, he pulled out his chair. It took him a couple of attempts to actually sit down.

'What do you think they did to him?' Gracie whispered to Dara.

She stared at her friend in disbelief. 'Are you kidding me?'

'No.' Gracie looked puzzled by Dara's response.

'What do *you* think they bloody did to him?' Dara couldn't quite believe that Grace didn't know.

Grace shrugged. She clearly had no idea why Dara was angry with her. How could she have? 'I'm sorry, Dar.'

Dara didn't say anything for a moment. She ate another spoonful of porridge as she thought about it. She shouldn't have snapped. It wasn't fair. Gracie was intelligent for her age, but she wasn't street smart, life smart. Grace was one of the lucky ones. Innocent. The way it should be. She only hoped that Gracie's mum would get her out of here soon, before it was too late.

'Nah, it ain't you that should be sorry, it's me,' Dara whispered. She smiled and gently said, 'They just hurt him really badly. In the way no one ever should.' That was all Gracie needed to know for now. All being well, it would stay that way for a long time.

Dara slid her hand across the table to Robbie, who was sitting opposite her. Their fingertips touched for a moment but he didn't lift his head to look at her.

Silently, everyone continued to eat their breakfast. The only noise in the freezing dining room was the sound of the children's spoons tapping against the metal bowls.

All of a sudden, the door handle rattled. It began to turn. Dara glanced over at Robbie, spotting his bowl *still* full of porridge. She leapt forward, quickly grabbed it and swapped it with her empty bowl, just before Barrows reappeared.

Robbie looked up and blinked at Dara, his eyes full of tears, and he mouthed a silent *thank you.*

Barrows took a deep drag of his cigarette and let the ash drop on to the floor. He rubbed it into the rug with his foot, and looked around.

'Why haven't you finished?' Striding over to Dara, he grabbed hold of her head, turning it so she faced him. 'You've been here long enough to know the rules.' He reached over and put his cigarette out in Gracie's cup of tea. 'Well?'

'I'm not hungry.' Dara shrugged.

'Not hungry? You ungrateful little bitch.' Without warning, Barrows dragged Dara's head back, then slammed it forward, pushing her face into the bowl of porridge. He held it there.

She squirmed, unable to breathe. She was dimly aware of Gracie screaming. She tried to fight, but Barrows held her down, and her lungs began to tighten.

'Get off her. *Get off her!*' Grace leapt on to Barrows back, pulling at his hand.

His hold on Dara eased. He swiped Grace away, sending her flying against the wall. She hit her head against the cutlery cabinet and slumped to the floor. Out cold.

Unaware of what had just happened, and feeling dizzy, Dara staggered to her feet, rubbing her chest and trying to catch her breath. Barrows shoved a napkin in her face, and wiped the porridge from her eyes. She blinked rapidly.

Seeing Gracie unconscious, crumpled in a heap on the floor, she tried to rush over to her, but Barrows blocked the way.

'Someone wants to see you, Dara. They're waiting in my office.'

Chapter Forty-Three

Samantha put her head round the door of her mum's room at midday. 'I've got to go to work, Mum. You'll be all right for a couple of hours, won't you?' She tucked her red scarf into the neck of her coat.

Phyllis shoved a large piece of Turkish delight into her mouth, chewing it noisily. 'I don't suppose I've got much bleeding choice, have I? I don't know why you need to go in on Christmas Eve. Can't those kids do without you for once? The amount of time you spend at work, I reckon Mother bleedin' Teresa has got it cushier than you.'

Samantha took a deep breath before she answered. To distract herself from her frustration, she looked around the room. It was like the Blackpool illuminations. Every surface was covered in gaudy red, green and gold tinsel from Woolworths. Her mum had wrapped fairy lights around each of her porcelain statues, which were flashing on and off. A small white artificial tree stood in the corner, its branches weighed down with silver baubles and chocolates. Next to the gas fire was a light-up Nativity scene her mum had insisted on ordering this year. The figurines of the three kings looked like they were off down the pub, rather than heading to Bethlehem.

'Actually, Mum . . .' Samantha handed her mum the copy of the

Radio Times she'd bought this morning from the newsagent's on the corner. 'There're usually more emergency call-outs at this time of year. So we're really busy.'

Phyllis sniffed, flicking through the magazine. 'Maybe I should call social services, ask them for help then. Tell them how you neglect me.'

Samantha wasn't even going to bother answering that.

'What about the mince pies, have you got them?'

'Yes, Mum.'

'And the turkey? Cos I don't want to be pouring gravy on to an empty plate. I ain't eating fresh air, you know.'

'Mum, it's fine, I've got the turkey, sausages, cranberry sauce, stuffing, potatoes, veg, Christmas pudding, crackers. I've got the lot.'

'Apart from the decency to spend some time with your old mum.' Phyllis tutted, took another large piece of Turkish delight, and folded her arms.

Samantha stared at Phyllis. Was she the only daughter who had such a cantankerous cow for a mother? Because right now, she'd be happy to do time for Phyllis.

Holding her tongue, Samantha gave her mum a peck on the cheek and headed out, not trusting herself to say a polite goodbye. She knew she'd regret any harsh words spoken in anger; her mother would never let her live them down.

And God knows, Samantha had enough grief from her mum already.

Phyllis heard the front door close.

She pulled out the pocket notebook she kept hidden down the side of her chair. Licking the tip of her pencil, she turned to a fresh page.

Loyalty

As she had been doing for the past week or so, Phyllis began to write down the time, the day and the date her daughter went out.

Because, after all, if she was going to be Jason's eyes and ears, she needed to make sure she had written evidence.

Chapter Forty-Four

Jason sat in one of the large leather chairs in Honey's. The club had been closed since last week's arson attack, and the place still stank like Guy Fawkes Night. The smoke damage was still evident, and the whole place would need to be redecorated in the new year.

'He could've killed you, Jakey.' Jason's voice was tight with anger.

'We've been over this. He could've done, but he didn't. It was a warning. Let's face it, if someone had turned *us* over, we wouldn't even bother with a warning.'

They'd been lying low for the past week, avoiding the Albanians, and it was the first time they'd been up to Soho since the incident. Jason knew what his brother was saying made sense. And it was true: Jason wouldn't think twice about putting a bullet in someone's head if the circumstances were reversed. But that didn't stop Jason being pissed off, to put it mildly.

He needed to feel like people respected him. In his book, allowing the cunts to get away with this shit sent out the wrong message. 'I still think we should've acted before now, shown them they can't mug us off, even if we'd just sent them a message back.'

Jake shook his head. 'And what good would that have done us? We're the ones in the wrong here, mate. If we go storming in and start an all-out war, who do you think's going to back us? Not a single fucking face. No one's happy with us. If we're not careful, we won't have anyone to do business with. It's us that looks like cunts, not Zef and Dren. So we need to sit on it and, as sour as it is, swallow it up. And let's see if we can sort out either offering their money back with interest—'

'And how the fuck are we supposed to do that?' Jason argued.

'*Or . . .*' Jake continued, without directly answering his brother. 'We get this deal off the ground somehow. But what we *don't* do, is go storming in, tooled up. I knew this was going to happen, Jase. I fucking told you not to have dealings with them.'

'Oh, turn it in, Jakey. You're like a broken record. That ship's sailed, mate. And let's have it right – this ain't them, it's Alan.'

'Whatever.'

Jason watched his brother intently as he paced around the club. Jake hadn't spoken much about what had happened with the gunman, just shrugged it off as *one of those things*. But Jason had seen Jake knock back a couple of shots of whiskey, something he hadn't done for a while. He wasn't judging, but Jake had been adamant he wanted to stay sober. For a start, his brother was unpredictable when he was on the booze, capable of things he wouldn't normally do. Like the day their father was killed.

He and Jake had both been boozing, both high, coked up, when their estranged father came into their club, accusing them of cutting him out of a deal to supply heroin to the area between Croydon and Crawley. In truth, Ray not getting the contract with the Russians had been fuck-all to do with Jason and Jake, and more to do with their father being an unhinged cunt.

But Ray wouldn't listen to anything they'd said. Fucking typical. A fight had broken out. Their father had pissed off, but then he'd come back hours later with his heavies in tow.

By that time Jason had left the club, and Jake was on his own.

251

Booze and coke, as they always did, had turned Jake into a different man. Given him that psycho edge where he didn't give a fuck, and half the time, he didn't even connect to what he was doing. The next thing Jakey knew, he was covered in blood. Their father's blood.

Jason had received a distraught call once Jake had sobered up. He'd helped Jake bury their father deep in Epping Forest. Good riddance to the cunt, that's what he'd said, but Jake hadn't seen it like that. Family didn't usually shed their own blood.

From then on, Jake had felt like he owed Jason something. He'd wanted to prove his own loyalty. Return his brother's. And he'd certainly done that over the years. No matter what. Loyal to the end, even if it had meant giving up Samantha. Which was why, if Jason *did* find out Jake was actually going behind his back with Samantha, well, that would make him no brother of his. Jake would soon be pushing up the ivy next to his father.

'I had a call from Alan this morning. Seems like the cunt's resurfaced,' Jason said.

He scooped up a small mound of coke on the tip of his knife from the bowl on the table. He flicked it on to the marble top, chopped it and snorted it with the gold monogrammed toot a business associate had given him. He swallowed the bitter taste and welcomed the rush.

'What did he say?' Jake looked surprised.

'The usual bullshit. What does Alan always say? He wants to meet us though. He's supposed to be calling back to arrange it.' Jason took another line, snorting it up hungrily.

'Fancy a Christmas blow job, Jakey?' Shelley grinned as she walked towards him.

She was embracing the holiday season to the fullest, dressed in a Santa outfit complete with sequinned hat.

'I'll make sure you get a white Christmas. I'll get it to snow, all right.' She licked her lips suggestively.

Jake winked and laughed. 'Thanks for the offer, Shell, but I'll take a check on that one, darlin'. There's somewhere I need to be.'

'Suit yourself, but you know where to find me if you change your mind.'

Shelley twirled around happily, flicking up the Santa minidress she was wearing to flash her lacy red crotchless knickers.

'I'll see you later, babe, and Happy Christmas, by the way.' Chuckling, Jake made his way out of the club.

Jake emerged into the alleyway, then checked over his shoulder before strolling down Walker's Court.

He was still feeling the effects of the brandy he'd drunk earlier as he wandered through Soho, weaving through the early-Christmas revellers. He popped a mint in his mouth to disguise the fact he'd been drinking. What had happened, well, that had fucked him up, and the alcohol made him feel better. He really had thought the gunman was going to shoot him. Instead, he'd fired past him, sending the bullet through the window and into the wall of the pie and mash shop.

He unbuttoned his coat, enjoying the cold air and the walk. Rather than taking a cab, he drifted down the Haymarket, cutting through to Pall Mall East, and letting the sleet drift down on to his face.

When he reached Victoria Embankment, Samantha was waiting for him by Cleopatra's Needle.

'I'm not late, am I?'

'No, I'm just early.' Samantha reached up and wiped the snow-flakes off Jake's nose.

'Was it difficult to get out without Phyllis asking awkward questions?'

'No, not really, she thinks I'm going to work, which is kind of true. I have to be at the office by three.'

Jake took in the information and glanced up at the obelisk. 'It's supposed to represent eternity and immortality.' He shrugged. 'Something my old man told me.' Then he looked back at Samantha, putting his hand under her chin to raise her face towards him. 'Thanks for coming, babe.'

'I wanted to see you . . . I could've lost you.'

He grinned cheekily. He was a handsome man, no mistake. 'Maybe I should've arranged a shooting earlier.'

'Maybe.'

They didn't say anything for a moment.

'You know, staring down a barrel of a gun has a way of changing the way you look at things . . .' Jake hesitated. 'Puts stuff into perspective. I fucked up before. I should never have agreed to stop seeing you. Hurting you is one of my biggest regrets. I need you in my life, Sam, *properly* in my life.'

'And what about Jase? He'd kill you, he'd kill both of us.'

This time he cupped her face in both hands. 'Look, if we're careful, he'll never know. And he's got no reason to suspect, has he? I'll make sure nothing happens to you. I promise. And then, when the time's right, we can make a life together.'

'I can't leave my mum. More's the pity.' Partly jokingly, she rolled her eyes

'I know, and I wouldn't ask you to. Plus, this whole thing . . . we'll go at your pace, whatever you want, Sam. I ain't going to be seeing anyone else, not even casually, not even hookers. I'll knock all that on the head.'

She laughed and shook her head. Could it work? Maybe. If they were careful, of course. It was what she wanted. No doubt about it. She'd missed him in her life.

'So what do you say, Sam? Will you give me another chance?'

The snow was becoming heavier. A group of carol singers scurried past, huddled up in coats and scarves.

Samantha scanned Jake's face. She took a deep breath and smiled. 'Yes, yes, I'd like that.'

He leant in and kissed her slowly.

And nothing else mattered apart from each other in that moment.

Chapter Forty-Five

Dara had waited until Gracie had come around. She'd checked her friend was all right, before getting changed out of her thin cotton dress – which was covered in porridge – into a burgundy polo-neck jumper and a pair of denim flares Brenda had lent her.

She made her way slowly along the stone corridor to Barrows' office. She was in no hurry. Thoughts of the screams from last night played in her head on a loop, and she was genuinely terrified of what might be waiting for her.

The door of Barrows' office was splintered and peeling, with strips of mahogany lacquer revealing the cheap pine underneath. Dara raised her hand, letting her fist hover in the air, trying to summon the courage to knock. She took a deep breath, exhaled and counted to ten, trying to stop her knees trembling.

Eventually, she rapped quietly on the door.

'*Come in.*'

And forced herself to hold her head high as she entered the room.

Barrows' office was full of cricket souvenirs and trophies. A fat old tabby cat Dara had seen pottering around the grounds lay curled up on a wooden chair in the corner. Barrows' desk was a mess of overflowing ashtrays and car magazines, along with several cups of half-finished tea.

Dara had felt sure Clemence would be waiting for her, and she was relieved that he wasn't anywhere to be seen.

Sitting behind his desk in front of the window, Barrows didn't waste any time. 'This is Mr Howard. And Nurse Pike.' He nodded towards the two other people in the room. 'Mr Howard has come to talk to you.' His voice sounded flat and uncaring, like he'd rather be somewhere else.

Dara peeked at Mr Howard. He was a big man; his legs stretched out like tree trunks in front of him, and his thighs struggled to fit on the wooden chair. He had a bald head with a nasty flare-up of eczema near the top of his left ear. His nose was wide and flattened to one side – it'd clearly been broken years ago – and Dara wondered what he'd done to deserve someone giving him a punch hard enough to break it.

Nurse Pike was leaning against one of Barrows' trophy cabinets, looking like she was enjoying the long, thin menthol cigarette she was smoking. She was somewhere around her mid-fifties, and she fixed Dara with a steely glare. Her short grey hair was permed into tight curls, and there were deep smoker's lines around her lips.

Mr Howard coughed to get Dara's attention.

'So, Dara, I'm from children's social services. I'm sorry I haven't been to see you before.'

Dara's heart rate sped up. She felt her face flush with excitement. Tommy, Rosie . . . Finally, she was going to get some news about them. See them maybe? Get out of Holly Brookes and be with them again. She could almost feel their hugs and hear their giggles, and for the first time in a long while, Dara let down her guard, and allowed the tears of relief to well up.

'There's no easy way of saying this. Your mother's dead.'

The word rang in Dara's ears. *Dead*. She must have heard that wrong. 'What?'

'Dead, Dara. Your mother. They found her in a park. Pedlar's Park, near where you used to live. I understand it was an accident. The police think your mother was drunk maybe, or on drugs. From what they can gather, she fell and hit her head on a stone. It took a while to identify her – that's why it's taken until now to inform you – but the tattoos on her neck helped.' Mr Howard smiled at Dara as if he'd just told her the time.

'No . . . no, you're lying.' Dara gazed at them all. She shook her head repeatedly, her voice starting to rise hysterically. 'I know you're lying, all of you are fucking lying. She ain't dead. She can't be . . . Don't tell me she's dead, *please* don't tell me she's dead.' The walls felt like they were closing in on her. 'Don't fucking play games with me. Where is she? Just tell me where my mum is.'

'I know you're upset, Dara. But try to watch your language, hey?' Mr Howard reprimanded her. 'The good news is, Mr Barrows has informed me there's room in Holly Brookes for you to become a permanent resident here.'

Dara began to shake. She stepped away, towards the door, as though she could distance herself from what they were telling her. 'I don't believe you.'

Howard checked his watch, and eased himself out of his chair. 'I'm sorry not to have better news.'

'Wait, you can't just go . . . what about Tommy, what about Rosie? What about all my little brothers and sisters? I need to see them. They need to see me.' She spoke quickly. Her words tumbling out on top of each other. 'We need to be together . . . I *promised* them.' She looked at Barrows, desperately appealing to him. To someone. To anyone. 'Please, I need to know where they are. I said I'd keep them safe. I can't stay here. I can't. Just tell me where they are.'

'They're in another home, Dara. Different homes. I'm sure you can understand, when there are so many of you, it's impossible to keep you together. And even if we could, maybe that's not the right thing for you all.'

'I said, *where are they?*' Angrily, Dara wiped her nose on her sleeve. 'Tell me.'

'We can't tell you that, I'm afraid.' Mr Howard picked up his briefcase and headed for the door.

Dara stood in front of him. 'What do you mean?' She didn't understand. Why were they being like this? 'They're my brothers and sisters, not yours. You *have* to tell me where they are.'

Howard stepped around her. 'Actually, Dara, we don't. They're in our care now, and as they're so much younger than you, eventually they'll be put up for adoption.'

Dara wailed, an animalistic cry of pain from deep within her. She flew at Howard, scratching at his face, kicking and screaming.

Barrows nodded to Nurse Pike, who quickly stepped forward with a syringe. With one brutal stab, she jabbed the needle into Dara's leg.

Dara blacked out.

Chapter Forty-Six

'Dar, Dar, wake up . . . Dar?' Gracie sat on Dara's bed in the dormitory. She stroked her head. 'Dar, it's me. I heard what happened, and I'm so sorry, Dar. And I know it's not the same, but you can come and live with me, when my mum's better. I know she wouldn't mind. She'll like you, Dar, I know she will . . . please try to wake up.'

Gracie was worried about Dara. After the pantomime dress rehearsal – which saw Barrows and Clemence make several kids cry – Gracie had come back up to the dormitory, but not before she'd heard the news about Dara's mum. When she'd heard she'd burst into tears.

Some of those tears, Gracie knew, were for herself, but most of them were for Dara. She could imagine what Dara was going through. When her dad had died, it felt like there was a constant noise in her head. It didn't go away for a very long time. Her mum had said it was wild horses running through her brain. She'd also felt a pain in her stomach; it hurt so much, she constantly felt sick. Even if she didn't have the right words for her friend, Grace still wanted to be there for Dara.

She'd found Dara asleep on the bottom bunk. Her arms were covered in fresh cuts. The scissors from the sewing room lay discarded on the floor. While Dara had been asleep, Gracie had tried to clean her arms up. She didn't think she'd done a very good job though. The cuts still looked sore, but at least they weren't bleeding now.

Grace had thought Dara would wake up when she'd started wiping her wounds, but her eyelids hadn't even twitched. She knew she was naive about a lot of things, but Gracie was almost sure that Dara had done this to herself. Though she had no idea why. In spite of that, she wasn't going to tell anyone. Gracie had already learnt that drawing attention to yourself in Holly Brookes would be adding fuel to the fire.

She stroked Dara's head again. It was hot and sweaty.

'Dar, wake up. You've got to get up.'

Finally, Dara stirred, only to turn on her side, with her back to Gracie.

'Go away.'

'Dar, *please*, you'll get into trouble. You have to come down to the pantomime, it's going to start soon.'

'I don't care if I get into trouble.' Her voice was slurred from the sedatives.

Grace was terrified that Dara might go back to sleep and never wake up.

She was now faced with a dilemma. She didn't want to push Dara. It had taken her a whole two weeks after her dad had died before she'd gone downstairs. So she understood how bad Dara was feeling. But she very much doubted Barrows would.

'You want me to sing to you, Dar? You know, that song you like?'

Dara didn't answer, she just lay in the dark, staring at the wall. There was a long silence.

Then Grace's singing cut through the darkness.

'*Lavender's blue, dilly, dilly, lavender's green, when I am King, dilly, dilly . . .*'

*

Dara listened and let her tears run across her nose and on to the side of her cheek, wetting the pillow. Then she slowly turned over to face Gracie. Even in the flickering light from the bare bulb, Dara could see how frightened Gracie looked. Her friend's eyes were wide with fear, and her voice was shaking.

Dara remembered how brave Gracie had been. Trying to stop Barrows from smothering her in the bowl of porridge.

Trying to smile, so as not to alarm Gracie any more, Dara pulled down her sleeves, hiding the cuts on her arms. She licked her lips. They felt sore and cracked.

'How's your head?' she asked Gracie.

Stopping in the middle of the chorus, Gracie looped her fingers between Dara's, holding her hand tightly. 'It's all right, I'm fine. It's *you* I'm worried about.'

Dara sat up, swung her legs off the bed, and nodded. It was weird, because she didn't quite feel in control of her own body. She was drowsy, and her thoughts were blurred at the edges. But Dara's thinking was clear enough to realise that if she didn't go to the pantomime, maybe Gracie would get into trouble herself. She'd clocked what that bastard Barrows was all about.

She didn't care about herself, not any more. She felt so empty. Everything was pointless now. She'd even thought about killing herself. She knew how to do it. She'd seen her mum slash her wrists once, when one of her pimps had left her. But if she could look after Gracie, keep her safe until her mum came to take her out of here, then maybe she'd wait. There was a reason to stay alive.

Yes, that's exactly what she'd do. She'd wait until Gracie left Holly Brookes, and then . . .

Well, then she'd do it.

Chapter Forty-Seven

By the time Dara and Gracie reached the hall, the pantomime had already started, and the audience was packed. Holding Gracie's hand to steady herself, still feeling woozy from the effects of the sedative, Dara groaned inwardly as she saw Barrows walking towards them.

'You're supposed to be helping out with costume changes, so get a move on, both of you.' He spoke without breaking his stride, and continued down the corridor behind the stage. His brown pull-on leather shoes made a squeaking sound on the polished floor.

Suddenly, he stopped and turned back round, clicking his fingers. 'Oh, and Dara, no more special treatment for you. You're part of Holly Brookes now, understand?' He didn't wait for a reply.

Ahead of them, they saw Robbie dressed in his duck costume, holding the large orange-beaked headpiece under his arm.

'What's the matter, Robbie?' Gracie got to him first.

Robbie looked how Dara felt. There was no colour in his face. It was ashen.

Dara looked at Robbie for a long moment. 'What's wrong?'

'They're there, Dar. In the front row.' He struggled to get his sentence out as he snatched at her hand and gulped for air.

'Who's there?' Gracie asked, frowning.

Robbie pressed himself against the wall. 'He is, they are . . . I can't do it. I can't do it.'

Dara walked to the side of the stage, trying to understand what Robbie was talking about. From the wings she stood in the dark, looking out into the audience. The rawness of fear ran through her. The audience was mainly men – patrons and other people she'd seen yesterday at the swimming pool opening – and she realised why Robbie was so terrified. On the front row, smoking a pipe and smiling up at the children on the stage, was Dennis Hargreaves and the other two men who'd been with him.

She hurried back to Robbie, who was still standing with Gracie. 'I can't do it any more, Dar.' Robbie was desperate. 'I can't.'

Dara found it painful to look at him. 'It's okay, Robbie, it's fine, you don't have to . . . I'll do it. They won't know it's me. Once I'm in the costume, no one's going to know, are they? Not with that big bleedin' duck head on.' She worked hard at managing a smile.

'It won't fit you, Dar. You're too tall.'

Gracie gave a tiny shrug. She wouldn't fit into it either. Robbie was so skinny.

Wondering what to do, Dara glanced around. 'Hey, Albie . . . Albie, come here.'

Albie, a short boy with a hard expression, wandered over to them.

'You need to play Robbie's part.'

'What?' His dark eyebrows knitted together. 'I ain't playing the duck. I'm supposed to be helping hand out the props.'

'Then you can do both, can't you? You ain't got to be Einstein,' Dara said firmly.

Pulling a face, Albie shrugged. Slightly boss-eyed, he glared at Dara. 'I don't know the lines. I ain't getting a battering from Barrows, not for Robbie.'

Exasperated, Dara sighed. 'Christ Almighty, all you need to say is, *quack, fucking quack*. Barrows changed his lines cos he couldn't remember them, so he ain't even looking for Mrs Hubbard in the cupboard any more . . . Just do it, all right.'

Albie, seeing that he had no choice, reluctantly snatched the duck head from Robbie. 'You owe me though, Dara,' he said sulkily.

Dara eased up on him. 'Okay, I do. Swear on it. And thanks, Albie. But make sure you keep the headpiece on, all right. So they don't know it's you.'

Once Robbie had got out of the costume, and helped Albie get into it, Dara told them her idea.

'You don't want Barrows seeing you, Robbie. So I reckon we should get out of here. Barrows saw me and Gracie five minutes ago, so he'll think we're somewhere helping out. We'll come back just as the performance finishes, and help Albie get out of his costume quickly, so no one will know.'

'Why don't we wait in the woods?' Robbie suggested. 'I know it's cold out there, but it isn't much warmer inside. And at least we'll have the trees to shelter us, and there's no way anyone will see us there.'

'Sounds like a plan,' Gracie said, taking Robbie's hand.

The three of them hurried round the back of the stage, and crept out of the hall. Outside, it had stopped sleeting. They ran along the gravel path that wound around the cottages.

'Dar, I'm sorry about your mum,' Robbie said shyly as they made their way across the grass. 'I've never had a family, so I don't know what that must feel like, but I'm glad you're here, cos I reckon you're the best.'

They sat silently under the trees for the next forty minutes, not even daring to whisper. The thought of being discovered truly terrified them. They watched the blue moon rising in the clear black sky, before eventually hearing the applause that signalled the end of the performance.

'You stay here, Robbie. We'll go and help Albie.'

Dara and Gracie rushed back across the grass, down the path and towards the hall. Just as they got to the door, Dara heard the sound of footsteps coming towards them.

'I think someone's coming. Can you hear that?'

Gracie listened. Yeah, there was definitely someone there. Without speaking, she nodded at Dara. They joined hands and ran to the unlit side of the building. Neither of them wanted to run slap bang into Barrows, and they scrabbled to stay hidden in the shadows.

'Come on, Robbie, stop struggling.'

Dara's heart leapt in her chest at the loud voice. Robbie? Oh God, they'd found him. Alarmed, she glanced at Gracie, who looked rigid with fear. Then very carefully, Dara tiptoed along the side of the building to see what was happening.

Hearing laughter, she peeked around the corner.

Immediately, she slammed her hands across her mouth to stop herself from screaming. Making their way to a big posh car, she saw Dennis staggering along with the other two men. They all looked drunk, and they sounded in the mood for a party.

'Quack, quack . . . Come on, Robbie.'

But it wasn't Robbie who they were dragging along, was it?

'Albie.' Dara whispered his name as she watched him, still fully dressed in the duck outfit, being bungled into the boot of the car.

'That should have been me.'

Dara jumped as Robbie came to stand by her.

'They think that's me, Dar.'

'What do you think's going to happen to him?' Gracie asked.

Neither Robbie nor Dara answered her.

As the car drove off and the tail lights vanished into the darkness of Christmas Eve, Dara wondered what she'd done. This was her fault. Whatever happened to Albie now, it was on her head.

At only thirteen years old, Dara realised she might have blood on her hands.

Chapter Forty-Eight

It was Boxing Day and Alan Carver sat in his Jaguar XJ6 in Brewer Street. He'd spent a quiet Christmas back home in Dulwich, with only a mound of cocaine and a Polish hooker with gigantic breasts for company.

He turned the heating up and switched the car radio on. Fucking Christmas music.

Alan hated *anything* to do with fucking Christmas. Everyone in the country tried to be way too happy, with every cunt sending useless Christmas cards to each other and forking out money on a shedload of presents no one wanted. And who the fuck actually enjoyed drinking mulled wine? Alan let out a long sigh. He, for one, was pleased to see the back end of the *festive* season.

Alan turned the radio off in disgust and stepped out of the car, pleased to be up town in Soho. The wind whipped around the bottom of his black wool coat, and he hurried along the street, battling the winter weather. Partway down, by the sex shop, Alan stopped. He suddenly had a feeling he was being watched. He looked back down the road. There was a scattering of tourists, a tramp huddled by the door of the Thai massage knocking shop, and a few lads joshing each other as they walked into one of the walk-ups. He couldn't see anyone else, but the feeling of being watched still lingered.

Turning into Walker's Court, Alan was shocked to see the boarded-up frontage of Honey's. He'd heard about what happened at the club, but this was the first time he'd seen the damage up close. The Albanians had properly done a number on it. Not for the first time, Alan wished to God he'd never gone anywhere near this deal with the Wakeman brothers.

Stupidly, he'd thought it was the best way to get rid of the Wakemans, by allowing them to buy the land. Hands down, it was turning into the worst decision Alan had ever made. He'd set in motion a fucking chain reaction he couldn't have seen coming.

He glanced at his watch. One thirty-five. He had no wish to see Jake and Jason, but it had to be done. Avoiding them wasn't going to make it go away. He just hoped they'd listen to his proposal.

Alan walked into the club and shook off the snow from his coat.

'Alan.' Jason grinned. 'How's the old mitts? Coping with nine little sausages, are you?'

Alan seethed inwardly. He nodded a greeting to Jake, who sat moodily next to his brother. He could see that Jason had been sniffing, which was never good, and oddly, Jake didn't look particularly sober. Was he back on the sauce?

'I'm fine, thanks, Jase. What's a finger between friends?'

'That's what I like to see, a sense of humour and no grudges.' Jason's eyes flickered darkly. He pulled out a chair for Alan. 'Why don't you come and take a seat.'

Jake still hadn't spoken. In truth, his silence made Alan more uncomfortable than he already was. And there was no fucking way he was going to sit between the two brothers.

'I'll stand, if it's all the same to you, mate . . . Look, I'm sorry.' Alan tried to sound more confident than he felt. 'But this is getting out of hand. This whole thing. Nobody wanted it to get like this, so I've got an idea.'

There was a slight beat before Jason spluttered with laughter. 'Al, are you winding me up? An idea? We don't hear from you for over a week, and when you do crawl out from under your stone, there's me thinking you were going to hand over a signed contract, or a wad of money. Not only to pay *us* back, but Zef and Dren too, *with* interest. And then there's the money it's going to cost to do this place up. But instead you walk in here like some trumped-up prick, with your hands full of fresh air, talking about fucking ideas.'

'Jase, I can see how it looks and where you're coming from, but if you'll just hear me out for a minute—'

Jason shot out of his seat and strolled up to Alan. His face was twisted in anger. 'My brother nearly got a bullet in his skull because of you, and you want me to hear you out?'

'This will benefit all of us, including Zef and Dren, if you—'

A loud noise came from the entrance. Alan turned in time to see the door being staved in.

'*Fuck.*' Jason raced towards the VIP area where he'd left his gun.

Jake jumped up and made a beeline for the bar where his shooter was kept.

Alan ran for the back entrance, but before he could get there, he was slammed to the floor. A boot kicked him in the side of his ribs so hard he groaned out in pain. 'What the fuck?'

Another kick to the side of Alan's body was followed by a steel toecap to his forehead. Pain rushed through him. His hair was grabbed in a fist-hold so tight it felt like his scalp was on fire. He was dragged upright, and came face to face with uniformed officers. Two of them grabbed his arms.

'What the fuck are you playing at? You've got this all wrong.'

Alan hissed through his clenched teeth. The deep gash across his forehead was dripping blood profusely.

'Oh dear, oh dear, is there a problem?' A tall officer strolled nonchalantly towards Alan, smirking. 'Hello, Mr Carver, I'm Detective Randall. We've heard all about you.'

'Well, whatever you've heard, it's total bullshit. Now I want to see your boss.'

Randall nodded to his colleagues. Then without warning, he punched Alan in the stomach.

Alan doubled up in agony, coughing his guts out. Before he was able to recover, a fist was driven into Alan's face with a powerful upper cut, loosening Alan's front tooth and flooding his mouth with blood.

'All your little dealings, Mr Carver. We've being watching for quite some time, and it's a very murky business.' Randall seemed to be enjoying himself.

It took another few minutes before Alan was able to straighten up. He was breathing heavily now, covered in blood, and he leant towards the officer, lowering his voice.

'I told you, you've got this arse about face. If I were you, I'd get your boss on the line. *Now*. You're going to regret this, understand? I want to see Chief Superintendent Lewis—'

'That's never going to happen.' Randall shook his head sorrowfully. 'Get him out of here, boys.'

The two officers started to drag Alan away, towards the entrance. Out of the corner of his eye, he saw the Old Bill dragging Jake and Jason out too.

'Alan Carver, we are arresting you for . . .'

But Alan wasn't listening to his rights being read out. He was too busy screaming objections.

'Get your fucking hands off me, you cunts! You're making such a big mistake. I'll have your fucking job, you hear me? I said, *get off me!*'

For his trouble, his arm was twisted painfully behind his back as he was marched to the nearby police cars.

Chapter Forty-Nine

Dara and Gracie stared across the lunch table at the empty chair where Albie usually sat.

'He ain't coming back, is he?' Grace looked scared. Christmas had come and gone, and there'd been no sight or sound of Albie since they'd watched the men take him away.

Grace wasn't sleeping well either; she kept being woken up by horrible nightmares, and soaked in urine from wetting the bed. She was so embarrassed. Her bedsheets were starting to stink, and it wouldn't be long before the other kids smelt it.

Dara gave the tiniest shake of her head. 'It don't look like it.'

She'd heard the whispering in the dormitories about Albie. Apparently, he wasn't the first kid to be taken and never come back. It had happened before. Dara didn't even want to think about the things the other kids were saying might have happened to him. She was only pleased that Gracie hadn't heard.

But how had they got away with it, time and time again? Brenda had said they were the lost kids, and no one cared enough to go looking for them.

Dara's head was a complete mess. Even the pain of knowing she might never see her siblings again had been overshadowed by the thought that she was responsible for Albie. It was her fault. If anything had happened to him, she and she alone had caused it.

Nobody else had forced him into that costume, had they? If Albie was dead, she had murdered him.

'Dar, are you okay?' Gracie looked at her. She didn't bother asking why Dara was crying, there were so many reasons to cry in Holly Brookes.

Dara hastily wiped her tears with her top. 'I was just thinking, they can't get away with it. I ain't going to let them.'

'What are you going to do?' Robbie sounded worried. 'Dar, you've got to leave it.'

'I ain't going to leave anything. Don't worry, Robbie, I'm not going to ask you or Gracie to help, but I ain't sitting here doing nothing.'

Gracie and Robbie exchanged glances.

'Do you remember the Yorkshire Ripper, a couple of years ago, when they were looking for him? It was all on the telly?'

Robbie shook his head, looking blank.

'My mum wouldn't let me watch it,' Gracie said. 'She was worried it would give me nightmares, so she always turned over when the news came on. But what's it got to do with Albie?'

'Well, they were always talking about his car number plate,' Dara explained. 'When I was watching all them police appeals about him, I found out that you can trace the owner of the car from their number plate.'

Gracie looked doubtful.

'I clocked the number plate when those men drove off with Albie, and I can still remember it. So it got me thinking. If we tell the police about what happened, and tell them the geezers' number, the Old Bill will be able to pull him in and maybe . . .' She shrugged and finished hopefully, 'Maybe they'll find Albie . . . or I dunno, it'll stop them from doing it again, won't it?'

'But how are you going to report them to the police, Dar?' Robbie was seriously concerned now.

'When they drove us here, I saw a telephone box near the turn-off. We can call the Old Bill from there.'

'*We?*' Robbie blanched.

'Like I say, you don't have to do nothing you don't want to.' Dara wasn't going to force him, not after what had happened with Albie.

'*Good afternoon, everyone.*' Barrows strolled in, greeting everybody loudly. He'd had a few days off over Christmas, but now he was back, and in charge.

He looked around the dining room, checking everyone had eaten their lunch. He stopped when his eyes lighted on Robbie. His smile turned into a nasty chuckle. 'You've got more lives than an alley cat, ain't you, Robbie?' He turned and walked out.

The moment Barrows had left the room, Robbie leant towards Dara. It was the first time she'd seen him looking angry.

'I'll come to the phone box with you, Dar. Cos you're right, they shouldn't get away with it.'

Chapter Fifty

Frank Baker was trying to enjoy the leftovers from Christmas dinner. All his favourite things. He sat at the kitchen table, his plate piled high with turkey, ham, roast potatoes, chipolatas – slightly burnt – all of which had been fried up in butter, along with chestnut stuffing and a bit of cauliflower cheese. Usually he'd be tucking in. But for once, Frank was finding it hard to digest.

Dancing in front of him, semi-naked, was Judy. The radio was on, and she'd been bumping and grinding to the Thompson Twins' 'Hold Me Now'. Frank couldn't actually think of anything worse.

Unfortunately for Frank, Judy loved sex. She absolutely adored it. It turned his wife into a different woman: wild, passionate, screeching and moaning at the top of her voice, to the point where Gloria next door often hammered on the wall. And right now, Frank could tell Judy was in the mood for a long session; she only wore that cream lacy dressing gown from Liberty when she wanted more than a quickie.

He sighed inwardly.

'You all right, darlin'?' Judy purred. 'You look a bit queasy.'

'Just got a bit of a headache, that's all.'

'I know a way of making you feel better.' Licking her lips, she sashayed round the back of him, rubbing his chest, nuzzling her face into his neck.

Frank just wanted to be left in peace to eat his cauliflower cheese. He almost cheered in celebration when there was a loud knock on the door.

'I'll go.' He shot up out of his chair

Judy pushed him back down. 'It's fine, I'll deal with it. It's probably those little bastards from next door but one. They were after some ciggies yesterday. I gave them a bit of tobacco, but believe you me, I'll be giving them a piece of my bleedin' mind today.'

Frank watched her go, and frowned. Judy had seemed different lately. Still his loving wife, of course, but the best way he could describe it, was secretive. Secretive and distracted. He put it down to Jimmy going missing. She must be devastated – on top of which, she'd been supporting Mandy through it. In Frank's opinion, it seemed a lot of fuss over nothing. No doubt Jimmy was stoned out of his nut, bunked up with some girl or other, and the lad would eventually skulk back home.

He shrugged dispassionately to himself, picked up his fork, and scooped up a mouthful of potato.

Judy closed the kitchen door behind her and hurried down the hallway. She'd had a telephone phone call this morning while Frank was in the bath, so she'd been expecting the knock.

Judy wasn't surprised to see the person who was standing on her freshly scrubbed stone step.

Lewis smiled.

Never one for small talk, he cut to the chase. 'We need a body.'

'Excuse me?'

He rubbed his hands together, trying to keep warm. 'I didn't want to say anything on the phone, in case Frank overheard us, but your sister is making a fucking nuisance of herself. I thought you said you'd sort it?'

Judy kept her voice down. 'I can't help it if Mandy is worried bloody sick, can I? I've told her not to keep phoning.'

'Yeah, well, that's clearly not working, is it? So we need to do something about it.'

'*We?*'

'Yes, *we*, Judy,' Lewis hissed.

Judy Baker was beginning to annoy the fuck out of Lewis. She was a hard-faced cow, but *for now* her loyalty to Frank was useful to them.

'It was your fucking nephew who was the loose cannon, and it's your sister who's starting to bring too much attention to Jimmy going missing. People are starting to sit up and take notice. They're not just dismissing her as some crazy bitch. The point is, we need to nip this in the bud. We need to make it go away . . . It's either that, or we get rid of Mandy as well.'

Judy thought about this suggestion. She'd led her nephew to his death, lied to her sister, comforted her, and all the time knowing exactly what she'd done. Some people might call that fucked up. But now Judy wondered, if she agreed to Lewis's latest idea, might she regret it?

'No, that ain't happening,' she said firmly.

Her nightgown fell open and, like Frank, Lewis felt his stomach turn over at the sight of her fat, hairy cunt.

'Okay, well, in that case, we'll need a body, to make this go away. And in the meantime, I need you to keep your sister under control. She can't phone the station any more, and she certainly can't come down there . . . I'll be in touch.' Lewis turned away and strode down the path.

'Wait.' Judy called after him, gesturing him back to the doorstep.
Lewis looked at her in anticipation.

'I might know someone.'

'I beg your pardon?' Lewis was cold, and he was getting antsy.

'You need a body, right? Well, I know just the person. Someone
who won't be missed.'

Chapter Fifty-One

Samantha pulled over her red BMW on the grassy verge and looked at the Road Atlas map on the passenger seat next to her. If she was right, she was only a mile or so away now.

She took a sherbet lemon out of the glove compartment, and popped it into her mouth. She'd never been the most confident of drivers, especially not in the powerful BMW Jason had bought her last year. She'd been more than happy with her old Ford Escort, but he'd given her no choice. And just to cement his point, he'd had her car towed away, getting it crushed at his mate's scrapyard in Streatham.

Crunching on the boiled sweet and tasting the bitter sherbet, Samantha threw the atlas back on to the seat. According to the map, she wasn't far away now. Ten minutes tops?

She checked in the wing mirror, before pulling out again on to the deserted country road, driving very slowly in the slush, hoping not to miss the turning to the rural village of Hambledon. She indicated left and drove over a small humpback bridge. She was beginning to wonder if she'd made a big mistake by coming here.

Samantha left her car parked by the entrance to a muddy field, and wandered down a narrow lane, passing a telephone box. She headed in the direction of the woods she'd driven past only moments earlier.

Another few minutes' walk, and she found herself staring up at the huge, dark rusting metal gates of Holly Brookes. The gates were locked, and there was no hope of getting over them with the barbed wire wrapped around the top. From where Samantha was standing, the whole place looked pretty difficult to get into. A high brick wall continued as far as she could see, with large oak trees screening the view on the other side.

The place was vast, and Samantha shivered. Maybe it was simply the weather, bleak and cold, but there was nothing warming about the place. Through the bars of the gates, she could see buildings way off in the distance. It reminded her of a prison camp, and it was miles from anywhere. Though maybe that was the point.

She wasn't sure what she'd expected, but certainly not this. What she'd imagined, or rather hoped for, was to see Grace and be able to talk to her. She hadn't thought it through properly. What had she been planning to do then? Just check that she was all right, she supposed. Because not a day had gone by when she hadn't thought about her, and wondered—

A hand slammed over Samantha's mouth.

Terrified, she struggled to get out of her assailant's grip as she was dragged towards the trees, down the lane. Her feet scrabbled underneath her, and she continued to fight, trying desperately to get away, but the grip on her was too tight.

Unable to turn to see her attacker, Samantha was pulled through a small thicket and thrown down on to the wet earth. Frantically, she clawed her way on to her feet, using a tree branch to help her. She spun round to face a wiry, dirty-looking man. He had a long raised scar running from the corner of his mouth right across his cheek. Even from where Samantha was standing, she could smell the alcohol on him.

He pointed. 'What the fuck are you doing here, poking around?'

'I was having a look, that's all. I'm staying with a friend, so I thought I'd come out for a little walk . . . but they know *exactly* where I am.'

Leering at her, he laughed. 'Is that right?'

Dara, Robbie and Gracie crouched down behind some trees, a few yards away from Samantha.

'*Sshhhh*, there's someone over there.' Dara peeked through the tall brushwood. 'Over by the oak tree.'

Gracie couldn't see. They still hadn't done anything about getting her a new pair of glasses.

'I can see them,' Robbie whispered. 'I think it's Clemence. Yeah, it is . . . look.'

'Oh *shit*, yeah.' Dara saw him too. As usual, he looked drunk. 'He's with some woman. He looks well angry, don't he? She don't look too happy neither.'

Gracie looked in the direction Dara and Robbie were staring in. The only thing she could make out was the outline of two people. 'What's happening?'

'It looks like he's having a barney with his girlfriend,' Robbie answered.

'No way. There's no way Clemence would have someone as classy as that,' Dara commented. 'Oh shit.'

'What?' Gracie asked, frustrated. 'What is it? What's going on, Dar?'

'She's just slapped him, and he's grabbed her again. Looks like he's hurting her.'

Dara searched around and picked up a large stone. Then she threw it as hard as she could.

It hit Clemence on the side of his head. Not as hard as Dara would've liked, but hard enough to surprise him for a moment, which allowed the woman to pull herself away. For the briefest of moments, she seemed to look through the bushes straight at Dara, but then she sprinted away.

'*Hide.* He's coming.' Robbie scampered off, followed by Dara and Gracie.

They dipped down, keeping low, making sure Clemence couldn't see them. He looked so pissed, Dara thought it was unlikely he'd be able to focus properly anyway.

They hid for another few minutes, watching Clemence stagger off in the other direction. They saw a red BMW drive past before emerging from their hiding place.

'Are you all right, Robbie?'

Robbie looked around. This was the first time he'd been outside the walls of Holly Brookes. His heart was working overtime. He was like a rabbit caught in headlights. Everything seemed so vast, it was like the world went on forever.

'Yeah, I'm fine. Ta for asking,' he said quietly.

Dara didn't think he looked fine, far bloody from it. She wasn't going to show him up though. She knew from the time he was born, Holly Brookes had been the only home he'd ever known, so even stepping outside the grounds must be a big deal to him. She understood that he needed to appear brave and feisty,

With Dara leading the way, they ran along the lane towards where Dara had seen the telephone box. She gave Robbie an encouraging smile as they hurried through the slush. They were exposed out here, with no trees to hide them. Dara, Gracie and *especially* Robbie wanted to be as quick as possible.

The phone box was covered with snow. It was surrounded by tall weeds, and the glass panes were laced with icicles, frozen and crispy.

Thinking of Albie, Dara glanced nervously at Robbie and

Gracie. 'Shall I do this then? You reckon we're doing the right thing?'

A silent agreement passed between them. They were scared, but they didn't want that to stop them from doing the right thing.

'I think you should, Dar,' Gracie said.

'Me too.' Robbie nodded.

Dara opened the heavy door of the phone box, and picked up the phone. She closed her eyes tightly. She'd always been taught never to call the Old Bill, no matter what. Threatened by her mum with a beating if she ever did. But someone had to help Albie, didn't they?

She opened her eyes and, going against everything she'd ever been told, she punched in the number.

'Hello, emergency services, how can I help you?'

Dara took a deep breath.

'I'd like to report a crime.'

Chapter Fifty-Two

'So, Jason, you're really trying to tell us that you didn't know the land deal with Alan Carver was illegal? You didn't wonder why you were getting it at such a cheap price, when it's prime land on the Embankment? Oh, come off it, do we look like mugs?'

The police interview room was filled with cigarette smoke. A half-eaten Wimpy cheeseburger had spilt ketchup down Detective Randall's tie, and now sat in its wrapping on the table. A days-old cup of Nescafé collected dust and mould on the side.

Jason leant back in the plastic chair, trying to ignore the smell of heavy sweat in the air. He rested his hands on his head and smirked at Randall. He knew how to wind him up. The Old Bill were all the same. They expected respect. Well, they were going to get fuck-all from him. 'Do you really want me to answer that, mate?'

Randall pulled deeply on his cigarette. It caught the back of his throat, and he stifled a cough. 'You see, if you help us, Jason, we can help you.'

'And how do you fucking make that out?'

Randall had a habit of stroking his moustache before speaking. He leant forward, elbows on the scratched table, staring at Jason. There was no love lost between them. 'Because if you tell us what you know, Jason, then we'll go easier on you and your brother.'

Jason's handsome face twisted into a snarl. 'I ain't telling you fuck-all, and you know why? Because there's fuck-all to tell.'

Since they'd been pulled in on Boxing Day, they'd been kept in the cells for the past thirty-six hours, waiting to be questioned. Jason knew that the Old Bill would have to release them soon, unless they could pin something on them.

He wasn't worried about Jake. His brother wouldn't be talking. He only hoped that cunt Alan wasn't either. Alan had done nothing but bang on the police cell door, like some little pussy. He wouldn't be surprised if Alan started crying, the way he'd been going on. Fucking hell, the geezer was a joke. Giving it the big one outside, larging it up, but when he was brought in by the filth, back against the wall, and looking at a stretch, he couldn't fucking hold it together.

Jason's scowl turned to another smirk. The Old Bill were clutching at straws, he was sure of it. They might have got a sniff of what was going on, but there was no way they had anything on the Wakemans. 'You're wasting all our time. You might as well let us go, because you won't get anything out of me and Jakey.'

Randall made sure he gave it a lengthy pause before speaking. 'No, maybe not, Jason, but someone else *has* been talking. Telling me all about what you've been up to . . .'

Jason wanted to kill Alan. He knew it. He had a feeling that fucking low-life scum would talk in the end, he'd do anything to save his own skin. *Cunt.*

'Little birds have been talking to us. Little Albanian birds.'

Jason tried not to look astonished. He blinked rapidly. 'What?' A ripple of unease filtered through him. This was the first time he'd felt any kind of concern.

Randall picked up on it straight away. 'Surprised?' He flicked through the grey file in front of him. 'You must have royally pissed them off, Jason. Because when we picked them up, it didn't take long for them to start singing. What did you do to them, hey?'

Jason couldn't believe what he was hearing. 'You're bluffing.'

Randall laughed. He stubbed his cigarette out. 'Am I? You see, that's what you *wish* I was doing, isn't it? But how else would I know *exactly* how much you paid for the land?'

Randall picked up the chewed biro next to him, and scribbled something on a piece of paper, pushing it across the table to Jason. Cocksure, Randall grinned. 'That's how much. I'm right, aren't I? The thing is, Jason, you're in deep shit, but not as much shit as Mr Carver. Seems like he's been selling off pieces of land for favours for quite some time. So why don't you help us with our inquiries, make it easy on yourself?'

'Go to fuck.' Jason clenched his teeth. He didn't appreciate being interrogated by this trumped-up prick. 'I ain't a grassing cunt.' He leant back in his chair. 'And besides, like I say, there's nothing to tell. So what, you've got a few numbers, but what does that mean? Nah, mate, if you had enough evidence, you and I both know you'd be charging us now.'

Randall held Jason's stare. He tapped the end of the pen against his teeth. Then reached for his packet of Silk Cut. Pulled out a cigarette, putting it in his mouth without lighting it. 'Oh, believe you me, it's only a matter of time, Jason.'

There was a knock on the door of the interview room. An officer popped his bald, shiny head around the door frame. He tapped his watch, and Randall nodded, before the officer disappeared again.

Randall picked up his file, shuffling the papers. 'It looks like time's up. You're free to go, Mr Wakeman . . . for now.'

Jason angrily scraped back his chair and walked towards the door.

'But Jason . . .' Randall threw his biro at Jason to get his attention. 'Trust me when I say, we'll be in touch.'

Jason felt a burning anger. He wanted to grab the cunt's neck and snap it. Though not as much as two Albanian necks he could think of.

He stalked out, listening to Randall laughing like a fucking hyena.

'Let me out of here . . . Jase, what's happening?'

Jason caught a glimpse of Alan shouting and banging on the cell door as he marched down the corridor, heading for the reception area where the desk sergeant would give him back his things.

'Jase . . . Jase, talk to me . . . what's happening . . . Jase . . . Why the fuck are you letting him out, not me? Hello! Hello!'

Jason didn't give two fucks about Alan.

The only thing he had on his mind was what to do about Zef and Dren. Because little birds that chirruped had a habit of getting shot.

Chapter Fifty-Three

It was Friday, the day before New Year's Eve, and the year was drawing to a close.

It was cold in the sanitised corridor of the coroner's office, behind the police station. Mandy stopped walking. She was unsteady on her feet from the Valium Judy had been dishing out to her since Jimmy's disappearance.

'Are you all right, darlin'?' Judy feigned a sympathetic smile.

Mandy was in no fit state to be out really. The vallies had made Mandy listless, barely functioning and struggling to get through the day without Judy's support, which certainly suited Judy.

'You should've stayed in bed, sweetheart.'

'It's not fair on you, Jude, to have to do this on your own, I wanted to come.' Mandy sounded slurred. Her eyes filled with tears, and the fear she'd woken up with this morning felt like it was pounding her skull.

Judy took in every detail of her sister's face, then searched in her handbag and took out a small bottle of pills. She unscrewed the top and shook out a couple of the blue tablets into her hand.

'Here you go, sweetheart, get these down you, it'll make you feel better.' Judy sounded full of concern.

Trembling, Mandy put up no objection, swallowing the pills

quickly without water. 'Thank you. I don't know what I'd do without you, Jude.'

'That's what sisters are for, aren't they?' Judy kissed Mandy on her cheek, and squeezed her hand. 'I hate that you have to go through this, but it's got to be done, darlin'. I'm so sorry, but at least this way, you'll know, won't you?'

'I don't *want* to know.' Mandy broke down in tears, collapsing on to the chair in the corridor. 'I'd rather think Jimmy's alive somewhere, shacked up with some little tart, than be told he ain't ever coming back . . . I don't think I can bear to look . . .'

As Mandy wept, rocking back and forth, unable to control her emotions, spaced out from too much Valium, Judy was trying hard not to throw up. The overpowering smell of peppermint in the air – intended to mask the nasty smells from any human remains being brought in and out – was making her feel sick.

'It's okay, Mand, you don't have to do anything you don't want to do,' Judy reassured her, continuing to play the dutiful sister.

'But I'm his mother . . .'

Judy disguised a sigh. She only hoped that the extra tablets she'd given Mandy would kick in soon. 'But I already told you this morning, I'll do it. I'll identify him for you, if you want me to.'

Judy almost believed her own sorrow. This morning, over her plate of scrambled eggs, she'd reminded herself that Jimmy had played the biggest hand in his own demise. If he'd done as he was told, right now none of them would be in this position. Jimmy could have messed things up for Frank, good and proper. If anything, Judy thought, she should be *angry* with him, not mourning his loss.

'Come here, darlin'.' She leant down and gave Mandy a hug as a glazed expression came over Mandy's face and her eyes started to close.

'Good afternoon, ladies.' Lewis's voice boomed down the corridor.

He strode along to greet them, carrying a large black bag. He focused on Mandy; she was slumped in one of the chairs, looking wrecked.

'Thank you for coming. I know how difficult this is.' Lewis, like Judy, gave a sympathetic smile

He was wondering how to make this as painless as possible for himself. He'd drunk too much last night and he had the headache from fucking hell. He certainly didn't want a whinging mother making it worse.

'I asked you here, because I've taken a personal interest in Jimmy's disappearance since the initial missing person report. When I heard a body had been recovered . . . well, I know how much red tape is sometimes involved. So hopefully, I can help by not prolonging the agony. I'm sorry to put it so bluntly, but we need to establish whether the body we've found is, in fact, Jimmy's.'

'What do we need to do?' Judy asked, going through the script in her head. Lewis had helped her rehearse it earlier.

'As I said on the phone this morning, we need one of you to identify the body. Sadly, I must warn you that the body has been badly disfigured so I'm afraid a strong stomach is required.'

Mandy was clearly struggling to take in anything Lewis was saying.

'What makes you think it could be Jimmy?' Judy followed the question up with a small smile to Mandy. One of her sister's false eyelashes had come unstuck and Judy gently pressed it back on her lid.

Lewis produced a see-through plastic pouch from the bag he'd been carrying. 'We found these things with the body.' He held the pouch up, which contained Jimmy's wallet, a comb and some house keys.

'They're Jimmy's. Oh my God, they're my Jim's.' Mandy cried out. Her eyes rolled back in her head. The extra Valium had well and truly kicked in. She hardly knew where she was, let alone what was happening.

Judy leant across and touched Mandy on the knee. 'Mand . . . Mand, let me do this, darlin'. You don't seem like you're really up to it. How about you stay here?'

Mandy could barely focus on her sister. She nodded, and muttered something incoherent.

Judy looked at Lewis, wanting to get this over with. 'I think I better identify the body, as my sister isn't up to it right now.'

Leaving Mandy in the care of a female liaison officer, Judy followed Lewis through a series of doors and into the viewing room. A white sheet was pulled over what was clearly a body laid out on a steel trolley.

Lewis yawned as Judy pulled the sheet down a few inches to look at the person lying there. She grimaced at the sight of his disfigured face. Even though the features were unrecognisable, Judy was relieved that Mandy hadn't insisted on identifying the body herself.

It was amazing what an extra handful of Valium could do.

Lewis looked at Judy. 'This should be the end of it now. Hopefully, it will shut your sister up.'

'Did he cause any problem?' Judy asked.

'No, we just picked him up from where you said he'd be. And then Charlie . . . well, he saw to the rest.'

Judy stared down at Kit, the tramp who regularly begged outside Vauxhall Station. She dreaded the sound of him rattling his tin cup as she walked past. He'd reached out a filthy hand once and grabbed hold of her, muttering that he had no family, and no place to call home. God knows, life on the streets was hard and dangerous. Violence commonplace. Well, this was one way to put him out of his misery.

Lewis made his way to his office, leaving Judy to bundle a weeping Mandy into her car. He was planning to collect his things and go home for the day. His headache was like a nagging bitch. Relentless. He needed to go and sleep it off. Closing his eyes for a moment, he let out a sigh. This had been a hell of a fucking year.

'Inspector.'

Lewis groaned and opened his eyes. 'What is it *now*?'

He turned around to see Timms, one of the control room sergeants. As usual, a cigarette hung out of the corner of his mouth, and a habitual squint distorted his lined features from the smoke drifting into his eyes. A solid beer gut hung over his unironed trousers. He scratched his crotch.

'This came in, sir.' He glanced over his shoulder before handing Lewis a note. 'I thought you might be interested in it.'

Lewis frowned, taking the piece of paper from Timms. He unfolded it, reading quickly. Yeah, this certainly was a hell of a year. And clearly it wasn't over yet.

'Do you know who called it in?' he demanded.

'No, sir. It came in the other day, apparently. It was an anonymous tip-off.'

Lewis mulled the information over. He reread the note carefully. A phone call about Dennis's car. About a child being bundled into his boot.

Who the hell could've known? Had someone been talking? Lewis knew all about Albie and what had happened to him. Not that he'd been directly involved, this time. The beauty of being part of the large group Lewis belonged to, which had members up and down the country, was their loyalty to one another. It also included sharing stories. Which was how he'd heard all about Albie, from Dennis and Frank.

'Thank you, Timms. I appreciate this. You're a good lad.' He patted him on his back gratefully.

'What would you like me to do with it, sir?'

He stared at Timms. Then crushed the note in his hand.

'We bury it.'

Chapter Fifty-Four

Alan ran down the stairs of Honey's nightclub, still fuming at the way he'd been manhandled. What those bastard coppers had done to him! He still had the cuts and bruises to prove it. Not only that, but they'd kept him banged up for the past couple of days like a fucking animal. He'd been stuck in an overheated cell with some stinking old wino who'd kept pissing and missing the toilet in the corner.

He was raging.

'Which one of you talked?' Alan yelled at the brothers.

Jason sat sipping a large brandy next to some tart with her tits hanging out.

'I see they finally let you out then, Al.'

'You think it's funny? Those cunts only just released me.'

Jason sniffed. 'You don't smell too good. And they've made a right mess of your face, ain't they?'

Alan dived forward, slamming his hands down on the table in front of Jason. He leant in, glaring. 'If anyone had seen me, my fucking reputation would be up the Swanee. None of this is a joke.'

Jason pushed Shelley off him. 'Do I look like I'm laughing?' He shoved Alan in the chest. 'Don't fucking come in here and give it the big one, Al. This is your mess . . .' He paused, recalling what

Alan had just said when he'd come in. 'Hold up, you think I bunnied? You think I'm a cunting grass?'

'I don't know what to think, do I?' Alan snarled.

Jason grabbed Alan by his jacket, bringing him close, and knocking over the small table between them, along with the drinks. He pulled his knife out from his back pocket, flicking open the blade.

He pushed the tip against Alan's lips. 'We've been here before, ain't we, mate? You ever imply that again, I'll cut your fucking tongue out. Understand me?' He pushed Alan with both hands

Alan stumbled backwards on to the sticky floor. He got up, wiping his hands on his trousers. 'I understand. But what I don't get, is why they let you lot out before me. I'm fucked if they can pin anything on me. That cunt Randall made it sound like someone's been talking.'

'And they have.' Jason shrugged matter-of-factly. 'Zef and Dren opened their mouths.'

Alan turned round on the spot. He pointed at Jason. 'You . . . you told me we could trust them.' Chewing on his lip, he shook his head. 'What the fuck, Jason, what the fuck . . . *Shit.*'

'We're sorting it.'

'How? How the fuck can you sort it?' Alan's face was red. 'I know I fucked up, but Christ Almighty, *this*, this is a shit show. You need to be careful who you do business with, Jason.'

'What the fuck did my brother just say to you, Al?' Jake had been quiet until this point, but now he stood up from his bar stool and sauntered over. 'He said it was all in hand, didn't he?'

Alan noticed Jake was drinking again. Whatever the hell was going on there, it wasn't good news. Alan had a long history with the Wakemans, and he remembered very clearly what Jake was like when he was on the booze.

'And what's *in hand* supposed to mean?' Alan demanded nastily.

Jake sneered with laughter. 'Listen, I'd be careful if I were you, no one's forgotten that you've been mugging us off as well. So don't play the hard-done-by bitch. No one wants a grass around, and the worst kind of grass for that matter. The kind that likes to save their own skin.'

Alan looked between the brothers. Even in the short time Jake had been drinking again, Alan could see he'd changed. There was an extra edge to him. A dangerous one. Something Jason no doubt appreciated.

'They ain't going to get away with it,' Jake promised. 'I've spoken to a few people, and it seems they're not happy either with having little birds knocking around that chirp. No one wants to do business when there's a firm around that's talking to the filth. But listen, Al, don't go too far. Expect a call later.'

Alan nodded and made his way out of the club, back down Walker's Court. He marched down Brewer Street, before turning into Wardour Street where a crowd of tourists milled around.

Alan barged through, shouldering people out of the way – he wasn't in the mood to take anyone's shit – and hurried down the street. At the crossroads he ran across Shaftesbury Avenue, weaving through the traffic, which was bumper to bumper. He made his way through Leicester Square, nodding at the concierge outside the private members' club on the corner of St Martin's Lane. The man tipped his hat and opened the door to let him in.

Making his way down the stairs, Alan stared across at the small group men standing and drinking at the bar, chatting and laughing.

He walked towards them.

'Well?' Lewis tilted his head to one side.

297

'The cunts fell for it. Hook, line and sinker. They really think it was Zef and Dren who grassed them up. They have no fucking idea. Pricks.'

'Alan, it's good to see you.' Detective Randall raised the glass of brandy he was drinking and grinned at him.

Alan glared. Everything had been a set-up, from start to finish, including the gunshot warning to Jake. It had actually been Charlie, Lewis's sidekick, who'd fired the gun.

But Alan's anger wasn't part of the set-up.

'Good to fucking see me? Look what you've done to my face, Randall. You could've split my skull open with that boot you put into my head.'

The police doctor had stitched up his forehead, but it was bloody painful. And they'd done a botched job of it; Alan was worried it would scar.

'And what's with keeping me in the fucking cell for so long, hey?'

Randall glanced at Lewis and smirked. He had crumbs in his moustache from the packet of ready-salted crisps in his hand. 'It worked, didn't it? I didn't know how great your acting skills were, Alan, so we had to make sure it looked authentic.' He shrugged, taking in Alan's battered face. 'Which we clearly did.' Randall laughed again and tapped his cigarette in the large crystal cut-glass ashtray. 'And the point is, Al, they fell for it.'

'Yeah, and I was nearly fucking killed in the meantime.'

'Oh, stop being such a fucking pussy. You wanted this to go away, and now it has.' Unconcerned about Alan's injuries, Randall shook his head and took a large mouthful of brandy.

Alan was now completely enraged. This whole idea had been Lewis's. After Alan had asked him for help, Lewis had come up with the plan. It had undoubtedly been a good one. The pressure

Zef and Dren were putting on the Wakemans to make sure the land deal went through – which, in turn, meant they were putting pressure on *him* – would now disappear. The Albanians would soon be a distant memory, if Jason had his way. And without the Albanians in the picture, it would be easier for Alan to keep the Wakemans sweet.

But there was no doubt in Alan's mind that everything Randall had done to him, including literally putting the boot in, had amused him no end. Sadistic fucking bastard. Lewis and he were certainly birds of a feather.

Alan held his temper in check and watched Lewis motion to the barman who was busily polishing the glasses. 'A bottle of champagne, please . . .' Lewis turned back to his companions and dug into his coat pocket, pulling out an envelope stuffed with money. He handed it to Randall. 'From Dennis, he appreciates your help on this . . . and thank your colleagues too. There's a little something in there for them as well.'

'You see, Al.' Randall narrowed his eyes, regarding Alan through the smoke of his cigarette. 'You should be thanking me, mate. We went to a lot of trouble for you and your shitty deal. The Wakemans think the Albanians grassed on them, which means you're off the hook, doesn't it?'

Lewis mockingly put his arm around Alan's shoulders. 'Not quite. He owes us now.'

Alan had no doubt that Lewis was serious. Out of the frying pan, into the fucking fire.

Chapter Fifty-Five

It was New Year's Eve, and Mandy had managed to make herself a pot of tea. She hadn't drunk it though. It sat on the table, going cold, surrounded by her belongings. Judy had helped her to pack them into boxes. She couldn't stay here any longer, not after what had happened to her Jimmy. There was nothing left for her in this house now. Staying was too painful. The idea that she'd have to sit among the memories for even another day was unthinkable.

He'd been the baby of the family. Little Jimmy, who'd always loved his mum. She knew Judy felt the same way about what had happened, though clearly her sister was better than her at hiding it.

Judy had arranged everything. Mandy was off to stay with her mate Janet, by the coast in Southend-on-Sea, for the time being. Once the house had been sold, she'd think about what to do next. Though for now, she couldn't think of anything beyond taking her next Valium.

There was a loud knock on the door, and Mandy was thankful for the interruption. Cigarette in hand, she struggled to the door. 'Just a minute, I'm coming!'

She opened it to see Becky and Larry, Jimmy's best mates, standing there.

'Thank you for coming.' As soon as Mandy spoke, she started crying again.

'I'm so sorry, Mrs Williams.' Becky's eyes were red from weeping. 'I can't believe it.' She snuffled loudly. 'I can't believe he's gone.'

Larry took over the conversation as Becky broke down on his shoulder. 'How are you doing?'

Mandy had always like Larry. 'I'll be better when I get away from this place . . . Anyway, here you go.'

Mandy stepped backed into the hallway. She pointed at a large cardboard box with a lid, along with Jimmy's metal detector.

'These are his things. I know he'd like you to have them. There's not much. His metal-detecting magazines, coins, bits and pieces, some records. You know what Jimmy was like, he loved to collect rubbish.'

'Are you sure, Mrs Williams?' Larry, although genuinely in pain from Jimmy's death, was trying not to look too delighted at being gifted his things, in particular Jimmy's metal detector. 'You might want all this one day.'

Mandy shook her head. 'No. Please, take it with you. Keep it, throw it away, do what you like . . .'

It suddenly all became too much for her. Images of the last few days were jumbled in her mind, along with memories of Jimmy as a baby, a toddler, a teenager . . . the young man she'd never see grow older.

Larry was mumbling his thanks as Mandy shut the door on his conversation. Holding her head in her hands, she slid down the wall, collapsing into a heap. It had been heartbreaking clearing his stuff out, and now it was over. Her son was dead.

Though as Mandy rocked and wailed in the empty hallway of her house in Fox Road, one item she had failed to mention to Becky and Larry was the piece of bone she'd found in Jimmy's drawer and had thrown into the box of his things.

Chapter Fifty-Six

Alan Carver was standing on the plot of land which had caused him so much grief. He stood on the side of a deep, muddy trench next to Jason and Jake. He looked down and smiled inwardly at the sight of Zef and Dren, who were bound and gagged, struggling helplessly in the dirt at the bottom. He'd arranged for a set of trenches to be dug earlier in the day. No one would question why a digger had spent the afternoon excavating a channel in the ground.

'I can't hear you? You best speak louder, mate?' Jason mocked them. 'What's that, Zef? You're sorry that you're a pair of grassing cunts, are you?'

Muffled noises came from the two men. Their eyes were wide and their pupils dilated, bulging with fear.

Jason roared with laughter. He was having the time of his life. No one was going to get the better of him, especially not these two. There'd be no repercussions, he'd made sure of that. Word had got round that the Albanians had grassed the Wakemans up. No one doubted it. A grass was the lowest form of scum. If Jason hadn't done it, they'd be dead meat anyway.

But that didn't mean Alan and the Wakemans had kissed and made up. Jason and Jake were still fucked off with him. Alan still owed them, after all the shit that had gone down.

Jake looked at his brother. He didn't bother saying anything. He had known all along that doing business with the Albanians was a stupid move. At least now, with this business behind them, he could look to the future. In more ways than one.

The weather was starting to change now, from snow to rain, and Alan gestured to a waiting concrete mixer. The drum was spinning noisily. Ten tons of fresh, wet cement sloshed around inside. The vehicle started backing up to the trench, with the orange lights flashing on the roof. The loud warning beeper sounded as it reversed slowly. It came to a stop inches from the trench.

Frank, wrapped up in his favourite red lumber jacket, climbed down from the driver's cab and walked to the back of the lorry. He blew on the tips of his fingers, to try to warm them up, and winked at Alan. Frank roared with laughter as Alan glowered back at him. Alan had fucked up badly, and with that cunt on the hook with so many people, Frank thought it was the best possible way to end what had turned out to be a very profitable year.

Frank swung the lorry's large metal chute out over the trench, and aimed it directly above Zef and Dren. He held his hand over the control panel, waiting for Jason to give him the nod to release the cement.

'So, I reckon this is *arrivederci* . . . I'll see you in hell.' Jason hawked up and spat a copious gob of phlegm at Zef and Dren. He nodded towards Frank, who pressed the green button on the side of the lorry.

A hydraulic pump began to lift the huge, spinning barrel of concrete, tipping its contents on to Zef and Dren.

Satisfied, and feeling no spark of pity for the Albanians, Alan walked away, leaving Jason and Jake to it. By the morning the whole plot would be concreted over. Just like Dennis had wanted. Secrets and betrayals would be buried together. All was not lost after all.

He strolled along the Embankment and around Pedlar's Park, not missing a beat. He breathed out, then in, taking the freezing air into his lungs. Fuck, it felt good. He'd got away with it. Even if it *had* been touch and go at times.

Jason had made it clear he was still pissed off, but the brothers had accepted this is how it was. He didn't even owe them money any more. The Old Bill regularly confiscated the booty they found and shared it out between them. Lewis's team had enjoyed a bumper year. He'd simply ordered them to hand over some of the spoils to him, to give to the Wakemans. Alan chuckled to himself. The police were as crooked as any villain he knew.

Alan came to a sudden halt. He stared across to the other side of the river. The Palace of Westminster. He didn't want a life of almosts and nearlys and could haves. No, he was going to make it happen, no matter what he had to do. He could virtually smell the green leather of his seat in parliament, and he felt the stirrings of an erection. The anticipation of power was a heady aphrodisiac

He checked his watch. It was nearly midnight.

He smiled to himself. All's well that ends well. And it had.

As long as Alan didn't ask himself the question: what would everyone demand of him in return?

Chapter Fifty-Seven

It was a couple of minutes to midnight and Samantha stared at her mother. Phyllis was happily downing a bottle of cream sherry. Samantha had already finished off the bottle of red she'd bought for herself. She was beginning to sober up now, which was making the evening excruciating.

She'd painted her nails a bright red, but hadn't been bothered to do her toes. She wasn't going anywhere.

Phyllis glared at her. 'Can't you take that bloody look off your face?'

Samantha rolled her eyes. 'I'll go and change it at the shop for you, shall I, Mum?'

'Don't take it out on me because your old man is shagging half the toms in London.'

Phyllis was vicious when she had a drink inside her. A vindictive cow. She stared spitefully at her daughter.

'And don't look shocked either, it's not news to you, is it?' She took another large gulp of sherry, and a bite of a mince pie, before saying, 'But you've only got yourself to blame. If you looked after Jason the way he should be looked after, he might be here with you now. But instead, you drive him away. You don't have the sense to keep a good man . . . you should be ashamed of yourself.'

That was it.

Samantha grabbed her coat. 'And before you ask, Mum, I'm going out to get a breath of fresh air, before I do something I'll regret . . .'

Phyllis narrowed her eyes. 'Threaten an old woman, would you?'

'If the old woman is anything like you, *yes*, yes, I bloody well would. And you don't need to call Jason to tell him either, because I'll be right outside.'

Samantha slammed out of the front door and stood in the garden, breathing in the cold night air.

It was always the same: seeing in the new year with her mother, listening to Phyllis complaining about everything she did. Well, this year, she refused to listen to the chimes of midnight with her.

God, what she wouldn't do to get out of here! Without a hint of self-pity, Samantha realised everyone was moving on, apart from her. Even Kit seemed to have done that. She usually gave him a Christmas card with a bit of money in it, but he'd clearly moved on too. Though Samantha wished him nothing but luck.

'Hello, you.'

She snapped her head around to see Jake. A smile played on Samantha's lips, and her heart beat faster, like a love-struck teenager. His hair, that crooked smile, the way he looked at her . . . Samantha had never stop loving him.

'What are you doing here?'

Jake winked. 'Don't worry, I left your husband with his head between Shelley's legs. We're celebrating a bit of finished business.'

In truth, while Jason had set about snorting coke and celebrating with Kitty and Shelley, Jake had knocked back a brandy. He was sure he could keep it under control. Although it wasn't about *how much* he drank, it was about what *happened* when he drank.

Samantha looked at Jake. She didn't care about Jason, she didn't give a flying fuck what he was doing. She glanced up at the moon, and her thoughts unexpectedly turned to Holly Brookes. As difficult as it was, she had to close the chapter on Grace now. She'd tried everything she could think of to help her. Grace's godmother hadn't been in contact, and it was clear that she couldn't do anything to move her out of Holly Brookes. It had been a waste of time driving down there. All she could do was hope that Grace was all right, and try not to dwell on it.

'Let's make this next year special.' Jake stroked Samantha's face.

The booze helped Jake wash his hands of the guilt he might have felt, knowing he was in love with his brother's wife. But it also stopped him recognising the danger he and Samantha might be in.

'You and me, darlin'. Like it always should have been.'

'Yeah, I'd like that.'

In the distance a cheer went up to mark the new year.

Samantha stood on her tiptoes, kissing Jake on the lips, trying to push away the sense that trouble was just around the corner.

Chapter Fifty-Eight

Gracie and Dara stood by the window in the evening light, watching the snow fall. The other girls in the dormitory played clap-hands, singing the song Gracie had taught them. Dara was pleased that Brenda had come to join them. Unlike Connie and the bitches she hung around with, the girls in her dormitory didn't want to fight; they were all just trying to survive.

Foolishly, Dara had hoped that something would've been done about Albie. But only yesterday she'd seen Dennis walking around the grounds with the new gardener, a man she recognised as one of his cronies, a man called Frank. It had turned her stomach to see them laughing and joking. She just had to believe that Albie would turn up one day. And that Dennis and the others would get what was coming to them.

She sighed and shook her head to dispel the thoughts about Albie. It was too raw. Instead, Dara thought back to last New Year's Eve. She certainly hadn't been playing clap-hands. She'd been trying to find some money for nappies, begging for hand-outs from the neighbours, knowing her mum would spend it on skag.

She didn't know how to feel about her mum dying. Dara couldn't even begin to get her head around it. She'd blocked so much out as a youngster, to protect herself over the years. Each night, before she closed her eyes, Dara said a silent prayer for her brothers and sisters. But she was having to teach herself not to think about them either. It was too painful. Every time her siblings came to mind, the feelings of anxiety would rush up inside her. The only way to stop it was to hurt herself, or take a few of the pills they kept dishing out to her. At least they made Dara feel removed from what was going on in her head.

'Do you think I'll hear about my mum soon?' Gracie clutched her hands together.

'I'm sure you will, babe.' Dara gently moved Gracie's hair out of her eyes. 'These things take time, don't they?'

Gracie paused for a moment. She looked thoughtful. 'You reckon we'll be fine, Dar? Being here, you think we'll be all right in this place?'

Dara held Gracie's gaze. She'd noticed Gracie was withdrawing into herself, day by day, not really wanting to talk about anything to do with the outside world. She was even quieter than before, and she had these weird little habits. Tidying, straightening things, making sure everything was a certain way. And if it wasn't, Dara could see how upset and agitated Gracie got.

Dara wasn't sure if they would be all right. This place was evil. No question. And there'd been no news from Gracie's mum, had there? Dara couldn't understand why? *Why* had no one told Gracie anything at all? Something wasn't right.

Dara took Gracie's hand. She wasn't going to say what she was thinking.

'We've got each other, ain't we? So, yeah, I *know* we're going to be all right. You and me.'

The light was switched on.

Clemence and Barrows stood in the doorway, swaying drunk.

They grinned, leering.

'Happy New Year, everyone. I thought we could have a celebration together, to see the new year in.' Barrows slurred his words.

Gracie flinched and started to tremble, and Dara stood rooted to the spot. She whispered to Gracie. 'Whatever happens, Gracie, just look at me. Keep looking at me, okay?'

Barrows staggered over to them. 'Happy New Year, Grace . . .'

He grabbed Gracie by the arm, pulling her towards him.

Clemence grabbed hold of Dara.

'Dar, Dar . . . *Dar!*'

While the other girls in the dormitory screamed, Dara struggled, but she couldn't get away.

She yelled to Grace. 'Gracie! Gracie, remember what I said . . . Look at me . . . whatever you do, just keep on looking at me . . .'

Book Three

1985
March

He tears me in his wrath, and hates me; he gnashes at me
with his teeth, my adversary sharpens his gaze on me.

Job 16: 9

Chapter Fifty-Nine

'Denny, *hurry up!* Fucking hell, I've seen faster slugs.' Barry laughed hard. He raced through the rain, darting between the trees.

It was a cold, wet March day, and they'd been playing hide-and-seek in the woods that formed part of the vast Holly Brookes estate. As usual, they'd lost track of the time. Now they were late for supper, and Barry knew they'd be in trouble.

Not that he cared. Barry was all about having fun. Playing with his mate was worth the grief – and the beating he'd get from Clemence. That was his life, and he just accepted it.

'Slow down, Baz!' Denny struggled to keep up.

He was certainly no match for Barry. He reckoned Baz was the fastest runner in Holly Brookes.

'No chance.'

'Going to catch you up, mate!' Giggling hysterically, Denny pumped his arms as hard as he could. He barely noticed that he was soaking wet.

'You wish!' Tasting the rain in his mouth, Barry panted and roared with laughter. He looked over his shoulder. 'You ain't ever going—'

His words were lost as he tripped over, tumbling forward in the air. He splashed down hard in the thick mud, knocking all the breath out of his body.

As Barry sat up, all he could hear was the rain pattering down, and Denny pissing himself laughing. He scowled for a moment, then thought better of it, and began to laugh as well.

'What a muppet!' Denny held his stomach, he was laughing so hard. 'Look at the state of you, Clemence is going to kill you, Baz, when he sees you!'

Barry threw a handful of mud at Denny. 'He can fuck off. It ain't my fault if I trip over a bloody tree, is it?'

He glanced around. The earth was saturated from the heavy rains – it had been one of the wettest months for a long while – and the woods were muddy and water-logged.

Barry's eyebrows snapped together. What the hell was that over there? There was something sticking out of the ground.

Standing up, he walked across slowly to the tree. 'Oh my God, oh fuck . . .'

'What? What is it?' Seeing Barry's face, Denny became serious too.

Barry stepped back. It wasn't a tree root he'd tripped over.

Fear rushed through him.

A few feet away from where he and Denny were standing, a decomposed body was pushing up through the mud.

Chapter Sixty

It was nearly eleven o clock at night when Barrows made the call about the discovery to Miller.

Miller, in turn, made the call to Lewis.

Lewis then phoned Dennis, to get his instructions.

Alan owed them, Dennis told Lewis.

And Frank, well, Frank was always happy to help.

Chapter Sixty-One

Alan Carver covered his mouth with the collar of his leather coat, trying not to vomit. He'd already retched a couple of times, and he was sure any minute now he was about to lose the entire contents of his stomach.

Frank was standing in the pouring rain in the middle of the woods, rubbing his hands together. He sneered at Alan from beneath his flap cap, the rain dripping from the brim 'You're like a fucking woman, Al.'

Alan felt too queasy to get into a ruck with Frank. There was no talking to fucking idiots anyway. Frank wasn't worth a cold cup of piss, and the less they had to say to each other, the better.

They had a job to do. Not that he'd wanted to do it, but Lewis hadn't given him any choice. He'd called him yesterday, telling him to pick up Frank and drive down to Holly Brookes. And now here they were. Christ.

Swallowing hard, he closed his eyes. How had it fucking come to this? Someone like *him*, having to be a fucking cleaner. Tidying up other people's shit.

It wasn't the first time Lewis and Dennis had snapped their fingers, expecting Alan to jump when they said 'jump'. The small seed of resentment he'd been harbouring had turned into white-hot hatred over these past couple of years. They continually used him to do their shit, like he was some fucking two-bit whore.

But what really pissed him off – something he'd been ruminating over lately – was the fact that at the heart of this shit was Dennis and his sick goings-on. There was a potential fallout as long as the fucking Thames, and being here in the woods, standing in nearly an inch of mud, just went to prove that.

Alan opened his eyes to see Frank standing directly in front of him – inches away – dressed in his dark blue wax jacket. The man's breath was rancid.

'Help me pick him up, Al.'

'Are you fucking kidding me?'

'Just *do* it.'

Alan didn't like the way Frank was speaking to him. 'I never signed up for any of this, pal.'

Frank smirked. 'And yet you're here. Now grab his fucking legs.'

Alan didn't move. He looked down.

The heavy rains had caused the earth to push up the body. Worms and insects had made it their home. The mud had partly preserved the corpse, but the way it had rotted, and the flesh had partly decomposed, gave the body a more disturbing look. It was semi-clothed: a jumper and jacket were still present, but there was no sign of trousers or pants.

'Doesn't it bother you, even in the slightest?'

Frank scratched his ear. 'Why the fuck would it?'

Alan held Frank's stare for a good few moments, appalled. 'You really don't know, do you?'

Frank appeared to be fucking clueless. Clueless that the body they were moving was that of his nephew, Jimmy.

Dennis had told Alan to keep his mouth shut. No, he wasn't

going to say anything, it was more than his life was worth. Not for the first time, Alan thought how much Dennis enjoyed playing games with them all. Pulling strings no one even knew were there, most of the time.

It was raining hard now, and almost dark. He was feeling edgy about getting caught. 'I'm not happy about being here, so let's fucking hurry up and do this, shall we?'

'That's exactly what I've been saying.' Frank chuckled.

Alan picked up the remains of Jimmy's legs, while Frank took the torso. They tried to lift his decayed body into the wheelbarrow Frank had taken out of the Holly Brookes gardening shed. It was trickier than they'd anticipated. Jimmy's height made it difficult to fit his body into the wheelbarrow. On their fourth attempt, they managed it.

Frank knew the woods well. He pushed the wheelbarrow towards where they'd parked the car, with Alan following behind.

Jimmy's hand dropped over the side of the barrow, dragging along the ground as the wheel sunk into the mud, making it hard-going for Frank. Eventually, they reached the lane.

'Wait there, I'll check no one's coming.' Alan hurried out on to the narrow country road. It was deserted, and he signalled the all-clear to Frank.

At the car, Alan stared at the boot of Frank's brown Vauxhall Cavalier. 'He's not going to fit in here, is he? What the fuck!' His heart was hammering hard. It would only take one car to come round the corner, and then they'd be discovered. 'Come on, hurry up, Frank. I want to get out of here.'

Frank shoved Alan out of the way. He glared at him. 'Stop fucking panicking, Al.' He grabbed a large, thick plastic sheet out of the boot along with some gaffer tape.

For a moment, Alan frowned, distracted by a rolled-up, tatty yellow ball of what appeared to be some sort of children's fancy-dress costume, stained with streaks of reddish brown, tucked at the back of the boot.

'Oi, Al. Keep your eyes on the prize.' Frank threw the sheet on the ground. 'Tip him up . . . come on, tip him up.'

Alan did just that, and Jimmy's body slopped out of the barrow.

Frank, using all his strength, grabbed Jimmy's leg, bending it upwards towards what had once been his face. He pushed down with all his weight, breaking what was left of Jimmy's limbs, making his whole body more compact. And without missing a beat, he rolled him up in the sheet, wrapping it tightly with the gaffer tape.

'Are you going to help me, Al? Or are you just going to stand there like a prick?' Frank wiped the rain from his face.

Seething with anger and revulsion, Alan assisted Frank to lift the bundle and throw Jimmy into the boot.

'I'll dispose of him later.' Frank locked the car, pulled out a packet of Benson & Hedges from his coat pocket, smiled and lit a cigarette. 'After all that hard work, I fancy a drink. What do you say, Al?'

Alan wouldn't normally have gone anywhere with Frank. But right now, a stiff drink was absolutely needed. Or several.

He pulled the cigarette from Frank's muddy fingers and took a deep, long drag. 'Where's the pub?'

Chapter Sixty-Two

Dara was wondering where she'd seen the man in the corner before. He was busily knocking back shots of whiskey as if his life depended on it. She certainly knew the bastard he was sitting with. She often saw Frank around the grounds of Holly Brookes these days. He was the full-time gardener and handyman now. But she also knew what else he was.

Dara turned away. She didn't want her vibe to be brought down. There was a good atmosphere in the pub tonight. It was packed, and cigarette smoke and music filled the air. Everyone, including herself, was having a good time.

Her head was swimming. The booze in her system, as well as the pills, made her feel warm. She reached across the table to grab a handful of peanuts. Even in her merry stupor, Dara was still self-conscious about the dozens of self-harm marks on her arm. She quickly pulled down her sleeve, and popped the peanuts in her mouth.

'You all right, Gracie? You're going for it tonight, ain't you?'

'I am a bit.' Grace smiled at Dara and threw back another vodka, enjoying the heat of the burn.

Saturday was definitely their favourite day. Barrows and Clemence went off drinking to the pub in the next village along, together with most of the house parents. Which meant they didn't reappear until late Sunday afternoon because most of the time, they were nursing their hangovers.

Gracie and Dara were under age. But a faceful of make-up, skanky cast-offs and a fuckload of attitude meant no one challenged them. And the local publican was happy to serve them. What did he care if the little scrubbers wanted to get off their faces? Barrows knew the older kids regularly snuck out on a Saturday night. Not that he gave a fuck either. Just as long as they avoided the pub where he was drinking, and were back by midnight.

'Fancy another vody, Gracie?' Dara giggled, looking at her friend from underneath her messy fringe. 'Hey, Robbie, get Gracie another drink, will you? And you can get me one too while you're at it.'

'Ah, what! I'm broke.' Robbie pulled a face.

Dara blew a kiss across the table to him. 'Liar. Don't you love us?'

Robbie blushed. 'Shut up, Dar.'

Gracie rested her head on Dara's shoulder, her warm eyes focused on Robbie. 'What do you reckon, D? You reckon his pockets are full of dough? I saw him doing some errands for Father Michaels, so I bet he's loaded. Think we should mug him?'

Gracie leapt forward and started tickling Robbie. The girls cackled as he turned an even deeper shade of red.

From the other side of the pub, Frank took a sip of his Guinness.

He glowered at the girls. 'Fucking slags. They're from Holly Brookes.' He threw a quick glance at Alan. 'They come in here most Saturday nights. Noisy little fuckers.' He grinned, showing off his broken, stained yellow teeth. 'Why don't you get in there, Al? They're easy meat. They'll open their legs for an escaped fart.' He let out a gruff, phlegmy laugh. 'Go on, crack on, they won't say no.' He nodded towards Robbie. 'It's just a pity the boy's growing up now . . . Still, plenty of fish and all that.'

Time might have moved on, but not Alan's loathing for Frank. 'Haven't you got any fucking shame?'

Frank took another sip of Guinness and thought about it. He shook his head slowly. 'Don't kid yourself, Al. You and I are both the same. Just because you don't eat the deer, doesn't mean you didn't help to shoot it.'

Alan knocked back another shot of whiskey in response. He could smell death on his clothes. He also felt sick. He'd drunk too much, and he was feeling wasted from the half-tablet of ecstasy he'd popped a short while ago.

'I need to go for a slash.'

Frank nodded. 'Outside . . .'

'For fuck's sake.' Alan stumbled towards the exit. 'What happened to being civilised?'

Gracie moved her chair slightly, frowning at the man who'd just pushed past her without bothering to apologise. She looked around, not that she could see very far. Holly Brookes had never bothered getting her a replacement pair of glasses. She'd stopped asking, a long time ago. Like she'd stopped asking about her mum. Or anything to do with the outside world. She couldn't . . . she couldn't even go there. Feeling the familiar pain in her stomach as the box opened in her head, Gracie quickly pushed down the unwelcome thoughts, concentrating instead on the night out.

'Oh fuck, I love this song.' Dara suddenly sprang up, laughing and singing loudly. '*You spin me right round, baby, right round . . .*' She yelled, out of tune, at the top of her voice, above the music.

A few of the customers stared at her, but she took no notice.

She didn't care. No one was going to stop her having a good time.

'Come on, girl, dance with me. Gracie, come on! Oh, don't be such an old woman, Gracie, please . . .' She began to drag Gracie up on to her feet.

'I'm too lazy, Dar!' Gracie let out a stream of laughter.

Gracie's giggles were contagious, and Robbie soon joined in.

'Hey, Connie, come over here!' Dara waved to a group of kids in the corner. 'Come and join us.'

Robbie frowned, looking up at Dara from where he was seated. 'What do you want to bring them over here for?'

She winked at Robbie. 'The more people, the better the party, doll!'

Connie frowned and called back across the pub snarkily, 'I'm picky about who I drink with.'

Dara twirled around. 'Yeah, that's why you're with that lot, is it?' She pointed to Connie's friends, who were all A-grade bitches. Then, not giving any more energy to them, Dara set about pulling Gracie up on her feet to dance.

'Gracie, *please*.' She grinned and gazed into Gracie's eyes.

At fourteen, Gracie was beginning to blossom and come out of her shell. Gone was the puppyish, shy girl, and in her place stood a confident, kind, slender girl. But there was also a part of Gracie which had retreated. A part Dara couldn't ever reach. She loved Gracie so much. She wouldn't have got this far if it wasn't for Gracie. Gracie was her reason to stay alive.

Gracie looked back at Dara and laughed.

They were joined at the hip. The best of friends, and God, Gracie couldn't love Dara more. The whole time they'd been in Holly Brookes, Dara had been the one to fight for them. Dara had battled for herself, but had also taken on Gracie's battles, by putting herself in the line of fire with Barrows and Clemence. Gracie had no doubt that Dara was the reason she was still here. She couldn't have survived without her.

But Gracie was worried about her friend. She knew that Dara drank a lot, nicking the booze from Barrows and Father Michaels. Not that they'd notice. Every week crates of beer were delivered for the house parents to share out between themselves. Dara went to bed drunk a lot of nights. And then there were the pills they dished out daily, simply to try to keep her quiet.

'Okay, okay, fine, I'll dance with you, after I've had a pee.' Gracie stood up, kissed Dara on the cheek, and pushed through the crowd.

Dara was too busy dancing to bother answering her.

'Last orders, everyone, please!'

There was a rush towards the bar, triggering Dara to glance around. Sweat ran down her back and her cheeks were flushed. She was happily drunk, and she swayed on her feet gently, trying to focus. She couldn't see Gracie or Robbie. Where'd they gone?

Connie was over in the corner with her mates, chatting to a few blokes.

'Con, have you seen Gracie?'

Connie stuck two fingers up as her reply.

Dara ignored it and continued to search for Gracie. Singing to herself, she headed for the other side of the pub. By the double glass doors leading out to the small car park, Dara caught sight of someone running.

Grace burst in. Looking shell-shocked.

'Grace?' Dara stared at her friend. 'Gracie, oh my God, what's the matter? What's happened?'

Gracie's top was torn, exposing her bra. Her skirt was hitched up and Dara could see red marks on her neck.

Dara felt the panic began to rise. 'Gracie, tell me what happened, baby.' She shouted, trying to make herself heard over the beat of the loud music. She stepped towards Gracie, taking in the dishevelled state of her. The blank look in her eyes.

A second later, Robbie ran in. Dara stared at him.

'Rob? Robbie, what the fuck happened to Gracie—' She stopped, noticing how upset Robbie looked. 'Rob, are you okay? What happened to Gracie . . . Rob?' Her words rushed out.

Robbie looked drawn, and he gave a tiny shake of the head.

'I said, *what the fuck happened?*'

And right then, Alan staggered in, doing up his zip. He was off his face on E. He wiped his mouth, and leered at Gracie, giving her a wink. 'You all right, babe?' He laughed.

A cold realisation hit Dara. She rushed at Alan, slapping his face. 'You bastard. You fucking bastard!'

Chapter Sixty-Three

'Leave it, Dar, *please*. Don't make it worse.' Gracie wept, while Robbie put his arms around her.

'Are you fucking kidding me? After what he's just done to you?' Dara raged.

Frank roared with laughter, patting Alan on the back.

'Alan, come on, let's leave these dirty bitches to it.'

'You're not going to get away with this.' Dara jabbed her finger in the air at Alan.

Frank grabbed hold of her hand, twisting it around. 'Your mate wanted it, just like you all do . . . Hey, Robbie.'

Incensed, Dara pulled herself out of Frank's grip, pushing him hard in the chest. 'Fuck off!'

Not caring that people were starting to look across, Frank continued to roar with laughter. 'Don't pretend you girls don't love it. Especially you.' He narrowed his stare and directed his words at Dara. 'Yeah, we all know how you always put up a fight, but you're really gagging for it.'

Tears pricked Dara's eyes. She wanted to kill him, and she flew at Frank, but Robbie held her back.

'One day, mate, you're going to get what's coming to you . . . Both of you are, you fucking bastards!' She screamed at Alan, who still had a stupid grin on his face.

Frank shrugged. He was half-cut and leered at them, showing off his nicotine-stained teeth. 'Piss off, before I report you to Barrows.' He looked towards the exit. 'Hey, Robbie, fancy one for old times' sake?'

Robbie shrank back, and this time Dara lunged at both men. But once again, Robbie stepped forward to pull her back.

'Dar, stop, *stop!* Leave it,' Gracie urged Dara. '*Please.* Let's just go.'

'You should listen to your friend, darlin',' Alan mumbled, barely coherent, still buzzing from the E.

The two men stumbled out of the pub.

Dara turned to Gracie, trying to hide her distress. 'What did he do, babe?' Though Dara could guess.

Gracie shook her head. 'I don't want to talk about it. I want to go back to the dorm.' She rearranged her clothes as best as she could.

'Rob, what did you see? Did you clock what he did?' Dara asked him gently.

A flash of anger crossed Gracie's face. 'I said, *leave it.*'

'But—'

'No,' Gracie interrupted. She wiped away her tears. 'No bloody *but*, Dara.'

Dara's stare criss-crossed Gracie's face. She was upset and frustrated. 'I only want to help. How the fuck is it okay for them to go around doing what they want to us?'

'It's not okay.' Gracie's voice shook. 'But that doesn't mean it's okay for you either, *not* to leave it.'

Dara took hold of Gracie's hands, but she pulled away.

'I can't bear the fact that he hurt you, Gracie. I'm so fucking angry.'

Gracie was crying hard now. 'This isn't about you, Dara. It's about *me*, and I won't tell you again, *just leave it.*'

Dara watched Gracie march out of the pub, with Robbie trailing dejectedly behind.

What Gracie had said was true: it wasn't about her. But that didn't stop Dara wondering how she could get her own back on Alan.

Chapter Sixty-Four

It was still dark outside, but the morning light threatened to break through.

Samantha turned over and smiled. 'Hello, sleepyhead.'

Jake smiled back. He stretched forward to kiss Samantha on her nose. 'Hey, you. Did you sleep well?'

'Yeah, did you?'

'Well, I might have done if you hadn't been snoring all night.'

Samantha laughed. 'We've talked about this before, I do *not* snore.'

'Yeah you do, babe. Oh God, you do . . .'

She slapped him playfully.

'But you know what, you could snore like a fucking Tyrannosaurus Rex, but that wouldn't stop me loving you, Sam. Nothing will. Ain't nothing going to come between us again.'

He stroked her hair, then moved in to kiss her on the nape of her neck.

Samantha shuddered and closed her eyes, responding to him. His lips pressed passionately against hers, and she kissed him back, feeling loved, and letting herself fall into the moment. She thought of nothing else, only Jake, as he moved down her body, his tongue circling her nipples, making her gasp.

Samantha opened her eyes to see him looking tenderly at her.

'You all right, doll?'

She grinned. 'I couldn't be better.'

His thick hair flopped endearingly over his forehead. His naked, muscular body lay on top of hers.

Samantha felt every part of him as he entered her slowly. She caught her breath again, responding to his touch in rhythmic motions, letting Jake take her mind and body to another place.

An hour later, Jake watched Samantha sleep. He smiled to himself. But in truth, his mind was already thinking about the day ahead.

Jason was away on business, arranging a shipment of coke, and he needed to get to the club early. There were contracts to be sorted, boring stuff, but the council had been breathing down their necks recently, keen to make good on a pledge to clean up the bars and clubs in Soho. Jase wanted to tell them to fuck off. Or tap someone in the council; pay them off, so they wouldn't have any hassle. But Honey's was the *one* legitimate business they had, and Jake wanted to keep it sweet. Everything above board, like it had been for the past couple of years.

Jake sighed and pulled on his dark denim jeans. He dressed quickly and slipped on his shoes. He crept out, closing the bedroom door behind him, and tiptoed downstairs, avoiding the last but one step. He'd learnt which one creaked.

As the days, weeks and months of sneaking around had gone by, and the affair with Samantha had intensified, his priorities had changed.

There was still that loyalty to Jason; that pull to be at his brother's side. And yet, he knew his relationship with Sam was the deepest betrayal of them all. Like knifing his brother in the back.

He loved Samantha, but that didn't excuse him from shitting on the ties that bound him. He and Jase were brothers. Blood and bone, to the very end. He'd tried to stay away from Sam – and Christ, he knew better than anyone how he'd struggled with his guilt over it – but Samantha was like a drug to him. And the drugs, like the booze, had won through.

'Jake?'

With his hand on the front door, Jake froze. His blood ran cold as Phyllis's voice broke through the silence.

'Jake, I'm in here.'

Jake turned and headed for the kitchen. Phyllis was sitting at the table, wrapped in a brown nylon dressing gown. Her two walking sticks rested against her large thigh. Her thin grey hair was tightly curled around small rollers and covered in a pink hairnet.

She pulled out a Silk Cut from the packet on the table and lit it, staring at Jake.

He kept his expression neutral.

She took a long drag on her cigarette. 'Make me a cup of tea. I think it's time we had a talk, don't you?'

Dutifully, Jake did as he was told. He filled up the kettle and flicked it on. Without saying anything, he opened the cupboard and took out two mugs. Grabbing the tea bags out of the tin, he threw them into the cups, added some milk and poured the boiling water on.

He slammed the cups down on the table, not bothering to stir them. Pushed one across to Phyllis and said, 'How long have you known?'

Phyllis's small, beady eyes narrowed. The cool chill of the March morning had made its way into the kitchen, and she took another drag of the cigarette. 'So you're not denying it then?'

'Would there be any point?'

The corner of Phyllis's mouth began to twitch. 'You're not as stupid as you look, Jake.' She smirked at him.

He didn't have time for this shit. He needed to know what the sanctimonious old cow wanted. 'This chat is all very lovely, Phyllis, but what's your game?'

'It's simple really. I want you gone. I want you out of Samantha's life for good. And the only way for that to happen, is to put as much distance as possible between you. I don't care what you do, or where you go, as long as you stay away from my daughter.'

Jake leant back in his chair and regarded Phyllis evenly. 'That's never going to happen.'

Phyllis knew exactly what she was doing. She'd thought about this moment for a while now. She'd waited just long enough.

She was enjoying seeing Jake squirm. Like a cornered rat.

Holding Jake's stare, she put out her cigarette and immediately lit another one. She pushed the dog-eared notebook across the table.

'Every date and every time.' She tapped on the cover. 'It's recorded in here . . . I've been his eyes and ears. Just like your brother asked.'

Jake blanched. He'd had no idea that Jase was using his mother-in-law to spy on him.

'Why now, Phyllis?' He glared furiously at the notebook. 'Why leave it until fucking now?'

Phyllis sucked her ill-fitting false teeth and contemplated the question. 'Because you've got comfortable.' She grimaced. 'And my daughter's happy.'

Jake stared at her in disbelief. 'You say that like it's a bad thing.'

'It is . . . when the person she's happy with isn't her husband. So you need to leave her well alone. I want you gone today, Jake. And don't come back.'

'And what am I supposed to tell Jase?'

'Anything you like. Because the alternative is me telling him what you've been up to.'

'You vindictive fucking old witch.'

Phyllis cackled. She had Jake by the balls, and by God, she was going to squeeze them.

Jake sat on the chair, trying to control his breathing. 'Jason is *never* going to accept me clearing off without a proper explanation.'

Phyllis shrugged. 'Then don't give him one.'

Jason rubbed his forehead. He clearly couldn't believe this was happening to him. He was being run out of town.

'So this is what you're going to do . . .' Phyllis had the upper hand now. 'You're going to clear out the joint business bank accounts, take all the money I don't doubt you have in various safes, as well as anything else of value. When Jason gets back from his little business trip tomorrow, he'll think you're a low-life thieving piece of scum, rather than a cheating one.'

Jake looked at her with hate-filled eyes. 'You've thought this all through, ain't you?'

Phyllis blew her cigarette smoke in his face. A twinkle appeared in her eyes.

'He's my brother, Phyllis. He's never going to believe I just suddenly woke up one morning and robbed him,' Jake objected.

Phyllis reached across and grabbed Jake's hands. Her hatred for him gave her a youthful strength, and she squeezed hard. 'The same brother whose wife you're bedding . . . Oh, trust me, Jake, I'm sure he'll believe it, once he sees you've made off with his dough. And as for Sam, tell her any old flannel . . . but you keep your mouth shut about this conversation. Understand?'

Jake couldn't bear to sit opposite her any longer. He got up and marched towards the door.

333

Phyllis's next words held him back.

'And Jake, if you're not gone by this evening, I'll tell your brother everything. It's your choice. But if you love my daughter, you won't try anything stupid. Because we both know if Jase finds out, not only will he kill you, but he'll kill Samantha as well.'

Chapter Sixty-Five

Samantha slipped her clutch bag under her arm and hurried down Kennington Road.

It was only five o'clock, but she wanted to be early. She'd taken the day off work, though most of it had been spent running errands for her mother. Phyllis had been in a strangely good mood, which always made Samantha suspicious. Still, she wouldn't worry about that now; she was just grateful she'd managed to get out of the house without a thousand questions.

Turning up Lambeth Road and heading for the bridge, Samantha tried not to worry about Jase coming back tomorrow. She didn't want it to spoil her mood. Instead, she wanted to make the most of her last evening with Jake for a while.

Jake wouldn't be able to stay over tonight, in case Jason made an early appearance. Samantha knew the risks only too well. She was still scared of Jason – that hadn't gone away – but knowing she had Jake, and loving him like he loved her, made life bearable. Jake made her feel safe. Safe and happy, which made the risks feel worth it.

Smiling to herself, Samantha crossed Lambeth Bridge. She weaved through the city commuters and quickened her pace as she made her way along Millbank towards the Beehive.

The bar had become their sanctuary when it was too dangerous for Jake to come to the house. Samantha had actually become friends with the landlady. Deana and Jake had history, and she was one of the few people Jake trusted. She was also the only person who knew about their affair.

Samantha was hit by the heat and the chatter as she walked into the bar. Bryan Adams was playing on the jukebox. The place was busy already with early evening drinkers, and Samantha waved to Deana at the bar.

Deana smiled, calling over to her. 'All right, darlin'. You fancy your usual? Just give me a minute, yeah?'

Samantha nodded. She had a lot of time for Deana. They could have a laugh, and she'd found herself opening up to the older woman about her life – something she never did, not even with Jake. It made her feel uncomfortable talking about Jase with him. Jake was protective of her, and so she was careful what she said to him. She played down the way Jase treated her, but with Deana, it was different. Sam had opened up about the hell she was living in, and she'd found it a relief being able to talk to another woman.

Deana sauntered over with Deana's wine.

'I'll put it on Jake's tab.' She placed the glass of red in front of Sam. 'Make him pay . . . Anyway, listen, doll, I'd love to have a natter, but we're run off our feet here, as you can see. But take a seat, and I'll catch up with you later.' She looked over Sam's shoulder, and shouted, 'Oi, mate, that table's reserved for this lady.' Then she winked at Sam as the disgruntled customers – who were already seated – got up and took their drinks and ciggies with them.

Sitting by the window, Samantha waited for Jake. She glanced up at the oversized clock on the wall. Five fifty. Jake was meeting her at six thirty, so not long now. She settled down in her chair with her glass of wine, smiling at the thought of seeing him.

*

'Deana, has Jake phoned?' Samantha was starting to worry now. It was almost eight o clock. 'It's not like him to be late. I know it's silly, but I'm starting to think something might have happened to him . . .'

'He's probably been held up on business, babe.' Deana picked up a couple of empty beer glasses from the next table. She gave Sam a tight smile

Something about the way Deana looked at her made Sam begin to panic even more.

'Deana . . . Deana, what aren't you telling me? Has something happened to him?'

'No, no . . . he's fine.'

'Then what?' Samantha could feel her cheeks flushing. 'Deana, *please*, if there's something I should know, just tell me.'

Placing the glasses down, Deana threw the chequered tea towel she was carrying over her shoulder. She slid into the chair opposite.

'He ain't coming, darlin'.'

Samantha blinked rapidly and stared at Deana. 'Sorry? What do you mean? You said he was fine.'

'He is . . . he's okay.'

'Then why? I don't understand.' Samantha searched around for words. 'I . . . I . . . I mean, is he held up at work or something?'

Deana reached over and placed her hands over Samantha's. 'He's not coming. And he's not coming, because he's seeing someone else, doll. I'm so sorry, Sam.'

It took a few seconds for what Deana had said to properly sink in. 'What? *No.*' She vigorously shook her head. 'No, no, he wouldn't. I mean, he isn't . . . He can't be.'

'Sweetheart, he is.' Deana's eyes were warm, and kindness shone through them.

'You must have got it wrong. There's no way . . .' Samantha hated the fact that she was beginning to cry. Deana handed her a paper napkin from the table behind her, and Sam took it, wiping her eyes as she talked. 'This morning, we were together and, well, everything was normal . . . He even said he loved me.'

'He's a player. Always has been, always will be.'

Samantha felt like she'd been hit by a truck. She began to shake. She felt sick and dizzy, and she had to take several deep breaths to stop herself from keeling over. She struggled to speak, and when she did, she sounded disbelieving.

'But . . . but why, why didn't he tell me himself? Why didn't he tell me this morning? Why has he got you to do it for him?'

Deana shrugged. 'He might be some tough geezer out there, but when it comes to this – to matters of the heart, babe – he's a fucking coward.'

Samantha didn't say anything for a moment. Had this been a game for Jake all along? Had she only been his plaything until he'd got bored and someone better had come along? Jesus, she'd been such a fool! He'd done this to her before. Just dropped her like she was nothing.

'I need to go.' She couldn't look at Deana, she just wanted to get out of the bar.

'Yeah, of course.'

Samantha got up, but her legs gave way, and Deana reached out quickly, to make sure she didn't fall.

'Are you going to be all right getting home on your own?'

'I'll be fine.'

'Look, take care of yourself, won't you, darlin'?' Deana let Samantha start to walk away, but grabbed her arm. 'Remember, they ain't worth it, babe. *Men.* Believe me, I was a brass for years, and they're all bastards. One way or another, they end up breaking our hearts. They're all the same.'

'The thing is, Deana, I really thought Jake was different. More fool me, hey?'

Deana watched Samantha leave. Poor cow. She only hoped she'd be able to get over him quickly, but something told Deana she probably wouldn't. The pain on Samantha's face was something she wouldn't forget in a hurry.

Sighing, Deana reflected on her own disastrous love life as she ambled through to the staff room. She walked slowly up the stairs to the tiny first-floor flat where she lived alone, above the bar.

She wandered into the kitchen, shook her head and grabbed the whiskey bottle off the table.

'So, did you tell her then?' Jake stared up at Deana.

'Yeah, yeah, I did. And I don't *ever* want to have to do that again. You should've seen her . . .'

He leant forward and tried to grab the bottle out of Deana's hand.

'Ain't you had enough?' Deana gave him a hard stare.

He looked smart in his expensive clothes. His hair was immaculate, but he also looked pissed. Pissed and feeling sorry for himself, when it should've been Sam he was feeling sympathy for. Deana tutted. Bloody men.

'I'll say when I've had enough, D.' And he lunged for the bottle again, taking a large swig. 'How did she take it?'

'How the fuck do you think she took it?' Deana dropped down on to the white wicker chair. Fuck it, if she couldn't beat him, she'd join him, and she took a swig from the bottle herself. 'She was broken, Jake. That girl loved you, and you made me lie to her.

Why make her think you're screwing around with someone else? Why not tell her the truth?'

He didn't even want to think about it. 'I just can't. And anyway, it's better like this, D.'

Deana was angry now. 'Better for who? Because let me tell you something, sweetheart, this ain't fucking better for her. So stop kidding yourself.'

Jake matched Deana's anger. His eyes flashed as he slammed his hand on the table.

'That old cunt said she was going to tell Jase . . . and you and I both know what would happen if she did that. I *am* looking out for Sam. Because even if we did a moonlight, no matter where she goes, he'll find her and hurt her. He'll kill her.'

Deana took another gulp of whiskey. She leant back in her chair, holding Jake's stare.

'Then maybe, Jakey, you need to start thinking about killing him first.'

Chapter Sixty-Six

'How the fuck did he just come and take the money out of the safe?'

Jason could feel the anger spiralling through him. Though anger didn't even come close to how he was feeling. What the fuck? He couldn't get his head around it.

'Tell me again, *exactly* what happened.' Jason spat out the words with loathing as he held one of his enforcers by the throat against the wall.

Martin had never thought twice about torturing someone to collect money. But even he knew not to cross Jason when his boss was losing it. 'There ain't much to tell.'

Jason's hand increased the pressure on Martin's throat. 'I never fucking asked you for your opinion. All I want is the facts.'

Martin nodded. 'So Jake, he came in here yesterday. He looked a bit off, like he'd had a heavy session, he said hello, then went into the back and straight into the safe.'

'AND WHY DIDN'T YOU FUCKING STOP HIM?' Jason's eyes were bloodshot and manic.

'With due respect, boss . . .' Martin breathed heavily. 'That's normal. He goes into the safe all the time, like you do.'

'Not to clear everything out, I fucking don't.' Jason was in no mood to listen to reason.

Because there was no possible reason for what Jake had done. Had someone been trying to turn him over, was that why he needed the money? No, was it fuck! Jake would've said. Or did his brother need the money to fund some business deal that had come up, and was just too good to turn down? Nah, of course not. There was only one possible explanation: Jake had wiped him out for no other reason than he was a disloyal, back-stabbing cunt. That was all there was to it.

What Jake had done should have shocked Jason, but his brother had changed. His boozing had seen to that. Jake was a different fucking beast when he was on the sauce. Look what'd happened with their old man.

'For fuck's sake, Martin, how can you let someone walk in and rob me right under your fucking nose? What the fuck am I paying you for?'

'But we're talking about Jake here. So when he went into the safe, I didn't think anything of it, boss.'

With a quick flick of his head, Jason headbutted Martin, tearing open the skin across his eyebrows. Blood spurted out, covering both men.

'*You didn't think anything of it.* You fucking cunt. And because you didn't *think*, he's cleared me out. The bank accounts, the gold, all the safes, the money in the warehouse, he's fucking robbed the lot. And if I don't get my dough back, you might as well get on to the funeral director. Cos, mate, you'll be six foot under.'

He turned to Kitty. She was off her face on E, and had been hungrily giving a blow job to a client when Jase stormed in. She was naked, and right now the sight of her tits and fat pussy on show annoyed the fuck out of him. He grabbed her by the hair, dragging her up.

Kitty screamed, yelping in pain. 'What the fuck have I done? Jase, you're hurting me.'

Jason slapped her. Once. Twice. Then shoved her against the wall. 'Has he said anything to you?'

'Who . . . who you talking about?' Kitty's eyes were glazed over.

Exasperated, Jason slapped her again. This time harder. 'Donald fucking Duck . . . Who do you *think* I'm talking about, you stupid cow?'

Kitty still looked blank. Jason gave up and threw her on to the floor. He booted her hard in the ribs, before storming out with murder on his mind.

An hour later, Jason was pacing up and down the front room of Samantha's house in Langley Lane. He was hard on the coke and getting angrier with Phyllis by the minute.

'My men are out looking for him. I swear to God, if I get my hands on him . . .'

Phyllis was dressed in a floral brown dress, and was finishing off her buttered crumpet. She wiped her mouth primly. 'I hate to speak out of turn, but he always was a sly bastard.' Her voice was mild and innocent.

Jason turned to her. 'You ain't saying anything which isn't true, darlin'. The worst thing about it all is that I never saw it coming. So I knew he was knocking the booze back a bit – has been for the past couple of years. But this, Phyllis . . . he's proper taken me for a mug. From this day onwards, he's no brother of mine.'

'I don't blame you, Jase.' Phyllis said this as she leant forward to grab her cup of tea. Her elbow knocked the books and magazines from the table on to the floor.

Jason, for all he was a cruel and manipulative bastard, enjoyed playing the gentleman at times. He began to pick everything up, placing it tidily back on the table. Christ, he needed to get hold of some better gear. The coke wasn't giving him any kind of a buzz, even though he'd already sniffed a couple of grams in the last two or three hours.

'Thanks, Jase. I tell you what, my arthritis makes me a clumsy mare.'

He winked at her, and picked up the last item from the floor, a tattered notebook, reaching up to place it back on the table. The pages fell open.

His hand stopped in mid-air. An icy chill ran down his spine.

What the fuck was Jake's name doing in Phyllis's notebook?

He glanced at Phyllis. She stared back at him with a startled look. Lowering his eyes slowly back down to the notebook, he flicked through the pages.

'What the fuck is this?'

'Jase, I can—'

'I said, WHAT THE FUCK IS THIS?' Interrupting Phyllis, Jason leant menacingly over her.

It crossed Phyllis's mind that maybe now wasn't the time to tell Jason the whole truth.

'You asked me to be your eyes and ears.'

Jason waved the book in the air. 'And you've waited this long to tell me?'

The anger had come back, but this time it was mixed with hatred. For Jake, for Samantha, for Phyllis.

'Jase, look, I . . . I didn't know how to tell you. I wanted to, but . . . but . . . the other day . . . I was going to . . . but you had to rush off.' Phyllis was floundering with her words. They sounded like a bag of poor excuses.

Jason laughed then. A loud, nasty sound.

'Shut the fuck up. I don't want to hear any more *shit* coming out of your mouth, understand me?' He was inches away from Phyllis's face, hating the interfering old cow. 'You're lucky that you're too old for me to bother knocking you out.'

He moved away, leaving her sitting terrified in her chair. Then he marched to the door and yelled up the stairs.

'Sam! Sam! Get down here.' He looked at Phyllis.

She was more than happy for Jason to focus his attention elsewhere.

'Sam, get the fuck down here, *now*.'

While Jason waited for Samantha to come downstairs, he rapped his knuckles on the door, imagining her lips around Jake's cock. Then he pictured his brother riding her hard, and by the time Samantha *did* step into the room, Jase was ready to kill someone.

His fist shot out and caught Samantha square in the mouth. She staggered backwards, unaware of what was going on.

'You fucking slag.' He brought back his clenched fist again and hit her in the jaw.

This time, she didn't stay on her feet. As she tried to scramble away on her hands and knees, Jason towered over her and grabbed her hair, ripping a clump out.

She screamed in agony. 'Jase, stop . . . Jase, *please!*'

Jason wasn't listening. He kicked her in the back of her head, then spun her around on her front. 'My fucking brother? You've been opening your legs to him behind my fucking back. You dirty, sly cunt.'

Samantha was crying now. 'Jason, stop, let—'

'Let you explain? Is that what you want to do, *explain*? Is that what happened when Jake was licking your pussy, did you *explain* how you liked it?' Beside himself with rage, Jason forced his knee into her chest. He rammed Phyllis's notebook in her mouth, shoving it in, jamming it past her teeth until she began to gag. 'This is for every time you fucking saw him, for every time he fucked you.'

Jason straddled her and began to rain down the blows.

Samantha felt the pain, then the sensation of her eyelid ripping open as she screamed for help.

'You fucking whore!' Jason's breathing was coming in heavy, rasping gulps.

Exhausted, but still not finished, he undid his belt, pulling it out of his waistband. He wrapped it around his hand, making sure he used the buckle to hit her, opening up the skin on her face.

Eventually, his wife stopped making a sound.

Samantha lay motionless on the floor in a bloody pulp.

It was only when Jason was gone that Phyllis called the ambulance.

As she put the phone down, she decided when they asked she'd tell them she didn't see a thing.

Chapter Sixty-Seven

It was mid-May, the clocks had gone forward, and the warm winds of spring had finally arrived. Dara was grateful that she no longer had to find ways of trying to keep warm. She'd never got used to the cold in Holly Brookes, and she doubted she ever would.

It was a sunny, balmy Friday afternoon, and Dara had been looking forward to a long weekend. There were no lessons scheduled – the house parents and teachers were watching the horse racing on TV – so Dara had been planning to steal some food from the kitchen, round up a few girls from the dormitory, and go for a picnic on the other side of the grounds, beyond the stream.

Dara was now standing outside the girls' toilets, gently tapping on the door.

'Gracie? Gracie, are you all right? Gracie?'

Dara waited for a minute and then she heard the sound of the door being unlocked.

Gracie appeared, looking pale and ill.

'Jesus, you look terrible, babe.'

Dara studied her. Gracie's long hair, which they'd dyed last week, turning her from a redhead to a bottle blonde, was stuck to her forehead with sweat. Her eyes were red. She was clearly upset.

'What's going on, Gracie?'

Dara had been worried about her friend recently. For the last few weeks, Gracie had hardly spoken to her or the girls; she'd even cold-shouldered Robbie, which was unusual. No matter what Dara did, Gracie just wouldn't join in. And she hardly ever smiled any more.

Dara had been hoping to cheer her up with the picnic, but it looked like that wouldn't be happening now. What was wrong with her?

Dara put her hand on Gracie's forehead. She frowned. 'You aren't hot, babe. But Barrows has been coughing everywhere lately, so maybe you've picked something up from him.'

Dara smiled and absent-mindedly stared around the green tiled bathroom. Every tile was chipped, the grouting was brown and dirty, and the small wooden window frame was mouldy and rotten.

'Maybe you're just tired, Gracie. That could be it?'

Gracie went to wash her hands. She threw some cold water over her face, then turned to look at Dara.

'It's not that, I'm not tired.'

'What is it then, babe? You know you can tell me anything.'

Gracie's eyes filled with tears.

'I'm pregnant, Dar.'

Chapter Sixty-Eight

Dara had thought things couldn't get any worse. She couldn't have been more wrong.

'Are you sure, Gracie?'

The dormitory was empty, and Dara sat on the bed with Gracie, shell-shocked and devastated for her friend.

'How many times are you going to ask me that?' Grace snapped. 'The answer isn't going to change just because you ask me the same question ten bloody times.'

Gracie sounded so raw. She covered her face with her hands, and Dara watched the tears run through her fingers.

'What am I going to do, Dar?'

Dara had no idea. But admitting that, well, it wasn't going to help Gracie. Right now, she needed to be as supportive as she could.

'We'll figure it out.' That was the best Dara could come up with.

Gracie dropped her hands and stared at her. 'How?'

Dara knew *all* the girls in Holly Brookes dreaded getting caught out. She'd seen a few pregnancies since she arrived, though most were the product of sex between the older kids. She was only aware of one pregnancy to do with Barrows. He and the other adults were canny bastards; they favoured oral and anal. No condoms, and no inconvenient consequences.

Dara knew only too well what had happened to each of the unwanted pregnancies. None had a happy ending. One of the girls had miscarried, and one had hanged herself. The others had gone through with the pregnancy, but their babies had been taken away at birth. They ended up in the nursery in Holly Brookes, awaiting adoption.

Dara had seen how the babies were mistreated and abused by the staff. Compared to them, it made Dara's mum look like Mary fucking Poppins.

'I just wish you'd told me before,' Dara said kindly. 'Do you know how far gone you are?'

Gracie looked utterly miserable. 'About eight, maybe nine weeks.'

'Whose it is, doll? Barrows'? Oh fuck, don't tell me it's Clemence's?'

Gracie shook her head and looked across to the window. The sun was shining but all of a sudden she felt cold.

'No, they ain't touched me for a while.' Gracie said it matter-of-factly. 'We're getting too old for them now, you know that.' There was disgust in her voice.

Dara frowned. She began to work out Gracie's dates, and as she did, the realisation hit her. She held Gracie's hand. Squeezed it. It was all beginning to make sense. Gracie hadn't been herself since that night in the pub back in March, had she?

'Oh my God, that bastard who was knocking back shots with Frank, he's the father, ain't he? It was at the pub, wasn't it? That's when it happened.'

Gracie couldn't look at Dara. She became agitated and tried to shut the conversation down. 'I don't want to talk about it.' She played nervously with a thread on her skirt.

'But I'm right, ain't I?'

'What's bloody wrong with you? If someone says they *don't* want to talk about something, just leave it. I don't even want to think about it, Dar.'

Dara was only half listening now. She jumped off the bed, grabbing Gracie's hand. 'I've got an idea. If you're only eight weeks or so gone, maybe it'll do the trick . . . Come on.'

She dragged Gracie up and out of the dormitory. Gracie didn't argue with her, and they ran down the stairs and along the corridor.

At the end door, Dara glanced over her shoulder. 'Keep an eye out, Gracie.'

'What are you doing?' Gracie was worried now.

'Just do as I say.'

And with those words, Dara opened the door and slipped into the storeroom, leaving Gracie to stand patiently outside, deep in thought. She just hoped she sounded more confident than she felt.

Frank wondered what the two little whores were doing.

He'd been fixing the ceiling leak in the dining room when he'd noticed them running down the stairs a moment ago. They looked thick as two thieves. They were clearly up to something.

He'd followed them along the corridor, and now the blonde-haired one was standing outside the storeroom looking very suspicious.

Frank thought about going back to the dining room to finish polyfilling the crack. He wanted to get off early today.

But the way the girl was loitering made him curious to find out what was going on.

He didn't have to wait too long for her friend to reappear. Frank frowned. She appeared to have a bottle of booze in her hand.

'Mother's ruin, ain't it?' he heard her say. 'A bit of this, and maybe your problems are over. Let's go.'

They moved towards the bathroom, all the time watched by Frank.

The bath was slow to fill up, but after ten minutes it was deep enough for Gracie to step in.

'Oh my God, it's fucking hot!'

'It's supposed to be.'

Gracie carefully lowered herself in. The water was scorching.

'Are you sure this is going to work, Dar? It all sounds like an old wives' tale to me. Drinking gin in a hot bath?'

Dara shrugged. 'It's worth a try. I mean, I've heard it works . . . brings on a miscarriage. That's what they did sometimes . . . to get rid. Back in the day.'

Gracie wasn't so sure.

'Thing is, Gracie, heat and gin is all we've got right now, babe.'

Dara tried to smile but her heart broke as she watched Gracie wince at the pain of the scalding water on her skin, turning it red and blotchy. It was burning her, Dara could see that.

'Look, just get it down you.' She handed Gracie the bottle.

Gracie could hardly bear to stay in the bath, the water was so hot, but she took the bottle of gin, unscrewed the top, and began to swig it down.

Dara stroked Gracie's head, listening out to make sure no one was coming.

'What if it doesn't work, Dar? What then? What if I have to go through with this pregnancy? I can't let them take the baby away. You've seen what they do to the babies here. The way they're treated.'

Gracie was starting to slur her words as the gin took effect. She was crying at the enormity of the situation she found herself in. Wide-eyed, she stared around the ancient bathroom with its yellowing plaster and brown carpet tiles. The steam rising from the bath was like a Turkish sauna.

Dara couldn't bear to think about it. When she was walking through the grounds, she often heard screams coming from the nursery. She knew the babies were neglected. But she feared there were even worse things than neglect.

'I know . . . we could always run away.' Dara was crying now. 'If this doesn't work, we'll fuck off out of here, what do you say?'

Gracie thought about it for a minute, wiping away the tears and snot from her face. Then she shook her head.

'There's nowhere for us to go, Dar. I can't have a baby on the street, can I? And the police would soon pick us up, I reckon.'

Dara hesitated for a moment, then asked as gently as she could, 'What about your mum? We could go and look for her?'

Gracie hugged her knees. The alcohol in her system took away the pain of the scalding water. 'She don't care. She left me here, didn't she? Anyway, I don't want to talk about her.'

Dara nodded. 'Okay . . . okay . . . Look, have some more of this.'

She passed Gracie the gin, but not before she'd taken a swig herself. She smiled again at Gracie, not wanting to show her own panic. She couldn't see a way out.

'I'm not surprised Daisy killed herself when she found out she was pregnant. I reckon that will be me soon.' Gracie sobbed big fat tears.

'Don't say that, don't even think that.' Dara sat on the edge of the bath and grabbed hold of her friend's shoulders. 'You hear me, Gracie. I never want you to say that again.' Dara thought quickly. 'Look, if this doesn't work, we'll hide it.'

'What?'

'At my old school, my mate once hid her pregnancy, no one knew until she had the baby. We can do the same with you.' She cradled Gracie's face in her hands. 'That's what we'll do, we'll *hide* your pregnancy.'

'What then? What happens when I give birth?'

'I don't know. But I promise, I swear on my life, Gracie, I'll look after you. I won't let Holly Brookes take your baby, *never*. No matter what I have to do.'

Chapter Sixty-Nine

Frank scooped up a large roast potato and shoved it in his mouth. He was a man who enjoyed his food, especially his Sunday roasts. Frank was also a man who enjoyed eating his food in silence. But since Judy had got off the phone to her sister, Mandy, she hadn't stopped telling him all the news.

'If you ask me, Frank, what she needs is a few weeks in the sun, you know, getting some R&R. Who knows, it might do the trick? But here's the thing, then she told me about Bernie, her neighbour, who thinks . . .'

Frank couldn't stand Judy's chatter about Mandy any longer. 'One of the girls at Holly Brookes is pregnant, I think.' He changed the subject.

Anything had to be better than listening to endless shit about Mandy, who was now living in Bournemouth. The stupid bitch was permanently strung out on Valium, and seemed to spend all her time having huge stand-up rows with the woman who lived opposite.

Frank took a sip of his tea from the new blue mug Judy had bought last week from John Lewis. 'Nasty little slags, both of them. Mouthy bitches as well. They get away with all sorts. A bit more discipline wouldn't go amiss.'

It did the trick.

Judy was no longer interested in talking about her sister. 'How do you know? I mean, how do you know she's pregnant?'

Frank shrugged. 'I saw them. I mean, I might be wrong of course.' He waved his fork at Judy. No need to tell her about the spyhole he'd drilled in the wall of the girls' bathroom so he and Clemence could take a peek whenever they felt in need of a little relief. 'But you tell me . . . hot bath, a bottle of gin.' He shrugged again, finishing his mouthful of peas. 'Mother's ruin, ain't it? I've seen it before in that place. Trying to get rid.'

'Did it work?' Judy frowned.

'Dunno, we'll have to wait and see. They'll need to hide it though . . . if they don't want Barrows to know what's going on.'

As Frank continued to tuck in, Judy noticed he had a smirk on his face.

'What's so funny?'

'I'm thinking about Alan. He'll get a fucking fright if she *is* up the duff. That'll put the cat among the pigeons. And it'll put an end to that cunt's ideas of grandeur. God, can you imagine the look on his face?' Frank let out a loud smelly burp, as if to emphasise his point.

Judy didn't understand what Frank was talking about. 'I ain't following you. What the hell has Alan got to do with it?'

'It was when we were at Holly Brookes, back in March.'

Judy pulled a face. 'What was Alan doing down there with you?'

Frank sighed. Judy always liked to ask a hundred questions, and he was now regretting saying anything at all.

'Don't ask me . . . Dennis needed him to go down for something.' As Frank said this, he pictured the body he'd sawn into pieces.

Thankfully, Dennis's bloodhounds – the ones he kept for fox hunting – had been more than willing to eat them.

'Anyhow, when he was down there, he got his leg over. Caused a right fucking commotion. Think the girl wasn't too keen on Alan jumping on her. Who fucking would be?' He roared with laughter, and almost choked on a stray pea. 'Maybe it's worked and he's firing silver bullets. Though who knows, with that lot? The father could be anyone.'

Judy played with her food in silence; she'd suddenly lost her appetite. She mulled over what Frank had just said.

'Frank, I want to show you something.'

'I'm still eating my dinner.'

She snatched his knife and fork from him and grabbed hold of his hand. 'It won't take long.'

Frank's heart dropped. He didn't want to leave a perfectly decent roast dinner. And the idea of having sex with Judy – if that's what this was about – turned his stomach. He grabbed his mug and drank his tea down fast, before Judy could take that out of his hand as well.

Reluctantly, he let her pull him up the stairs. He was surprised, and somewhat relieved, when she led him into the spare bedroom.

'Wait there.' Judy seemed nervous.

Frank stood in the doorway of the room, which had been freshly wallpapered in pale Windsor cream. He watched as Judy opened the doors of the two large built-in wardrobes. He'd been on the verge of saying something about his dinner getting cold. Open-mouthed, he stared in silence as Judy frantically pulled out box after box. She rushed across to the matching chest of drawers, and violently wrenched them open, pulling out baby clothes, blankets, bottles, dummies and teddies.

Panting, she turned to him. 'We've all got our secrets, and this is mine, Frank . . . All those miscarriages I had, pregnancies with no babies to take home and love . . . it's not fair, Frank, not when those little whores are opening their legs and getting up the duff in their sleep.'

Tears rolled down Judy's face. She walked over to Frank, looking angry and upset.

He was shocked by her confession.

'I've always been here for you, Frank, looked out for you, more than you will *ever* know, darlin'. And now I want *you* to do something for me in return.'

'Anything, Jude.'

She smiled at him and stroked his face. 'I want that girl's baby, Frank. If the gin don't work, I want you to get me that baby.'

Book Four

1985
Winter

Oh, what a tangled web we weave,
When first we practise to deceive.

Sir Walter Scott, *Marmion*

Chapter Seventy

It was PE, and Dara was bunking off. Gracie hated PE as much as Dara did.

The girls sauntered through the woods of Holly Brookes, then stopped to lean against the old oak tree. Dara pulled out a packet of cigarettes from her games skirt, took one out and lit it.

'Turn to the side, doll,' she instructed Gracie. She looked her up and down. 'Shit, I can see it.'

Gracie glanced down at her stomach and tried not to cry. She was sick of herself. All she seemed to have done for months was cry and feel sorry for herself. They'd tried so hard at the beginning of her pregnancy to get rid. She'd sat in the bath with a bottle of gin more times than she could remember. But in the end, it was just an old wives' tale. So without any other options available to them, they'd set about trying to hide the pregnancy.

Keeping it a secret had felt impossible to Gracie, especially in the first few months when she was dealing with exhaustion and morning sickness, and all the while trying to hide her ever-growing bump. Dara had been amazing throughout. Whenever Gracie started to panic – which she'd done a few times – Dara was there to comfort her. But it had come at a cost for Dara, Gracie knew. Although she also knew that Dara would never admit it.

'Is that better?' Gracie rearranged her jumper.

It had been difficult through the summer months, wearing bulky oversized sweaters. She'd been sweltering; but it had worked. The more layers of clothing she'd added from lost property, the less noticeable the changes to her body were. And now the first fall of snow had arrived, Gracie was grateful to be able to keep warm.

Dara studied her. 'Nope, you need to pull the band tighter.'

She kept the cigarette in the corner of her mouth and walked behind Gracie, lifting up her top.

'Here, let me do it.'

Dara pulled on the home-made belly band Gracie had stitched together. It acted like a corset; she wore it under her clothing, to help support her stomach and hold everything in place. In any case, Gracie was skin and bones now. They'd decided that the best course of action, apart from the belly band, was a strict diet to keep any excess weight off.

'You don't think this will hurt the baby? It's so bloody tight.' Gracie looked worried.

Dara took the cigarette out of her mouth, and kissed Gracie on her cheek. 'I already told you, it has to be tight.' She spoke quickly. 'We've come this far, we don't want Barrows or anyone finding out, do we? And I *promise*, it's not going to hurt either of you.'

Dara didn't know if this was true or not. But she didn't want to frighten Gracie and make her more anxious than she already was. *Especially* as Gracie had started to fall in love with the baby growing inside her. From the very first time she'd felt a kick.

'Thanks, Dar. You're the best.'

Dara smiled. She felt protective of Gracie. She reckoned it was a small miracle that no one had found out about the pregnancy. Holding on to any sort of privacy in the dormitory was hard, and always caused a lot of fights and arguments. But having to keep a pregnancy secret . . . well, it had made things doubly difficult.

The responsibility of keeping her friend safe had taken its toll on Dara. She went to bed every night feeling petrified, dreading the night terrors when she would wake up screaming, covered in sweat.

Her self-harming had become worse. Not only were her arms covered in angry cuts, so too were her legs. It was the only way Dara felt she could cope.

Dara stared at Gracie's top. 'Yeah, that's perfect, you wouldn't know you were preggers. Just make sure to always pull your jumper down.'

Dara wished Gracie would let her confide in Robbie. But Gracie was adamant she didn't want anyone else to know. She'd thought, over time, Gracie would open up, but now the only person she really spoke to was Dara.

It was beginning to snow now, light, feathery flakes drifting down, and it was bitterly cold. In the distance, Dara heard the bell for the end of the lesson.

'We better go. Morgan might not give a shit that we've bunked off PE, but Mr Jacobs will have a fucking fit if we miss his stupid art class.'

'Yeah . . .' Gracie nodded. She looked ill and malnourished. Black circles sat under her eyes. 'I need to go for a wee first, I'll see you in class.'

Dara watched Gracie jog towards the toilet block. Their plan had worked well so far, though there was one major flaw. One subject they'd both been too scared to address.

What were they going to do when the baby was finally born?

Chapter Seventy-One

Frank stood by the tool shed watching them. Feeling the sleet trickle down the back of his neck, he pulled up the collar on his wax coat. He'd been given strict instructions by Judy to find out *exactly* what was going on. And although he was too far away to hear what was being said, he'd seen everything he needed to.

Frank had been in bed for the past few months, laid low with a bout of pneumonia. During his absence from Holly Brookes, he'd hoped, but not really believed, that Judy might forget about the baby. But ever since he'd first mentioned it, back in May, she hadn't stopped mithering him.

Frank thought he needed a couple more weeks off work; the cold weather wouldn't do his chest any good. But Judy had other ideas. She'd as good as dragged him out of bed, eager to find out whether or not that little tart had flushed the baby down the toilet.

From what he'd seen now, not only had she failed to get rid, but she was hiding her bump so no one would notice she was knocked up. And it looked cooked enough to drop.

'Oi, I want a word with you.' Frank stepped into Dara's path.

She jumped. Seeing it was Frank, her mood darkened. 'What the fuck do you want?'

Frank sneered and grabbed hold of her chin, squeezing it hard.

'I'd watch that filthy mouth if I were you, before it gets you into trouble.'

She hit his hand away. 'Like I told you, *fuck off.*'

'Be careful what you say to me.' Frank's eyes narrowed. 'You don't know who you're talking to.'

His words were loaded, and his expression told Dara that she needed to go carefully, he was violent and dangerous.

Dara had never backed down in the face of bullies, and she wasn't going to start now. 'Oh I know who I'm talking to, mate, and one day . . .' She hissed through her teeth. 'One day, you're going to get what's coming to you.'

'Rude little bitch, aren't you?'

'Pervert, aren't you?'

Frank slapped her hard across the cheek. He saw the look of hatred flash across her face. But then she glanced around the woods – they were so isolated here – and she realised it wasn't a good idea to goad him right now.

It didn't stop Dara from trying to push past him, but Frank wasn't about to let her go so easily. He yanked Dara by her top, dragging her towards the tree, and pushed her hard against it.

'Get off me. Get the *fuck* off me.'

He pressed his body against Dara, giving her a faceful of bad breath. He couldn't stand little slags. That's what she was, in his eyes. A slag, reminding him of his fat bitch of a mother. She was a whore in the making.

He grinned a spiteful grin, which made him look uglier. 'I've seen your mate's belly.'

She panicked, and this time she shoved Frank hard enough to get away. 'I don't know what the fuck you're talking about.'

'Is that right?' Frank called after her. 'Well, let's see if Barrows knows what I'm talking about, shall we?'

He walked away, heading for the cottages.

'Wait, Frank . . . *wait*, okay. You can't speak to Barrows.' She sounded desperate.

Frank smiled before he turned around. The wind was beginning to get up.

Dara wiped the sleet from her face. 'What do you want?'

'That's more like it.' Frank stepped towards her. 'Now I want you to tell me *everything* you know about this baby.'

Chapter Seventy-Two

Judy sat in Alan's office enjoying the piece of Victoria sponge cake Reenie had just handed her. She was also enjoying watching Alan squirm.

'Thanks, love.' Judy sucked the crumbs off her fingers and beamed at Reenie.

Reenie said nothing. She kept her eyes down as she passed a cup of tea to Frank.

'Thank you, Reenie, that will be all now,' Alan snapped at her in irritation.

'Yes, sir . . . of course, sir.' Reenie spoke softly. She smiled at him, though the smile didn't reach her eyes.

Alan noticed her hands were trembling. He watched her totter off. These days, Reenie had a different look about her. There was a sharpness to her. A disapproving edge. Though what the fuck Reenie had to be disapproving about, Alan couldn't imagine.

The minute the door clicked shut, Alan dropped the niceties.

'What the fuck do you think you're doing coming to my office?' He glared at them both, seething inwardly, and walked around his desk. He snatched the plate from Frank, who was just about to take a bite of cake.

'I don't appreciate you waltzing in . . .' He jabbed his finger at Frank. 'And bringing Judy along like a fucking bodyguard.'

Martina Cole

Judy placed her cup and saucer on top of a small pile of books on the side table. She settled her green leather handbag on her knee and looked around the office, appraising the walnut wood and the tones of regal blue.

'Nice work, Alan. You've done well for yourself. Who'd have thought a scrote like you from South London could get this far?' She moved her gaze back to him. 'Though you and I both know none of this would've been possible without help, would it?'

Alan ignored the question. He leant against the edge of his desk and adjusted his pinstriped trousers – which were slightly tight around his thighs – before taking a step forward.

'What is it you want, Judy? Because I know you aren't here just to enjoy the view. So go on, tell me, why *are* you here?'

Judy looked him up and down disdainfully. 'I want a baby, and I want you to get it for me.'

Was the woman fucking insane? Alan rolled his eyes at Frank, the poor bastard.

He laughed nastily. 'The maternity hospital is down the road. Now do me a favour, stop wasting my time and get out of my office.'

'I don't think you'd want us to do that, Alan.' Judy didn't move. 'You see, I don't think you want everyone to know you forced yourself on a young and vulnerable girl, do you? And if I do get up and walk out of here, that's exactly what's going to happen, and everything you've worked for is going to disappear overnight.'

Alan's expression darkened. 'What exactly is this about?'

'That night in March, when you went down to Holly Brookes, I heard you were a very naughty boy. But unfortunately for you, Alan, you left a little present.'

'I have no idea what you're talking about.'

'She's pregnant.' Judy smirked. 'That girl you met in the pub.'

368

Alan looked between the two of them and rubbed his face. 'What?'

'You hit the bullseye.' Frank's shoulders moved up and down as he laughed heartily.

Alan could only stare ahead in disbelief.

He'd tried several times to remember exactly what had happened that night, though it only came in snatched waves. The booze he'd drunk, and the ecstasy he'd taken, had wiped away most of that night. He recalled Jimmy's body . . . then a pub . . . then the girls, loud and obnoxious. Could he picture chatting to one of them outside, then a struggle? Maybe. The image of her semi-naked body kept popping up in his mind . . . *Shit*.

Alan was shocked. 'So . . . so let me get this right, Judy: you want that girl's baby?'

'*Your* baby, Alan.' Judy beamed at him.

'Don't fucking say that.'

'Yours . . . hers . . . who cares? As long as it becomes mine.' Judy's eyes narrowed. 'You need to persuade this girl to give you the baby. And then you give it to me.'

Alan needed a drink. He strode across to the decanter and poured himself a large whiskey, knocking it back. 'Do you know how fucked up this is?' He turned to look at Frank. 'You agree with this shit?'

'Of course he does.' Judy replied before Frank had a chance to get a word in. 'He wants to be a father every bit as much as I want to be a mother. Try not to look so stressed, Alan. Your job is easy.'

'How the fuck do you make that out?'

'Frank chatted to the girl's best mate yesterday. No one knows about the pregnancy, they've been hiding it, and they're desperate to keep the baby out of the Holly Brookes nursery. Seems to me, they're in a bit of a predicament, and that's where you come in. Play on their fear, Alan.'

Judy was the coldest woman Alan had ever come across. There wasn't a hint of emotion in her eyes.

'Do you *actually* understand what you're asking me to do?' Alan was nonplussed.

Judy nodded. 'Certainly.' She gave him the widest smile. 'Oh come on, you're not going to start feeling sentimental about this baby, are you?'

'Absolutely fucking not.' Alan was quick to answer. He meant every word.

'So there's no problem then, is there?' She stood to go, brushing the stray cake crumbs on to the carpet, then poked Frank to do the same.

Alan wiped his hand over his sweating face. 'What you're suggesting is madness. Why don't you have one of your own?'

Judy glared at him. 'We've tried.'

'Adoption? What about that? For fuck's sake, there must be some other way . . .'

Judy looked at Frank, then back at Alan. 'I'm sure you, of all people, can understand that sometimes you'd rather not have people poking around, inquiring into your background.'

Alan was pacing now. A thought occurred to him. 'And anyway, how the fuck do you know it's mine?'

'She's adamant it is.' Frank spoke up at last. He stared at Alan from underneath his cap.

'Oh come off it, it could be anyone's. She probably doesn't even know herself . . . I bet she's been spreading her legs for every man who walks into that pub.'

Judy shrugged. 'That may be so . . . and who knows? She might have got it wrong. But that's merely a technicality, ain't it? Because at the end of the day, her mate is telling Frank it's yours, and that *you* forced yourself on her. And like I say, you wouldn't want that getting out, would you?'

Alan ignored the threat. 'What I don't understand is, why don't you get her to give the baby to you? Why the fuck do I have to get involved?'

There was a pause from Judy. She gave Frank a small sideways glance. 'I think, maybe . . . it's probably better coming from you. Let's just say, if she's heard certain lies about my Frank, she may not be so accommodating about handing it over to us.'

'And what if she doesn't agree?'

Judy reached for the door handle. 'Then you have to make her agree, Alan. Frank will take you down there tomorrow. But this stays between the three of us. No one else, not even Dennis. I need that baby, Alan, and I don't want anything to get in the way.'

Alan shook his head to dislodge the fog that was threatening to scramble his brain. This crazy series of events all stemmed from that little piece of land along the Embankment, which was now a playground. It had become a hornets' nest.

'And if you don't succeed, Alan, and get me what I want, believe you me, darlin' . . .' Judy smiled vindictively. 'The whole world will know what you did to that poor fucking girl.'

The worst of it all was, Alan knew Judy wasn't bluffing.

Chapter Seventy-Three

Alan was watching Frank closely.

They'd been waiting in the woods for the past hour and a half, and they'd barely said two words to each other. Alan shoved his hands deeper into his pockets. It was freezing.

Frank nodded towards a group of girls emerging from the main block.

'So you've got it clear then? If any of the house parents see you, just say you're a friend of Frank's.'

Alan sneered at him. 'I think of all the lies told up to this point, that one not only feels like the most unbelievable, but it also sticks in my fucking throat.'

Frank responded with a loud belly laugh.

Alan was already wound up, but he knew he had to keep a lid on his temper. His balls were in a vice, and there was fuck-all he could do about it.

'There she is.' Frank pointed to two girls who had left the group and were walking towards them. 'I'll go back and wait in the car, I don't want them to see me.'

'Hold on, Frank, which one is she?'

Frank looked genuinely surprised. He scratched his chin, absent-mindedly picking the scab off a spot. 'You really don't know?' He patted Alan on the back. A large grin spread across his face. 'Fuck them and leave them, hey, Al? I like your style. Though it's a shame for you, this time you left a little something behind.'

'What the hell are *you* doing here?' Dara stood with her hands on her hips.

The bastard who was responsible for ruining Gracie's life was walking towards them, blocking the path to their cottage.

She hadn't told Gracie about her conversation with Frank yesterday. She didn't want to worry her. The situation was a mess already, and telling Gracie that Frank knew all about the pregnancy would freak her out for sure.

She also hadn't wanted Gracie to be angry with her. But what other choice had she had? Frank was a nasty bastard, and Dara didn't doubt he would've gone and spilt the beans to Barrows if she hadn't told him.

'I've come for a word with Gracie.'

Dara was taken aback that the man knew her friend's name. 'Well, she doesn't want a word with you.'

'Look, I can understand why you're angry, but I want to be honest with you, I can't remember exactly what happened, but—'

'Stay away from her, okay?' Dara cut in. 'Now do one, *mate*.'

It struck Dara that the man being here *now* wasn't just a coincidence after the conversation yesterday with Frank. She was curious to know what he wanted – she'd rather know what they were dealing with – though she had to make sure Gracie wasn't part of the conversation.

'Can you put your fucking dog on a leash?' The man spoke to Gracie, pointing at Dara. 'I haven't come here to get my ear chewed off.'

'Who the fuck are you calling a dog?' Dara's face flushed red, and she stepped closer to Alan.

Gracie began to pull her away. 'Please, leave it, Dar. We don't want any trouble, do we?' she mouthed quietly.

Turning her back on the man, Dara kept her voice down as well. 'I can't stand the way he talks to us, especially after what he did to you. He needs to be put in his place.'

'Yeah, but not by you.' Gracie's eyes implored her. 'You promised me, Dar, you said you'd leave it. And I told you *I* don't want to talk about it. What's done is done.'

When Dara saw how upset Gracie was, she began to calm down. 'Okay, look, why don't you go and find Brenda? I'll get rid of him. We don't want him talking to Barrows or anyone, do we?'

Gracie looked scared. 'Do you think he will?'

'No. Try not to worry, all right. I'll make sure he doesn't. Anyway, what's he going to say? He doesn't know about the pregnancy, does he? No one does, apart from us.' Dara lied well. 'We'll be fine. Trust me.'

Dara pushed her fingernails into her palms to stop herself from screaming. She couldn't cope. She didn't know if she'd be able to stop what was happening; everything had started to feel like it was beyond her control.

At the beginning of the pregnancy, Dara could pretend none of it was happening, but now it was all too real. She didn't know what she was going to do, or how she was going to keep Gracie and the baby safe. And what with Frank knowing, she was terrified. A flash of Tommy and the rest of her siblings shot through her mind. She'd let them down, hadn't she? Betrayed them by not looking after them the way she should've done, and there was no way she was about to do the same to Gracie.

'I'll see you in a minute.' Dara smiled reassuringly at Gracie.

Gracie walked off, looking back over her shoulder before disappearing around the corner.

'Where's she going?' Alan demanded.

'She doesn't want to talk to you. Anything you have to say, you can say it to me.'

She was a mouthy bitch. So he let her have it straight.

'I know your friend is pregnant. Frank told me everything.'

He must have been out of his fucking mind to go anywhere near her skanky little friend. Gracie, was it? That E certainly had a lot to answer for.

Come to think of it, both girls looked ill. Scrawny and sickly. This little bitch reminded him of someone, her eyes, the way she was looking at him seemed familiar somehow, though he couldn't quite put his finger on it. She was wearing clothes far too small for her. The sleeves of her cardigan were too short, and tight, and Alan noticed the angry, fresh self-harm marks.

As for the other one, she'd looked emaciated, like she'd been starving herself. She'd had sunken eyes and cheeks, and her arms and legs had been stick-thin. And even though Alan knew she was pregnant, he hadn't been able to tell.

But now he remembered why he was here, and he made an effort to turn on the charm.

'I want to help . . . er . . . Gracie. I want to face up to my responsibilities. I intend to do the right thing.'

Chapter Seventy-Four

Dara was feeling sick. The words that had come out of the man's mouth were something she couldn't possibly have foreseen.

'You want me to get Gracie to give you the baby? Have you completely lost it, mate?' Dara didn't know whether to laugh or cry.

The man gazed around. It was beginning to snow, but even a dusting of pure white snow couldn't do anything to change how bleak and grim Holly Brookes was.

They'd walked across to the woods to talk, but so far it didn't seem like they were making any headway.

'Maybe I need to speak to Gracie, not you,' the man said.

'I already told you, mate, you keep away from her. She ain't going to say anything different to what I'm saying. She didn't even want to stay and look at your sorry face, so she's hardly going to listen to this shit, is she?' Dara stared at him in disgust. 'How could you? How could you come here after what you did to her? You should be locked up.'

'Things got out of hand, but I'm willing to step up. I want to do right by my kid.' He looked like he meant it.

Listening to him, Dara shook her head. She kicked at the ground and let out a bitter laugh. 'You're a fucking joke. I know guys like you and Frank. I know what you do to kids.'

The man jumped in then. 'Hold up, hold up a minute. I am

nothing like that prick. Look at me . . . go on, look in my eyes, and see if I'm telling the truth.' The man spoke passionately. 'I may be a lot of things, darlin', and I'm certainly no angel, but believe me, I would never and have never touched a little kid.'

Dara didn't know if she was being stupid or not, but there was something about the way he said it that made her feel like maybe, *perhaps*, he was telling the truth. 'He's your mate though, ain't he? You hang about with him. Why else did he tell you about Gracie?'

'Let's get one thing clear right now. He's not my friend. Never will be. We know a couple of the same people, that's all. I was down here on business, that's when you saw me in the pub, and Frank tagged along. Nothing more. And as for telling me . . .' The man paused and chose his words carefully. 'Well, he's an arrogant cunt who thought it was funny to wind me up. But there's nothing funny about it, I know that. That's why I'm here to help, the best way I can.'

'But you know what he is, you know what he does, yet you still talk to him.'

'And it makes me sick.'

'Then why don't you do anything about it?' Dara stared at him wide-eyed.

The man stretched out his arm to touch Dara on the shoulder, but she jumped back, not wanting him near her.

'No one would listen . . . no one would believe me. That's what happens when men in power abuse their position.'

Dara could feel he was beginning to reel her in.

'Look, have you ever heard any stories about me around here? Have you heard *anyone* say that I'm like Frank?'

Dara thought about it. She hadn't. Not from Robbie, not from anyone. 'No, but you still did what you did to Gracie.'

'I know, and I'm holding my hands up in the air, it was wrong.

Whatever I did was wrong, but she's hardly a nine-year-old boy, is she? How old is she, sixteen?'

'Fifteen, *nearly*. Only fourteen when you . . .'

Shit. Dara couldn't say it.

The man looked stricken, as if he'd had no idea.

'The point is, if you . . . if *Gracie* lets me have the baby, it isn't going to come to any harm. I'll look after it. Give it everything it needs. I don't know how we're going to manage it all. But Gracie's hidden her condition well so far . . . so maybe, when she goes into labour, somehow we can get her into hospital.'

'No . . . *no!*' Dara was adamant.

She'd not thought about it. She covered her face with her hands as tears filled her eyes. She hadn't wanted to show any emotion to this man, but she was confused and scared. She wanted to do what was right by Gracie. She needed to look after her, but she had no idea what to do, or where to go, or what to say. She had no one to talk to, and in her entire life, Dara had never felt so alone as she did now.

She felt the man lower her hands. She stared at him, and he fixed her with his gaze, and this time Dara didn't try to get away.

'I'm sorry, I really am. Holly Brookes should be shut down, and I know it's too late to rescue you, darlin', from being here . . . and too late for Gracie. But it's not too late for the baby.'

He was laying it on thick. Could she trust him, or was it just about saving his own skin?

'It's not ideal, but what other choice is there, sweetheart? No one in their right mind would want their baby to end up in this place. And unless you've got a fairy godmother lined up, I'm as good as it gets, darlin'.'

The man went into his pocket and pulled out a note. 'My name and number are on there. Think about it, and don't leave it too long. Babies have a habit of coming sooner than expected . . . Trust me, this is all for the best.'

It had been another forty minutes after Alan left before Dara found the strength to get up and go back to the cottage. She'd spent the time sitting in the cold in the woods, deep in thought. She hadn't been able to face Gracie. She'd felt completely broken.

On the way back to the dormitory, she'd gone the long way round, past the nursery, and had listened. Watched. Seen the babies in Holly Brookes' care.

Ten minutes was all it had taken for her to have seen enough, and she'd backed away, drenched in fear. This place had always made her feel like she was a nobody The idea of that happening to Gracie's baby turned Dara's blood cold.

The fight that was usually in her had disappeared. She'd looked at the piece of paper in her hand. There was nothing else for it . . . apart from give Gracie's baby to Alan Carver. Gracie's attacker. Gracie's saviour. Though it didn't even matter any more what he was, did it? Surely he wouldn't harm his own flesh and blood?

And as Dara sat in the bath now, cutting into her flesh with the razor blade, letting it take her pain away, she realised there were no winners.

Alan had been right: it was too late for them. And in order to save Gracie's baby, she'd have to break her friend's heart. Dara would have to sacrifice one for the other, and she wasn't sure she had the strength to see it through. She didn't know what to do for the best. Which one was the lesser of the two evils: Holly Brookes or Alan Carver?

It was clear to Dara that, whatever choice she made, she would still be choosing evil.

Chapter Seventy-Five

It was a grey dawn. Judy lay in bed staring at the ceiling. She had no idea where the past month had gone. Yet another Christmas was on the horizon, and she hadn't even started to think about what to get Frank.

Judy had had plenty of opportunity to buy something. She'd spent most of the past few weeks going up to the West End, mooching around the shops, daydreaming about how it would feel to push a pram around with her *own* baby in it.

She remembered when Jimmy was little; she'd always enjoyed taking him out, often pretending he was hers when people came up to coo over him. But in her heart, Judy knew it wasn't the same as having one of her own, was it?

With a loud sigh, Judy sat up in bed and swung her legs around. She slipped her feet into her pink fur-lined moccasins. It was chilly. She'd go downstairs, put the fire on and make a nice mug of tea for herself. She might even give Mandy a ring. Her sister was always up early too, especially now she was on her medication.

Judy pulled on her dressing gown and looked across at Frank; he was still fast asleep and snoring loudly. She smiled and pottered out of the bedroom, not wanting to wake him.

She was walking down the stairs, when she heard a loud banging on the front door. She frowned, wondering who on earth it could be at this time in the morning. She hurried to answer it, only to be knocked flying . . .

Six policemen broke down the door and came racing in.

Judy scrambled up, took one look at them, and began to hurry back towards the stairs.

'Where is he?' one of the officers shouted at Judy. 'Where's Frank?'

'Leave him alone, he ain't done nothing wrong—'

She tried to block their way but they pushed roughly past her and charged up the stairs.

There was yelling from the bedroom and the sounds of a struggle.

Frank was dragged out, dressed in a stained white vest and brown paisley-patterned Y-fronts.

He stared at Judy. 'Call Dennis . . . *Now.*'

Chapter Seventy-Six

Dara was worried. Very worried. Gracie had been asking her what they were going to do, and Dara didn't have an answer.

Alan Carver had been on her mind. She'd thought of nothing else since their conversation last month. She'd been tempted to call him so many times, but on each occasion, she'd held off.

There were no two ways about it: Alan was a bastard. Each time Dara pulled the band tighter around Gracie's growing stomach, or watched Gracie making herself vomit, so as not to put on any weight, Dara was reminded of what Alan had done. Could she really hand over Gracie's baby to him? More to the point, would Gracie let her? Dara wished she had someone to talk to. Someone to help her make the right decision.

She knew that Gracie was relying on her to do what was best, to decide what was right. Dara had thought long and hard about this: what was best, and what was right, were two different things. Gracie couldn't face what the future held, so she was leaving it to Dara to sort out what was going to happen. But Dara also suspected that, deep in Gracie's heart, she still hoped for a happy ending.

'Dar, are you all right? Why are you out here? It's snowing.'

Robbie came and sat next to Dara on the bench. It was break time and a lot of the younger kids were running outside to mess around in the first proper snow of the season.

She glanced at him. 'I needed to get some headspace.'

'You want to talk about it?'

Dara shook her head. She appreciated Robbie's concern. Looking sideways at him, she suddenly broke into a smile. Robbie was wrapped up in a long, oversized trench coat and a black pork-pie hat.

'I see you've been raiding the lost property box again, Rob. Though I'm not surprised they left those behind. I would, if I owned them.'

Robbie looked down at what he was wearing, and shrugged. 'It's freezing, I couldn't care less what I look like.'

Dara laughed warmly. 'It's a good job.'

'I think one of Dennis's mates must have left the coat. When they were pissed up, last time they came here . . .'

Dara went cold. She jumped at Robbie, tugging the coat off his back. 'Get it off . . . Get it bloody off . . . *now!*'

'Dar, let go . . . Dar, please, stop.' Robbie began to get upset.

'Just take it off!' She grabbed the hat from his head and flung it into the flower bed of plants which were covered in snow. 'Robbie, I'm being serious! How can you wear that?' She was crying angry tears.

'Dar, no . . . *Stop!* Stop it!'

But Dara continued to grapple the coat from Robbie, and without warning, he slapped her. They both froze.

Robbie's eyes filled with tears. 'I'm sorry, Dar . . . I . . . I . . . It's just that you were pulling at my clothes and . . .' He trailed off, devastated by what he'd done.

Dara stayed silent.

'Dar . . . Dar, please say something. I'm so sorry.'

Dara felt terrible too. 'It's not your fault, I shouldn't have pulled your clothes like that.' She rubbed her cheek. 'Can I ask you something?'

Robbie nodded and swiped fiercely at his tears.

'You've been here all your life, haven't you? Do you think there are worse places for a child to grow up?'

Robbie fell silent for a minute. His pale face was ashen and drawn.

He gave the smallest shake of his head. 'No, I don't. I'd rather be in hell, Dar . . .' He shrugged, remembering something he'd once read. 'Cos hell is empty, ain't it? And all the devils are here.'

She looked at him, taking in the pain etched across his face. 'Thank you, Robbie.'

He sounded surprised. 'What for?'

'For helping me make up my mind.'

Chapter Seventy-Seven

The noise of the wind rattling the window panes woke Dara up. She watched the snow building up on the outside of the window.

She shivered, knowing she'd find it hard to get back to sleep. Barrows had started locking the room where they kept the booze, so she hadn't been able to medicate herself as much as she'd have liked to. She'd managed to pinch a bottle of whiskey from Father Riley's office. But she was saving it for Gracie.

Dara leant over the side of the bunk, looking down to see if Gracie was awake or not. Lately, Gracie had been having trouble sleeping because of the baby kicking.

Gracie's bed was empty.

Dara scrambled down the ladder from the top bunk, and crept out of the dormitory. She tiptoed down the hallway to the girls' bathroom.

'Gracie? Gracie, are you there?' Dara whispered.

There was no reply.

Dara was just about to head back to the dormitory when she heard a groan.

'Grace? Is that you?'

She hurried into the bathroom and found Gracie sitting on the toilet with the cubicle door wide open. Her face was pinched in agony, and she was holding her stomach.

'Dar, Dar, I think it's coming.'

'Oh shit . . . oh *fuck* . . . Are you sure? I mean . . . er . . . er, hold on.'

'Where are you going?' Gracie was breathless. 'Dar, don't go . . . *Dar!*'

As Gracie let out another groan, Dara ran out of the bathroom, stopped, and immediately ran back in.

'Will you be all right, Gracie?' She was trying not to panic, but she didn't know what to do, her head was all over the place. It suddenly felt like everything was out of her control, going too quickly.

'*Help me, Dar!*' Gracie leant forward, doubled up in agony.

'I will . . . oh, *shit* . . . wait there . . . I won't be long.' Dara spoke quickly.

She ran down the corridor again, then down another set of stairs. Dara kept looking over her shoulder, making sure none of the house parents were roaming the hallways. Certain she was alone, she quietly opened the door to the boys' dormitory and tiptoed in.

She hurried across the room to a bed by the window. 'Robbie?' Dara leant over his sleeping form. 'Robbie?'

Robbie's eyes shot open. He scrambled back, terrified. 'Get away from me, leave me alone.'

'It's okay, Robbie, *sshhhh* . . . it's okay, it's only me.'

'Dara? Dar, what are you doing here?' Robbie was confused.

'I need your help. It's Gracie . . . she's having a baby.'

Robbie blinked rapidly. 'What? A baby? What the hell are you talking about?'

'I haven't got time to explain.' Dara whispered, sounding out of breath. 'She's having the baby, *now*. Right now . . . she needs us, come on.'

Without waiting for a response, Dara grabbed Robbie's hand.

386

He leapt out of bed, grabbing his clothes and shoes from a pile on the floor, dressing himself as he followed Dara back to the girls' bathroom.

They ran in together.

'Dar, is that you?' Gracie's voice was quiet but was filled with pain.

'Yeah, I'm here.' Dara rushed over to her.

Gracie was still sitting on the toilet. She looked up with a grimace. Her pained expression flashed with anger.

'What the hell is he doing here, Dar?'

'I'm sorry, Gracie, but we need his help.' Dara turned to look at Robbie. 'Rob, listen to me. You need to get her to the shed, the one over near the river, okay? I'll come and find you soon.'

'Where are you going?'

'I'll tell you later. I'll be back as quick as I can.'

'Dar, wait.' Robbie called her back. 'I can't . . . I can't do it.'

'What are you talking about?'

Robbie's face was grey with fear. 'I can't take her . . . I can't do the dark, Dar . . . I just can't.' He shook his head and Dara could see he was trying not to cry.

She didn't have time for this, no matter how much her heart went out to him. She grabbed hold of his shoulders.

'Robbie, *you have to*. You have to help her, because if you don't, then Barrows will hear her. And then we're all dead.'

Chapter Seventy-Eight

'Hello?' Dara could see her breath in the cold air as she stood in the phone box. She fiddled absent-mindedly with the telephone cord, wrapping it around her fingers.

'Who is this?' The voice on the line was gruff.

'It's Dara.'

There was a pause . . . followed by warm words.

'Hello, Dara, it's good to hear from you . . .' Alan held the phone away from him to finish off snorting up the fat line of cocaine. He swallowed hard, enjoying the familiar taste of the bitter powder at the back of his throat. He put the phone back to his ear. 'Sorry, what was that, darlin'? The line went a bit funny.'

'I said, Gracie's in labour.' Dara wiped away the fat tear running down her cheek. Overwhelmed, she rested her head against the coin box and took in gulps of air. 'I want to take you up on that offer.' Dara spoke hurriedly. 'But you need to come here now, otherwise it'll be too late.'

He rolled his eyes. It was Christmas fucking Eve, and the last thing he needed was some kid giving birth.

'So can you come now?' Dara sounded desperate.

'Yeah, of course, of course I can . . . and thank you . . . this is wonderful news, Dara . . .'

Alan winked at the hooker sitting naked on his bed, waiting for him. Hers was the worst boob job he'd ever seen, but she gave the best head.

'Sorry, say that again, sweetheart?' He attempted to sound interested.

'I want you to promise, *promise* me, you'll take good care of the baby?' Dara struggled to talk. She was taking deep breaths to control her emotions.

'Yeah, yeah, of course . . . You have my word, darlin'.'

Dara chewed on her lip. She had to get back to Gracie. 'There's a river on the edge of the woods. Meet me by the bridge tonight. I don't know how long it'll take . . . Wait for me there, and I'll bring the baby to you. But Alan . . .'

'Yes . . .?'

'Once I hand the baby over, you've got to swear that you'll *never* come to Holly Brookes again. Ever. And if you ever see Gracie or me again after tonight, walk past us. Pretend you don't know us. Can you do that?'

That was easy. It suited him just fine. 'Yeah, of course.'

'And you won't tell anyone?'

'No, I won't. It can be our little secret.'

The line went dead, and Alan smiled.

He needed to make a call.

Chapter Seventy-Nine

'Why's there so much blood, Dar? *Dara*, why's she bleeding like that?'

'I've already told you, I don't fucking know, okay . . . but it'll be fine. *She's* going to be fine.' Dara stared at Robbie.

'But how do—'

'Jesus Christ, Rob, just shut the fuck up, *please.*' She spoke in an urgent whisper. 'And don't ask me any more questions, okay?'

His panicking was making everything worse for her. Not that this situation could really get any fucking worse than it was already, but she didn't want to hear anything else he had to say. For the past half hour, she'd been trying to convince herself that she wasn't frightened, though that was a big fat lie. She was petrified. It was like she was caught in a waking nightmare.

She was determined not to show her fear. She bit hard on the inside of her cheek, willing herself not to cry. She just hoped that Gracie would think her trembling was down to the cold December night.

'What shall I do then, Dar?'

'Just . . . just fucking go back over there, and tell me if you hear anything.'

Robbie was supposed to be on lookout, holding the door of the woodshed closed, in case anyone came along. They couldn't risk being caught hiding out here.

Robbie nodded. In the dim, flickering light of the single candle burning in the corner, Dara could see how wide and fearful his eyes were. Even though he was turning fifteen, he looked much younger.

Dara hated snapping at him. But right now, she couldn't worry about Robbie. God, she had enough to think of. Dara looked at her hands, quickly wiping the blood off them. She hadn't realised there'd be so much blood either. It had seeped out across the floorboards of the old woodshed, creating a trail in the dirt.

Gracie was lying on the floor, groaning in agony. Her usually timid features were contorted aggressively into lines of pain as her swollen stomach contracted and hardened.

'You know you're amazing, I'm *so* proud of you, babe.' Dara still kept her voice to a whisper, but she managed to force a smile.

'Are you, Dar?'

'Of course I am, look how well you're doing.' Dara fought against the tears. The back of her throat felt scratchy. Maybe she was being stupid, but she could almost taste the fear. She wished she could do more to help. She felt fucking useless. The only time she'd seen anything like this, was when her mum's mate had helped some stray dog in the park give birth to a litter of puppies. Some fucking good that was to her now.

'It hurts, Dar . . . it hurts so fucking much. It feels like it's stuck. I don't know if I can do this any more.' The skin on Gracie's stomach was taut and shiny, and she moaned loudly.

'You can, I know you can . . . but try to keep quiet, okay?' Dara wiped away the snot from Gracie's nose on her frayed nylon jumper.

'Is it going to be all right, Dar?' Gracie sounded terrified.

Dara thought about Alan, then pushed him out of her head. 'Yeah, of course it's going to be all right. Anyway, I'm going to look after you, aren't I? Trust me, babe, everything's going to be fine.'

Dara concentrated hard on keeping her voice steady. She hoped what she'd said sounded convincing. She just wished she could believe it herself.

'Now keep pushing, okay? You've got to keep pushing.' Dara wasn't entirely sure if it was the right thing to say or not. But what could she do? She couldn't just stay silent.

'She don't look well, Dara.' Robbie spoke to Dara in a soft voice. 'Are you sure we shouldn't go and get some help?'

'Are you fucking stupid?' Dara glared at Robbie. 'You know what will happen if they find out. And anyway, I've already told you, *shut up!*' She scowled and turned away.

A large black spider was floating in a pool of blood. She hated them, at the best of times, but seeing it drowning in the middle of a gummy blood clot, like a glob of jelly, made her feel sick.

'Dar, Dar, it hurts . . . Oh my God, Dar, help me, help me, I think it's—'

Dara slammed her hand down over Gracie's mouth, but her heart broke for her . . . for her and her child, struggling to be born. '*Sshhhh*, listen to me, Gracie, you can't make a noise, remember? If they catch us they'll . . .' She trailed off, too frightened to finish that sentence, then she moved her hand away slowly.

'It bloody hurts though . . . *Please*, Dar, just get it out, I can't take this pain. *Please*.' Gracie's sobbing was getting louder in between the contractions.

Panicking, Dara knew she had to do something to try to keep Gracie quiet. She unscrewed the cap on the bottle of whiskey she'd stolen from Father Riley's study.

'Get this down you, babe, it should make you feel better. Go on, take a swig.' Dara forced another smile.

She hadn't really planned for Gracie to be drunk, not yet anyway. Dara needed her to be able to concentrate on pushing the baby out, but more importantly, she needed Gracie to be as silent as possible.

'Dar, I'm scared. You won't leave me, will you?'

'Never, ever, ever. I'd never leave you, babe. I promise . . . Now drink some more . . .'

When over half the bottle of whiskey had gone, Dara leant forward, kissing Gracie on her forehead gently. She held her lips there for a moment, listening to her let out another groan. Somehow she needed to keep her completely quiet. The whiskey was doing its job, but she couldn't expect Gracie not to make any noise at all.

Dara shivered again. The powdery snow was blowing through the gaps in the wood and there was just no escape from the freezing temperatures. She was certain this was the safest place for them to be. If anyone noticed they were missing from the dormitory, she doubted they'd think of looking in here.

'Dar . . . it's burning, Dar. My fanny's burning hot. Oh God . . . Dar, what's happening to me?'

'I think that's normal,' Dara answered quickly. 'I dunno, but I guess if I was being stretched open to pop out something the size of a fucking melon, I'd frigging burn too.'

Dara spotted a pile of tatty rags in the corner. They were stained with oil, but they'd have to do. She got up, hurried over and grabbed one, then rushed back. It stank of kerosene, but hopefully it would do the trick. 'I'm going to put this in your mouth, okay, babe. Just bite down on it when you need to scream. But on the next contraction, push really, really hard, like your life depends on it.' She stuffed the rag into Gracie's mouth.

'Okay, now push . . . That's it . . . That's it . . . Oh fucking hell, fucking hell, Gracie, fucking hell, you're doing it . . . Oh shit, *shit* . . . shit, I can see the baby's head. I can see the top of its bleeding head! *Robbie*, look!'

Robbie gave the briefest of looks but immediately began to retch.

Dara whispered fierce encouragements. 'Once more, babe, just one more push, you're doing great . . . That's it, you've got it . . . Oh my God, you've done it . . . shit, *fuck*, Gracie, you've actually fucking done it!' Dara was filled with a mix of excitement and pride.

'What is it, Dar? Tell me what it is.' Gracie smiled. Her words sounded slurred from all the whiskey she'd drunk.

'It's a boy. You've had a boy.'

Chapter Eighty

The baby lay silently on the cold dirty floor. His skin was all blue and mottled, covered in blood and a cheesy white substance. His wrinkled hands were pulled up in a tight fist.

Dara looked over to Robbie. 'Pass that axe.'

'What?' His face drained of colour. 'What do you mean? Dar, what are you going to do?'

'Just pass me the fucking axe. *Now!*' Dara raised her voice as much as she dared, watching Robbie pull the axe out of the log it was embedded in.

He ran across and gave it to her.

She nodded, then without a second thought, brought it down in an arc, severing the umbilical cord. A look of relief passed over Robbie's face. Dara frowned at him but didn't bother saying anything.

Tutting, she scooped up the baby in her arms and wrapped him tightly in the blankets she'd brought along. Oh my God, she could feel the unknitted bones in the baby's crown, and the soft curls at the nape of his neck. Dara said a little prayer and hoped one day God would forgive her.

'Show me, Dar, show him to me . . . Dar, *show* me.'

Dara stood up and drew the baby close to her. She looked down at Gracie as more tears began to blur her vision. How was she going to tell her? She swallowed hard.

'I'm sorry, Gracie. I'm so sorry.'

'What do you mean, *you're sorry*? What are you talking about? Dara, what's wrong? Tell me what's wrong.'

As Gracie began to panic, Dara edged towards the door. 'He didn't make it, babe. He isn't breathing. He just ain't breathing . . . I'm so, so sorry, babe.'

Robbie stared at Dara. She gave him a cold stare in return.

'No, don't say that, Dar . . . No, no, please . . . Pass him to me. Let me hold my baby. Let me take a look at him. This is my fault, ain't it? This is my fault for starving myself and using that band.' Gracie was becoming hysterical. She buried her head in her hands, rocking from side to side. 'Let me see him, let me just see his face, Dar.'

Dara opened the door of the woodshed as swiftly as she could, and shook her head. 'I don't think that's a good idea. It's probably best you don't.'

She stepped outside and turned to Robbie, speaking fast. 'Stay with her, Rob, and give her some more booze, but make sure she doesn't make a noise. When I get back, we'll clear this mess up. Will you be all right?'

Robbie stared at the candle flickering. As long as there was light he'd be fine. 'What are you doing, Dar? Where are you going?'

'Well, I can't exactly leave it here, can I?' Dara began to back away. 'I have to get rid of it.'

'But—'

'But nothing.' Dara narrowed her eyes. 'Do as I fucking tell you. We haven't got long, we need to get back before they miss us, okay?' Glancing around and making certain no one was about, she rushed off deeper into the woods. She wasn't sure what time it was, but she knew it was getting late, so she had to be quick. She just hoped she hadn't been too long.

Although it was dark, thankfully the moon was bright tonight. It lit up the snow, making it easier for Dara to see where she was going. The scene was beautiful and pure, which only made what Dara was about to do even uglier. She darted through the trees. Her lungs filled with the cold air and her heart raced. She hated everything about what they were doing . . . what *she* was doing. But it was better this way.

Eventually, she came to the clearing by the stream. Her gaze moved around slowly. On the other side of the river, Dara spotted a large black car, parked under the trees. She froze, then moved back into the shadows as quietly as she could. The muffled crunch of snow underfoot, amplified by the stillness of the night, added to Dara's fear.

She stood and watched for a moment, then saw the car head-lights flash on and off. From where she was standing, Dara glimpsed the silhouette of a man getting out of the car. He walked over the small wooden bridge and strode purposefully towards where she was hiding.

She stepped forward. 'Alan—'

She stopped and stared at the person in front of her. What was going on? This wasn't Alan.

'Who are you—?'

'No names.' The man cut in quickly. 'The least said, the better. Don't you know, the night has ears, sweetheart . . . Alan sent me, he thought it would be better like this. He didn't want anyone to see him.'

Dara stared at him. 'Why didn't he tell me?'

'If there's a problem, I can go.' The man shrugged.

'No, no wait . . . it's fine.'

Dara couldn't think straight, but she nodded. She watched him tap out a cigarette, light it, take a drag, drawing the smoke into his lungs.

He narrowed his eyes. 'What about the mother?'

Dara knew he didn't really care. But then, none of them did. They were all bastards. Mean fucking bastards. But she knew better than to say that, so she glanced down at the baby, listening to him beginning to gurgle.

'She thinks he's dead.'

'*Dead?* Why?'

Dara wiped her runny nose on the back of her hand and thought about the question. Her plan had been to hand the baby over to Alan, but she hadn't thought through how she was going to take the baby away from Gracie.

When the baby hadn't cried straight away, she'd taken the opportunity – without really thinking – to pretend to Gracie that he hadn't made it. It was the deepest betrayal, but Dara told herself she was doing it out of love. It seemed the kindest thing to do for Gracie, because there was no way the baby could stay with her. And Dara didn't want Gracie to feel like *she* did about Tommy and the rest of her siblings: knowing they were out there somewhere, but never being able to reach them.

Shrugging, she sniffed. She didn't want to cry in front of this man. 'It would have destroyed her. Giving him up. This way, it makes it easier for her, thinking that he's dead.'

He chuckled and flicked the cigarette butt into the snow. Then he stretched out his arms for the baby.

Dara told herself again, this was the lesser of two evils. Even so, for a moment she didn't move. She kissed the baby on his head. He was so tiny.

'You'll keep him warm, won't you? He needs to be kept warm.' Dara's words tumbled out. Shaking with emotion, she reluctantly handed him over. 'He would've been loved, you know. If Gracie could've kept him, she would've been the best bleeding mum in the entire world.'

Cradling the baby in one arm, the man laughed nastily. 'You keep telling yourself that, sweetheart. He's probably well fucking rid of her.'

He turned to go, but she grabbed his coat. Every instinct in Dara told her to rip his eyes out. Who the hell did he think he was? But she kept a lid on her emotions. 'You will tell Alan to look after him, won't you? Tell him not to let anything hurt him.'

He pushed her roughly, and Dara stumbled, falling backwards into the snow. He hawked up loudly, forcefully spitting a lump of saliva and phlegm from the back of his throat into Dara's face.

'Happy Christmas, darling. Now do me a favour and *fuck off*.'

Trembling and angry, Dara wiped her face as he marched towards his car.

Watching it drive away, her heart began to beat faster. Panic rushed through her. Clarity. What had she done? What the *fuck* had she done? Her fear had made her take the wrong decision. How could she possibly think it was all right to give away Gracie's baby to a stranger?

She scrambled up quickly and started to run. 'No, wait! *Wait* . . . Please wait! Please, come back . . . Come back, I've changed my mind . . . Please. Oh my God, *please*.'

Even though the car was beginning to speed up, Dara continued to sprint after it, slipping in the fresh snow that was falling, already covering the icy tracks as the car disappeared into the night.

'No . . . No, *wait*. Wait, come back! *Come back!*'

'Dar?'

She spun round and saw Robbie staring at her. He stood holding the flickering candle. His cheeks were flushed red. In that moment, shame and guilt overwhelmed Dara, but they quickly turned to anger.

Crying hysterically, she ran up to him. She snatched hold of his arm, and shook him like a rag doll. The candle flame went out.

'Why are you sneaking up on me, Rob? Why are you fucking spying on me? I told you to stay with her.'

'She . . . she started to bleed again, Dar. I didn't know what to do, so I followed your tracks, because I thought you better come and see her.'

The wind began to get up, whipping the snow into their faces. Dara looked around. She stared into the darkness of the woods. A sense of unease crept over her. She squeezed Robbie's arm hard. 'What did you see? What did you see, Rob?'

'Enough. I saw enough . . .' He paused. A look of bewilderment flashed through his sunken eyes. 'Why, Dar? Why did you tell Gracie the baby was dead?'

'Because . . . because it's better this way. I thought it was for the best. She won't have to watch him suffering now. All those things that happened to you . . . I didn't want that for him . . . So you keep your mouth shut, *understand*?'

Robbie nodded as tears rolled down his cheeks.

'And if I find out you've told anyone, even if it's in ten, twenty, thirty years' time, I swear to God, Robbie, I'll kill you.'

Chapter Eighty-One

'Do you think this is what I bleedin' want either?' Judy hissed down the phone to Alan. She wasn't going to budge on this. 'It's impossible.'

'Here's the thing, Judy, I don't actually know what you want any more. I did what you asked me to do, even though I think it's some fucked-up madness. I still did it, but now, *now* you're saying you can't take the fucking baby.'

'Don't you dare talk about him like that.' Judy was incensed. 'And let's have it right, Alan, the only reason you agreed was to save yourself. So wind your neck in and stop making out like you did me a favour.'

'What part of this are you incapable of understanding, Judy? I can't have it here.'

'And I can't have it here with me – not yet. Give it a few days, maybe a week.'

'A week, are you kidding?'

Judy looked through to the lounge and the small Christmas tree by the hearth.

What had happened the other day, well, it wasn't the first time their house had been raided looking for images of Frank's '*tastes*'. Conveniently, like all the other times, Dennis and Lewis had made sure all charges were quietly dropped.

Frank had eventually arrived back home, to be greeted by a worried Judy. Of course he'd feigned innocence – even though she knew the police had found and taken away the shoebox of photos he hid behind the outhouse in the backyard.

But now it wouldn't be prudent to bring the baby home. The Old Bill would likely pay them another visit in the next couple of days, to put the pressure on. They'd done that in the past: popped in to have another little *chat* with Frank. Was Judy being paranoid? She wasn't sure. But she'd read in the papers recently that the police had set up a special division to start cracking down on men's *indiscretions*.

Judy wasn't going to take the chance. She didn't want them to find a newborn baby here and start asking questions she couldn't answer.

It had been awkward enough explaining away all the baby paraphernalia she'd amassed. The police had presumed it was some sort of sick fetish of Frank's. And even when she'd told them it all belonged to her sister – who'd recently had a nervous breakdown after poor Jimmy's death – they'd carried on as if there was something not quite right about having baby stuff without a child. Trying to tarnish it with their own filthy minds. Disgusting pigs.

'Judy? Judy . . . are you still there?' Alan's voice boomed down the phone.

'Of course I'm still here . . . I was thinking.' She was so close to getting what she'd longed for, but she was going to have to be patient. 'Look, I'll be in touch, all right. In the meantime, I'm going to send Frank around with some supplies.'

She stared at the bags of baby clothes, bottles, nappies and the Silver Cross pram in the hall.

Well, he'd need that, wouldn't he? Little Frank Junior.

*

Alan slammed down the phone. He was sitting at his kitchen table. He reached for the large glass of whiskey he'd only just poured, and knocked it back in one. This was not how he imagined celebrating Christmas fucking Day.

He looked across at Jason. 'Stupid bitch. That woman is off her fucking nut.'

He stared at the baby. It was tiny, and it hadn't made any noise, apart from a few gurgling sounds. But he wasn't feeling a rush of paternal fucking affection for it. As far as Alan was concerned, it was merely an inconvenience. An unwelcome intrusion that had royally fucked over his Christmas.

Alan frowned. 'Maybe you can help.'

'Me?' Jason scoffed. 'What do you want me to do with it?'

Of all the jobs Alan had asked Jason to do, driving down to Holly Brookes to pick up a baby was the strangest gig. But Alan had made it worth his while – and since Jake had taken him to the cleaners, it was just as well.

'Do I look like the fucking Christmas stork to you, Al?'

Alan poured himself another glass of whiskey. He was going to need several.

'Well, do *I* look like someone who runs a fucking nursery? Jesus Christ, Jase.'

But right then, Alan suddenly had an idea . . .

A few hours later, Jason strode into the house in Langley Lane.

'Okay, so it wasn't the Star of Bethlehem I followed – rather the A202 from Dulwich – but I still come bearing gifts, sweetheart.'

He placed the Moses basket on the table and smiled nastily.

'Happy Christmas, Sam. Never say I don't bring you nothing.'

Chapter Eighty-Two

'Oh my God.' Samantha stared at the baby. 'Jason, what is this?'

He lit a cigarette. He was tired and he didn't want any of Samantha's shit. 'And there's you working with kids, I thought you would've known a baby when you saw one.'

She glared at Jason. Sarcastic bastard.

She scooped the baby up in her arms. 'It must be only hours old.'

Jason shrugged. Like Alan, he didn't care. '*He* must be hours old.'

'Yeah, well, *he* needs to get checked out at the hospital as soon as possible. What about the mother, where is she? Is she all right?'

Jason stepped towards her, and nervously she backed away. The fight in Samantha had been extinguished long ago.

'Don't ask me, Sam, I'm not a fucking midwife.'

She turned up the heating on the thermostat on the wall, grabbed a couple of tea towels, and wrapped the baby up. 'What's his name? Who does he belong to? Jase . . . Jase?'

Jason clearly didn't want an interrogation from his wife.

He squeezed the bridge of his nose. 'Shut the fuck up, Sam.' His voice darkened. 'I don't need my fucking ear chewed off by you. Now I brought him here, so you can look after him, that's all.'

'But Jase, he needs someone to look him over.'

'No, he doesn't.' He poked Samantha in her chest. 'That's your job . . . *You* need to make sure he's all right. There's nappies, milk powder, bottles, clothes, I've even got a fucking pram in the back of my car. So you've got everything you need for the next week.'

Samantha blinked rapidly. 'Jason, what's going on?'

'Just do what I've told you.'

'Jase, *please*, I can't do this.' She shook her head. 'I can't just look after someone else's child without knowing what's going on.'

She looked down at the baby's face. Thankfully, some colour was coming to his cheeks. She placed him gently back into the Moses basket and turned on the gas under a pan of water, to sterilise the bottles as best she could.

She looked over at Jason. 'What about the mother?' She asked him the same question again.

'Who fucking cares? She doesn't want him, but somebody else does.' He stubbed out his cigarette in the teacup on the draining board.

Samantha took a risk by speaking up. Jason had been bad enough before, but since Jake left, the wind changing direction was a good enough excuse for him to get handy with his fists.

'What do you mean, *somebody else does?*' She frowned. There was something very wrong here. 'What's going on, Jase? Seriously, who does he belong to?'

She watched the anger flash across Jason's face. He had the urge to slap her. Hard. Really hard. She braced herself.

But it seemed he couldn't be bothered to put her in her place. More likely, he was eager to get back to whichever whore was waiting for him at the club.

'All I know is, his mum's some little scrubber, and they've made arrangements for him to go to some couple who wants him.'

'You mean she's sold him?'

'Sold him, bought him, swapped him. I don't give a shit . . . It's all the same, ain't it?'

Samantha was shocked. 'Who to? Jase? Who's he going to? Do you even know who this couple are?'

'Don't worry, sweetheart, they're friends of Dennis Hargreaves. Now enough with the fucking questions.'

Sam heard a tiny sound from the baby. She rushed across to him, picking him up again, holding him close.

Jason turned to go. 'Make sure nothing happens to him, all right. If it does, it's on your head.' There was a clear threat to it. 'I'll be back in a few days to check everything's all right. If you want me, I'll be at the club. Oh, and say hello to Phyllis for me, will you?'

She heard the front door click shut, then looked down at the baby.

A chill ran through her. Dennis Hargreaves. A name no child should be linked with.

Chapter Eighty-Three

'All right, all right, I'm coming . . . Fucking hell, *hold on*. What's the emergency? No one can be that thirsty for a pint.'

The door of the Beehive swung open.

'You do know we're closed, I . . .' Deana trailed off and stood open-mouthed.

'Hello, Deana.'

'Sam? Oh my God, Sam . . . come in.' Deana stared at Samantha's face.

Her left eye was half closed from the scarred and damaged skin that had grown over it. Her cheek was indented with dark marks and more scars. One side of her mouth, although it had healed, had clearly been badly mauled. It was pulled down and disfigured, making her look like she was recovering from a stroke.

'Jesus Christ, Sam . . .' Deana stood on the concrete steps outside the Beehive, not even noticing the cold. 'Please tell me that Jason didn't do that to you.'

Samantha, who was in constant pain now from her injuries, bristled. Over the past couple of days, she'd thought about coming to see Deana, but each time she'd changed her mind. She hadn't wanted to face her, because she'd been worried about Deana having *exactly this* reaction. But when Samantha had thought of the baby and Dennis Hargreaves – of what that actually meant – she'd forced herself to come and see her.

Samantha didn't know the identity of the couple who'd been lined up to take the baby, but she'd heard the rumours surrounding Dennis. Anyone who was a friend of Dennis's would never be a friend of hers, nor would they *ever* be suitable parents. Somehow, Samantha had to stop it . . . though for that, she needed help.

'Look, I'm not here to talk about that, all right?' Samantha was firm.

Deana nodded. 'Of course, sorry. It's so good to see you. Can I get you a drink, darlin'? Come in. Let's have a tipple and a catch-up—'

Deana suddenly stopped, noticing for the first time the pram Samantha was pushing. She frowned, then looked up at Samantha.

'Is he . . .?' But she didn't finish. This wasn't her business.

'I need to get in contact with Jake.'

This time, it was Deana who looked awkward. She was also surprised.

'I don't know where he is, love. Last time I saw him, he was in a bad way. Boozing too much. I think it hit him harder than he thought it would, you know, losing you.'

Samantha shook her head. 'Are you for real, Deana? He never lost me, he got rid of me, remember? As I recall, you were his messenger.' She was bitter but more than anything else, it still hurt.

'Yeah . . . sorry.'

The two women stared at each other. There was so much they wanted to say and ask. But instead, the silence between them made them feel like strangers.

'Jake once told me if I ever needed him, I should call him. And I know . . .' Samantha took a deep breath, trying to control her emotions. 'I know things might be different now that he's with someone else, but I really need to speak to him.'

Deana averted her gaze. 'Like I say, darlin', I really don't know where he is. I'm sorry I can't help you.' She looked at the baby again, but said nothing. 'Sam, please let me get you a drink. Come in from the cold.'

Samantha shook her head. 'No, no, thank you. I need to go . . . But if Jake does happen to get in touch, tell him, I was looking for him . . . *Please*.'

Watched by Deana, Samantha walked away, pushing the pram through the light covering of snow on the pavement.

Deana wrapped her blue cardigan around her tightly. She stared up at the sky. It looked like there was going to be a storm. She hurried inside, and moved behind the bar, picking up the phone.

It was answered on the second ring.

'Hello, darlin', it's me, Deana . . . I've got something I need to tell you.'

Chapter Eighty-Four

It looked to Dara like an infection had set in. Gracie's temperature was raging hot, and she was still bleeding heavily. It was five days since she'd had the baby, and Dara didn't know whether or not that was normal. She was no doctor, but even Dara could see how ill Gracie looked.

'What the fuck are we going to do?' Dara spoke quietly, with fierce urgency.

Robbie, who had sneaked into the girls' dormitory, sat on the bed with Dara, staring at Gracie. She seemed delirious, muttering incoherently to herself.

'What did Barrows say?' he asked quietly, not answering Dara's question directly.

'Nothing much, he thinks that she's picked up a virus. Winter cold. Told her to stay in bed. He doesn't give a shit, does he?'

'Yeah, but maybe that's a good thing?' Robbie wondered. 'We don't want them checking her over, do we? They'll know.'

What Robbie said made sense, but that still didn't help Dara know what to do for the best. She had convinced herself that, after Gracie had given birth, everything would go back to normal, including Gracie's body. She hadn't known she would continue to bleed, and her boobs leak milk.

'But I do think we need to get her to hospital, Dar.' Robbie turned to Dara. 'She looks in a bad way. We don't want anything to happen to her, what if . . . what if . . .?'

'Don't say it!' Dara knew exactly what Robbie was alluding to, and she didn't want to hear it. 'Just don't . . . She'll be fine. We'll keep an eye on her.'

Dara touched Gracie's forehead. Gracie moaned slightly but kept her eyes shut. Since she'd had the baby, she'd barely uttered a word. Within hours, her temperature had shot up. And since then, it hadn't gone down – if anything, Gracie felt hotter.

Robbie grasped Dara's arm. 'Dar, what if she isn't though? You can't just pretend this isn't happening.' He stared straight into her eyes. 'Dar, I love you, but this ain't right. Look at her, she's in a bad way. She needs to see someone.' For once, Robbie was firm.

'Do you think I don't know that?' Dara snatched her arm away.

She was angry. Not because of what Robbie had said, but because of her own guilt. It was eating her up. Guilt about the baby. Guilt about Gracie being ill. This was all down to her.

'But how? Come on then, Rob, you tell me, how the fuck are we supposed to get her to hospital? Because they're never going to take her, are they?'

Everything in Holly Brookes stayed behind the locked gates. That way, they could control everything. Dara had rarely seen any sort of proper medical care in the place. A few months ago, one of the younger kids had broken her leg when Clemence had pushed her downstairs. He'd refused to let her be seen by anyone other than the nurse who worked here and the doctor who visited twice a week, with his wandering fingers, and who smelt of booze. As a result of their useless care, the leg had healed badly, and the poor kid had ended up with a pronounced limp.

'Dar, please don't get angry with me. I want to help.'

Dara put her head in her hands. 'What am I going to do, Robbie?' She didn't want him to see her crying.

'Dar, it's okay . . . I know you're doing the best you can. But you know as well as I do, we can't leave her like this, even if it means telling them about the baby.'

Dara dropped her hands and glared at him. 'No. I've already warned you, we tell no one, *ever.*'

'So you'd rather let her die?'

Dara pushed Robbie with both hands. 'You think that's what I want? You think I want Gracie to die?'

'No . . . but . . . but we've got to do something before it's too late.'

Dara wiped her eyes. She didn't even want to look at Robbie right now. She was so mad at him. 'Since I found out she was pregnant, I've done *nothing* but try to keep her safe.' She turned back to him. 'Have you any idea what it's been like, keeping a secret so big?'

Robbie looked away, and his shoulders dropped.

'So don't you fucking dare say that to me, you hear me, Robbie? Don't you *ever* say I want anything bad to happen to Gracie . . . I'll sort it, okay? I'll fucking sort it . . . I'll make sure, somehow, I get Gracie to a hospital.'

Chapter Eighty-Five

A hand slammed over Samantha's mouth, and she began to struggle, fighting as though her life depended on it. Images of the beating Jason had given her came into her mind as terror rushed through her body.

'Sam . . . Sam, *sshhhh*, it's okay . . . it's me.'

Samantha froze. The hand over her mouth was removed. In shock, she blinked.

'Jake?'

She swallowed quickly, not wanting to give away any of her emotions.

'Yeah, it's me, I got your message from Deana. She said you needed to speak to me.'

Jake reached over, and switched on the light on Samantha's bedside cabinet. What he saw shocked him.

'Oh my God . . . I'm going to fucking kill him.'

Jake turned for the door, but Samantha leapt across the bed, grabbing his coat.

'No. Jake, no. *Stop*. Stop . . . wait . . . Don't you dare. Don't you dare turn up here and suddenly decide you're going to play the hero of the bleedin' hour.'

'Sam—'

'*No!*' Samantha interrupted firmly. 'You stay away from him. I didn't ask you here for that. You're not going to leave me to pick up the pieces when you disappear again.' Her voice caught in her throat.

Deana clearly hadn't told Jake about Samantha's injuries. She must have thought it was for the best; she knew he would've hunted Jason down.

He couldn't take his eyes off the scars all over her face. His hand rested on the door.

'Jake, don't do it . . . *Please.*'

Jake didn't move for a moment, and Samantha appealed to him again.

'Jake, I'm asking you . . . For me, *please*, leave it. What's done is done.'

He nodded and sat on the bed, then touched her face, moving his finger gently over the damaged and scarred skin. 'When did this happen?'

She pulled away. 'The day you left. He found out about you and me.'

Samantha knew she was lucky to be alive, but didn't say it. Jake was visibly distressed, consumed by guilt.

'How . . .? How did he find out?'

Samantha let out a bitter laugh. 'My mum.'

'So she told him, after all.'

'What do you mean?' Samantha was puzzled. 'You knew that my mum had found out about us? And what . . . you didn't think to say anything?' Her voice was rising, but she covered her mouth. She didn't trust herself not to scream.

'It wasn't like that.'

'No? You left me here, knowing that, at any time, she could open her mouth and tell Jase.'

'She promised.' Jake was ashamed. He looked away.

'Promised? We're talking about *my mum*. Phyllis. When has she ever kept her word?'

Jake became defensive. 'Sam, I already told you, it wasn't like that.'

'Then what, what was it like, hey? Because I know what it was like for me when Jason was beating the shit out of me, and you were holed up with your new fancy woman. Oh I know what that was like, all right.'

'Samantha, please, I—'

'No, I don't want to hear what you've got to say, Jake. And you know why? Because I don't need to talk about it with you.' She was angry now. 'I'm reminded of what happened every time I look in the mirror. Every time I blink, I feel it. I'm in pain . . . constantly. It hurts, but none of it hurts as much as me turning up at the Beehive, only for Deana to tell me that you had someone else. That scar runs so deep you can't see it. So you can keep whatever it is you've got to say to yourself.'

'Sam—'

'I said, *no*.'

Just then a sound coming from the corner of the room made Jake turn. He hadn't noticed the cot before. Walking over to it, Jake didn't say anything.

'That's why I needed to see you. I didn't know what else to do.'

Jake nodded. 'Why didn't you tell me before?'

'What do you mean?'

'Why didn't you come and find me before? You didn't have to do this on your own.'

'I . . .' She wasn't sure what to say because, in truth, she wasn't absolutely certain what Jake meant.

He looked at her straight. 'I take it he's mine?'

Samantha was taken aback. She'd had no idea Jake would leap to this conclusion. No idea at all. But she supposed it made sense. Why else would he think she was getting in contact, now that he'd seen the baby?

She opened her mouth to correct him, but she suddenly stopped, and thought about it . . . What if, when she told Jake the truth, he didn't want to help her? Could she really risk that? What if he *refused* to get involved, and walked away? What would she do then? How could she protect this baby, if there was no one to help her?

She was no match for Jase, and she daren't even report it. There were so few people she could trust. She couldn't prove it, but Samantha knew there was a network of power. Miller, her boss, was part of it, she was sure. So there was no one to turn to.

But there was also no way Samantha could let this couple, these '*friends*' of Dennis's, have the baby. No way at all . . . over her dead body.

She scooped the baby up into her arms, rocking him back to sleep. She smiled at Jake. How many lies had already been told? What difference would one more make?

'Yes, yes, Jake, he's yours.'

Chapter Eighty-Six

'Robbie, help her. Quickly. Help lift her up.'

Robbie looked at Gracie, then back at Dara, who was busy giving him orders. Gracie didn't look well at all; she was pale and sweating, and Robbie wondered if she was going to throw up again. She'd already vomited several times.

'What are we going to do, Dar? I don't think she can go anywhere, not like this.'

Dara was stressed and frightened. She glared at Robbie, keeping her voice down. 'She's got to. And anyway, you were the one who said she needed to see someone,' she reminded him.

She knelt by Gracie's feet and took her friend's face in her hands, lifting her chin up gently until their eyes met. 'Gracie, baby, I'm going to get you out of here, but I need *you* to help me, all right? You have to stay awake for me. Can you do that?'

Gracie didn't answer, but she gave the tiniest nod of her head.

Dara manoeuvred her shoulder under Gracie's arm, and gestured for Robbie to do the same. Then they made their way as quietly as possible, heading out of the dormitory, along the hallway and down the main stairs, stopping occasionally to let Gracie rest.

At the back door, with Gracie leaning her weight on Dara, Robbie turned the handle. The door was jammed. He rattled it again.

'Shit, Dar, it's locked.' He glanced around for the key, which was usually on the hook, but it was nowhere to be seen. 'What now?'

'Let's go through the kitchen. That door's never locked.'

Dara walked with Gracie, holding her up. It felt like she was getting drowsier as she leant more weight on Dara.

'Here, you hold her up.' Dara left Gracie with Robbie and hurried to open the heavy door. She was hit by a blast of icy wind. 'Come on, Rob, we need to hurry, it's getting late—'

'*Where do you think you're going?*'

Dara turned around to see a swaying Clemence heading their way, a tumbler of whiskey in one hand, an unlit cigarette in the other. His face was twisted in hatred. 'So come on then, what's so important out there?'

He stepped forward, inches away from Dara's face, blasting her with the stench of booze. 'What are you up to?' Flecks of his saliva sprayed her face.

'Robbie, go . . . *go!* Take her!' Dara shouted, pushing Clemence back, allowing Robbie and Gracie to get out.

Clemence staggered but regained his balance, dropping his cigarette.

He lunged at Dara, sending kitchen utensils crashing to the floor. Dara managed to grab a pan. She swung it wildly and hit Clemence hard over the head.

Enraged, and holding his head, he charged at her. 'You fucking stupid bitch! *Come here.*'

Clemence caught hold of her clothes. He pushed Dara against the large cooker, trapping her beneath his weight, and turned on the gas flame.

Dara tried to fight as Clemence began to force her hand towards the fire.

'No, *please*, no . . . *don't.*' Dara begged.

Clemence's laughter was cruel. He held her hand above the flame, searing the skin on her palm.

Dara screamed, the pain rushed through her. 'Let go, *let go!*'

Dara had never felt pain like it, and she continued to struggle. From out of the corner of her eye, she saw the glint of steel. Instinctively she reached out her arm, her fingers scrabbling to snatch the knife.

Managing to grab hold of it, with one rapid swipe, Dara plunged it into Clemence's leg.

'*FUCK!*'

Clemence fell to the floor, holding on to his leg. Blood poured out.

For a moment, Dara was frozen. She let the knife slip out of her hand and fall to the floor with a resounding clatter. The sound triggered her to snap out of her trance and begin to run.

It was sleeting hard now. The wind had picked up, cutting into their faces.

It wasn't until they got to the road, where the light was better, that Robbie stared at Dara's hands.

'What happened? Dar, what's that?'

She looked down and saw her hands were covered in blood. Clemence's.

'Nothing.' She wiped her palms on her jeans, wincing as the scorched skin brushed against the coarse denim. 'I cut myself on the barbed wire when we were coming through the woods.' She shrugged.

She wasn't about to tell Robbie what had happened. She only hoped that Clemence wouldn't call the police – that's, of course, if he made it.

419

'It's no big deal. I just want to get out of here . . . Come on, this way.'

They continued walking for a couple of minutes, Gracie leaning her weight on Robbie. They were moving much slower than Dara would've liked. They needed to get as far away from Holly Brookes as possible.

All of a sudden, Robbie stopped. '*Shit*, what are we going to do now? Maybe we should go back into the woods?' He stared at the car parked up by the phone box. The lights were on, the engine running, and smoke was billowing from the exhaust.

'It's fine.' Dara continued to walk in the direction of the car.

'Dar, wait . . . be careful . . . Dar, *stop*, what are you doing?' Robbie called out after her.

Dara, watched by Robbie, opened the car door. She gestured to him to get in. 'Come on, give Gracie a hand. Robbie . . . Robbie, get in, it's fine.'

Robbie was unsure, but he did what Dara asked. He helped Gracie in first, before getting in himself.

With Gracie on one side of her, and Robbie on the other, Dara spoke to the driver from the back seat.

'Thanks for picking us up.'

Alan Carver turned round.

'You hardly gave me any fucking choice, did you?' He was seething. 'But like you said on the phone, no one wants any more trouble.'

Dara remembered the late-night call to the number scribbled on the piece of paper. She'd threatened to expose what they'd done if he didn't help. Would she have gone through with it? She didn't know. But she'd relied on Alan not wanting to take the risk.

He looked at Gracie. 'I hope she's not going to die on me.'

'Then you better get us to the hospital quick . . .'

As Alan drove off, Dara gave one last backward look at Holly Brookes. There was no going back now. She squeezed Gracie's hand. There was no denying she was afraid, and what she'd done to Clemence was weighing on her mind, but no matter what happened, Dara supposed nothing could be worse than Holly Brookes.

That nightmare was finally over.

It had taken a couple of hours to get to London. The bad weather hadn't let up the whole journey.

Thankfully, they were outside St Thomas' Hospital now. And looking at Gracie, how ill she was, it couldn't have come soon enough.

Dara shuffled forward in her seat. She stared out. It was strange to be here. Strange to see how life had continued to roll on, while her life felt like it had stopped. Two years ago, her whole life had changed. She'd been driven from here to Holly Brookes . . . and nothing would ever be the same again.

Alan had driven the whole way in silence.

She clicked her fingers. 'I need some money.'

He fished out his wallet and grabbed a wad of notes. He slammed it into Dara's hand.

'Thanks. You'll never hear from us again . . .'

As they got out of the car, Robbie caught Alan's eye.

A look passed between them of pure hatred.

Chapter Eighty-Seven

'We need to get out of here. Don't bother grabbing anything, we can sort out everything we need later.'

Jake spoke urgently to Samantha while she held the baby in her arms. Right now, he didn't have time to think about it all. What it meant to have a son. To be a father. But Jake did know he was going to do right by the child. By both of them. He was going to look after Samantha, and make sure she wanted for nothing, ever again. Though right now, they needed to get as far away from London as they could. As fast as they could.

Samantha was tense. It was all happening so quickly. She hadn't known what to expect – she hadn't expected Jake to even show his face – and now, not only were they running away, but Jake thought they were the parents to this tiny bundle.

She smiled down at the baby, listening to him gurgling away. He looked healthy now, with a rosy colour in his cheeks. Although Samantha didn't like to judge, she decided whoever the *real* mother of this child was, not only did she not deserve him, but she should be ashamed of what she'd done.

'Are you sure it's going to be all right?' she asked Jake.

'If you're talking about Phyllis, as much as it sticks in my fucking throat, doll, I'll make sure to send someone around in the morning to sort her out.' He shrugged. 'Whether that's a care home . . . who knows? But she'll be fine.'

'I don't mean Mum.' Though that didn't stop Samantha being relieved that Phyllis, for all that she was, would be all right without her. 'I mean, leaving like this. You and me. How do I know you aren't going to disappear again?'

Jake tried to ignore the anger that rose up in him like a red mist every time he looked at Samantha's face and saw what Jason had done to her. 'Sam, I never stopped loving you.'

She turned away. Some things she didn't want to talk about.

'Let's go.' Jake smiled at her and kissed her head, then leant down to kiss the baby. 'We haven't even thought of a name.' Jake was full of pride. 'Once we have, we can sort out his papers, birth certificate and all that. I know some people who ain't exactly friends of Jason's. They'll be more than happy to help us, so we don't have to worry about him finding us.'

Samantha could smell the booze coming off Jake in waves, and she briefly wondered how much he was drinking these days. But she just smiled, and didn't say anything. All she cared about in this present moment was the prospect of finally being able to escape her life. And while it was based on a lie, some things were worth lying about.

Samantha placed the Moses basket on the back seat, strapping it in. 'I'll drive, Jakey.'

'I can't let a woman drive for me.' He winked at her.

'Yeah, well, this time, you have to. You've been drinking.' Good-humouredly, Samantha put out her hand. 'Come on . . . keys, mister.'

He threw them over and grinned. God, he'd missed her.

Settling herself behind the wheel, Samantha realised she had no idea where they were headed.

423

'Where to?' She turned to Jake. 'I've always fancied the coast myself.'

'Then the coast—'

There was a loud bang on the bonnet.

Samantha and Jake looked up at the same time.

'The prodigal son returns.' Jason was leaning on the bonnet in the pouring rain. 'Come on, get out, you fucking cunt . . . GET OUT of the fucking car.' He slammed his fist down again.

'You're about to get what's coming . . .' Jake spoke the words more to himself.

He went to open the door, but Samantha put her hand on his.

'Leave it, don't do anything stupid . . . Jake, *please* . . . Jake, let's just go.'

Before Samantha had time to switch on the engine, Jake leapt out of the car.

'*JAKE!*' Samantha yelled, but it was too late.

Panic gripped her. She knew what Jake was like when he was on the booze, and she was terrified of what he might do. But she was more afraid that Jason would blurt out the truth about the baby.

The rain beat down on the windscreen as Samantha watched them talk. Within seconds, Jason swung his fist at Jake, sending him stumbling backwards, crashing to the ground, the booze clearly making him less stable on his feet.

Panicking, Samantha reversed. She rolled down the window. 'Jake, get up, get up . . . come on, get in, *get in!*'

Jason spun around to look at her. The rain ran down his face. His eyes blazed with anger. 'You fucking stupid bitch, you are one dead whore.'

Samantha glanced at Jake, but he was struggling to get up. She fumbled in the dark with the gears.

In front of her, Jason smiled maniacally. He walked slowly towards the stalled car. 'I'm going to enjoy this.'

Samantha's heart raced, and she turned the engine back on, revving it loudly. She glared at Jason.

He locked his merciless stare on her face. He took one step closer to the car.

Without thinking, she put her foot on the accelerator, driving forward at speed, into Jason, throwing his body into the air.

'Oh my God . . . oh my God.' She gripped the wheel and stared at Jason's motionless body.

She jumped as the car door opened. Jake got in. He stared ahead.

'Jake . . . I'm—'

He turned to her, his eyes dark, and simply said, 'Drive. Just drive.'

Chapter Eighty-Eight

Judy was beside herself with excitement.

She looked around the room. Checking everything, again.

The temperature was perfect. Not too hot, not too cold. The yellow blankets had been washed, softened, then hung out to air. The terry towelling sheet on the white wooden cot was the best-quality cotton the House of Fraser sold. The full-length curtains, which were yellow too, were satin and lined to keep out draughts. Judy had even got Frank to take up the old carpets and lay some new vinyl flooring that could be easily washed to get rid of any dirt or dust. The last thing she wanted was for Frank Junior to get a cough.

Judy felt butterflies fluttering in her stomach. She couldn't believe it. She wrapped her arms around herself and let out a burst of delighted laughter.

Judy gasped when she heard the front door click. She hurried out of the room, rushing down the stairs to meet her family.

Judy beamed. 'Welcome ho—' She stopped. The half-spoken word was lost. Puzzled, she stared at Frank. 'Where is he?'

Frank took off his cap, and placed it on the hallway table. He unzipped his wax coat and slowly took it off, hanging it up on the hook.

'Frank . . . I said, *where is he?*' Judy hurried over to him. She grabbed his arm. 'Frank, tell me what's happened? Is he ill? Has something happened to him? Frank, please.' Judy was desperate, and even without knowing quite what was going on, she felt tears prick her eyes. 'Talk to me . . . Frank, tell me.'

Frank sniffed. He regarded Judy, who was wide-eyed now. 'He ain't coming.'

'What?' Her voice was almost too quiet for Frank to hear.

Her knees buckled and Judy held on to the wall to prevent herself from falling. Snot ran down from her nose. Her eyes filled with tears. 'What are you talking about? No, I've got everything ready. I even ordered some of that blue elephant wallpaper for him.'

'What else can I say, Jude? I don't know all the ins and outs, but it's messy. According to Alan, the woman who was looking after him did a moonlight flit.'

'She can't have . . . She can't have taken my baby.' Judy banged her head against the wall. 'No, no, no, *no!*' She stopped and turned to glare at Frank. Trembling, she pointed to him. 'This is your fault. *YOURS.*'

'What?'

'This. Him, gone . . . This wouldn't have happened if it wasn't for you and your friends . . . You filthy, filthy fucker.' She screamed at Frank. 'If the police hadn't raided the place, looking for your secret stash, then I would've been holding *my* baby in my arms.'

'He's not *your* baby.' Frank was angry now.

'He is! He's *mine.*' She wailed and bent over. 'He's mine.' An animal sound was coming from her.

Frank had heard enough. He grabbed his coat and hat and headed out.

'Don't you walk away from me. Don't you dare FUCKING

walk out on me.' Judy bellowed after him. 'I want you to go and find him. I want my baby back. *Our* baby. You hear me?'

'It's over, Judy. He's gone. Accept it.'

'No, no . . . no, don't say that. DON'T SAY THAT!'

'Fuck this.' He went to open the door.

'Where do you think you're going, *Sidney*?'

Frank clicked the front door closed again. 'What did you call me?' His voice was low.

'You heard me . . . *Sidney*.' Judy spat out his real name again.

He turned around, his eyes dark and cold.

'Yeah, I know who you really are.' Judy was full of hatred. 'Oh, what, are you surprised, *Sidney*? I've known all about you for a *very* long time.'

He walked towards her slowly. 'Is that right, darlin'?'

'Yeah, yeah it is. So what you need to do is, get out there and find my baby. You wouldn't want the police to know all about you, would you? Because by the time I've finished, no one – not even Dennis, not even Lewis – no one will be able to help you.'

He grabbed her by the throat, slamming her against the wall. He laughed at the fear in her eyes. His Judy. 'You've just made one very big mistake, threatening me.' He leant forward and whispered in her ear, then bit down hard on the lobe.

Judy squealed in pain and dropped to the floor. He booted her in the back, then turned her over, and before Judy had a chance to scream for help, he brought his foot down on her face. He stared at her in disgust. She was a fat, stupid bitch. A loud-mouthed, interfering cunt. All fluttering eyes, fat jiggling tits, and a big fat pussy that made him sick to his stomach. He booted her again, watching the blood trickle from her ear.

'Not so mouthy now, are we, Judy?'

He sneered at the way her legs, with their purple veins, moved in rhythm to her pain, making her cheap green paisley dress ride up her legs, past her thighs, exposing her dimpled flesh.

'My Judy. My little Judy . . . a stupid, blathering cunt.'

Judy was about to scream when he raised his foot and brought it down hard, breaking her jaw. The sound of her bones shattering resonated so loudly in the little hallway, it startled even him.

Through the excruciating pain, and the warmth of her blood – which was now choking her, instead of giving her life – Judy felt the impact of Frank's toecap as it smashed all her teeth, brutally forcing its way to the back of her mouth, filling her lungs up with blood. She'd never imagined this sort of pain was possible, yet as he dragged her through to the kitchen by a clump of her hair, there was more to come.

By the time Frank was finished, Judy was unrecognisable.

He wiped down his hands on the baby blanket thrown over the back of the chair, then walked to the phone, picking it up to dial a number.

'Hello, it's Sid. I've made a little bit of a mess. I'll explain everything when I see you, but I was wondering if you could come around and help me clean up.'

Chapter Eighty-Nine

Lewis and Dennis sat in the back of the Rolls Royce on the edge of Epping Forest. Frank was in the front seat, next to Dennis's chauffeur. The heater was turned up high, and the classical music Dennis enjoyed filled the car.

'It's a shame really, I liked Judy. She was loyal,' Dennis reflected.

He glanced out into the darkness and took a sip of his sherry. A tipple he regarded as essential for every journey.

'I'll be sorry not to see her again. Still, there are worse spots to be buried.' He leant forward and tapped Frank on his shoulder. 'Loyalty is the most noble of traits, don't you think? You see, without loyalty, Sid, there is no trust. And I find loyalty never grows in the heart of a traitor.'

Frank shuffled around in his seat to look at Dennis. He frowned but didn't say anything, letting Dennis continue.

'What you did behind our back, it makes me very uncomfortable, Sid. Buying babies? Whatever next?'

'We didn't buy it, I told you. No harm was done.' Frank rubbed the stubble on his chin.

Dennis chuckled. 'Is that what you told Judy, when you pounded her brains out on the kitchen floor: no harm done? This circle we're in . . . you of all people, Sid, should know that trust is *paramount*, and without trust . . .' Dennis paused to take another sip of his Tio Pepe sherry. 'We have nothing. Going behind our back like you did, was wrong. It could've caused a lot of problems . . . and so, I'm sure you'll understand why I need to do this.'

Dennis turned to Lewis and gave a nod.

Lewis pulled out a thick plastic bag from the footwell. He swiped it over Frank's head, and pulled it down, twisting firmly.

While Frank struggled for air, scratching and clawing at the bag as he slowly suffocated, Dennis – becoming aroused – turned the music up, closing his eyes as the opening bars of Mozart's *Eine Kleine Nachtmusik* filled the air.

Chapter Ninety

In hospital, it had only taken three days of intravenous antibiotics before Gracie's infection began to improve. She'd felt better and had been relieved to be discharged with a packet of painkillers and more antibiotics. Gracie hadn't given her real name, and she'd added a few years on to her age. Though she needn't have bothered; the nurses had been too busy to show much interest in the details.

Gracie now stood with Dara and Robbie outside the house she hadn't seen for over two years. The house she'd once called home.

'Are you sure you're okay doing this?' Dara asked.

While Gracie had been in hospital, she and Robbie had spent the nights in a dive in the Elephant and Castle. She hadn't wanted to spend a lot of Alan's money, they needed to be careful. Even though the walls had been crawling, the carpets filthy, and the mattress stained, to Dara the freedom had felt like heaven. Though her heart had raced every time she'd heard a police siren.

Gracie rang the bell again. 'No one's in. Maybe my mum's popped out to the shops or something.' She shrugged.

Gracie still looked pale and very thin. The light had gone out in her eyes.

'You want to come back later?' Dara asked gently.

Gracie didn't answer; she stood staring at the house, lost in her own thoughts.

'*Hello!* Can I help you?'

A voice came from the other side of the fence. The next-door neighbour hurried down her garden path and came round to snoop on the visitors.

'Can I help you? This is—' But she stopped, open-mouthed. 'Well I never. Grace Perry, is that you? I never thought I'd see you again. How are you doing? Where've you been?' The girl looked like she'd been in a prisoner-of-war camp.

Grace blinked, unable to see who it was properly.

'It's me, love, Mrs Stevenson.' She was a large woman, out of breath, but clearly delighted at this golden nugget of gossip she'd be able to pass on. 'What are you doing here?'

'I came to see Mum.' Gracie recognised the woman now. Being here felt so strange. 'I was hoping she'd be in.'

Mrs Stevenson stumbled over her words. '*Y-your mum* . . .? I . . . I . . . don't know what to say . . . I assumed you knew . . . She died. A couple of years back now. Let me think . . . Just after Christmas 1983. That's right. She was taken to hospital, and never came out . . . I'm so sorry, darlin'.'

Gracie looked stunned. She struggled to catch her breath, and Dara grabbed hold of her, supporting her so she wouldn't fall.

'I've got you . . . Gracie, I've got you.'

Gracie sat down and covered her face with her hands.

Robbie pulled Dara to one side, making sure Gracie couldn't hear. 'They must have known – Barrows and Clemence, and all that lot – they must have known about her mum and not told her. That's why they were able to do what they did to her.'

Dara glanced at Robbie then looked away as the memories came flooding back. She felt sick.

'There was something else . . .' Mrs Stevenson spoke to Dara and Robbie. 'A woman came here, after the funeral. She left her number, said she was Gracie's godmother. I've got the piece of paper behind the clock still. But nobody seemed to know where Gracie'd gone. *She* didn't know – and no one would tell her when she tried to find out.'

A deep, loud sobbing came from Gracie. God knows, she had enough to weep for. The mum she thought had turned her back on her. The abuse and neglect she'd suffered since she walked through the doors of Holly Brookes. And the baby she'd lost.

It was another five minutes before Gracie had calmed down enough to speak. 'Would it be all right if I called her?'

'Of course.'

Gracie looked at Dara.

'It's fine, we'll wait here.' She smiled, and stepped back to shelter underneath the porch roof.

Robbie wrapped his scarf tighter around his neck. He'd found it on a chair in the hospital, and was grateful for its warmth.

'It feels strange.'

'What does?' Dara was genuinely interested.

'Being here. In the outside world. Not being afraid.'

'You're not frightened?'

Robbie looked up, letting the rain fall on his face. 'Nah, I reckon now, nothing will ever frighten me that much again.'

Dara smiled and right then, Gracie came back out. 'What's happened, did you speak to her?'

Gracie nodded. 'She cried when she heard my voice.'

Dara shrugged. 'That's good then, ain't it?'

Gracie shook her head. 'She wants me to go and stay with her . . . she doesn't want all three of us . . . only me. But I told her, I said, I'm not going anywhere without you.'

Dara walked over to Gracie. She wiped her tears away for her. 'You listen to me, you *have* to go. I don't want you worrying about me, all right? I've got some money, and I've always fancied going up West. Maybe I'll get a job, waitressing in a bar . . . the point is, I'll be fine.' Dara didn't add, she felt like she was dying inside. How could she face life without Gracie?

'No, I can't, I can't.'

Dara stared into Gracie's soft eyes. 'I love you, and I am not going to let you stay here. You go and live your best life.'

There was the clatter of travellers making their way through King's Cross Station. A group of New Year's revellers were making an early start while a couple laughed raucously, swilling back a bottle of cider as they made their way towards the kiosks.

The train times flicked around on the departure board. Dara looked up, noticing a line of pigeons sitting on top of the board, watching them. 'You better go. The train to Newcastle leaves soon.'

'Dar . . .'

'*Sshhhh*, it's okay, it's going to be all right.' Dara stroked Gracie's hair.

Tears rolled down their faces and they clung to each other.

'I can't, Dar. I can't do it.'

'Gracie, you can.' Dara rested her forehead against Gracie's. She whispered. 'Do it for me. You'll be safe now. You're free.'

'Thank you . . . thank you for loving me. Thank you for everything you've done, Dar.'

Guilt rushed through Dara again and she stepped back from Gracie. 'Look, you've only got five minutes.'

They'd bought her ticket with some of Alan's money, though Dara hadn't told Gracie who had driven them to the hospital.

She'd been too out of it to remember, and Robbie had been sworn to secrecy.

'Bye then, Gracie.' Robbie hugged Gracie awkwardly.

'Goodbye, Gracie.' Dara couldn't look at her.

'You've got my godmother's number, so you'll call me, won't you, Dar?'

'You try stopping me.'

Dara turned her back. She couldn't watch Gracie go.

'I love you, Gracie Perry, never forget that.'

And Dara still didn't turn to look.

'Do you think we'll ever see her again?'

The train had left, and Robbie linked arms with Dara as they walked away from the station.

She wiped her nose on her sleeve. 'I don't know, Robbie. Maybe, maybe not.' She attempted a smile, but she felt a physical pain in her heart.

'What are we going to do now, Dar?'

Dara looked up at the clock; this year had almost finished. Another year gone by.

She glanced at Robbie and kissed him on his cheek. 'I'm not sure yet. But we don't look back. We never look back to where we've come from, and what happened in that place, okay? I never want to talk about it again.'

Robbie nodded. 'To new beginnings then?'

'Yeah, to new beginnings.'

Dara swallowed her tears. She didn't know what the future held, but she was determined that this would be the start of the rest of her life.

Book Five

2007
April

Hide nothing, for time, which sees all and hears all, exposes all.

Sophocles

Chapter Ninety-One

Gracie parked up outside the small two-bedroomed bungalow she owned in Hexham. She laughed and turned to speak to her ex-sister-in-law, Tracey, who'd slept most of the journey home.

'Wake up, sleepyhead, we're here.'

Without bothering to cover her mouth, Tracey yawned widely and sat up from the back seat. 'Remind me next time to walk, pet. How long did that take?'

Tracey glanced at her watch. She was a good-humoured woman, although a plain-looking one, but Gracie found her easy company.

'Howay, man, three and a half hours, for a one-hour trip.' She laughed as she said it. Her voice was light and warm, with a strong Geordie accent.

Gracie grinned. 'What can I say?'

She'd never been the best driver, and certainly not the fastest. Gracie put that down to only having had her driver's licence for the past year. Before that, her husband, Jeremy, had driven her everywhere. Though of course after their divorce, it was a matter of learning to drive or relying on public transport.

Like everything in Gracie's life these days, she'd made sure the divorce proceedings had been amicable; there'd been no huge arguments, no recriminations. They'd simply grown apart after thirteen years of marriage. They were still good friends. In fact, she and Tracey had just enjoyed spending a few days with her ex at his large, sprawling house on the Northumberland coast.

'I'll get the bags. And then what do you say to a nice, large glass of wine? Your brother gave me an expensive bottle of red. I've been saving it for a special occasion, but now's as good a time as any to crack it open.'

Gracie enjoyed her life. There was no drama – and most of all, it felt safe.

She stepped out of the car, flicked open the boot and grabbed Tracey's suitcase before getting her own.

'Bloody hell, Trace, what have you got in here?'

Tracey, who lived over in Carlisle with her deadbeat husband, was staying with Gracie over the weekend. She was looking forward to having a giggle for the next couple of days before having to go back to work on Monday.

Gracie shivered. For an April day, it was cold.

She was about to carry the bags into the house, when she felt her phone vibrate in her pocket. She pushed her glasses up her nose, fumbled for her phone and pulled it out.

'Hello . . . Yes, this is Grace.' She listened for a moment, smiling.

Tracey was busy taking a large bite out of the cold sausage roll she'd bought at the motorway services.

'Yeah, okay . . . no, I understand . . .' Gracie carried on talking, then closed her eyes as her smile disappeared.

'Grace? Grace, what's going on?'

Tracey stopped chewing and looked at Gracie in alarm.

Gracie slowly opened her eyes again. She blinked, snatching for air, feeling colder than ever.

'That was my doctor, Trace . . . The cancer's come back.'

Chapter Ninety-Two

Dara was laughing her head off. She was getting the club ready for the party later that night, but as usual, she was enjoying having a banter with the girls who worked there. The place was already buzzing. The music was deafening, and some of the pole dancers had just started their shift.

Semi-naked girls gyrated onstage. They were all good-looking, with pert tits – most of them fake – and supple, curvaceous bodies to bring the punters in. But what Dara prided herself on the most was that none of them were underage, nor were they strung out on gear. Not the dancers, not the servers. She made sure of that. She wanted the place to be classy, not some seedy dive; there were enough of them around Soho. Dara didn't want to be part of that world. Having minors in the joint was never going to happen. Not on her watch. Not in a million fucking years.

'Unlike you not to be drinking, Dara.'

Sharon was one of the dancers. She was a loud-mouthed, big-breasted girl from Birmingham, popular with the punters. She sashayed over to Dara, ignoring the fact she was late for her shift – again – and pursed her lips.

'I'd have thought you'd be knocking it back today, Dara, getting some Dutch courage, what with your old man being let out later. Fucking hell, we all know what he's like . . . he'll be raging, always is, when he's done a bit of bird.'

Sharon was right: Dara wasn't looking forward to Archie coming out today – or any day, for that matter. The past three months had been peaceful. It was just a shame they hadn't kept him in for longer. Archie had previously served nine months for handling stolen goods. Dara just wished his brief wasn't so good at getting him lighter sentences.

'I'd watch your mouth if I were you.' Dara looked evenly at Sharon.

'Oh come on, when have you not fancied a drink? You're like a fucking fish. What's with the orange juice all of a sudden?'

This time, Dara had to turn her gaze away, trying not to take offence. Mainly because it was true. But no one liked to be reminded of something like that, did they?

Over the years, the drinking and the pills had gradually taken a tight hold of her. There was a part of Dara that suspected Archie preferred her when she was bang on it. It made it easier for him to control her.

Since Archie had been away, Dara had been trying *really* hard to knock the booze and the pills on the head. She'd even been to meetings. Several of them. Not that she'd told anyone, fuck no, she didn't need to advertise the fact that she was trying to quit.

But avoiding the booze, especially when she was working in the club, was proving really fucking difficult for her. The benzos the doctor had given her helped – she'd even reduced her self-harming – but she still felt imprisoned by the craving for booze and pills. One day at a time though, hey.

Dara looked around the club she ran with Archie, taking deep breaths and making sure she was in control of her temper before she answered Sharon. The club had been refurbished last year in shades of silver and grey, with new drinking booths and private rooms. Archie had even insisted the bar be ripped out and replaced with a flashy black bit of kit.

Even though, by rights, it was Archie's name on the lease, and the freehold was owned by a man called Jake Wakeman, Dara was fiercely proud of this place, and the hard work she'd put in to get here. After years of living in squats with Robbie, waiting on tables, cleaning offices and shops, selling knock-off gear down Berwick Street Market, making sandwiches in the greasy spoon in Bateman Street and taking any job she could, just to survive, it'd finally paid off. She'd got a job here, and worked her way up to deputy manager.

And never once did she get tired of walking through the doors of the club, or to the flat upstairs. No, the only thing she was tired of was Archie.

Feeling calmer now, she smiled at Sharon, keeping her tone upbeat. 'I just don't fancy it, that's all, Shaz.'

Sharon raised her voice above the music pumping out of the speakers. 'Yeah, and I'm a fucking nun. Go on, take a sip.' She pushed her glass underneath Dara's nose. 'You know you want to.'

Dara smelt the alcohol. How easy would it be to take just the tiniest sip of Sharon's vodka? One sip couldn't hurt . . . She swallowed hard, staring at the drink. Her mouth was salivating at the mere thought of it.

She quickly snapped herself out of it. 'What the fuck are you playing at, Shaz? Jesus, when someone says, *no*, they mean, *no*.' Annoyed, Dara moved away from Sharon, grabbing her black leather jacket from behind the bar. 'I'm off out. I'll be back soon . . . Oh, and if you're late again, you can think about getting yourself another fucking job. There are plenty of clubs looking for a loud-mouthed cow.'

Sharon was surprised at Dara's reaction, but she didn't take offence. Everyone who worked at the club knew Dara was a decent boss – unlike Archie. She looked after all the girls, treated them with respect and backed them all the way. If there was ever any aggro from the punters, she'd be right there in the thick of it.

'What's got in your knickers – apart from your old man tonight, that is?'

'Do me a favour.' Dara tutted and walked away. Why couldn't Sharon just shut the fuck up?

She pushed through the small crowd of guys who'd just come in. She needed to get out and get some headspace.

'You sure you should be going out?' Sharon called out. Leaving her drink on the bar, she hurried to catch up with her. Dara stepped out of the way for a couple of guys making their way into the club. She checked her watch: she still had time, if she hurried,

Catching up to Dara, Sharon grabbed hold of her gently. 'What shall I tell Archie if he comes back while you're out? Isn't he due soon, babe?' There was genuine concern in her voice.

Dara shrugged. 'I dunno, tell him anything. Tell him I've run off with the postman.'

Sharon cackled. 'Are you fucking kidding? He's already taken . . . *by me!* Have you seen him, the geezer's got buns of fucking steel. I mean, I wouldn't say no.'

Dara raised her eyebrows. 'When do you *ever* say no?' She grinned and began to move away.

'Wait . . . Dara, I'm being serious. He'll kill you if you're not here when he comes home. You know he always likes a homecoming.'

'Let me worry about that, yeah . . . but thanks, I appreciate you looking out for me.' Dara pushed a strand of her bleached-blonde bob behind her ear, and a twinkle came into her eyes. 'And Sharon . . . get your butt on that stage. Because however nice you're being to me, it won't wipe out the fact that you're late *again.*'

They both laughed as Dara hurried off. She rushed through Soho, turning into Old Compton Street, which was packed and full of tourists. The noise of the pubs spilt out on to the pavements, and groups of people stood outside smoking and drinking, making the most of the balmy April evening.

Running across Shaftesbury Avenue, dodging the motorbike courier speeding down the road, Dara broke into a jog, turning right at the dim sum restaurant on the corner of Gerrard Place.

After weaving through Leicester Square, Dara spent another ten minutes to making her way down Charing Cross Road, across the Strand and finally into Craven Street.

Outside a large red-brick building, Dara came to a stop. She looked over her shoulder, making sure no one was around, took a deep breath, and pushed open the heavy green door.

Chapter Ninety-Three

Dara walked up a narrow flight of stairs leading to the second-floor landing, and wandered down the corridor to another door. She hesitated for a moment, geeing herself up. Then she pushed the door open, slipping in quietly and taking a seat at the back on one of the empty chairs.

'Hey, how are you doing, Dara? Good to see you again.' The man sitting in the chair next to her whispered his greeting. He had a ruddy, worn-out face – a lifetime of stories, no doubt – with a broken nose and eyes slightly too close together. He was well built and looked like he could hold his own.

'You too,' she whispered back, non-committally.

She had to keep an eye on the time, she couldn't be late. All hell would break loose if she wasn't back before Archie. But she needed to do this. Sharon putting that drink in front of her had triggered something: the craving to drink was overwhelming. Attending a meeting was the only way she had any chance of staying on the wagon. Even so, the next twenty-four hours would be a struggle.

The AA meeting she usually attended was across town, over in Notting Hill. Dara wasn't comfortable attending one so close to home, even if it was a good twenty minutes' walk away. She had to be careful, and she only came here if time was short and she was struggling, like now.

Resting her hands in her lap, Dara bowed her head and listened attentively to the person on the front row who'd begun to speak.

'I'm Devon, I'm one month sober today . . .'

There was a round of applause.

'I'm an alcoholic and I've been surrounded by heavy drinkers all my life. My dad's an al—'

Dara glanced up at the voice. She recognised it. The name too.

She leant slightly forward, to peer round the head of the large Black woman in front of her with a huge mane of dreadlocks. Yes, it was definitely him. She'd seen him regularly in the club over the past year, with his drinking buddies. But unlike them, he wasn't a lairy idiot. She'd had the occasional laugh with him, and he'd always shown respect to the girls in the club.

Looking at him now, Dara reckoned he was quite a few years younger than her. It was hard to tell, as he was sporting a beard, not something she was usually keen on. But she had to admit, it gave him a rugged, striking look.

Dara smiled to herself: each time he came into the club, Sharon had her tongue hanging out. Devon's handsome looks – his green eyes and strawberry-blond hair – and his muscular body on a tall frame, had all the girls lusting after him. Even Dara, who'd seen it all, had come across all girly when he first spoke to her. Though of course, she could never let *anyone* catch a glimpse of her flirting with another man. To put it simply, Archie would kill her.

Dara slumped down lower into her chair. She didn't want to be recognised by Devon. There was no way she was going to risk her attendance at an AA meeting getting back to Archie. She'd give it another five minutes maybe, then sneak out.

In the end, she waited until the assembled group began to recite the Serenity Prayer. It seemed the sensible moment to start heading out without being spotted.

'... *God grant me the serenity to accept the ...*'

Dara was almost at the door, when her phone rang. *Shit.* She'd forgotten to put it on silent. A few heads turned, and she hurriedly darted into the hallway, pulling the phone out of her pocket.

Frowning, she stared at the familiar number. She rushed down the stairs and out into the street.

'Hello . . .?'

Chapter Ninety-Four

King's Cross Station was an absolute shithole. It was almost empty, apart from a few people hanging around on the benches waiting for trains. Some of the homeless congregated in the corner over by the ticket office, sitting on flattened cardboard boxes, as though they were futons. There'd been some talk of a regeneration programme in recent years, but the plans had come to nothing. The place was a run-down mess: rife with drugs and hookers, and a spot where runaway kids hung out.

Dara pushed her purse further into the front pocket of her leather jacket. Street gangs were working in the station, and she didn't need any more grief today by getting her money lifted.

She felt her phone buzzing in her pocket. It was probably Sharon. She'd called over a dozen times already. Dara's blood had run cold when she'd heard Sharon's worried voice.

Babe, where the fuck are you? Archie's here already . . .

Archie ain't happy. Fuck me, that's an understatement, doll . . .

Call me back, will you? Better still, get back here . . .

I told Archie you've gone to pick up some supplies for the club, but I don't think he believed me . . .

Where are you? Jesus . . .

You've clearly got some sort of death wish . . .

Dara didn't need to listen to the rest of the messages. She got it.

Jesus. She got the fact that she was totally fucked. But what else could she have done? She'd had no choice.

'Dara?'

Dara turned around. All the worry fell away from her. Her face softened, and she smiled.

'Gracie?'

The two women stared at each other.

How long had it been? Ten years, maybe twelve? And even then, it had been the quickest of visits. Though Dara blamed herself for that. Stupidly, she'd taken Archie along to meet Gracie and Jeremy over dinner. They didn't even get to the desert menu. To say the husbands were like chalk and cheese was an understatement. Even now, Dara couldn't look back on that evening without shuddering at the way Archie had behaved.

Not one day had gone by when they didn't think of each other, first thing in the morning, and last thing at night. But it was complicated. Their love was as strong and as unbreakable as it had ever been, but seeing each other hurt: the memories, the shared history, needed to stay buried for them to be able to live any sort of life. Though not seeing each other was just as painful. They each had a space in their heart that could only be filled by the other.

Dara took a step towards the sophisticated, well-dressed woman standing in front of her; her hair was a light brown now, gone was the brassy red. But all Dara saw was little Gracie, on that first day they'd met, all those years ago.

Dara touched Gracie's face.

'Thank you for coming.' Gracie spoke in a hush.

The world around them stopped.

'I've missed you, babe.' Dara could barely get her words out. They stuck at the back of her throat, and she didn't bother even trying to stop her tears from falling.

'I've missed you too.' Gracie meant it.

Noticing that Gracie was wearing the delicate gold necklace she'd sent her a few years ago, Dara smiled.

'Is everything all right? What gives? I mean, don't get me wrong, there doesn't have to be a reason for you to come and see me, *ever*. I'm so pleased to see you. But why now, after all this time?' Dara's words rushed out.

She smiled again, because although being here – and not back at the club for Archie's homecoming – was going to cost her dear, Gracie would always come first.

Gracie smiled back and held Dara's face in her hands.

Dara looked different, and yet the same. Her hair was bleached blonde, cut short, immaculately styled; gone were the straggling, ragtag locks. Dara was certainly a beautiful woman, dressed in expensive clothes, smelling fragrant, but Gracie saw only the imp-like girl, feisty and strong, with dirt engrained in her skin, standing before her, like the first day they'd met.

'I needed to see you, Dar.'

Dara smiled. She hadn't heard anyone call her that for many years.

But it was the look in Gracie's eyes which troubled her. The look of fear which had haunted them throughout their whole time together.

'What's going on?'

Gracie blinked. 'I had to see you, to say it to your face . . . I'm dying, Dar.'

Chapter Ninety-Five

'No, no, *no*.' Dara shook her head.

She paced up and down underneath the train timetable board, like she'd done on the day she'd waved Gracie goodbye.

'You don't fucking get to come here, after all this time, and tell me that . . . like it's nothing. You can't just drop it on me out of nowhere.'

'Dar, *please*. It's okay. Don't be angry.'

Dara couldn't see Gracie for her tears. '*Don't be angry*? Are you fucking kidding me? Of course I'm fucking angry. It's not fair. Why you? Why does it have to be you? Why not me? You don't deserve this.'

'No one does, Dar. These things happen.' Gracie's voice was quiet.

Dara grabbed hold of her hands. She spoke out of shock.

'But why? I don't get it . . . I mean, you don't deserve this, Gracie. The rest of us, well, the rest of us . . .' She paused and pulled her hands, wiping her tears on her sleeve. 'Well, I'm just not a good person, Gracie.'

'What are you talking about? I feel blessed you came into my life. I love you so much. You're my hero, Dar.'

Dara shook her head. 'Don't say that, don't say it . . . If you knew who I really was, what I've done over the years, you wouldn't be saying that.'

'Stop, Dar.' Gracie was gentle but firm with Dara. 'There's nothing you could say that would stop me believing you're the *best* thing that ever happened to me in my life.'

Dara couldn't look at Gracie now.

They didn't say anything for a while.

'If I could do something about this, Dar, I would.'

Dara snapped her head back around to look at Gracie. She stared at her friend. It was happening again. That sense of powerlessness, that sense of being out of control, came flooding back to her. The feeling of being unable to help someone she loved. It crushed Dara.

'Are you sure . . . I mean, are you sure they ain't got it wrong? You hear it all the time, don't you? Misdiagnosis. And look, I've got some money put away, you can use that, yeah?' Like she always did when she was scared, Dara spoke quickly. 'You can get to see some proper quack then, not some arsehole who thinks because they've gone to university, they know everything. Are you even sure he's a proper doctor? There are some sick fuckers out there you know, Gracie. Just look at that doc a few years ago, who killed all them people.'

Even though Gracie was frightened herself, and saying it out loud made it real, she couldn't help but smile. 'Dara the fixer. Always wanting to make it right. You've always been like that. Always trying to sort everything out for me. But there are some things even you can't fix. It is what it is, Dar.'

'*The next train at platform six will be the nineteen thirty-five to Glasgow . . .*'

The tannoy announcement crackled out through the station and Dara fought to be heard above it.

'You might want to accept it, doll, but I don't. I fucking won't, I—' Dara caught herself. What the hell was she doing? 'I'm

453

sorry . . . I'm sorry, Gracie, this isn't about me, is it? I'm being fucking selfish, as usual.'

Dara covered her face with her hands, but a moment later, she felt Gracie begin to pull them away gently.

'Dar, it's okay.'

'But it's not though, is it? And anyway, it should be *me* helping *you*, but I can't. I don't know how to. Tell me how I can make it all right.'

Absent-mindedly, Gracie watched a small group of people hurrying past, carrying a mountain of suitcases. 'Dar, that's all you've ever done since I've known you: help me. But we're not kids any more, you don't have to be the strong one. I can be that.' She wiped more tears away from Dara's cheeks with the palm of her hand.

Dara bowed her head. 'What am I going to do without you though, Gracie? How am I going to live, knowing you're not here any more?'

'I'm here now though, aren't I? So let's make the most of it, shall we?' Gracie's voice was warm. 'Come on, my train isn't for a few hours.' She held Dara's hand. 'Why don't we go and get a drink?'

Dara bristled. The thought of downing a bottle of vodka right now certainly appealed to her, and although she knew she needed to stay off the booze, she wasn't sure if she could.

'Let's go and talk like old times, hey?' Gracie added.

Dara tilted her head. She gave Gracie a wry smile.

'Okay . . . maybe not like old times.' Gracie returned the smile and giggled. 'But let's have a catch-up. I want to know everything that's been happening in your life.'

They linked arms, the way they used to all those years ago. And they headed out of the station towards Euston Road, passing St Pancras clock tower.

Dara looked up. It was getting late, and she felt a cold chill of anxiety rush down her spine.

Now wasn't the moment to tell Gracie what was *really* going on in her life, and why she needed to get back to the club. Dara's phone began to buzz, but she quickly switched it off.

If Gracie could be brave about what was happening in her life, Dara could be brave about what was happening in her own. After all, like Gracie had said, *it is what it is*.

Chapter Ninety-Six

Dara and Gracie had walked into the first bar they'd come across. It was a piano bar, a throwback from the late eighties. The quiet, downtown Manhattan late-night-drinking vibe wasn't her style. She preferred a loud, raucous atmosphere – a noisy buzz – it gave her less time to think. The sound of her own thoughts was something Dara tried her hardest to avoid.

'You sure I can't get you anything stronger?' Gracie looked at Dara's empty glass of ginger ale.

Sitting by the window on the tall, black leather bar stools, Dara smiled, and gave Gracie the same sentence she'd used on Sharon. 'I just don't fancy it.'

Unlike Sharon, Gracie accepted it straight away. Dara was grateful; she was sure that if Gracie had pushed it, she would've given into temptation.

'Anyhow, carry on telling me about you and Jeremy.'

Over the years, they'd spoken on the phone, marking high days and holidays, and sent cards to each other. But Dara had always withheld the truth about her life. The conversations had been careful on both sides, rather than strained, making sure nothing was said that might shake their fragile existences.

'You loved him, right? That time, that disastrous dinner we had.' She shook her head.

Gracie laughed.

'Well, you seemed happy enough then,' Dara continued, wanting to talk about anything but Gracie's illness.

Gracie swirled the ice in her Mojito around the glass, and took a small sip before answering. 'Well, we weren't unhappy, and in a way I still love him. He's a good man, Dar.' She took another sip, put her glass down, then smiled. 'But God, he was boring.'

Dara roared with laughter so loud the customers on the next table turned around to stare at them.

'But that's what I needed. I needed someone quiet, someone predictable, reliable, someone who liked the same meals every week. No surprises. Someone who only wanted sex on a Sunday.' Gracie shrugged and gave a self-deprecating giggle. 'It was perfect, Dar. I was happy. I've had a happy life. No complaints.'

Dara frowned. 'Then why divorce him?'

'It wasn't fair on him. Jeremy needed someone who wanted him for himself, not just for a safety net . . . Maybe if I'd been able to have children, things would've been different . . .' Gracie faded off into her own thoughts.

Dara stiffened. 'I didn't know . . . You didn't say anything. I'm so sorry.'

'Don't be.' Gracie played with her glass. 'It's my fault anyway.'

'How do you make that out?' Dara reached across the table and touched her hand.

It was the first time that evening Gracie had cried. 'What I did back then, it—' She stopped, unable to finish what she was going to say. 'What about you, Dar? Did you ever hear from Tommy or your other brothers and sisters? You always said you were going to try to find them again. Did you get any leads?'

'No.' Dara's reply was clipped. 'I kept hitting dead ends, and it was too painful, you know, to carry on looking . . . You know how it is.'

Gracie knew exactly what that was like.

They fell into silence again.

'Enough of this doom and gloom,' Gracie suddenly said, trying too hard to sound cheerful. 'I want to hear all about your love life. How's Archie doing?'

'Nothing to report . . . He's fine, nothing new.' Dara started to feel awkward.

'I know he never saw eye to eye with Jeremy, but I love it that Archie treats you properly. Breakfasts in bed . . . Paris in January . . . Madrid last summer. Dar, I'm so happy for you. He's like the whirlwind you deserve.'

Dara chewed on her lip, trying to ignore the tightness in her stomach. She'd forgotten that she'd created such a romantic story for Gracie. But it was hardly as if she could tell her the truth, was it?

'Whirlwind? Hardly. He's not that exciting. He's boring, like your old man was. Anyway, who wants to talk about men? I know I don't.' Dara could hear herself being short with Gracie. 'So, listen, aren't you going to miss your train? It's probably the last one this evening. I'll sort out coming up in a few days. Then we'll really sit down and talk properly. I want to be there for you, Gracie, as much as you want me to be.'

'There's no need.' Gracie downed the last of her drink, then crunched on a piece of ice.

'Gracie, don't say that, *please*. I want to be there for you.'

Gracie smiled. 'You can be. What I mean is, there's no need to come up and see me, because I'm going to stay.'

'What?' Dara felt the colour drain from her face.

'Oh don't look so happy about it, will you?'

'No, it's . . . it's not that. I just mean . . . Haven't you got somewhere you need to be?' Dara's heart raced.

'No.' Gracie shook her head. 'I can do what I like.' She grinned broadly. 'I've got work, but who cares? What are they going to do? Sack me?' She laughed. 'No, Dar, I don't have to answer to anyone, not any more. I've been scared for so long, making sure that I never feel out of control, that everything's planned. That's how I've had to live my life, Dar.' Gracie thought about what she was saying. 'And the truth is, it was probably *me* who was the boring one. *Me*, not Jeremy.' She leant over and kissed Dara on the cheek. 'So now, for once, I'm going to do something spontaneous, and stay with you for a little bit . . . if you'll have me. It's going to be fun.'

Dara didn't say anything, but *fun* was certainly one way of putting it.

'Oh my God, is this it? It's amazing, Dar.'

It had begun to rain, and Gracie glanced quickly at Dara, then back at the frontage of the club. She stared up at the sign, illuminated in ebony and gold. *Straycats*.

'I like the name. I'm so proud of you, Dar. A club in Soho. You've done so well. You and Archie. It's brilliant.'

'Gracie, there's something I need to tell you.'

'I know it's a strip club, Dar. I'm not a complete prude.' Gracie moved towards the door. She giggled.

'It's not that, Gracie . . .'

'Okay, pole dancing then.' She shrugged and laughed, as though she didn't have a care in the world.

'No, Gracie, I really need—'

But Gracie had already walked through the entrance. Dara briefly closed her eyes before rushing after her.

The party in the club was already in full swing, and the whole place was packed. The drinks were flowing, and topless waitresses in gold thongs walked around carrying champagne on silver trays. The music was deafening, banging out Old Skool beats, as the pole dancers writhed around onstage, and cigarette smoke was thick in the air.

'Where the *fuck* have you been, you stupid bitch?'

Before Dara could react, a fist slammed into her head. She was sent flying, crashing into the table. She heard Gracie scream. The next moment, Dara was dragged up by her hair, her top ripped as she was shaken about.

'Am I some sort of fucking mug? I've been banged up. And you can't even be bothered to be here to say hello to me.'

She was slapped around some more, a vicious backhand across her face.

'What geezer expects to come out and find their missus not here? Fucking whore. A right fucking welcome home, this is. I've got a mind to put your head through the fucking wall.'

Dara was shoved hard on to the floor. She stared at Gracie.

Gracie stared back, open-mouthed.

'Gracie, you remember Archie, don't you?'

And with those words, Dara picked herself up and wiped the dripping blood from her mouth.

Chapter Ninety-Seven

'What the fuck is she doing here?' Archie snarled at Gracie.

He remembered her and her pussy of a husband from the dinner they'd had years ago. If it wasn't for the fact that he'd been out on bail for GBH at the time, he would've rammed his fist down her fella's throat. No question. Condescending cunt. Though Gracie hadn't been much better. The way she'd looked down her nose at him, when he'd dug the waiter out for trying to give it the big one around Dara.

'It's nice to see you too.' Gracie's voice dripped with sarcasm.

She was in shock at what had just happened. She fiddled with her necklace and stared at Archie. He had dark eyes, and a thick, stocky build. He looked like a thug. His shaved head and the Celtic cross tattoo on the side of his neck gave him a threatening edge. He'd been a prick at the dinner, but she'd never believed he would behave like this. Dara hadn't said. In truth, she'd made out the opposite.

Gracie turned to Dara. Her lip was bleeding, and her immaculately styled hair was a mess. Even though the lights in the club weren't very bright, Gracie could still see the expression in Dara's eyes, pleading for her not to say anything else.

'I'm sorry, Archie . . . I'm sorry I wasn't here.' Dara tried to smile. 'As you see, we've got a visitor. I went to pick her up.' She tried her best to sound casual.

'Why are you apologising to him, Dar?' Gracie spoke without thinking.

The roles felt reversed. Throughout their childhood, it was always Dara standing up for her. Dara, her strong, feisty, brave friend, prepared to take on any battle. Gracie couldn't understand what had happened. How had it come to this? Dara was almost cowering in front of this man.

'Gracie, *please*, leave it—'

'I think you better do what she says.' Archie leant in towards Gracie, showing off his gold tooth.

'Gracie, I'm begging you,' Dara pleaded.

Gracie looked between Archie and Dara, and gave a tiny nod of her head. She turned away but was immediately stopped by a hand on her arm.

'If you know what's good for you, Gracie, don't come here and start any trouble, understand me?'

Gracie looked Archie up and down in disgust. 'Get your hands off me.' She held his stare.

The hatred between them was palpable.

A slow, nasty smile appeared on Archie's face. Then he let go of Gracie and walked away without saying anything else.

Gracie immediately turned to Dara.

'Dar, why didn't you tell me what was going on? Why lie to me? Why pretend he treats you like a Disney princess? Is this why you've never asked me to come down here?' Gracie dabbed Dara's lip with the clean tissue she'd pulled out of her pocket.

Dara thought about it. By rights, *she* had been the strong one all along, trying not to give a shit about anything. Though when it came to Gracie, Dara cared. God did she care what Gracie thought. She always had done, which was the reason she'd never invited Gracie to stay. In fact, if anything, Dara had discouraged it. Because she'd always known, in her gut, that Gracie would never have approved of what was going on. At the end of the day, she was ashamed of her lifestyle and the woman she had become.

Yes, she'd done good by running the club, and she'd worked bloody hard to get where she was. Though shacking up with Archie was a mistake. She'd been drawn to him – or was it his violence she'd been drawn to? After all, it was what she knew. It was what she understood. And deep down, it was what she felt she deserved.

On top of which, she was a mess. A functioning mess. She might not admit it, at least not out loud, but Dara knew what she was. She'd had a pill habit as far back as she could remember, she had a booze habit, and the two combined . . . well, it made her like her mother, didn't it? The mother Dara had despised, had thought of as weak, loving the drugs and the alcohol more than she loved her kids. But somehow along the way, when Dara wasn't watching, she'd turned into the woman she'd hated all her life.

'As you say, Gracie, *it is what it is*.' Dara shrugged, attempting to play it down.

'No, you can't brush me off by saying that.'

'*You* did.' Dara was defensive. 'And I'd say, you coming down here and telling me what you did, is much worse than *me* not telling *you* about what was going on with Archie. And I was right not to. I knew *exactly* how you'd react, judging me, and that's why I didn't tell you.'

Gracie shook her head. 'Dara Tailor, I know you too well. We may have gone our separate ways over the years, but you're in here.' Gracie pointed to her heart. 'You're a part of me, Dar, you always will be, so I know you. I know you too well. So don't try and fob me off with some bullshit.'

Dara was getting annoyed now. Probably because Gracie had hit the mark. 'You're not my judge and jury, darlin'.'

A customer carrying some drinks back from the bar banged into them, and Gracie pulled Dara out of the way.

'No, but I'm your friend, Dar. And all I'm asking is, *why*? Why let that bastard treat you like this? I mean, what were you thinking of, getting involved with someone like Archie?'

Dara's eyes filled with tears. She licked her mouth, tasting the blood from the oozing cut.

'You want to know the truth, Gracie? How it happened?' She became emotional and words tumbled out. 'It happened because you left me, Gracie. You got on a train and went to your god-mother's and never looked back. Now I ain't saying that I wasn't pleased for you. Cos I was . . . genuinely fucking pleased, doll. You being safe was all I wanted. But while you were safe, sweetheart, I was left *here*, with nothing, only Robbie. And I had to take care of him . . . but I could hardly take care of myself. I had no home, no job, nothing. We lived in squats, hand to mouth, then I met Archie. He said he'd look after me, and in a way he did. I was tired, Gracie, so tired, and I needed help . . . Problem was, there was a heavy price tag.' She grabbed the tissue off Gracie. 'So now you've got your answer, you can fuck off with your judgement, because that's my husband you're talking about.'

And just like that, Dara walked away.

Chapter Ninety-Eight

Dara's hands were shaking. Yeah, she and Gracie were friends, the best of, but did that give Gracie the right to judge her? To look down her nose at her? No, it fucking didn't.

She marched behind the bar, grabbed a glass from the shelf and stuck it under the bottle of vodka. She pushed it against the chrome dispenser, measuring out a double shot.

'You sure you should be having that?'

Glass in hand, Dara spun around.

'Excuse me?' She frowned, and glared at Devon.

His handsome face was lit up by the club's neon lights, and he leant nonchalantly across the bar. 'I saw you.'

'I beg your pardon?' Dara snapped at him.

'I saw you at the meeting.'

'Keep your fucking voice down.' Nervously, Dara's eyes darted around the club.

Archie was over in the far corner, busy pawing one of the new girls who didn't know to stay well clear of him. He was knocking back the whiskey, which was never a good sign. As for Gracie, she'd been hijacked by a very drunk Sharon, and was deep in conversation with her.

Her gaze returned to Devon. 'What the fuck is it to do with *you* what I do?'

'I don't want to see you doing something you'll regret, that's all.' His voice was smooth and even. 'You attend those meetings for a reason.'

'Not here . . . for fuck's sake.' She looked across again at Archie, making sure he was completely preoccupied. 'Round the back.' Dara gestured towards the storeroom.

She put down her glass and waited for Devon to go through the double door, before quickly following him.

The corridor was badly lit, and Dara stood facing Devon, hands on hips, by the boxes of crisps, stacked almost to the ceiling. He towered above her.

'Who do you think you are?' she demanded. 'Anyone could have been listening. What the fuck are you playing at, Devon?'

'Only what I said – I don't want to see you making a mistake.'

'Who are you, all of a sudden, my fucking keeper?'

Devon shook his head and ran his fingers through his thick hair. 'I'm looking out for you, that's all.'

Dara raised her eyebrows. What the hell? 'I didn't ask you to; I don't even know you. Yet somehow you think because you come in here occasionally with your mates, and you've seen me at a meeting once or twice, it gives you the right to stick your nose into my business. What is it with people today? What makes them think they can go around judging others? Glass houses, mate.'

'Fine, go out there and have a drink then, if that's what you want. But I think, deep down, you're probably pleased that I was here to stop you putting that glass to your lips. Because I know, if you did, tomorrow you'd wake up hating yourself.'

'Has anyone ever told you that you're an arrogant bastard?'

Devon gave Dara a lopsided smile. 'Now I come to think of it, *yes* . . . Look, I'm sorry if I overstepped.'

He stared at her, and Dara felt herself blushing. He reached over to the roll of paper towel lying discarded on a crate of lager. He ripped a piece off, then, like Gracie had done only a short time ago, he gently dabbed Dara's lip, which was beginning to bleed again.

'Are you all right?'

Dara winced at the sting of the cut. She held Devon's gaze, catching her breath. 'I'm fine, thank you . . . And I appreciate you, well, you know . . .' She trailed off with a shrug.

'Not a problem . . . any time. I'm sure you'd do the same for me.' They fell silent.

Dara was aware that if Archie came through, they'd both be in the shit. But something about Devon made it hard for her to move away.

'Can I ask you a question?' He stepped in closer to her.

'Only if it's—'

The sound of a loud crash brought Dara back to her senses and sent her running through to the main bar. She heard the screams and shouts from the girls before she knew what was happening. Most of the customers in the club were either cowering or had left the bar.

Dara's first thought was Gracie, and she searched for her in the crowd. Thankfully, she saw her huddled in safety by the DJ booth with some of the dancers. Archie wasn't so fortunate: Dara spotted him standing inside a circle of men armed with baseball bats. With a sinking feeling, she recognised them.

'Nice to see they let you out, Archie. Though perhaps by the end of the week, you'll wish you were back inside, mate.'

Mad Angus was an ex-crackhead-turned-loan shark. He trailed a baseball bat down Archie's face, resting the end of it on his chin.

'Right now, Arch, I'm toying with the idea of whether or not I fancy getting the boys to give you a proper pasting, so we can put an end to this charade.'

'Do what you like, mate. If that's what you want, crack on, but it won't help you get what you want any quicker, will it?'

Dara knew Archie well enough to know he was putting on an act of bravado. She also knew she had to stand back and keep her mouth shut.

'But you owe us a lot of money, Archie, and each day that goes by, it accrues more interest. You owed it me before you went in. And now you're out, I'm still not seeing the readies in my hand.'

Angus, a small man with a lot to prove, pointed his baseball bat around the crowd. He enjoyed the attention. He'd clump anyone, given half the chance, kill them for less.

'Problem with you, Arch, is that you either like to stick it up your nose, or you like to put it on the gee-gees, but what you don't seem to like, is paying it back. Now you have until the end of next week, and that's me being generous. Otherwise what will happen . . .' Mad Angus looked across at Dara and winked at her, then brought the baseball bat back hard, swinging it into Archie's stomach.

Dara watched her husband double up in agony.

Angus bowled over to the bar, walking behind it as if he owned the place.

'Club's looking good, Dara.' He winked again at her, at the same time pressing the cash buttons on all three tills. The drawers sprang open. 'Don't mind if I help myself, do you, darlin'?'

Laughing, Angus ripped out the club's takings for the night – fifties, twenties and ten-pound notes – sticking them in his pockets.

All Dara could do was watch.

When his pockets were full, Angus waved the remaining notes around in the air. 'This will go some way to what you owe me, Archie . . . well, it'll cover today's interest.'

As Mad Angus and his men walked out, Dara glanced briefly at Archie. He was coughing his guts up and looked in serious pain. The few regular customers who were left, having seen a lot go down in the club before, drifted back to their tables, carrying on with their conversations. The strippers returned to the stage.

Dara strolled over to Archie.

He was beginning to stand up straight. His face was bright red. He grimaced and wrapped his arms around his stomach.

She hissed at him. 'What the *fuck* are you doing borrowing money from Angus? Jesus Christ, Angus of all people. What the hell are you going to do now?'

Viciously, Archie stared at her. 'You mean, what the hell are *we* going to do now? For better or for worse, remember?'

'The thing about that, Archie, is I can't remember any *better*. All it's ever been since we got hitched, is worse, and worse, and worse.' And she gave him a cold stare and marched away to where Gracie was. She was angry, not to mention worried. 'So go on, Gracie, tell me, are you still glad you came now?'

Gracie gave Dara a small, sympathetic smile. 'What will happen if Archie doesn't get the money for that guy?'

'For Mad Angus? To put it bluntly, he'll kill him . . . Welcome to my world, Gracie.'

Chapter Ninety-Nine

The Kaiser Chiefs were blasting out over the speakers. It was late now, gone two o'clock in the morning, and Mad Angus had been forgotten by Archie.

He was very drunk. Not only drunk, but also bang on it. Speed and coke. Making up for lost time.

Chloe and Layla sat on his knees. They were young girls – eighteen, maybe nineteen. Dara didn't care that they were draped over Archie semi-naked. But she'd have to warn them. Archie was like a cactus. Anyone who got near him would be badly hurt.

Sighing, she turned her attention to Gracie.

They were sitting together at one of the tables by the bar, and for the past ten minutes, Gracie had been trying to get Dara to take what she was saying seriously.

'. . . Come on, Dar, you don't need to be around this.' Gracie spoke quietly but her manner was forceful. 'You could pack up your things tonight, and tomorrow we could leave here. We can go back to mine, Dar. It's quiet where I live, and I've got a beautiful little bungalow. What do you say? And look, when I've gone . . .' Gracie smiled sadly and took a deep breath. 'Well, you can have the place. You can start afresh.'

Dara took in Gracie's worried face. 'It sounds lovely, Gracie, it really does, but I can't just get up and go.'

'Why not? Give me one good reason why you can't. You and Archie run this place, you don't own it. You can do what you want—'

'Gracie?' A voice came from behind Dara and Gracie. '*Gracie?*' They turned at the same time.

Behind them stood a tall man. His head seemed too big for his skinny body, and his eyes bulged out, froglike. He had a scrappy goatee, and his skin looked engrained with grime. His dark greasy hair hung limply over his forehead. He wore a blue denim shirt and faded jeans that were too baggy for his frame. And his fingernails were black with dirt.

Dara's face lit up, but Gracie looked confused.

Seeing Gracie's face, Dara laughed. 'Gracie, don't you know who it is? It's Robbie.' She beamed with pride, seemingly oblivious to the state Robbie was in.

'*Robbie?*'

If Dara hadn't told her who he was, Gracie wouldn't have recognised him. Never in a million years. Though she did recognise a chronic drug addict when she saw one.

'Robbie, oh my God, how are you?' She stopped at the phrase *you're looking well*. He clearly looked anything but.

Robbie's eyes darted around the club, and he shuffled restlessly on the spot. He leant in, to give Gracie the briefest of hugs.

'Fucking hell, Dara, why didn't you tell me she was coming?' He chewed on the knuckle of his left thumb.

'I didn't know myself. Nice surprise though.' Dara rubbed Robbie's back cheerfully.

Noticing Dara's split lip, Robbie frowned, but he didn't say anything. Instead, he turned his attention back to Gracie.

'Yeah. It's weird though, ain't it? It does my head in a bit. You know, us three back together.' He shrugged, trying to get to grips with seeing Gracie after all this time.

That was the nearest any of them had ever got to mentioning Holly Brookes since they'd run away that night, all those years before. It was buried in their past, and all of them wanted to leave their demons locked away.

'So how come you're here, and how long are you staying?'

'She doesn't know yet.' Dara got there before Gracie could. 'And the girl can visit, can't she, without a reason?'

'Mmmmm?' Robbie had already lost concentration and was busy looking around the club again. Spotting the person he wanted to see, he began to make his mumbled exit. 'I'll see you later, if you're sticking around then.'

Dara grabbed hold of his shirt. 'Rob, not tonight, hey? *Please*. Why don't you hang out with us. We could get a takeaway or something. How about a curry from the Taj Palace? They were all right last time. My treat.'

'Nah, maybe tomorrow.'

'Robbie, please, I'm asking you not to.' Dara was upset.

'Don't start chewing my ear off.' He looked towards Gracie then back to Dara. 'I've told you before, stop treating me like a kid, okay?'

'Then don't fucking act like one,' Dara snapped. 'Sorry . . .' She had to try to keep calm. 'I just think you should be careful, that's all. The girls were telling me earlier that Colin's been cutting his shit with all sorts of crap.'

'Who isn't?' He pulled away from Dara, itching to buy a fix, and stomped across to where Colin – one of Archie's mates – was sitting.

Dara sighed. She didn't move her gaze away from Robbie as she watched Colin hand him a wrap of heroin.

'That's why I can't get up and disappear,' Dara said, without looking at Gracie. 'I can't leave Robbie. He needs someone to look out for him. He's bang on chasing the dragon, as well as sniffing.'

'He's a grown man, Dar. You're not responsible for him. You're not responsible for any of us.'

Dara bristled. 'But what's he supposed to do? If I leave, Archie isn't going to have him around, is he? The only reason Robbie's got a job is because of me. He'd be out on his ear otherwise. He'd have nowhere to go, and I can't do that to him. He'd end up in a crack den . . . and within no time, he'd be dead.'

'Are you kidding me, Dar?' Gracie pulled on her hand, to force Dara to look at her, because she couldn't believe what she was hearing. 'I'm not saying my heart doesn't go out to Robbie, but this is about *you*. You are staying here, in danger of being beaten senseless by Archie, because you want to stay loyal to Robbie . . . Robbie must know that, but he's clearly doing nothing about it. Though that's nothing new . . .'

'What does that mean?'

Gracie shook her head. 'I don't want to go there, but it makes me angry, Dar. It's not right . . . You shouldn't have to look after him.'

'You're right, Gracie, I shouldn't, but that's the way it is. Someone has to.'

Gracie was getting frustrated. 'You're not thinking straight. It's like you've dug yourself into a hole, and you can't get out of it. But I can help you. I've still got time . . . Dar, I want you to be safe, like you made sure I was.'

'*Oi!*'

Before Dara had time to think about what Gracie was saying, let alone answer her, Archie yelled over.

'*Oi!* Oi, Dara, what's with the long fucking face? Is this what I've come home to? Your boat race looking like a slapped fucking

473

arse?' Archie's words were slurred. He looked between Gracie and Dara, and pointed the lit end of his cigarette at them. 'Oh, I see, is Gracie whispering poison in your ear? Is that it?' He sneered at Gracie. 'Nasty toxic bitch, ain't you? You jealous, is that it? Your old man ain't got what it takes?'

Gracie snorted with derision. She gave Archie a withering look. 'Jealous? Oh my God, jealous of what? Of you? Or Dara being married to you? Which one, Archie?' She laughed again. 'You think I'm jealous of Dar? I actually feel sorry for her. I feel sorry that she's got such a good heart, and none of you lot can see it.'

Archie prickled with anger. He didn't like to be challenged, especially by a woman. 'I can see what you're about, you've just come here to cause trouble between me and my missus, ain't you? Fucking dog.'

'Don't you dare talk to her like that,' Dara snapped at him. She'd had enough.

Dara's response had Archie jumping up out of his seat, sending the two girls on his knees flying. He knocked over the table he was sitting at. The wine and beer glasses smashed to the floor, along with a line of speed.

'Who the fuck are you talking to, you cheeky cunt!' He charged towards Dara. 'Come here . . . I said, *come here*.' Archie spoke through gritted teeth, and talked to his wife like an errant dog.

Dara didn't move from where she was. All eyes were on her, though everyone knew better than to interfere. They'd seen how this played out too many times.

Taking a deep drag of his cigarette, Archie swayed on his feet. 'Don't let me have to drag you. I'll give you one more chance to get your arse over here.'

Dara scrambled out of her seat. 'Arch, why don't we do this tomorrow, babe?' She tried her best to appeal to him.

'My party's *today*, you cunt, it ain't TOMORROW. And you, my sweet little bitch, are spoiling my fucking buzz.'

'Leave her alone, for God's sake, Archie.' Gracie stood by the side of Dara.

'Keep out of it, you nosey cunt.' He snapped at her, a look of fury on his face. 'In fact, I want you *gone*. I want you out of here.' He began to walk towards her.

Dara had never let anyone talk to Gracie the way Archie was speaking to her, and she wasn't going to let it happen now. 'I'll say who comes and goes, Archie.'

The open-palm slap to Dara's cheek whistled through the air. Archie grabbed hold of her blonde bob in his fist. She yelled in pain. He was pulling on her hair now, dragging her head backwards and causing more agony.

'Get off her, Archie, get off her!' Gracie shouted, tugging on Archie's arm.

She fully understood she was the only one in the club who was going to try to do something to help. The girls watched, while Robbie, looking upset, nervously made his exit, leaving Gracie clawing at Archie. But Archie was far too strong for her, and all it took was one punch to Gracie's face to send her staggering backwards.

'Archie, *no!*' Something inside Dara snapped, seeing Gracie being punched. She fought back harder, harder than she'd done for a long time, and in return, Archie beat her more savagely.

He shook her like a rag doll, pushing her up against the bar. 'When are you going to learn that I'm in charge around here? *Me.* Your old man. Got it?' He panted, wide-eyed, the speed and the booze mixing together in his bloodstream.

Breathing hard, Dara glared at him. 'You need to lay off the whiskey, Arch. You're a fucking nutter on it.'

'Nah, nah, that ain't the problem. The problem is *you*, you're the one who needs a drink, darlin'.' He grabbed hold of Dara's chin, squeezing it hard. 'It's you that needs it, you fucking miserable cow. You couldn't even raise a glass for me coming out, and you have the front to say *I'm* the problem . . . Well, we'll soon sort that.'

Archie leant over the bar and grabbed the bottle of ouzo they kept behind there. Still holding on to Dara, he unscrewed the cap with his teeth, spitting it out on the floor. 'Get that down you, it might stop you being so fucking moody.'

The small cut on Dara's eyelid was bleeding, and the blood ran into her eye. 'Let me go.'

'Not until you open up . . . Go on, open up your fucking mouth.'

She shook her head.

'I said, OPEN UP.'

Pulling Dara's head back again, with his fist in her hair, Archie pushed the bottle on to her lips.

She kept them firmly closed, but Dara could feel the pressure as Archie twisted the bottle. As much as she tried, she couldn't hold her lips closed any longer. The next moment, Dara felt the bottle smash against her clenched teeth.

She tried again to knock it out of Archie's hands, spluttering as he managed to pour the ouzo into her mouth.

'Now swallow it. Come on, you stupid bitch, *swallow*.'

Dara turned her head and spat it out. She was crying loudly now. 'I don't want to . . . I don't want it.'

'I said, *drink it*. Fucking drink it. *NOW*.'

'I don't want to . . . because I'm pregnant.'

Chapter One Hundred

Devon couldn't find his wallet. He remembered having it at the bar, moments before his conversation with Dara.

He walked back down the stairs into the club. Straight into the scene playing out between Dara and her mess of a husband. It didn't take him long to realise no one was doing anything to help.

Devon came to stand behind Archie. His stance was powerful. 'What are you doing putting your hands on a woman?'

'Leave it, Devon, it's fine.' Dara could have kicked herself the moment the words left her mouth.

The way Archie slowly turned his head to look at her, smiling broadly, told her everything she needed to know: she'd made one very big mistake.

'Devon? It's Devon, is it? That sounds very cosy.' He pushed his nose hard against Dara's, licked his lips, then turned back to glare at Devon. 'If you know what's good for you, mate, you'll get out of here.'

'Not until I know she's all right.' Devon stood a few inches taller than Archie and clearly wasn't intimidated by him. 'And what the hell do you think you're doing, forcing her to drink?'

Archie blinked rapidly. His laugh competed with the loud music. 'Fucking hell, this speed must be some good shit for me to find myself in the Twilight Zone. Cos that's where I must be, mate, for you to come into *my* club and tell me what *I* should and shouldn't be doing with *my* missus.'

'Your club, is it?' Devon pulled a face. 'Are you sure about that? News to me.'

Archie's eyes darkened. 'What the fuck is going on here? Have you got a death wish? You've been watching too many movies, mate. Coming in here on your white charger . . . Do me a favour. Maybe you've forgotten, the heroes always die at the end.'

Without any warning, Archie took a swing at Devon and made contact with his jaw. He started raining down blows at close range, bloodying Devon's face, and forcing him backwards.

The taste of blood in his mouth seemed to act as a trigger for Devon. All of a sudden, he sprang into action. He clenched his fist, and aimed a punch, landing a heavy blow on the side of Archie's head.

The contact was hard and powerful, and Archie was stunned, swaying on his feet like a boxer about to go down. Devon took the opportunity to throw an upper cut. The punch snapped Archie's mouth shut, causing him to bite down on his own tongue.

'Anyone who beats up on women, in my opinion, is the lowest form of scum.' Devon was disgusted. He nodded to Dara and walked away.

'*Archie*, no! Devon, look out!'

Devon heard Dara shriek.

He began to turn back round, but he felt a pressure in his shoulder, then a warm sensation, followed by a sting, and an excruciating pain rushed through his body.

Devon dropped to his knees, feeling dizzy and strangely weak. He touched his shoulder with his fingers. He blinked, looking surprised, as he turned to hold Archie's stare.

'You stabbed me.'

The next moment, everything went black.

Chapter One Hundred and One

'Get him out of here. Put him in the alleyway.' Archie pointed at Devon and barked out his orders.

Dara ran in front of him. 'What are you going to do? Look at me, Archie, what the fuck are you going to do to him? You can't just dump him somewhere . . . Arch, *Arch!* I'm talking to you, for fuck's sake. You need to drive him to a hospital.'

Archie poked Dara in her chest. 'I don't need to drive lover boy anywhere.'

Dara swiped his hand away. 'Then I will.'

'I don't think so. You ain't going anywhere.'

Panicking, Dara glanced at Devon. She watched him being hauled up by a couple of the bar staff who worked at the club.

'Arch, come on, what if he bleeds to death?'

Archie was scornful. 'It's only a fucking scratch. He's a pussy. A bit of pain and he's fainted. It's nothing.'

Dara didn't think so. She could see the back of Devon's cream shirt covered in blood. She had to do something. She needed somehow to persuade Archie to let her take Devon to hospital.

'Think about it, Archie, even if you don't give a crap about him, you don't want the Old Bill sniffing around here because they've found a corpse in the alleyway, do you? They'll be on you like flies around shit, sweetheart. You know that as well as I do. You'll be back inside before you know it. Is that what you want?'

'You're getting on my nerves now.' Archie clenched his fist. 'I don't need this shit from you, so shut the fuck up. Or pregnant or not, you'll be in for a battering.'

'Then I'll take him.' Gracie spoke up. 'I'll take him to hospital . . . Dar, where's your car?'

Dara kept her eyes firmly fixed on Archie, she didn't trust him not to lash out at her. Or Gracie for that matter.

'You'll find the keys upstairs, in the drawer under the television. If you go out of the club and turn left, you'll see my car parked on the corner. It's a black Range Rover.' Dara gave Gracie the registration number.

Gracie nodded. 'Great, and maybe one of the girls can come with me, give me directions . . .?' She paused and stared at Archie. 'And before you say it, I'm not your wife, and I'll do what I like and go where I choose. And I'm taking him to hospital, whether you like it or not.'

She kissed Dara on her cheek and squeezed her hand. 'Oh, and Archie . . . You're a prick.' She walked out of the bar and through the back, leaving Dara with Archie.

'I want that bitch gone, understand?' He was breathing heavily.

Archie looked down at Dara. It wasn't what Dara would call a warm look, but it was certainly kinder than he'd been for a long while.

'Why didn't you tell me you were pregnant?' He grinned and wiped Devon's blood off his face. 'I think this is cause for a celebration, don't you?'

Dara's heart plummeted.

Archie reached out and grabbed the bottle of ouzo. He took her hand roughly and pulled her upstairs, into their bedroom.

'Arch, please.' Dara looked at the bed. 'I'm tired.'

'Then it's a good job there's a bed here.' He pushed her down on to the mattress.

'Archie, I'm not in the mood. I don't want to—'

'I don't fucking care what you want.'

He stripped off his clothes, exposing his muscular body. His tattooed penis was standing erect. He grabbed her by her ankles and dragged her down the bed towards him, before forcing her legs wide open. He knelt on the bed and roughly pulled up her skirt, pushing her lacy knickers to one side. He raised his hand and slapped her hard in the mouth.

Dara squealed, but tried not to react. She didn't want to get into any fist fights with Archie, especially now she had to think of the baby. And Archie had always liked rough sex.

'I've just got out after three months inside, and I'd say I was within my rights to fuck my missus, wouldn't you? I mean, what the hell do you expect me to do, fuck one of your skanky strippers? Why don't you relax? Who knows, you might even enjoy yourself.'

He grabbed her by the throat, playing hard and heavy, as he always did, then she felt Archie's penis enter her. He moaned loudly as he pumped away, thrusting faster and faster. The sweat dripped into Dara's face as she lay looking up at him. And as Archie climaxed, she closed her eyes.

Maybe Gracie was right. Maybe she needed to get the hell away from Archie, to keep her and her baby safe.

Chapter One Hundred and Two

Two days had passed, and Mad Angus was deep in thought. As usual, he was plotting someone's downfall. And today it so happened to be Archie's.

Wearing his black velvet Crockett & Jones slippers, Angus lounged in front of the heatless flames of the faux fireplace in the garishly decorated red-and-gold dining room of his large mansion in Billericay. Angus had done well for himself. There was no disputing that. Earning money from people who were in desperate need undeniably paid top dollar.

The interest Angus forced them to pay was eye-watering. A loan of a hundred pounds could easily have them paying over a grand or more in return. With or without a broken leg, depending on how long it took them to cough up.

Angus had always enjoyed money. Even as a kid, he'd rather save his school-dinner money than spend it. He'd thought nothing of stealing the Save the Children collecting tins from the porch of the local Catholic church. The way he saw it, Mother Mary was smiling on him.

As for women, Angus had been celibate for many years, out of choice . . . financial choice. Having a wife was too expensive. They were leeches, extracting money for treats and clothes, wanting flowers and gifts on their birthday. And as for prostitutes, well,

Angus saw them as a complete waste of his hard-earnt money. Masturbation was far cheaper, and much more convenient. It was a policy he stuck to, several times a day.

Indeed, the minute Angus smelt money, he was like a pig in a trough, which was why waiting on the money Archie owed him irked him so much. He took a sip of whiskey, to take the sting out of the thought.

As a rule, Angus would never allow so many weeks to go by without full repayment. Prison had got in the way of course, but now there was no reason for Archie not to have called him. Being ignored was something Angus didn't appreciate, especially as he'd given the stupid cunt enough time.

He looked over at the gun lying on the table.

People who didn't pay up were a waste of space. There was no place in this world for welshers.

Reaching across to the walnut cabinet, Angus picked up the phone.

He needed to make a call.

Archie's numbered days on this earth were about to come to an end.

Chapter One Hundred and Three

It was Saturday afternoon already, and Dara stood with an armful of magazines at the door of Devon's room.

'Devon, hey, how are you doing, babe?'

'Dara!' Devon was surprised. 'Hi.'

'I hope you don't mind me coming to see you in hospital? I wanted to make sure you were all right.' Dara smiled. She decided to come straight to the point. 'I'm so sorry about Archie. He can be an idiot.'

She hadn't been sure how Devon would react to seeing her. She was pleased he hadn't told her to fuck off. Though there was still time for that.

Devon sat up in bed, wincing as he put too much weight on his shoulder. 'You're a sight for sore eyes, or rather, sore shoulders.'

Dara rolled her eyes at his bad joke.

'Come in.' He gestured to her. 'To what do I owe this pleasure?'

Dara didn't answer straight away. Instead, she placed the magazines on the windowsill and went to sit by his bedside.

'Well, I had to come and check on you, didn't I?'

Devon tilted his head, looking intently at Dara. She was annoyed to find herself blushing.

He laughed, and Dara wondered if he knew the effect he had

on her. Men like Devon were players; using their good looks and charm to their advantage. Still, Dara couldn't help warming to him.

'I'm being serious,' she insisted. 'Let's face it, you wouldn't be here if it wasn't for me, would you?'

'I'd say it was your husband who stabbed me, not you.'

Dara gave a tight smile. Over the years, Archie had caused a lot of aggro, getting into fights, cheating and robbing, and making a lot of enemies. There were lots of pies that Archie had his finger in. Most of them left a bad taste in everyone's mouth.

There was no doubt about it, Archie spelled trouble for everyone who knew him. There were a lot of people who actively hated him. Herself included. How many times had she pictured him in his coffin? It was a daydream that often kept her going during the darkest of times. But it was beginning to look like a tempting reality.

'Yeah, well, Archie's sorry too.' This was a lie.

Devon was incredulous. 'You and I both know that's not true. Why are you covering for him? I'm betting you he doesn't even know you're here?' He took a sip of water from the plastic cup on his locker, keeping his eyes fixed on her.

Dara briefly thought about denying it, but who was she kidding?

'Okay, no he doesn't,' she admitted. 'But why point it out?' She became defensive. 'Is this your way of trying to humiliate me?'

'Of course not.' Devon was quick to answer. 'Archie is lucky to have you on his side.'

'Look . . . are you going to press charges?' Dara said this with her head bent.

'Oh, I see, so now we're getting down to it. You only came here to make sure I kept my mouth shut.'

Dara couldn't deny that it was the real reason for her visit. Doing Archie's dirty work was something she'd got used to. But she never felt comfortable with it. She kept her head down as Devon continued to talk.

'I'm surprised you don't want me to press charges though. It's an easy way to get rid of Archie for you.'

'Who said I want to get rid of him?'

'Come off it, he's an arsehole. Think about it, he'd go down for a long time, and you'd get to live your life in peace.'

This time, Dara did look up at him. 'It's not as simple as that. He'll deny it . . . no witnesses will come forward . . . and it'll cause a lot of problems. Especially for me.'

Dara watched Devon take this information in. He finished off his water.

'Well, it's a good job I'm not a grass then, ain't it?' A twinkle came back into his eyes. 'Besides, I think my family would disown me if I did.'

'You told them what happened?' Dara asked, surprised.

She let her gaze wander around the room. It was plain and simple. Two blue wipe-down chairs stood by the window, with a view across Regent's Park, and there was a small wall-mounted television and an en-suite bathroom. The smell of bleach was overpowering, and it took her back to a place where she didn't want to go. Digging her fingernails into her palms, Dara worked hard to stay focused on what Devon was saying.

'*No.* Fuck, no.' Devon shook his head. 'That wouldn't end up very pretty for Archie, if my family got involved. And like you say, it would have consequences for you, as well as that deadbeat who hangs around you.'

'Don't talk about Robbie like that. You know nothing about him.' Dara's eyes flickered with hostility.

Devon raised his eyebrows, surprised at quite how protective Dara sounded. 'Sorry, I shouldn't have said that . . . but anyway, point is, I said I got jumped on in the West End. Like you, I want an easy life.'

Dara didn't ask any more questions. She didn't want to get involved. All that mattered was that Devon wasn't going to go to the Old Bill.

'Thank you. I appreciate it.' Dara was genuinely grateful.

'Any time . . .' He paused a moment. 'You been to any more meetings . . . sorry, that's none of my business.'

'No, it's fine, and no I haven't . . . It feels weird to talk about it. Although you clearly don't have that problem.' She grinned.

Devon laughed. 'I think it's probably because, between us, my whole family at one time or another has done more trips to rehab than to Clacton-on-Sea.'

There was no bitterness in the way Devon said it, and they fell silent.

Dara studied him. There was an arrogance about him – or rather, a confidence – which made him seem older. And yet, in this light, and despite his short, well-kept beard, he looked a few years younger than she was. Though she had to confess, she was attracted to his self-assurance.

'I'm pleased you came, Dara,' Devon said after a time.

Dara caught her breath. She couldn't remember the last time she'd allowed herself to be drawn to someone.

Flustered, she got up quickly. 'I better go . . . and thanks again, Devon.'

'You don't have to rush off, you know.' Devon was matter-of-fact.

'It's fine. I'll see you around.'

She moved towards the door.

'Dara.' He called her back. 'Give Archie a message from me, will you? He needs to be careful who he crosses, because one day, he's going to pick the wrong person.'

At the entrance of the hospital, Dara waited for a well-dressed couple to exit the revolving door before she stepped into it herself. All of a sudden, a distant memory she couldn't quite place came into her mind. It faded away too quickly, leaving her uneasy.

God, she felt sick. Fucking *morning* sickness, even though it was the afternoon. Still, it was going to be worth it. Excitement suddenly hit her. She was going to be a mother. Though within moments, the excitement turned to fear: fear that she wouldn't be good enough. The prospect of turning into *her* mother terrified her. How would she navigate being a parent, when she'd never been parented herself?

She closed her eyes and breathed in slowly. God, she could do with a drink. A double vodka and tonic.

It was a sorry tale, but Dara was determined not to give in. She just had to get through today.

Chapter One Hundred and Four

It was gone six by the time Dara finally arrived back in the club. She'd called Gracie, checking in with her and making sure Archie wasn't about. The last thing she needed right now was a thousand questions from him, wanting to know where she'd been.

Dara felt a sense of disquiet. She wasn't sure what was wrong with her. Maybe it was simply that she was worried and upset about Gracie's diagnosis. She hadn't had time to fully process it yet. Though perhaps stopping drinking hadn't helped. And then there was the stress of Archie's homecoming. For the first time since she'd been living at the club with Archie, Dara felt no sense of pride or joy when she walked in. The only thing Dara felt as she looked around the empty bar was a sense of being trapped.

Trying not to dwell on it too deeply, Dara hurried up the stairs to the flat. She threw her bag down on the large white kitchen table, and picked up the letters Archie never bothered to open. They were mostly bills and junk mail. As usual, nothing of interest. Yawning widely, Dara flicked on the kettle, grabbing herself a mug from the draining board to make herself a decaff coffee.

It was quiet in the flat. Dara was beginning to relax, waiting for the kettle to boil, when it occurred to her she hadn't heard from Robbie since last night. He'd made a drunken phone call, apologising for not intervening between her and Archie the previous evening.

Not bothering to make herself the drink, Dara made her way to Robbie's room: it was a safe space where he could crash out. She tapped lightly on the door. 'Rob? Robbie, it's me, babe.' She pressed her ear against it, but heard nothing. She tapped again, harder this time. 'Rob, it's me, hun, you in there?'

There was still no answer.

Dara opened the door, popping her head around it. There was a distinct smell of burnt heroin; a sweet, sickly smell that lingered in the air.

'Oh *shit!* Robbie . . .'

Robbie lay on the bed, curled up in a foetal position. There was a pile of dried vomit on the pillow next to him.

'Rob?' Dara tried not to panic as she rushed over and gently shook him.

His breathing was shallow and erratic. They'd been here before.

'Rob, can you hear me, babe?'

Tiny beads of sweat showed on his forehead, and a belt was tied tightly around his arm. She glanced at the floor, and saw the all-too-familiar evidence. Robbie had been burning smack on a spoon lying next to a blood-covered syringe.

'Robbie.' Sitting on the bed, Dara stroked his hair. 'For fuck's sake, *why*, babe?' She hated this. Hated seeing him this way.

It reminded Dara of her mother. But this was who Robbie had become, wasn't it? And the only way she could stay close enough to look out for him, was by accepting it.

She kissed his head. His once thick brown hair was a mass of knots and grease, and his skin, previously flawless, was scarred by the crusted remains of angry red spots.

'Robbie?' Dara raised her voice slightly louder.

He groaned. His head rolled back and lolled against her thigh.

'Dar?' Mumbling, Robbie opened his eyes slightly. A lopsided smile appeared on his face. He let out a small chuckle. 'I'm going to be an uncle . . .' He reached out with a great deal of difficulty to touch her stomach.

'Yeah, yeah you are, Robbie. So you and I need to get our shit together, don't we, babe? I don't want to bring a baby into this world, with us bang on it, do I?'

His eyes were glazed over. 'You won't leave me, will you?'

'No, never, Robbie, you know that.'

'Don't leave me in the dark, Dar . . . not in the dark.'

He was mumbling, and Dara had to lean down to hear him properly.

'No, baby, no, I'll never leave you in the dark again.' She cradled his head.

He muttered something else – a few words Dara didn't quite catch.

Noticing him suddenly wincing, Dara quickly asked, 'Robbie, are you all right?'

Robbie consumed drugs like candy. Coke and heroin were his drugs of choice.

'My stomach. *Fuck*.'

He winced again, groaning much louder this time.

'Robbie? Robbie, what's going on?' He didn't reply, but Dara could see how much pain he was in. 'Have you taken anything else? *Rob*, have you taken anything else?'

Gritting his teeth, he nodded.

'Tell me what else you've taken? For fuck's sake, talk to me. *Rob*.' Dara was scared for him.

'*Bags*.' It was a mumble.

'What do you mean?' Dara frowned . . . then it dawned on her.

She looked frantically around the room, before getting up and rushing towards the en-suite bathroom. She stood in the doorway.

'Oh my God . . .'

Her stomach turned as she saw the unwashed balloons, filled with what she knew was heroin, covered in shit and lying on the floor.

She shouted over her shoulder. 'How many bags did you swallow . . . *Rob*, for fuck's sake, HOW MANY BAGS?'

'Ten,' came the quiet reply.

'And how many did you get out? Robbie, *how many*?'

Once again, Robbie didn't answer.

Dara hurried to where the balloons were lying in a filthy heap. Not wanting to touch them, she used the toe of her shoe to move them around and count them . . . seven, eight . . . nine. *Fuck*, there were only nine.

'Robbie, are you sure it was ten bags?'

She ran over to him and tugged at the waistband of his joggers, looking down the back to see if he'd shat out the tenth balloon without knowing. The massive amount of laxatives he must have taken to get the balloons out of his system, combined with him getting high, meant he'd lost control of his bowels.

Dara was used to Robbie soiling himself when he got totally wasted, and she often cleaned him up. From what she could see, the missing balloon wasn't there.

'Rob, I'm going to get my phone, all right . . . Why the *fuck* did you take a hit when you'd swallowed some bags?' She muttered this more to herself than Robbie.

'What's going on?' Archie bowled down the corridor. He had a spring in his step.

Dara guessed he was on coke, which always gave him an edge. He watched her hurrying for the kitchen.

'What's all the fucking drama about?' he asked, staring at Robbie.

'I think one of the balloons might have popped in his stomach. He's in a lot of pain, and I'm worried he's OD-ing. I dunno . . . I need to find my phone.' Dara turned towards the countertop where she'd left her bag.

'For fuck's sake, so you're telling me he's lost some of my money?' Archie sounded annoyed. He needed to pay Angus, and a bag blowing in Robbie's stomach was a clear waste of notes.

Dara's heart was racing; she was terrified for Robbie. 'No, I'm telling you Robbie could be in a lot of trouble. He's been shooting up as well.' She shook her head, struggling to keep her temper under control. '*Why*, Arch? Why get him to mule for you, when you know he's bang on it himself?'

Archie's eyes always went beady when he was angry. 'Oh, it's my fault now, is it? Robbie's a fucking waster!'

'Don't say that about him.' Dara reached for her bag.

'And *you* don't be so fucking cheeky.'

'I asked you not to . . .' Dara searched for the words as she rummaged to find her phone. 'Why make him swallow it, anyway?'

This was all Archie's fault. Though she knew better than to say it. She hated the way her husband treated Robbie, like he was nothing.

'You know why. The Old Bill is watching everyone right now, they're cracking down across London, picking everyone up and giving them a dust-down to see if they're carrying.'

'*Please*, Arch, don't ask him again, okay? Give him anything else to do, but not that.'

Archie roared with laughter. 'And what exactly should that be? How am I supposed to get that little prick to pay his way? He's hardly an employer's dream, is he? Fuck me.'

His words had a savagery about them as he came to stand next to her. He wrenched the phone out of her hand.

'Arch, give it back, *please*. I need to call the ambulance, or at least the doc—'

'*Archie, please, please, save my little friend. Boo-hoo, I'm so worried about him.*' He made fun of Dara, putting on a mocking falsetto voice.

She grabbed for the phone, and immediately felt the impact of a fist. The pain exploded as the sovereigns on Archie's fingers came into contact with her eye. It was like a needle had been thrust straight into it. He was vicious thug.

She squealed, bending forward, covering one side of her face with one hand.

'You're lucky I'm in a good mood, Dara, and you're carrying my kid.' He pulled her into him. 'Now let's get Robbie to the hospital, shall we? But no ambulance, we can take him ourselves. And Dara . . .' He smiled at her.

If she didn't know better, the way his eyes lit up softly, she would think it was genuine.

'This fiery, defiant shit, this attitude you have towards me, has to stop, all right? We don't want the baby thinking you're a cunt, do we?' He kissed the top of her head.

As his lips brushed her hair, Dara thought once again about the daydream she often had of Archie lying in a coffin.

What would it take for her to find the courage to change that dream into a reality?

Chapter One Hundred and Five

Dara was aching. She'd spent the night in A&E, waiting for news of Robbie, and now her back was killing her from lying on the plastic chairs.

When they'd brought Robbie in, the medics had taken him through straight away, trying to get his blood pressure under control and stop the seizures he'd started having. They'd done a CT scan to check his stomach for anything else as well, and now they were keeping him in for forty-eight hours under observation.

Dara knew Robbie would discharge himself the moment he was feeling better, but at least right now he was in the place he needed to be. Over the years, they'd been through this before: the careless overdosing and the hospital dashes.

Unsurprisingly, Archie had done a disappearing act, leaving Dara to answer the doctors' questions. She'd been vague about her exact relationship to Robbie.

Dara walked into the ward on the fourth floor and smiled at Robbie. He was in the end bed, looking like a ghost. All the colour had drained from him. Robbie was everything to her, and she had to battle hard not to burst into tears.

'You gave me such a fright.' She plonked herself down on the bed, and grabbed his hand. 'Don't do that to me again, babe. You hear me?'

Chewing on his knuckle, he shrugged. 'Fucking hell, Dara, is this what I've woken up to, you fussing?'

'I care, that's all.' Dara tried not to feel hurt.

'Maybe try caring less. I love you, Dara, but sometimes it becomes too much.' A faint smile tugged at the corners of his mouth, but his eyes were lifeless and dull.

'I love you too, so much, Robbie. But I'm scared. I'm scared that one day I won't be there when you need me.'

'You've always been there for me, Dara. You don't have to worry about that.'

Dara stared at him. 'But I do, and if you don't want me to worry, then slow down on the smack, and stop being one of Archie's mules. It's going to kill you.'

He rubbed his face. God, he looked like shit.

'It hasn't so far.' Robbie shook his head. 'So there's no reason why it should now.'

'No, because I've been there looking out for you. But what if, one day, I'm not? What then?' She raised her voice, but lowered it when she saw the nurse in charge looking over. 'Robbie, for me, please, *stop*. I can't keep doing this. I know I've been bang on it, but I wasn't shooting up, and I get that it probably does your head in, me nagging you, but I don't want anything to happen to you. I want my baby to know his amazing uncle.' She wiped away her tears.

Robbie reached across, putting his arms around her. She leant her head on his chest.

'I appreciate everything you've done for me, Dara. I wouldn't be here if it wasn't for you, and I can see how much it means to you, so okay, I'll stop.'

She turned her head to look at him. 'The drugs?'

He gave her his usual lopsided grin. 'No . . .' At least he was being honest. 'I'll stop being Archie's mule, I'll think of some fucking excuse, give him some bullshit, and I'll try to pull back on the brown. I can't promise, but I'll give it a good shot.'

It was exactly what Dara needed to hear. Robbie had been taking drugs for years, but right from the start it had taken a hold of him. Robbie had never been a functioning addict. He'd sat around stoned out of his head, while she'd gone out looking for jobs, and places to live, providing food for them both. Not that she regretted it, nor would she have done anything different. She loved Robbie with all her heart. But the problem with love, like drugs, was it often made people do things they shouldn't.

He kissed Dara on her cheek. 'Thank you. What would I do without you, hey?'

She kissed him back. 'Then it's a good job you don't have to—'

'Can I have a word?' A male voice interrupted.

Dara looked up. It was the Old Bill. *Fuck*, she'd been hoping to get out of the hospital before they turned up. She knew it was only a matter of time.

'I'll see you later, Rob.' She scooted up from the bed, picking up her bag.

'Are you the lady who brought him in?' The officer stared at her from beneath his peaked cap.

'Don't know what you're talking about, mate.' Dara shrugged and turned away, hurrying out of the ward.

'*Hey* . . . Can we have a word?'

Dara heard the officer calling her back and she broke into a sprint, rushing along the corridor. Without looking behind her, she sprinted for the lift. *Shit*. She didn't have time to wait for it.

She barged through the double doors leading to the stairs and ran down them, hoping the Old Bill wouldn't come after her.

By the time she reached the pharmacy on the ground floor, Dara was breathing heavily. She stopped to catch her breath. Jesus, she was unfit. She peeked behind her. No sign of the Old Bill.

As her heart rate returned to normal, she felt suddenly light-headed. Perhaps she'd grab herself a cup of coffee, and perhaps a sticky bun. After all, wasn't she supposed to be eating for two? Dara headed for the hospital canteen.

With none of the cakes or sandwiches looking appealing, she waited for the coffee machine to finish making her a cappuccino.

She grabbed her drink, pressing a plastic lid on it. '*Fuck*.' Hot coffee shot out on to her hand and sleeve.

'Here you are, sweetheart, I did the same myself yesterday.' The man queuing behind Dara handed her a wad of napkins from the side. 'Fucking hurts, I can tell you.'

She took the tissues and smiled. Looking at him properly, Dara wondered where she'd seen him before. Then she remembered: he was one half of the well-dressed couple coming through the revolving doors when she visited Devon.

'I wouldn't mind if it was a decent cup of coffee,' Dara said ruefully.

Her phone rang and she turned away, pulling it out of her pocket. It was Archie. She didn't answer it; he'd assume she was still stuck in A&E. Although she *did* need to get home as soon as possible. She didn't like the thought of Gracie being alone in the flat with Archie.

Dara took a sip of coffee and headed up the stairs, hurrying out of the hospital and on to Euston Road to hail a cab. As the fresh morning air hit her, so too did another vague memory, of a voice, a face from the faraway past. But like before, it faded as quickly as it had appeared. She frowned and momentarily glanced over her shoulder at the hospital.

She dug her nails into her leg, desperate to stop the rising sense of being pulled back into a place she didn't want to revisit.

Chapter One Hundred and Six

Dara tapped on the door of the guest room.

She'd hadn't slept well after visiting Robbie. She was plagued with strange dreams that woke her, then faded before she could grasp them.

'Gracie, hey, Gracie, it's only me.'

Archie was out cold in the bedroom next door. After a heavy session of drinking and snorting coke last night in the club, he'd hauled himself up to the flat. He'd normally have gone out on the town, but Dara suspected Archie wanted to lie low because of Angus. She couldn't argue with that. No one wanted to be on the receiving end when Angus flexed his muscles.

There was no way it was ever going to end pretty.

Taking a deep breath, she knocked on Gracie's door again. She struggled with Robbie not being here – it felt like a part of her was missing – but at least she had Gracie to distract her, and this was the perfect opportunity to have a catch-up with her in private. They *still* hadn't actually talked about her diagnosis, but that didn't mean it wasn't very much in the forefront of Dara's mind.

'Hi, come in,' Gracie called out.

Dara opened the door, carrying the breakfast tray she'd prepared. A steaming-hot cup of tea, a couple of slices of crisp, buttered toast and a runny boiled egg. Cooking had never been her strong point, though she had prepared everything with love.

'I hope I didn't wake you.' Dara was apologetic.

Gracie sat up in the small double bed.

The room was decorated in shades of lemon and cream, with Habitat furniture and made-to-measure wooden blinds. It was a long way from the chaos and squalor of Dara's childhood.

'No, I've been awake for hours.' Gracie smiled as Dara placed the tray on the side and opened the blinds.

'I thought you might want a bit of brekkie. But don't blame me if the egg isn't cooked, fuck knows how long you're supposed to do it for . . . And it didn't help that I had to stop to be sick a couple of times.' Dara began to laugh, but it soon turned into a frown. 'Are you all right, babe?'

Gratefully, Gracie reached for the mug of tea. She blew on it. 'Truthfully? Not really. I try not to think about it . . . you know, about what's going to happen. But I get scared, Dar.'

Dara sat on the bed. 'You want to talk about it?'

Gracie shook her head. 'Not really, not right now . . . And I was thinking, maybe I should go. Go back home.' She took a sip of tea. 'I don't want to outstay my welcome. Not that there's been any welcome from Archie.' She shrugged.

'Fuck Archie.' Dara laughed uneasily. 'You're my guest, not his. And look, babe, if there's anything you need – clothes, shoes, make-up – you can use mine. Help yourself . . .' She looked Gracie straight in the eye. 'I don't want you to go back yet . . . you make me feel safe, Gracie. And somehow, having you here, well, I find it easier to look after Robbie as well. You know, because you understand.'

Gracie shook her head. 'I don't know if I do, Dara. I know it was tough for Robbie, but—'

'You had a better start in life.' Dara interrupted. 'He was born in that place, so what do you expect? Robbie might be walking free now, but there's a part of him that's never really left it. His foundations are built on trauma, babe. So you can't judge him, not you as well . . .' She fidgeted nervously. 'I still remember his screams when they used to put him in that shed in the woods . . .'

Dara didn't say any more. Instead, she curled up on the bed with Gracie. 'Remember that song you used to sing to me?'

Gracie laughed. 'What song?'

Dara scrambled round on her stomach to gaze up at Gracie. 'You sang it to all of us. I used to love it. It helped me hold on to the belief that, one day, we'd all have a better life.'

Dara began to hum, then broke into quiet song.

'Lavender's blue, dilly, dilly, lavender's green, when I am King, dilly, dilly, you shall be Queen. Keep me from harm, dilly, dilly. Keep me from—'

'I don't like to think about it, Dar,' Gracie interrupted and looked away, gazing out of the window. 'I try not to go back there in my head. Robbie wasn't the only one who found it difficult.'

Dara noticed Gracie's eyes filling with tears. 'I'm so sorry.'

Gracie didn't look at her. 'It's not your fault.'

They fell into silence.

Gracie continued to sip her tea. As Dara watched her, an idea came into her head.

'What you need is to have a good time. We need to get you out of yourself a bit. Dust those flies away from your nunny.' She laughed, hard and real.

Gracie grinned. 'Go on?'

'Devon.'

'Devon? What are you on about?'

Dara sat up. 'You. You and him.'

Gracie was still puzzled. 'What are you talking about?'

'How about you go on a date with him?'

Gracie spluttered with laughter. 'Dar, you've lost it. For a start, I don't know him. He probably wouldn't want to. And anyway, have you seen him? I mean, how old is he? In any case, the last time I saw him, your other half had just plunged a knife in his back. I wouldn't say that's off to a great start, would you? Plus . . .' Gracie tilted her head. 'I thought maybe you liked him?'

'Me?' Dara shook her head.

'Dar, come on. I saw you two chatting in the club the other night. There was definitely something there.'

'Well, there isn't.'

'Dar, you deserve so much better than Archie. Archie the meathead.' She pulled a face.

They both giggled, as if they were young girls.

'But seriously, Dar, you've battled for so long, for so many people, taking care of them. It's actually you who should be having the good time.'

Dara smiled at Gracie again. She appreciated what she was saying. But she didn't need any more complications in her life. She did like Devon, she liked him a lot, but there was no way she could go there, even if she wanted to. Besides, seeing Gracie happy and having some fun would always be her number one priority. Gracie and Robbie came before anyone. And anyway, Devon was perfect for Gracie.

'Thank you, but no thank you. Could you imagine if Archie found out? But nothing's stopping you . . . and you were the one who said you were going to be impulsive, right? And what better way than Devon? No one's asking you to marry him, doll, or get serious with him, I just want you to have some fun. I mean, you said it yourself, you and Jeremy were boring fuckers.'

Gracie laughed so hard she nearly choked on her tea.

Dara took hold of Gracie's hands. 'So will you?'

'He probably wouldn't even want to, Dar. I'm sure he has his pick of any woman. So why would he want to go on a date with me?'

Dara leant forward and pushed a strand of Gracie's hair out of her eyes and behind her ear. 'Why *wouldn't* he? Gracie, you're beautiful, and any man would be lucky to take you out.'

Gracie blushed. 'I love you, Dar. You've always had a way of making me feel special.'

'I love you too . . .' She studied Gracie's face. 'So is that a yes then, *Mrs Robinson*?'

Gracie laughed at the reference.

'So can I?' Dara continued. 'Can I play matchmaker for you?'

Gracie took a deep breath. 'Fine . . . But don't be surprised if he says no, and runs the other way.'

Chapter One Hundred and Seven

Dara was tired and her back was still aching. She'd promised herself a long, hot soak in the bath when all her chores were done.

Sighing, she carried a crate of empties out of the club. She'd leave them in the tiny pedestrian alleyway for the guys from the brewery to take in the morning. She gazed around. Soho was beginning to come alive, the sex shops opposite were starting to get busy, and tourists were milling around.

'Shit . . . *Shit* . . .' Dara cursed out loud to herself as she saw Angus and a couple of his men making their towards the club.

She ran inside and darted down the stairs, through to the back where Archie was busy auditioning a couple of girls for the club. Their tits were on display, and they were fanny-naked. They were shivering and covered in goosebumps as they stood in the middle of the room. Archie was inspecting them as though they were cattle in a market.

'Archie, quick, run . . . *run* . . . Angus is here. I've just seen him, walking down the street.'

'Fuck.' Archie scrambled out of his chair.

'Out the back . . . *now.*' Dara grabbed him, pulling him along, out of the office and towards the exit at the back of the club. She tugged open the fire door, charging down the small alleyway with Archie, barging past the crates of empty wine and beer bottles.

The alleyway took them to St Peter's Street, where Dara looked up and down the road, making sure no one was coming. They ran across to Wardour Street, and Dara hailed a black cab.

'Go over to Ray-Ray's, stay there for a bit, I'll call you later, okay?' She bundled Archie inside.

He nodded at her. 'Yeah, all right . . . and cheers.' It was the nearest Archie got to being civil.

Not wanting to go back to the club yet, in case Angus was hanging around, Dara strolled through Chinatown.

Out of nowhere, tears welled up in Dara's eyes. She leant against the display window of a mobile phone repair shop. What the hell was the matter with her? This pregnancy seemed to be playing havoc with her hormones. She wiped away the tears fiercely with her hand. Her anxiety levels were through the roof. It was the same sort of worry that used to sit in her stomach when she was a kid, and it had never left her.

Trembling, Dara fumbled in her pocket and pulled out the bottle of benzos the doctor had given her. He'd said they were the safest pills while she was pregnant to keep her off the booze and control her cravings, but she still felt guilty taking them. She shook a couple out, popping them quickly into her mouth.

'Hey.'

'*Fuck.*' Dara jumped. She put her hand on her chest. 'Jesus, has anyone ever told you not to give people a fright like that?'

Devon stared at her. 'Hey, are you all right? You been crying?' He used his thumb to gently wipe away her remaining tears.

'I'm fine, just tired, that's all. I always cry when I'm exhausted,' Dara lied.

She attempted a smile; she knew she had to keep the feelings she had for him locked away. But it was harder than she'd imagined.

'Anyway, it's good to see they finally let you out,' she said breezily. 'And it saves me the trouble of trying to contact you.'

He stood very close to her. 'Then that makes two of us, I was about to pop into the club and see whether you'd come across my wallet at all? Black leather? That's why I popped back the other night, though I never actually got round to asking if anyone had found it.' He shrugged, and laughed, giving her a droll grin.

'Nothing's been handed in behind the bar, but I'll ask the girls to keep an eye out.'

'Thanks . . . are you walking back there now? I'll walk with you.'

'*No.*' Her reply was too quick.

Devon looked at her and frowned.

'No, we're not open yet, and I wanted to get some fresh air, and a coffee from the new Italian.'

Devon tilted his head to one side in a characteristic gesture. 'So were you waiting for me?' He winked.

She felt herself blush. 'Kind of . . . well, yes.' Now it came down to it, Dara suddenly felt awkward. 'Yeah, I wanted to ask you something.'

'Name it.'

'Will you take my friend out to dinner?' Dara blurted it out and laughed at how random it sounded.

'Your friend?'

'Yeah, Gracie. The one who took you to hospital.' She raised her eyebrows and stared at him cheekily. 'Well?'

'Well what?'

Dara watched a group of teenagers walking by, then looked back at Devon. 'Well, will you take her out? I know it sounds a bit childish, but she doesn't know anyone down here, and you'd be perfect. A change of scenery will do her the world of good.'

'Do you often ask your customers to take your friends out to dinner?'

'Only the ones who get stabbed in my club.'

Their easy laughter mingled in the open air, and Dara wished, once again, things were different.

Devon shook his head. 'I'd rather not, I can't even remember her, so I might take a rain check on that, babe'

'Then call it a blind date . . . Look, between me and you, she really needs some cheering up. There's stuff going on which . . . well, just stuff . . . and hey, she did save your life.' Dara was teasing him, though it was partly true.

Gracie had stepped in when no one else had dared to go up against Archie.

'Surely that deserves a dinner, Devon, even if it's only a *thank-you* dinner. It doesn't have to be a date. And you'd be doing me a favour.'

He shoved his hands into his pockets. 'I dunno.'

'Look, she's only down here for a short time. She needs a laugh, and right now, I'm hardly the best company.'

Devon looked away for a moment, then leant against the wall, staring at Dara. 'You don't get it, do you?' Absent-mindedly, he licked his lips. 'It's you I want to take out for dinner, not your mate.'

Dara was thrown, though she managed to recover quickly. 'I'm flattered, but I'm taken . . . And like I said to Gracie, I'm not asking you to marry her. Take her out for a meal, to say thank you. That's all. She stood up to my arsehole of a husband for you, and she didn't have to.'

Devon didn't say anything. He breathed in deeply, then nodded his head. 'Fine. Fine . . . I'll take her out. Happy?'

Dara grinned. She wasn't, but like hell would she ever say. 'Thank you. Oh, and be at the club tomorrow at eight.'

'No problem.' Devon headed towards Shaftesbury Avenue. He raised his hand as he walked backwards, still facing Dara. 'Bye then . . . I can't believe I've agreed to this, you know.' He was laughing.

Cheerfully, she called after him, 'You won't regret it. It's a great idea.'

'Yeah right, that's what they said about the maiden voyage of the *Titanic*.'

Chapter One Hundred and Eight

Dara stood looking at Gracie, aghast.

'What the hell are you wearing? You look like you're going to work in the office.'

Gracie was standing in Dara's guest room, getting ready for her date with Devon. She looked down at the navy suit she'd bought earlier that day from Fenwick.

'What's wrong with it? I spent a good few quid on it.'

Dara laughed. 'You need to start asking yourself what's *right* with it, Gracie . . . Jesus, you look like a schoolteacher who hasn't got laid in a few years.'

Gracie grinned. 'Sounds good to me.'

'No. No way are you going out like that . . . come with me.' Dara grabbed hold of Gracie's hand.

She pulled her along the hallway, giggling, and led Gracie into her bedroom. It was decorated in grey and silver, with opulent crushed velvet and glitzy accessories.

Dara went into her wardrobe and riffled through the racks. She grabbed a red sequinned crop top and short denim skirt.

'What about this? This should look good.'

Gracie was horrified. 'Yeah, if you're a hooker from the seventies. Dara, I'm in my thirties, not a sixteen-year-old kid . . . Maybe this isn't a such a good idea, after all.'

'Of course it is . . . Look, we'll find you something else to wear, all right?'

Dara good-humouredly threw the skirt and top on to her king-sized bed. She hunted through her large fitted wardrobe again, searching for something Gracie would feel comfortable in.

'Bingo! What about this? It's from Harrods.'

Dara held up a black satin Azzedine Alaïa bandage dress.

'That looks too expensive, Dar.'

'Don't worry about it. And anyway, I've got a few of them in different colours – my mate nicked them all. Let's call it a souvenir from Harrods . . . Go on, try it on.'

Gracie shrugged off her Fenwick suit and pulled the dress down over her slim figure.

Dara's face lit up. She was so proud of Gracie.

'You look amazing. Devon will be drooling. You'll be walking like a cowboy tomorrow.'

'Dar, I'm not going to sleep with him.'

Dara kissed Gracie on her cheek. 'We'll see.'

They stared at each, bursting into laughter at the same time.

Gracie put her hand on Dara's stomach. 'I'm hoping I'll still be around for this little bean.' She grinned. 'I'm so pleased for you, Dar. You being a mama, it's going to be brilliant. You were born to be one, babe. I would've loved to have been a mum . . . you know, again. If things had been different, of course, but that infection I got afterwards, well, it put paid to that.' She shrugged.

Dara tensed and moved away from Gracie. The thought of Gracie's loss was like a sharp pain. There were a lot of subjects Dara couldn't deal with, and so many things going on with her right now. If she stopped and thought about it, she became overwhelmed.

'Oh, Dar, I didn't mean to upset you. I'm fine . . . Look, this dress is great. It couldn't be better. And you know what? I'm actually looking forward to tonight . . . Dar, what's wrong?'

'Nothing.' It sounded more uptight than Dara intended. 'Let's go. We wouldn't want to keep Devon waiting, would we?'

At the top of the stairs leading down to the club, Gracie stopped. 'Will Archie have a problem with Devon taking me out for dinner, do you think?'

'Yes, but who cares.' Dara giggled again.

She tried to push away the constant anxiety that gnawed away at her. Though strangely enough, she was feeling more like herself than she had for a very long time.

The club didn't open until nine on Tuesdays, so it was still empty apart from a handful of staff getting the place ready.

Dara saw Devon first.

He wore a black shirt, denim jeans and Chelsea boots. She had to admit, a tiny part of her was envious of Gracie going out with him.

'Jesus, Dara, I don't know if I can do this,' Gracie confessed.

They both stared at him.

'Yes, you can. Go on, Mrs Robinson, go have a good time.'

'Oh my God, stop calling me that!' Gracie chuckled nervously. 'You make me feel old.'

'You'll be fine.'

Spotting them, Devon walked across. 'You look great.'

And Gracie did. She held herself with more confidence than she felt.

'Look after her, won't you, Devon? Otherwise you'll have me to answer to.' Dara was only half joking. 'Oh, and Gracie, make sure you do *everything* I would.' She winked and trilled with laughter.

Dara was left standing in the empty club. Like Gracie had done, she touched her stomach, rubbing her hands over it.

Birth and death were too closely linked for her liking.

Chapter One Hundred and Nine

Dara finally felt well enough to start getting the bar ready for the evening.

She'd vomited at least four times, and felt like she was constantly on the verge of retching. Tiredness was also kicking in, but perhaps that was more to do with not having eaten much. And the little she had, she'd thrown up into the toilet.

'Dara. *Dara!*' It was Archie.

He'd come home late last night from Ray-Ray's, after she'd given him the all-clear. Thankfully, Angus hadn't done anything to the club, apart from leaving a calling card of piss. Though knowing Mad Angus, he'd be planning his next move already.

Sharon had told Dara she'd heard Archie speaking to Mad Angus on the phone, *begging* for his life, telling Angus some tale about having the money for him by Friday. Who knew if that was true? Dara wasn't sure how Archie was going to pull it off. But she was certain Mad Angus didn't make idle threats.

'Dara, where are you?'

Dara sighed before answering. She just wanted a little peace. 'Yeah, what? I'm in here . . .'

She didn't bother to look up at the sound of footsteps coming down the stairs to the main entrance. She yawned again. She could actually do with resting on the sofa for a couple more hours, she was knackered, but she'd wanted to do a bar inventory while the club was quiet. But now Archie had arrived back, and put an end to that.

'Dara. Got a visitor for you.' Archie's voice was firm, and this time Dara *did* look up.

She was taken aback when she saw who was with him.

Archie threw her a hard stare. 'Aren't you going to say hello? My wife isn't usually this rude, are you, *Dara*?'

The man shrugged. 'Don't worry about it . . . Maybe it's because we've already met. It's a small world, ain't it?'

Archie seemed puzzled.

'Me and Dara, we had a good old moan about the hospital coffee the other day, didn't we?'

'Sorry, yeah . . . that's right, at the coffee machine.' Dara nodded, but she was thrown by seeing him here.

She watched in surprise as he glanced around the empty club, taking in the stage and the strippers' poles, the private drinking booths. He nodded in what seemed like a gesture of approval. Then, much to Dara's astonishment, he casually walked around the bar and took a glass from the shelf, sticking it under the bottle of whiskey to dispense a shot.

'You've done a nice job here.' He downed the whiskey in one, then measured himself another shot. He stared at Dara again. 'Your old man says you're the brains behind it all.'

He pulled out his cigarettes, and she watched him tap one out, light it, drawing on it deeply. Through a cloud of smoke he narrowed his eyes at her.

'So what are you planning—'

But his words faded out and Dara stopped listening to what he was saying. Her heart began to race, and she held on to the edge of the bar behind her for support.

She stared straight into his eyes. 'Sorry, sorry . . . I have to go . . . I've . . . I've just remembered something.'

She ran out of the club and through to the back. She closed her eyes, leaning forward, taking gulps of air.

'What the fuck's wrong with you?' Archie marched through after her. 'What was that about? Do you want to embarrass me?'

She stood up again, looking at her husband.

Archie scowled then. 'You look like you've seen a fucking ghost.'

'What does he want?' Dara whispered.

'What do you mean, what does he want? I already told you he was popping by, you dozy cow. Now get out there, and make yourself presentable.'

Dara was shaking. 'Who is he?'

Archie grabbed hold of her arm tightly. 'If this pregnancy is going to turn you into some ditzy mare, you can get yourself down to the clinic and get rid.' Exasperated, he sighed. 'Like I said, he's the fucking owner, so sort yourself out.'

'*What?*'

Since they'd taken over running the club, they'd done everything through a managing agent. Dara had never had anything to do with the owner – or even thought about him. Until now, of course.

'You heard me. Now go and say hello properly. I don't want him pulling the fucking plug on us because you've got a face on.'

Dara shook her head. 'No.'

'What is your fucking problem? Get out there, and make him think you're not a crazy bitch.'

'I said, *no.*'

Archie nodded. 'Okay.' And with a swift movement, he grabbed Dara's head, smashing it against the wall.

She fell to the floor, feeling the skin above her eyebrow split open.

And as Archie slammed out of the corridor, back into the main club, Dara staggered up and ran towards the fire exit, rushing out into the alleyway.

Chapter One Hundred and Ten

The French restaurant Devon had taken Gracie to in Glasshouse Street was deceptive. The outside was drab, with a tatty sign that was barely legible. But customers were treated to an entirely different experience the minute they walked through the door. There was a luxurious Art Deco splendour to the interior: wood-panelled walls, sweeping red velvet curtains trimmed with gold, and subtle lighting. Jazz music was playing softly in the background.

Gracie and Devon sat in one of the private alcoves, lit by candles. It crossed Devon's mind that this place was completely over the top for a simple thank-you dinner. So why had he chosen to bring Gracie here?

Gracie took a sip of her glass of Pinot Noir. Her conversation so far had been rather boring, after years of unexciting small talk with Jeremy. She didn't want to pry too much by asking Devon probing questions. She didn't really know anything about him – apart from the fact he was a good-looking guy, and he'd been stabbed by Archie. Both subjects seemed to be inappropriate for a first dinner. And Gracie heavily suspected, by the way things were going, this would also be the last.

Devon sat nursing a large glass of Pepsi with ice. Gracie was looking at him, probably wanting him to say something, rather than sit here in awkward silence. He'd usually have the gift of the gab, employing the old cheesy chat-up lines, before taking his date back to a hotel, where he'd fuck her brains out, leaving in the morning before she woke up.

But with Gracie, it didn't seem right. She had a sophistication about her. It wasn't so much that she was slightly older than him, he didn't care about that. He loved women, no matter what. His mum always called him a 'ladies' man' – which, in Devon's books, made him sound like some old fucking sleazebag. No, it was that Gracie commanded a respect that, to his shame, he didn't always give.

'So what do you do? Dara didn't tell me.' Jesus, could he be more boring?

Gracie took a bite of her fillet steak – medium rare – and immediately regretted it as she began to chew on a tough bit of gristle. She could see Devon was waiting for her to answer, and she tried to chew faster, but it was so tough her teeth couldn't get through it. It was also too large for her to swallow whole. She felt herself starting to go red as Devon sat patiently watching her attempt to finish chewing her mouthful. In the end, Gracie had no option but to grab the napkin and spit the piece of meat into it.

'I'm so sorry, Devon . . .' She felt mortified. 'Oh my God . . .'

Devon burst into horrified laughter.

For a moment, Gracie didn't know whether to be offended or not, but she soon erupted into fits of giggles too. They were laughing hysterically, the ice finally broken.

'Look . . .' Devon said, still snorting with laughter. 'Why don't we get out of here? Maybe go and get a Maccie D's instead? What do you say?'

Gracie nodded. Beaming with happiness. 'Yeah, I'd like that. I really would . . .'

*

'Oh my God, where have you been, Gracie?'

It was late – three in the morning – and the club was still open, though the last of the strippers had been onstage. Dara tried to sound cheerful as she tapped her watch.

She was an emotional wreck, but she was trying not to show it. She'd struggled hard not to come back to the bar and pour herself a large glass of vodka.

'We took a slow walk back from Trafalgar Square.' Gracie strolled up to Dara. 'Jesus, Dara, what happened to your face? Did Archie do that? As if I need to ask! Of course he bloody did.' She shook her head, looking frustrated and upset for her friend. 'You need to leave that man. He can't keep doing this to you.'

Dara touched her face. She'd managed to stop the bleeding from the cut above one eye, using some Steri-Strips, so she hadn't needed to go and get any stitches. Her face was sore and bruised, and her eyes were blackened, but she'd live. She'd certainly had worse. But this time, it was going to be different. She'd make sure of that.

'Yeah, I do . . . and I was thinking, maybe . . . well, maybe I'll take you up on your offer to come to your place. Get away from here. Perhaps you could go back sooner, on your own? And we'd follow you later. I . . . I need to persuade Robbie, of course, and then we'll both come and stay. Devon could even join us.' Dara spoke quickly. 'That would be perfect.'

'Really?' Gracie was surprised, although pleased at this change of heart. 'That would be amazing! But what if Robbie won't come? Please tell me you're not going to stay here and let Archie continue to treat you like this.'

Gracie stopped talking, and pulled Dara in for a hug.

'Dar, you're shaking.'

'I'm fine.' Dara eased herself gently out of the embrace. 'Anyway, I want to talk about how *you* got on . . . Go on, tell me, what was it like?' She sat Gracie down at one of the tables by the door. 'More to the point, what happened?' Dara tried to push the fear circling in her mind to one side.

'I didn't kiss him, Dar, if that's what you're asking.' Gracie played with a lock of hair between her fingers. 'But I had the best time. Thank you, Dar.'

'What for?'

'For being the greatest friend anyone could ever want.'

It was too much for Dara. She got up, and ran out of the club, bursting into guilty tears.

Chapter One Hundred and Eleven

'What time are you going out? You don't want to be late.' Dara lay on Gracie's bed, watching her get ready.

It was a Thursday evening and, thankfully, all had been quiet, with Archie lying low at the club. But that hadn't stopped Dara feeling like she was going out of her mind with worry.

'Anyone would think you wanted me out of here.' Gracie grinned.

It was actually the truth. Dara *was* trying to get Gracie away from the club as much as she could.

Dara laughed uneasily. 'It's not that. I have to go and pick up Robbie, he's being discharged from hospital later. I'm actually surprised he didn't walk out himself, but I reckon he's been enjoying the meds they're giving him.'

She tried to make light of it, but she desperately wanted Gracie out of the way. Who knew if the owner of the club was going to turn up again? She had to get Gracie as far away from Soho as she possibly could.

Dara was hoping somehow to persuade Robbie to leave London. She knew she'd have her work cut out, and of course she wouldn't go up north without him, but they needed to be gone. Gracie had noticed that Dara was increasingly preoccupied. Though thankfully, she had assumed the situation with Angus was at the root of her friend's troubles.

'You look lovely, by the way, Gracie.'

Gracie watched Dara as she sprayed herself liberally with Chanel Nº 5. She sat on the bed, slipping on the new shoes she'd got from Selfridges, and smiled. 'It should be fun tonight, we're going to go out with a couple of his friends – as well as his dad, I think – and we might even go on one of those river cruises for a laugh. And you were right, Dara, this is exactly what I needed. So thank you for pushing me out of the Jeremy zone.'

'I'm pleased – now go on, you'll be late.' Dara was almost shoving Gracie through the door.

'All right, I'm going. I'm going.' Gracie laughed and grabbed her handbag from the chair where she'd thrown it last night.

Dara frogmarched Gracie down to the club. She could relax a bit once she'd gone. Then she'd pick up Robbie and work on persuading him. She waved Gracie off before going into the office to grab her car keys. *Shit.* She'd forgotten. Devon's wallet. The cleaner had found it, and she was supposed to hand it to Gracie to give it back to him.

Grabbing the wallet off her desk, Dara ran after her friend, heading through the club and out on to the street. It was raining and the sky had darkened.

Dara looked around.

All of a sudden, she spotted Gracie about to get into a car on the corner of Brewer Street, with Devon at her side.

'Gracie! Gracie! *Wait up.* Gracie!'

Gracie turned around, and walked back towards Dara.

'Here, give this to Devon, it's his wallet.'

'Thanks, I will . . . Look, I better go, his dad's driving us to the restaurant, I don't want to piss him off. First impressions and all that . . .' She giggled.

'Well, have fun.'

Loyalty

Dara stood on the kerbside, watching the car speed past her, with Gracie and Devon in the back seat.

Dread seized Dara as she noticed who the driver was. Realisation hit her.

The pieces fell into place, and as they did, Dara began to vomit.

Chapter One Hundred and Twelve

'I don't fucking care if he's busy or not, I want to see him, *now*.'

Dara paced around the carpeted foyer of the offices on Temple Street. They were a stone's throw from the Thames, on the Embankment, and the rain was lashing against the glass.

'I've already told you, Ms . . .' The receptionist paused deliberately, so she could look Dara up and down in disapproval. 'I can't disturb him. If you haven't got an appointment with him, well, there's nothing I can do. I'm sorry.'

'No, you're *not* sorry, but believe me, darlin', you fucking will be.' Dara gritted her teeth. It was all she could do to stop herself from punching the woman in her smug face. She leant her weight on the reception desk and glared at her. 'Listen to me, you snotty-nosed cow, you can stick your fucking attitude up your arse, because I'm not going anywhere until you get him down here.'

The receptionist wasn't so smug now. She fiddled with the top button of her burgundy woollen two-piece suit. 'I really don't think that's possible.'

Dara was raging. 'Oh, I think it is, sweetheart, especially if you tell him it's about Holly Brookes, then you'll get him to listen. So pick up that phone, and tell him it's Gracie's friend from Holly Brookes, and I want to see him, NOW.'

A group of bureaucrats had been chatting quietly over in the corner of the foyer. They glanced across at Dara.

She saw them looking, and heard them tutting in judgement. 'Yeah, what? You got a fucking problem or something?' she growled at them.

As Dara turned to blast the receptionist again, the person she wanted to see walked around the corner. His faced blanched.

Dara pointed at him. 'Hello . . . Remember me? What's it been, twenty-odd years? You don't look any different. Still the cunt you always were . . . Now I think you and I need a little word, don't we, Mr Carver?'

Alan Carver stared, speechless. And he realised, in that moment, the nightmares of the past were returning to haunt the present.

An hour later, Dara rushed out of Alan's office and ran down the stairs into the foyer. She pushed past a crowd of people to get out. She needed some fresh air. Her chest was tight, and she was struggling to catch her breath.

She ran through the revolving glass door, bending forward and taking deep gulps of air.

'You went to Holly Brookes?'

A voice from behind Dara made her turn round. 'What the fuck is it to do with you?'

'I was wondering if I could have a word with you . . .'

Dara shook her head. She didn't have time for this. She couldn't even think straight. What she'd just heard had sent her world spinning.

Ignoring the woman, Dara began to walk away.

'Please *wait* . . . I'd really like to talk to you. You see, I went to Holly Brookes too. I know exactly what it was like . . . and what happened in that place . . . I'm Reenie, by the way, I work for Alan. I think you'll be interested in hearing what I have to say.'

Chapter One Hundred and Thirteen

'Hey, Dara, how come you're not open tonight?'

Gracie walked happily down the stairs of the club with Devon. They'd gone out for lunch, and had ended up whiling away the afternoon and evening together, enjoying each other's company until after dark.

She looked around and frowned. 'Has something happened?'

Dara shook her head, battling really hard to force her words out. 'No, no . . . er, the . . . the electricity kept cutting off. Er . . . the whole of the street was down.' It was a lie, but the only one Dara could think of. She was listless, and gave Gracie a nod for no particular reason, staring down at her hands.

'Dar, Dar, what's going on, babe?' Gracie rushed over to her. 'What's Archie done now . . . Dar, tell me, what's he done? I can't stand to see you like this . . . Dar, *please*.' Gracie looked down at Dara's arms and noticed blood seeping through the sleeves of her blouse. She quickly blocked Devon's view; she couldn't imagine Dara wanted him to see.

She dropped her voice to a whisper. 'Dar, why have you hurt yourself?'

Dara couldn't answer.

'Dara, you're frightening me. *Please*, tell me what's happened.'

Dara managed to slowly lift her eyes to meet Gracie's. 'I love you, Gracie. I always have.' Her voice was a hoarse whisper.

Gracie smiled, fighting back her own tears at seeing Dara in such distress, but she was also puzzled. She cupped Dara's face in hers. 'And I love you too.' She looked over her shoulder and smiled at Devon, before turning back to Dara. 'Look, I'm dying for a wee, I should've gone before we started walking back to the club. Will you be all right for a minute?'

Dara nodded. 'Of course. I'm tired, that's all.' Her eyes were full of tears.

'I'll be back in a sec.'

Gracie rushed out through the staff door.

The minute she'd gone, Dara sprang into action. She spun around to glare at Devon. 'I want you out of here,' she snarled at him. 'I want you fucking gone, and I don't want you coming back, do you understand me?'

'What?' The shock on Devon's face was obvious. 'What the fuck are you talking about?'

Dara ran over to him, pushing him back towards the entrance. 'You heard me.' She was screaming now, hitting his chest. 'GET OUT, GET OUT, *GET OUT!*'

'What the fuck is your problem, you crazy cow?' Devon's eyes darkened.

Dara heard the door opening. Gracie was coming back. 'Just do it, *please, just do it, Devon.*' It was a whispered cry. 'Just go.'

Devon didn't move.

Spotting Gracie out of the corner of her eye, Dara panicked. She jumped forward, and out of nowhere, started to kiss Devon passionately on the lips.

'Dar? Dar, what are you doing?' Gracie looked at her friend in disbelief.

At that moment, Robbie strolled in. He looked shocked, but not as shocked as Devon.

Dara glanced at Robbie. He shrugged at her, bemused.

She turned back to Gracie, scrambling for words. 'He's no good for you. I swear I was telling him to get out . . . but then *he* kissed me, and . . . and I kissed him back . . . but . . . but, I know I shouldn't have done it . . . but that just shows he's no good, doesn't it?' Dara was crying.

'She's lying, Gracie.' Devon grabbed Dara's wrist. 'I don't know what the fuck is wrong with you. Have you lost your fucking mind?' He said this to Dara, then turned to Gracie, who was visibly upset. 'I swear I didn't kiss her, Gracie. It's true, she was telling me to get out, but then all of a sudden, she kissed me. I'm telling you, *she* was the one who kissed *me*, Gracie.'

Dara shook her head. 'Gracie, come on, who are you going to believe? Me or him?' She was trembling.

Gracie thought about it. She nodded and threw a hard stare at Devon. 'Yeah, well, Dara's not going to lie to me, is she? So I think she's right. I think you *should* go.' She was bruised by what she'd seen. 'Anyway, let's face it, who am I kidding? You're too young for me . . . So go on, *go*.' Gracie folded her arms.

'Okay, okay, I'll go, if that's what you want, but I need you to know, I *didn't* kiss her. I wouldn't disrespect you like that.' He glared at Dara. 'You're fucking off your head, you know that? Why don't you tell her the truth?'

Dara wiped away her tears. '*I am* telling her the truth . . . and you know full well *you* kissed *me*—'

'What the fuck are you talking about?' No one had heard Archie come through into the club. He glared at Devon. 'You kissed my missus, after everything? You fucking kissed my missus, you cunt?'

Archie was drunk. Drunk and enraged. The worst combination, as Dara knew to her cost. He grabbed a bottle, smashed it on the side of the bar, and pointed the jagged edge at Devon, stepping towards him.

Dara ran over to Archie, desperate to stop him from attacking Devon. Somehow, she had to try to stop things spiralling out of control. 'Archie, *please*, it's not like you think.'

Archie pushed her away, sending her crashing into the bar.

She managed to keep her balance, and she rushed back towards him. 'Archie, Arch, look at me . . . I told you, it's not what you think.' Dara grabbed hold of his shirt, trying to restrain him. 'Devon, go! GO NOW.'

Archie walked menacingly towards Devon, dragging Dara with him. 'I'm going to kill you.' He fixed a look of hatred on Devon, then stared down at Dara with nothing but contempt.

'You have to listen. Archie, *please* . . . Robbie, do something,' Dara pleaded.

Robbie stood frozen by the bar.

A nasty smile appeared on Archie's face. 'He ain't going to do anything, are you, Rob . . . I've seen more backbone in a plate of fucking jelly . . . Now come here.' He gestured to Devon. His face was red and twisted in anger. 'I'm going to break your fucking neck, do you hear me?' Archie bellowed at the top of his voice.

Dara was desperate. She knew Archie was serious. 'Please, Arch, don't do anything stupid. *Stop*, just *stop it!*' She tried to block his way. 'Look, I swear, it's not what you think.'

Archie wasn't interested in anything Dara had to say. He lunged at Devon, who was strong, but was no match for Archie when he was bang on it. Archie dragged and twisted Devon around, and imprisoned him in a tight necklock.

'Let him go . . . For fuck's sake, let him go, Arch!' Dara pulled on Archie's arm.

'Do something, Dar!' Gracie screamed across the club at her.

Devon's face began to turn a bright red as he struggled for air.

'Archie, please, I had to get Devon out of here, that's all. I swear that's all it was. Nothing more.' Dara was hysterical. She pulled again at Archie's arm, but it was impossible to release his grip on Devon. 'Robbie, help me!'

'What the fuck are you going on about?' Archie snarled at her while he continued to squeeze Devon's neck.

'Tell him! Dara, enough now, just tell him!' Robbie was watching Devon's eyes becoming bloodshot. 'He's killing him, Dar! For fuck's sake, tell him, otherwise I will—'

'Robbie, *no*. No! I'm begging you!' Dara screamed at Robbie while Gracie watched on helplessly.

Robbie ignored Dara and aimed his next words at Archie.

'She needed to get him out of here because—'

'Okay, okay, *okay!*' Dara interrupted, screaming into Robbie's face. 'Because Devon's—'

At that moment, footsteps were heard coming down the main stairs into the club.

Archie dropped Devon, who fell to the floor, coughing and spluttering, holding his throat.

'Because Devon is . . .' Dara couldn't finish the sentence.

'Devon is what?' Jake Wakeman, the owner of the club – the same guy Dara had seen at the hospital, and later driving Gracie and Devon off in his car – stood angrily staring at them all. 'Come on, because Devon is . . . what?'

'Because Devon is not your son.' Dara spoke these words in

a whisper, finally giving voice to the terrible secret she'd been bur-
dened with for all these years.

'*What?*'

'He ain't your son.' Dara turned round. 'He's yours, Gracie . . .
Devon is *your* son.'

Chapter One Hundred and Fourteen

'What the fuck is she talking about? Can someone tell me what she's on about? Because I fucking don't know. I came to hurry Devon up, and I walk into this . . . Gracie, help me out here, do you know?' Jake Wakeman looked at Gracie.

Gracie barely glanced at Devon's dad – or the man who, until a few minutes ago, she'd thought was Devon's dad. 'I . . . I have no idea what she's talking about.'

'You better stop talking shit and start explaining yourself, darlin'', Jake snapped at Dara.

'Dar, what you're saying is impossible. Look at him.' Gracie's hand shook as she pointed at Devon.

'How old are you, Devon?' Dara whispered. 'Tell Gracie how old you are.'

Devon looked between them. He was only just recovering from Archie's attack. He managed to croak the words: 'Twenty-two.'

Devon certainly didn't look his age. He looked easily ten years older; the beard gave him a rugged look of maturity.

'Gracie.' Dara's eyes filled with tears. 'It's true.'

Jake stepped forward, grabbing Dara, and shaking her. 'You are fucking insane. I want you to pack your things and get out of my club.'

Dara pushed Jake off her, and stepped nearer to Gracie.

'Gracie, I am so sorry.'

Gracie stepped away, shaking her head. She held on to the pillar in the middle of the club for support. 'My son is *dead*. He's dead.' Tears began to roll down Gracie's face while her whole body started to visibly tremble.

'No, Gracie, he's not.' Dara turned her head to the side. 'This is your son, right here.'

'No, no, no, no, no, *no!*' Gracie held her hands over her ears. 'My son's dead . . . YOU told me my son was dead. *YOU* took him away, you held him in your arms, and you told me he was dead, and I never even got to hold him . . .' Gracie covered her mouth.

'That's what I'm trying to tell you.' Dara's voice was so quiet. Shame and guilt were consuming her. She pointed to Jake. 'I gave your baby to his twin brother. I thought Alan was going to take him and look after him. That's why I had to go and talk to Alan when I saw Jake with Devon. I got mixed up and I thought he was Jason . . . but Alan explained it all to me.'

'Alan?' Jake stared at Dara. This was starting to sound serious.

'I was trying to keep him safe, Gracie. I swear I was only trying to keep your baby safe. I know it's a mess, but . . .' Dara didn't know what else to say. 'I . . . I didn't want it to come out, not like this . . . but how was I supposed to know that Jake was going to show up?'

'Oh, I'll make you so fucking sorry I turned up, darlin',' Jake snarled.

He strode across to Devon and helped him up from the floor. With his arm around *his son*, he stared defiantly at Dara. What he was hearing couldn't possibly be true.

Archie was watching Dara, ready to silence her with his fists if necessary, while Robbie stood rooted to the spot.

But Gracie was hardly listening to what Dara was saying. She bent over, wrapping her arms around her stomach. She wailed a painful cry, from deep inside her.

'Gracie.' Dara went to try to comfort her.

'Don't touch me . . . Don't you fucking touch me.'

'I didn't know what to do Gracie. *Please.*' Dara fell to her knees. 'Gracie, please, please, please forgive me. I was scared. I was scared for us all, but mostly I was scared for your baby. I didn't know what else to do. What else could I have done?'

'NOT THAT.' Gracie stood up straight and wiped away her tears. Her eyes flashed. 'Anything but that.'

'Please, Gracie, don't you see, I couldn't let them do to him what they did to Robbie. You know what they did. You saw it. We all did. Barrows, Clemence, Dennis, all of them. There was no escape. I thought it was the best thing to do . . . to pretend he was dead. I wanted you to have the least amount of pain . . . Gracie, I'm so sorry.' Dara got up off her knees, and tried to reach out to Gracie again.

'I've told you, get away from me.' Gracie backed away, pointing at Dara. 'I grieved for him . . . I've grieved my entire life for him, but the whole time he was alive . . . How long have you known?'

Dara took a deep breath, trying to steady herself. 'When I first saw Jake and a woman at the hospital, it triggered some memories I couldn't place. Then I saw him again, and something didn't feel right. And then he came into the club – I didn't know he owned this place, but it was the way he looked at me. He looks so like his brother. That's when everything I've tried not to think about for so many years started to come back to me. And then . . .'

Dara paused, summoning the strength to continue. 'I saw him

driving the car with you and Devon in it, that's when it all connected.' She turned and looked at Jake. 'Your eyes. It was your eyes. That night, in the snow, when your brother took Devon away, the way he looked at me, as if I was nothing. I'll never forget that.'

Gracie suddenly looked at Robbie. 'Did you know this part of it? DID YOU? Did you know she'd given away my baby?'

Robbie went to answer.

'No, he didn't.' Dara shook her head. 'It was all me, Gracie, all me.' Even under extreme pressure, Dara continued to be loyal to Robbie.

'But he let it happen . . . didn't you?' Gracie pointed accusingly at Robbie.

'What?' Dara didn't know what Gracie was talking about.

'That night, he saw what was going to happen, but he ran away and hid, didn't you, Robbie?'

'He was a kid, Gracie, a frightened kid.'

'*I was* a kid, we were all kids, and I was frightened too . . . but of course, when it comes to your precious Robbie . . .' Gracie sounded hurt and bitter. 'He can't do any fucking wrong, can he?'

'Gracie, please, it's not his fault.'

Gracie was trembling, in shock. Her face was soaked with tears. 'You know, all this time, I blamed myself, Dara. I thought he'd died because of what I'd done. I thought *I'd* killed him. Do you know how that feels? Do you know what it feels like to blame yourself for something like that? But all along, I should have been blaming *you* for taking my baby away.'

'I only did it because I loved you so much. I loved both of you, always . . . I would have put my life on the line for you, and I *did*, I did, Gracie, so many times, I did. And I was trying to save your baby from Holly Brookes, not take him away . . . Gracie, please forgive me'

Gracie walked up to Dara. She nodded her head, and stared at her. 'You are dead to me, like my son, *MY SON*, was dead to me.' And with those words, Gracie ran out of the club.

Chapter One Hundred and Fifteen

'Gracie . . . Gracie, *wait!*' Dara screamed after her friend.

But she knew it was no good. The way Gracie had looked at her, with nothing but hurt and hatred in her eyes, told Dara everything she needed to know. Gracie wasn't coming back.

Robbie, Jake and Devon had gone after her, leaving Dara staring at Archie. 'You did this . . . This is all your fault.'

Archie burst into drunken, bitter laughter. 'Me? No, darlin', this is *your* fault. Like Gracie said, you're the one to blame, you're the scheming cow.' He poked her hard in the side of her head as she silently wept. 'You stupid bitch. Don't you see what you've done? You've lost us this club. After what's gone down tonight with Jake Wakeman, there's no fucking chance I can talk him round.'

Dara batted his hand away. 'Is that all you care about?'

'What else should I be fucking caring about?'

'*My friend!*' Dara screamed in his face, deep sorrow pouring out of her. 'Not this fucking club.'

Archie was incensed. 'You really are a stupid cunt.' He flew at Dara with his fists flying. He kicked her until she was on the floor, then pulled her up like a rag doll. He grabbed her by her hair, dragging her along, and smashed her head against the edge of the bar with all his strength.

Dara's knees gave way as the room began to spin. She lurched backwards, the pain rushing through her face like it was on fire. She fell to the floor again, and tried desperately to crawl away, but Archie slammed his foot down on her spine. She collapsed in an agonising sprawl and lay prone as Archie brought his foot back again and booted her in her face.

Dara's mouth was filling with blood, and she tried again to crawl away, but it was useless. Archie followed right behind her, laughing. 'You pathetic bitch.' He jumped up on the spot, this time bringing both feet down on her back.

Dara screamed. Archie's eyes were wild; he was a man possessed, battering her senseless, one kick after another.

She managed to roll over on her side, in an attempt to guard her stomach. It was only when she blacked out that Dara Tailor stopped trying to protect the baby she so desperately wanted.

For a moment Dara didn't know where she was.

She attempted to open her eyes. The pain was excruciating, and she could hardly see. Her mouth was torn, and her tongue was bruised and swollen.

She staggered up, using a chair to help her.

She froze as she caught a glimpse of herself in one of the mirrored pillars of the club. She didn't recognise her own face, it was red and purple with bruises, her eyes almost closed, like a boxer's after a brutal fight.

Dara's injuries made her look grotesque, beyond recognition. She winced as she tried to breathe. No doubt her ribs were broken.

And then Dara felt something else. She looked down.

Panic gripped her.

There was fresh red blood trickling down the inside of her legs.

Chapter One Hundred and Sixteen

'Help me . . . *help me* . . . please, somebody help me.'

Dara staggered into A&E. The sight of this battered and blood-ied creature had the nurses staring at Dara in horror.

'Please help me . . . *please.*' Dara held on to her stomach, the pain ripping through her as her body tried to expel the baby grow-ing inside.

'Please, someone . . .'

She was bleeding heavily now – her legs, and even her shoes, were covered in blood. Crying, Dara held on to the wall for sup-port. Terror overwhelmed her.

'Please help me, I'm begging you . . . I'm losing my baby . . .'

Chapter One Hundred and Seventeen

'When were you going to tell me, hey? How many more years were you going to fucking wait?'

Jake kicked open the kitchen door of his sprawling manor house in the Oxfordshire countryside.

Samantha had been making herself a nightcap. She stared at her husband, puzzled by his outburst. Jake's face was red, his expression strained, although his features were as smooth and handsome as ever. The love she'd always felt for him was constant.

'What's the matter with you?' Sam frowned. 'Tell me this isn't about the car. Okay, I admit, I banged into a bollard in town, but I spoke to—'

'This isn't about a FUCKING bollard, you stupid cow!' Jake yelled, interrupting Samantha.

'Jake, what's going on, babe?' Samantha was nonplussed. He rarely raised his voice to her, let alone swore.

Jake ran his hand over his face. Then, without warning, he took a swipe at the pile of clean plates Samantha had taken out of the dishwasher. They smashed to the floor, scattering pieces of porcelain everywhere. 'I should be asking you that question.' He was breathing heavily now.

Samantha glanced at Devon. He'd just walked into the kitchen behind Jake.

'Devon? What's happened?'

Devon shook his head and didn't answer. It crossed Samantha's mind that he looked ill.

'Can someone tell me what's happening, *please*?' She asked again.

Jake started to pace. He pointed at her and went to say something, but seemed unable to find the right words. He lit a cigarette, drawing the smoke deep into his lungs, and eventually he managed to say, 'Who the fuck are you, Sam?'

'What?' Samantha was bemused. 'Devon, what's wrong with your dad?'

'I ASKED YOU A QUESTION, not him.' Jake was almost blinded by rage.

Samantha reacted. 'If I knew what you were talking about, I'd be able to answer you, wouldn't I? If this made any sort of sense—'

'Made sense? Oh that's rich, coming from you, darlin', because all of a sudden my life doesn't make *any* fucking sense at all . . . I don't even know who you are any more. I mean, who have I been sleeping with for the past twenty-odd years?'

'What the hell are you talking about?'

Jake rushed over to her with his fists clenched, and punched one of the kitchen cabinets behind her.

Samantha was frightened. Jake was behaving like a madman, but right now, he looked to be in too much pain to care.

'I'm talking about Devon.' He leant forward to whisper in Samantha's ear. 'He ain't my son, is he? He ain't even yours, Sam.' It was husky whisper.

Samantha began to tremble, and she backed away. She reached for the bottle of wine next to her, but Jake grabbed it out of her hand, throwing it across the kitchen. Red wine dripped down the walls.

'Oh no you fucking don't, you ain't going to booze yourself out of this one. You're going to tell me exactly what the *fuck* you thought you were doing. Stealing babies from a young kid, are you out of your mind? You and my brother. Is that why you mowed him down, Sam? Were you worried he was going to spill your dirty little secret?'

Samantha covered her mouth, rocking back and forth on the spot. She turned to Devon.

He shook his head and turned away from her.

'And you can stop those fucking crocodile tears, darlin', cos that ain't going to wash with me!' Jake snapped at her.

'Why couldn't you leave things in the past?' Samantha was distraught now.

Jake burst into bitter laughter. 'Are you having a bubble? None of this is my doing . . . How the hell did I know there was a Pandora's fucking box waiting for me to open?' He was furious, but he was also hurt, bellowing at Sam like a wounded animal. 'And anyway, Sam, everything *was* left in the past. I let people manage my club, manage my businesses, and I was fine about that, because I thought we had a happy-ever-after, but all we had was a fucking jackanory . . . You've been lying to my face for years.'

'It wasn't like that.'

Jake slammed his fist on the counter. 'THEN TELL ME HOW IT WAS.'

'I'm sorry.'

'Sorry?' Jake spat out the word. 'You're sorry. Is that all you can say? I trusted you, Sam.'

A spark of anger rushed through Samantha and ignited something inside her. She pushed him, hard. 'Don't you dare, don't you dare talk to me about trust, because *I* trusted *you*. I trusted you and you left me, you fucking left me for your brother to do what

543

he liked with. Look at my face, Jake, look at it. That scar, however faded, is a constant reminder of me trusting *you*, because that's what happened when I did. You left me to drown . . . so don't you dare come in here and take the moral high ground.'

He stared at her damaged face, and Jake knew what she was saying was the truth.

'All right . . . all right. I'll own that, I know I let you down, but that still gave you *no* right to do what you did. You took some young kid's baby. What the fuck?' He tapped the side of his head, not understanding.

'No, no I didn't, not like that . . . I took the baby *Jason* brought to me. The baby I was *supposed* to hand over to Alan. And then Alan was going to take him to some friend of Dennis Hargreaves.'

Jake looked blank.

'Dennis was, and for all I know, he still *is*, head of one of the biggest paedophile rings in the country. Alan was going to give Devon to him. Think about that . . . I couldn't let that happen, not to him.' She took a deep breath. 'It was going on right under my nose, Jake, and I couldn't stop it. I tried. I really, *really* fucking tried. But I had no one to turn to, because the people I *should* have been able to trust, like my boss, the people in the council, people in the police force, people in government, so many of them were involved in it, Jake.' She turned and gave Devon a small smile, then looked back at her husband. 'What was I supposed to do? I had this little baby in my care, a few hours old, and I had a choice: do I let them have him, or do I do *everything* in my power to save him?'

'You could have told me, Sam, you didn't have to lie to me.'

'I *did* have to lie. I DID. And you know why. Because like I told you, I didn't trust you, and trust is everything, Jake. You'd already disappeared on me *twice*, and I couldn't risk it. I couldn't risk it for

Devon. I needed you to help, no matter what. I needed you to make sure he was safe. And yes, yes, I lied to you, because I stayed silent when you presumed he was yours. Your fucking macho ego presumed you had a son.'

'That ain't fair.'

'None of it's fair, Jake. Not for Devon, not for those kids in Holly Brookes, not for every single person who gets turned away when they cry out for help and there's no one there to listen . . . So yeah, I let you believe what you wanted to believe. And you know what? If I had to do it again, I'd make the same choice.' Samantha stood defiantly, with her head held up high.

Jake stared at her, then turned and walked away without saying anything.

'You aren't going, are you?' Devon's voice stopped Jake at the door.

Jake looked over at Devon and saw the unease and pain on his face.

He strode towards him, and putting his hand under Devon's chin, he smiled sadly. 'You will *always* be my son, Devon. You hear me. That will *never* change. I love you, and I will *never* stop loving you. I will never stop being your father, you understand me? But right now, son, I need to get my head around it all, and then I'll be back, and when I am, you and I will pick up from where we left off, all right?'

Jake pulled Devon into him, holding him tighter than he'd done for a very long time. He kissed him on his head, the way he'd done when Devon was a baby, and marched out, slamming the front door behind him.

Chapter One Hundred and Eighteen

'Where the fuck are you?'

Jake strode into the offices opposite the Embankment. It was early in the working day, and he'd spent the previous night in his car going over everything in his mind. Samantha had called him several times, but he hadn't answered. He couldn't yet bring himself to speak to her.

He'd pick up the phone to her soon. He loved her – that hadn't changed, nor would it – but he wasn't quite ready. He was angry. Not with her – not now he knew the circumstances – but with himself.

He couldn't speak to Samantha right now. It wasn't what she'd *done*, it was what she'd *said* that hurt so much. Because she was right. He'd failed her completely, and he was bloody ashamed of it. His trust, his loyalty had been completely inadequate, yet his ego had been out of control, like his drinking. He only hoped that one day Samantha could forgive him.

Devon had called him last night. Jake had texted to say he loved him, and he was proud to call him *his son*.

'Where are you? Where the fuck are you?' Jake bellowed, walking past the mostly empty offices.

He opened the doors along the carpeted hallway, booting them open and sticking his head into each one in turn. At the door before last, on the fourth floor, Jake walked into a suite with a small reception area.

He glared at the woman sitting at her desk. 'Where is he? Come on, darlin', make it snappy, where the fuck is he?'

Reenie was shocked. 'I'm sorry . . . I don't know who you're talking about? And you shouldn't be in here. I'll have to call security . . .'

Jake sneered. 'I'm looking for Alan. Where the fuck is he? And as for your security, maybe if they weren't so busy having a fag around the side, they'd know who was in the building . . . Now are you going to tell me where he is or not? You know what, don't bother . . . I'll find him myself.'

Jake looked at the door behind her and walked in without knocking.

Alan's face dropped.

'Hello, Al, long time no see, mate.'

'Jake, what . . . what—'

'Let me finish that sentence for you, shall I . . . What am I doing here?'

Alan nodded.

'Well, let's just say, it's not to have tea and cake and bit of polite fucking chit-chat. You and me are going to talk about how you took a baby from a kid, and wanted to give him to some nonce . . . And believe you me, Al, you're going to tell me everything you know.'

Jake put his hand in his pocket and pulled out a metal knuckleduster. 'I ain't used this beauty for some years, but hey, now is the perfect time to see if I've still got what it takes.' Jake blew on it, smiled, and kicked the door shut behind him.

Even from where she was sitting, Reenie heard the first thud of the knuckleduster connecting with Alan's face. She looked at the phone. She should really call the police. But she smiled to herself: what she *should* do, and what she was *going to* do, were two very different things.

She stood up from her desk, got her coat and bag from the hook, and like Jake had just done, she quietly closed the door behind her.

She hummed to herself as she walked down the stairs and out into the fresh air. She decided that occasionally in life, there was no need for *direct* revenge.

Sometimes it was a matter of just sitting back and waiting.

Chapter One Hundred and Nineteen

It was early evening when Dara walked out of the hospital. Her clothes were covered in blood still, as were her shoes, but she didn't care that she looked as if she'd been in a car crash.

Her face was completely swollen and coloured with dark purple-and-black bruises. Her eyes were almost closed from the swelling. She ignored the shocked stares from passers-by as she walked into the mini-mart halfway down Tottenham Court Road.

Dara went straight to the counter, and pointed. 'I'll have a bottle of that vodka, please.'

'No problem.' The shop assistant grabbed the bottle from the shelf behind him and placed it down on the counter. 'That looks nasty . . . been in the wars?'

'Fuck off.' And with that, Dara slammed twenty quid on the counter, and walked off without waiting for her change.

Dara was only dimly aware of the fact that it was raining as she staggered, drunk, along the street and headed back to the club. She banged into people as she walked, taking large swigs of vodka from the bottle.

She rested against the wall, swaying on her feet as she struggled to drag her phone out of her jacket pocket. Pulling it out, and still clinging on to the bottle of booze she'd tucked under her arm, Dara drunkenly pressed dial.

She heard it ring. Then a beep, and she muttered her message incoherently.

'Gracie . . . Gracie, it's me . . . I'm sorry, Gracie . . . Gracie, are you there? It's Dar . . .'

She let the phone slip out of her hand, then she staggered forward to pick it up, taking another gulp of the vodka, before setting off again towards home.

Not knowing quite how she got there, Dara stumbled down the stairs of the club. The place was still empty – just the cleaning staff finishing up, and a few of the girls getting ready for their shift. 'Get out . . . Get out of my fucking club.' She screamed at them all, waving the bottle in the air.

'Dara, are you all right?' Sharon rushed over to her. 'Dara, do you want to sit down?'

'Why the fuck would I want to sit down? Where's Robbie?'

'I dunno, he and Archie had a row, and I haven't seen him since . . . Dara, please come and sit down.'

'I said, *I don't want to* . . . Now get out. *NOW* . . . And Sharon . . .' Dara called after her. 'Put the fucking *closed* sign on the door on the way out.'

'All right, okay.' Sharon was clearly flustered.

Rumours had been flying around the club, and everyone knew Archie was handy with his fists, to say the least. But Dara looked like she'd barely survived this latest beating. Sharon wondered if she should pass on the message, but decided it was better if Dara knew. Not that she was in a fit state to do anything about it.

'Dara, Angus came in when you were out . . . he was steaming, he was looking for Archie again. Arch wasn't here, but I don't know what Angus would've done if he'd got his hands on him . . . He says he's going to come back later. Archie's upstairs now, but he better be gone by the time Angus . . .' She trailed off, unsure if Dara was taking any of it in.

Dara gave a drunken shrug. She leant forward, slurring her words and spitting out a thin string of saliva. 'I don't care, I hope Angus gets him, in fact no, I hope he doesn't, because I want to be the one who kills him. I am going to kill that fucker . . . Now fuck off.'

Hearing Sharon leave, Dara stumbled to the bar. She rummaged in the ice box, pulling out the handgun they kept discreetly hidden in there. She stared at it, trying hard to keep her focus. Then she grabbed a bottle of whiskey, and sat at one of the tables in the empty club. She unscrewed the cap, and like the vodka, began to drink it out of the bottle.

What difference did it make what she drank?

Now she was no longer pregnant.

Chapter One Hundred and Twenty

Dara attempted to open her eyes

By God, it hurt. She rolled her tongue around her mouth, trying to conjure up enough saliva to ease the sticky dryness.

Her head pounded, and her sinuses throbbed; even taking a breath was painful. Dara couldn't recall how much she'd drunk, but judging by how she was feeling, it was one hell of a lot.

Her thoughts were hazy, her mind numb, but then Dara remembered the reason she'd got pissed in the first place. Tears sprang up, and she felt a physical ache in her body. She touched her empty belly. This was her punishment for what she'd done to Gracie.

Maybe it was for the best that this had happened to her. She would never have been a good mother, would she? But God, how she'd wanted to be. She would've loved her baby. But that was the point: her love wasn't, and never had been, good enough.

Dara took a deep breath, wincing as it hurt her head. She realised she'd vomited, and she wiped it off her chin. She tried to move, and she struggled to push herself up slightly.

She must have collapsed on the floor last night, between the door and her bed, which was where she was lying now.

Dara felt a sudden wetness on her arm. She inched over enough to see that Archie was next to her. 'Archie? Archie . . . Arch . . .' She trailed off; talking made her head hurt.

Carefully, she shuffled forward on her bum, leaning over Archie. She frowned. His face was mottled, a strange colour, and then Dara saw it.

'Oh my God . . . *oh my God!*'

She scrambled back, pressing herself against the wall. The side of Archie's skull had collapsed. Fallen away. Leaving a huge gaping hole the size of her fist. It oozed fluid, and blood, and as she moved her leg away, part of Archie's brain fell out and on to the floor.

Her panicked stare landed on her gun lying next to him.

What had she done? What the *fuck* had she done?

She gave a long-drawn-out cry. Her screams shattered the silence of the club.

'Archie . . . *NOOOOOOOOO.*'

The next moment, the door was flung open.

Chapter One Hundred and Twenty-One

'We'll go through this again, Dara, shall we?'

The detective stared at Dara across the table in the tiny interview room of Charing Cross Police Station. The room hadn't been painted for many a year, and the magnolia walls were stained with cigarette smoke and etched with graffiti. The room stank, mainly of sweat, but there was also a faint smell of urine.

It felt to Dara like they'd been at it for hours. She'd been hauled in a couple of days ago, thanks to one of her staff calling the Old Bill, and the rest had been a whirlwind. They'd bagged her clothes, taken swabs and thrown her into a cell with some pissed-up old hag who'd shat in the corner before making a dirty protest. Even now, Dara could swear the smell still lingered in her nostrils.

'No matter how many times you ask me, I'll tell you the same thing. I *didn't* do it, all right.' She stared with hostility at the round-faced detective.

The man was overweight, and clearly not partial to any exercise. His brown suit was cheap, and it seemed like he was wearing yesterday's shirt; it was creased and the collar was too large, ringed with grey sweat marks.

'You're really trying to make us believe, Dara, that you had nothing to do with Archie being shot? Yet you were found in possession of a gun, next to the victim, covered in his blood.'

Even to Dara it sounded bad. And the truth was, she had no recollection of the night. None. Well, not exactly. Because the one thing she *did* remember was getting the gun from the ice box. Oh God, that part of the night she could remember clearly. It was going around on a loop in her head.

Dara wasn't stupid. She wasn't about to mention retrieving the gun. She hadn't even told her solicitor, Mr Marshall. He seemed decent enough, but she didn't entirely trust him. Mr Marshall was a posh brief from a firm in Kensington. He was tall, on the bony side of slim, with a sharp, angular face, and a thick barnet of wispy white hair. When he'd shown up, taking over from the duty solicitor assigned to Dara, she'd been excited. She'd thought Gracie must have sent him, which meant Gracie didn't hate her.

But it turned out Jake Wakeman had sent him and was covering the cost. Marshall and Goodwin were Jake's solicitors, and had been for many years. Jake had sent the senior partner along, and Dara was duly grateful.

'My client has already told you the reason for that, Detective. She'd been asleep next to him all night.'

'Do you often make it a habit, Dara, of sleeping on the floor next to the man whose brains you've blown out?'

Mr Marshall scribbled on his notepad, then raised his eyes to regard the detective again. 'To repeat myself, my client is denying having *anything* to do with the murder.'

The detective threw a Polo into his mouth, missed, and let it fall on to the floor. 'A lot of people say they saw you drunk, Dara, the previous night.'

'That ain't a crime, is it?'

'Not unless it leads to murder.'

Dara sighed. 'I didn't touch Archie.' She tried to sound confident, but even she was starting to doubt herself.

The detective leant back in his chair and smiled as it let out a loud creak. He stared at her, taking a moment before speaking. 'I wouldn't blame you if you did, Dara. What Archie did to you is criminal. Your injuries, they're shocking. A lot of people would want revenge.'

'He didn't do this.'

The detective laughed. 'We have witnesses to say that your husband often beat you, we *also* have witnesses to say that you were threatening to kill him.'

'No comment.' Dara spoke firmly.

'And what about enemies? Did Archie have many?'

Dara steadily held the detective's gaze. There was a list the length of Oxford Street. Archie had pissed a lot people off, not to mention cheated them and treated them like shit.

'No comment.'

'Tell me about this Angus geezer.'

Dara chewed the inside of her cheek. As much as she would've liked to give him up, there was no way she was about to start grassing on Mad Angus. No way at all. Angus had been hungry for Archie's blood, hadn't he? But then, she'd been drunk, hadn't she? Drunk, and angry, and hurt. She knew what she was like when she was pissed. She and booze had a bad relationship. Over the years, there'd been so many times – too many times – when she'd woken up after a heavy session, with no memory at all of what she'd done the night before, piecing things together from the evidence in front of her. Why was this time any different?

The stakes were the highest they'd ever been. This wasn't some mouthy mare she'd had a fight with, and couldn't remember, or some flash cunt's car tyres she'd slashed with a knife, and had no recollection of doing. This was her husband, Archie, who'd had half his head blown away. And much as she might deny it to the Old Bill, there was a strong possibility she'd killed him.

'You look like you know the name, Dara.' The detective tilted his head to one side. 'What do you know about Angus?'

'No comment.'

'And the gun, Dara, it had a number of fingerprints on it we can't match, it's as if it's been used in a game of pass the parcel.' He smirked at her. 'But it did have your prints on it. You do know having an unlicensed firearm is illegal.'

'No comment.'

'We'll be checking your clothes for gun residue, Dara, are you aware of that?'

Mr Marshall gave the detective a long, withering look. 'You and I both know, Detective, when a weapon is discharged, gunshot residue is created within the environment and easily transfers to other people. As the victim was shot at point-blank range, no doubt he will have residue on his clothes, which could certainly have found itself on to Ms Tailor's clothing when she was lying against him during the night. So that's no conclusive proof of what did or didn't happen . . . I rather think, if there's no other evidence, bail should be granted.'

It was the detective's turn to give Mr Marshall a withering look. 'This is a murder investigation, she's the prime suspect, and she doesn't stand a chance in hell of getting bail.'

An hour later, Dara stood in the corridor of Charing Cross Police Station making a phone call. With her back turned to the duty officer, Dara cupped the phone in her hand, listening to it ring.

Finally, it was answered.

'*Hello?*'

'Reenie? Reenie, it's me . . . Dara. I need your help . . .'

Chapter One Hundred and Twenty-Two

Reenie had her best coat on.

She'd changed several times that morning, but she hadn't known quite what to wear. She'd put it down to nerves. In the end, she'd chosen the purple outfit she'd worn to Ascot last year.

And now here she was, sitting in the overheated office, and feeling a tad overdressed for the occasion. Although, Reenie did wonder what the dress code was for meeting a piece of scum from the past.

'I'm glad you decided to meet me, Inspector. I think you'll agree, it is in your best interest—'

'*Chief* Inspector.' Lewis stared at Reenie with sheer loathing.

He sat across from her, behind his imposing desk, a gift from Dennis, to mark over thirty years in the force. He'd spoken to Reenie a number of times over the years, when he'd called or visited Alan. The unfortunate man was now in a coma in intensive care after single-handedly tackling an intruder in his office. But he'd *never* expected that the day would come when he was being held to ransom by a two-bit secretary.

He pointed at her, looking at Reenie over the top of his gold-rimmed glasses. Age caught up with everyone.

'Let me get this fucking straight, you think you can waltz into Scotland Yard dressed like a Quality Street, and coerce *me* into agreeing to this absurd proposal? Do you realise what can happen when you try to bribe an officer of the law?'

Reenie sat up straight in her chair. She crossed her ankles neatly, placed her hands in her lap, and carried herself with a confidence that didn't come naturally to her.

'I am sure, Inspector, that in your time, not only have you *taken* bribes, but you've also been the *instigator* of them . . . and far worse besides. Now the choice is entirely yours, of course, but I know that you're not a stupid man. And you'd be risking a lot if you refused to entertain my suggestion.'

Lewis was seething. He spun round in his leather chair, and stood up abruptly. He walked across to the bureau, to pour himself a large glass of brandy.

'What you're asking is impossible. Maybe a few years ago . . . but there's simply no way I can bury a murder case.'

'Inspector, I haven't asked you to do that. I've asked you to *assist* with granting bail.'

He knocked back the brandy. 'You're playing with fire, you know that?'

Reenie shrugged. 'Maybe I am. But I assure you, Inspector, nothing can ever scar me as badly as I've already been burnt in my life.'

He looked at her quizzically, but didn't ask anything further.

Reenie got up. She'd already been speaking to him for a good half an hour. But it seemed like they were going around in circles.

'Inspector, you're wasting my time. But let me tell *you* something . . . if Dara doesn't get bail by this evening, I will make sure every newspaper, every television channel, every news network, receives all the evidence I have about you and Hargreaves, which I have been sitting on for years . . . Times are changing, Inspector, and the people who used to protect you are no longer there. I will make sure I destroy you, like Hargreaves destroyed a part of me. I have waited for decades to make sure the evidence I've got on you isn't buried, like it so often was, in the past. Your time is coming to an end, mark my words.'

Reenie walked out of Lewis's office and marched along the corridor. She got into the lift, and pressed the button for the ground floor.

It was only once she'd emerged on to the busy pavement that she allowed herself to start shaking.

Chapter One Hundred and Twenty-Three

It was seven o'clock in the evening when Dara walked out of the police station into the visitors' car park.

Jake was standing by his Range Rover, waiting for her.

Dara wished Gracie was there, though she knew that would have been asking a lot. 'Thanks for picking me up, I appreciate it, Jake . . . I appreciate everything you've done. And I'm grateful for you checking on Robbie as well. He's all right, isn't he?'

Jake nodded. Dara treated Robbie like a kid, even though he was a grown man: a drug addict who probably cared more about drugs than about Dara.

'Oh, and thanks for the clothes, by the way.' Dara was grateful that Jake had dropped off some fresh clothing, no doubt organised by Sam, once they knew Dara was being bailed.

'How long did they give you?' Jake asked.

'Forty-eight hours, then I have to report back, sign in. It's better than nothing, ain't it? Reenie played a blinder . . .'

He nodded again and opened the car door for her. Dara noticed his knuckles were bruised, but she said nothing.

He sauntered around to the driver's side, and jumped in.

'Have you heard from Gracie?' Dara was worried about her. Even if Gracie wouldn't speak to her, she needed to know she was all right.

Jake settled himself behind the wheel and put the car into drive. 'Nothing.' He shook his head. 'We've left a few messages though.'

'*We?*'

'Well, I did, you know, to check in on her . . . and Devon did too.' He looked at Dara. 'But it's a lot for him to get his head around. I'm just glad she didn't do a full Mrs Robinson on him.' He whistled. 'Can you imagine? And then my missus did as well,' he continued. 'She contacted her.'

'Your missus?'

'Yeah, she's a good woman, she wanted to have a chat. I dunno, it's difficult, ain't it?'

'Was she the woman you were with at the hospital?'

'Yeah.' Jake did a left turn.

'I'm sure I've seen her somewhere before, you know.'

He gave Dara a quick sideways glance. Archie had done a proper number on her face, and although Jake didn't say it, he was pleased the bloke was on a slab with a tag around his toe. Scum like Archie, like Jason, deserved what they got. 'Maybe you have, she used to work in children's social services, a long time ago.'

'Yeah, perhaps that's it.'

They drove in silence for a while, passing Canary Wharf, and the old Dagenham depots, speeding towards the open roads beyond.

'What about you, are you all right, girl?' Jake eventually asked. 'None of this can be easy.'

'I don't know how I feel . . . a bit numb, I think . . . and I'm not saying I'm pleased it all kicked off. But the stuff with Gracie, well, I've kept that secret for so long, it was eating away at me, affecting everything I did. So in a way, I'm glad it's out now . . . Secrets are like a cancer growing deep inside you, aren't they?'

Jake thought about his own brother, Jason . . . about how he himself had harboured a secret. He'd been seeing Samantha behind his brother's back, and for all Jason's sins, keeping that from him had still eaten away at Jake.

Jake lit a cigarette and opened the window. 'Can I ask you a question? And I'm not judging, but did you do it? Did you blow your old man's brains out? I mean, if you did put a bullet in his head, I for one, girl, would be clapping you all the way to the funeral parlour.'

Dara took a deep breath. 'Honestly? I don't know. All the evidence says I did . . . *Fuck.*' Dara covered her face, the reality of everything hitting her. 'I'm hoping, by some small miracle, that something turns up to prove to me – and to the Old Bill of course – that I didn't do it . . . But I know what I'm like on the booze, and that's the thing that keeps playing out in my head. Why wouldn't it be me? I hated Archie. So maybe I should throw the towel in, and accept I killed him.'

Panic began to rise in her. Her heart raced. It made her feel sick. But then she looked at Jake's knuckles again. Fresh bruises.

'What about you?'

'Me?' He laughed hard. 'You think I did it? Sweetheart, you're clutching at straws.'

'That's not an answer.'

Jake stayed silent, taking a drag on his cigarette.

'He stabbed your son. He threatened to kill him, he nearly broke his neck.' Dara shrugged. She didn't know a lot about Jake, but she guessed he would find it easy to put a gun against Archie's head.

'No, I didn't kill your old man.'

At the traffic lights, they stopped and looked at each other. Each one doubting the other's truth.

When the lights changed they continued in silence.

Twenty minutes later, they pulled up outside a large house in Billericay. Jake turned off the engine.

'Are you sure you want to do this?' Dara asked.

He nodded. 'I've been out of the game for a long time, by choice, but believe you me, right now is as good a time as any to get back into it . . . Come on, let's go and see this Angus, find out what he has to say.'

Chapter One Hundred and Twenty-Four

Jake and Dara banged on the front door of Angus's house. They waited for a couple of minutes.

When there was no answer, Jake looked around the affluent street, making sure the coast was clear. He reached into his coat, pulled a gun out of the inside pocket, and fired it at the lock, busting it open.

Angus was walking towards them from the kitchen, dressed in a silk paisley dressing gown and holding a cream cake in one hand, delicately poised above a bone china plate. He looked shocked as Jake bowled down the hallway.

'What the fuck? Who the fuck are you?' he screamed. 'Whoever you are, mate, you're making a big mistake . . .' He snarled at Jake, seemingly unconcerned by the gun in Jake's hand.

Angus clocked Dara, and for the briefest of moments, he was taken aback by her battered appearance. '*You.*' Somehow Angus managed to convey complete and utter contempt for Dara in that one word. 'I hope you're here to give me the money your old man owes me . . . Being dead ain't a reason not to pay your debts. Like the sweetest memories, they live on, darlin'.'

Jake poked Angus in his fleshy chest with the barrel of his gun. 'We're not here to pay you anything.'

'Then I suggest you stop playing Bonnie and Clyde, and get the fuck out of my house.'

'Be careful how you speak to me, mate.' Jake's tone was dangerously low. 'I haven't driven all the way here only for a fat cunt like you to talk shit in my ear. So listen up, and take some advice. You need to speak to me carefully, just like you need to answer carefully . . . I want to know *exactly* what you did to Archie.'

Angus stared at Dara, then back at Jake. 'What I did to him? What are you on about?'

'There's a lot of noise surrounding you. A lot of people heard you threatening to kill him.'

Right then, Angus had a light-bulb moment. He burst out laughing. 'You think I did it, don't you? I *wish* I had. I gave that fucker too many chances, and where's it got me? Out of fucking pocket, that's where. But too right, I wish I'd pumped that cunt full of lead.' Angus's face darkened. 'But I didn't, so now get out.'

Smiling, Jake rubbed his neck. 'You think I'm just going to take your word for it?'

'I don't care what you do.'

Jake stepped towards him. 'Then you're as stupid as you look, aren't you?' He jabbed Angus again in his chest with the gun.

Maybe it was the way Jake stared at him, but this time, Angus's colour began to drain from him.

'Look, what do you want?'

'I told you, I want the truth,' Jake said firmly. 'And I've got a feeling you won't tell me that, not unless you *really* have to.'

'What's that supposed to mean?'

Jake aimed the gun at Angus's kneecaps.

'Come on, mate, come off it. For fuck's sake, there's no need for that, is there?' Angus's words rolled out quickly. 'Okay, okay, I'll tell you what I'll do, I'll wipe the slate clean. How about that? She doesn't have to cough up the money. She doesn't have to pay me what her old man owed.'

'She was never going to pay you anyway, *mate*.' Jake shrugged as he continued to point the gun at Angus's knees.

'I swear I didn't do it.'

'I hear you, but let's see if you're really telling the truth, shall we?' And without hesitation, Jake pulled the trigger.

Bone and cartilage blasted everywhere.

Jake was splattered with blood. He wiped it off his face with his sleeve, and leant over Angus, watching him writhe in agony on the white marble floor. 'I'll ask you again, mate, were *you* the one to put a bullet in Archie's head?'

'No . . . no . . . I swear.' Angus thrashed around in a pool of his own blood.

Jake pulled a face, and pointed the gun at the other knee.

'I didn't . . . I didn't . . . *Please*, I didn't . . . I swear.'

Jake pulled back the trigger, resting the nozzle of the gun directly on Angus's kneecap this time. 'Are you *sure* about that? Because I don't want to leave here, and then find out you were lying to me, and have to drive all the way back here. Fuel's expensive, you know.' Jake grinned.

He was enjoying, even briefly, being back to his old ways. Life in the Cotswold countryside was lovely, but it didn't quite give the same buzz as kneecapping someone.

Angus was crying like a baby. 'You've got to believe me.'

Jake shrugged, and pulled the trigger again.

'*FUUUUUUUCCCCKKKKK!*' The scream from Angus filled the hallway.

'I'll ask you once more, did you do it?'

'*NO!*' It was a shriek of pain.

Jake leant down and wiped the gun on Angus's silk dressing gown, before replacing it in his inside pocket.

He stared at Dara as they walked out of the house.

'I've never known a grown man who didn't tell the truth when he was getting his knees blown off. I'm sorry to say it, doll, but I don't reckon Angus is your guy.'

As they walked towards the car, the dreadful realisation clamoured in Dara's head. It was looking more and more likely that *she* had been the one to pull the trigger.

The only question now was what to do about it. Should she run? Or should she stay and face the consequences?

Chapter One Hundred and Twenty-Five

Dara lay down on her bed. She was exhausted, not to mention scared.

Why the fuck couldn't she just bury her fear like she usually did? Like she'd done all her life?

She had to work out her next move. Should she pack up and get out today? She was supposed to surrender herself tomorrow at the police station. If she went now, maybe she could get to Ireland by the morning. She'd have to take Robbie with her. She couldn't leave him behind.

It would mean starting again. But that would be fine, wouldn't it? After all, it wouldn't be any harder than when she and Robbie had been teenagers, doing whatever it took to get by, going from one crappy job to another. Besides, for a long time, it had felt to Dara like she was drowning. She'd tried to leave Archie before, but whenever she thought about it, there was always something inside her holding her back. And then there was Robbie. But maybe now he'd come, if he saw she was desperate.

Going to Dublin could be her chance; not only to get away from the Old Bill, but also to reinvent herself. Her and Robbie, together. A new life. Perhaps she could ask Jake for money? She'd send it back to him when she could, but that would be one way of getting to Ireland quickly and easily. Yeah, maybe she'd call him later.

She sighed and yawned. Her eyes were beginning to close. It was strange coming back to the club. Everything in it felt dirty. The remaining evidence of a crime scene had been cleaned up, but the idea of strangers raking over her flat made Dara feel uncomfortable.

She was dozing off when she heard her phone ring. She reached for it without opening her eyes, and groaned as she knocked her mobile on to the floor. '*Fuck.*' She sat up sleepily, got off the bed, and knelt down unsteadily to pick it up.

The phone had skittered under the chest of drawers. Dara reached for it. Her fingers snagged something else, and she grabbed whatever it was at the same time as dragging out her phone.

'Hello?' She thought it might be Robbie, but she was distracted by the necklace tangled around her fingers. She frowned. It didn't make sense. Then she quickly brought her focus back to the call.

'Dara, it's Devon, you better come here quickly . . .'

Chapter One Hundred and Twenty-Six

'Where is she?'

Dara rushed through the grand doorway of Jake's manor house. It had taken just under a couple of hours to drive up from London.

'She's through there, in the front room. She's just been standing there for the past couple of hours.' Devon was worried.

Only now did Dara see how young he actually was. Gone was the bravado, the macho swagger, and in its place was a frightened young man.

'Where's your dad?'

'He's on his way, but he's stuck in traffic.'

'Okay, thanks . . . And Devon, it'll be fine. I'll make sure it's fine. But you stay here, all right?' Dara gave him a quick smile and hurried through to the opulent gold-and-cream lounge. Dara was shocked by what she saw but she didn't show it. 'Gracie . . . Hey, Gracie, it's good to see you, I've missed you . . . but I tell you what, why don't you put the gun down, yeah?'

'Dar.' Gracie wiped her tears away with one hand. With the other, she was pointing the gun at the woman Dara had seen at the hospital. 'Do you know who she is, Dar?'

Dara glanced back at Gracie. 'I think she's Jake's wife.'

'LOOK AGAIN!' Gracie screamed.

'Okay, okay, baby, I'm looking, I'm looking. I see her.' Dara tried not to sound puzzled.

Gracie spotted Dara's confusion. 'Look harder, Dar . . . *Look* at her . . . That's Samantha. That's the woman who said she was going to help me, but she left me in Holly Brookes, so she could take my baby.'

'It wasn't like that—' The woman spoke softly.

'SHUT UP.' Gracie stabbed the gun in the air.

Dara stared at Samantha. She could see she was terrified. 'I'd do as she says, if I were you.'

'She left me there, Dar. She left me there so they could hurt me. I shouldn't have been there, Dar, *none of us* should have been there.' Gracie sounded on the edge.

'I know, baby, I know . . . But what I need now is for you to put the gun down. Can you do that for me?'

Gracie shook her head. 'No, because she's not going to get away with it. *This bitch* didn't tell me my mum had died, she didn't tell me my godmother phoned her house, trying to get me back.'

'I didn't know.' Samantha was pleading now. 'Gracie, I didn't know. I thought about you *a lot*, and I *did* try. I tried to find out about you.'

'YOU SHOULD'VE TRIED HARDER.' Gracie was trembling. She turned to look at Dara. Her eyes were clouded with tears. 'They all left us there, didn't they? They all knew what was happening, but they left us there, because they thought we were nothing.'

'But they were wrong, Gracie, they were so wrong. We weren't nothing. None of us. We were warriors . . . survivors . . . Gracie, listen to me, I don't think she did it on purpose, did you, Samantha?'

'No, I swear, Gracie, I didn't know it was your baby. All I knew was, when I saw him, I couldn't let this beautiful child be any-where near the people they were going to give him to. I am so sorry, Gracie.'

'Gracie, she risked everything to give Devon a good life. Jake's told me all about it. She was saving him, darlin', not stealing him.'

'Saving him.' Gracie spoke to herself through her tears. She nodded, staring down at the floor. 'That's what I was trying to do.'

'What do you mean?' Dara asked gently.

'You saved everyone else, Dar, but who was going to save you? That's why I did it, Dar, but I've gone and made everything worse, haven't I?'

Dara wiped her face. 'Did what, Gracie. What did you do?' Her words were quiet and slow.

'I couldn't bear it, I couldn't stand it. The way he treated you, Dar. That night, you'd left so many messages on the phone for me, and even though I was angry, I couldn't stand hearing you in so much pain . . . So I came back, and you were drunk. I saw what he'd done to you, and I just wanted him to stop . . . I wanted Archie to stop hurting you.'

'What?' Dara covered her mouth.

'You had a gun on the table next to you, but you were so drunk, you'd fallen sleep. Archie was upstairs, so I took the gun. I went to tell him that he had to stop, but we got into a fight, and I could tell he wasn't *ever* going to stop hurting you, Dar. And you were *never* going to leave because of Robbie. But Archie was slowly kill-ing you, and I love you too much to let that happen . . . I had to put an end to it . . . So I shot him. It was me . . . But I was always going to confess, Dar, I was never going to let you take the blame. Everything just got out of hand.'

Silence filled the room.

It now made sense to Dara. That's why she'd found Gracie's

necklace under the chest of drawers in her room. Archie must have ripped it off her neck when he got into a fight with Gracie.

The wail of approaching sirens broke into Dara's thoughts. 'Who the fuck called the police?' Fear made her voice shrill.

'I did,' Gracie said. 'Just before you arrived.'

'Oh my God, what did you say to them? Gracie, what did you say?'

'I told them I was going to kill the woman who lives here as well.'

'Did you tell them your name?'

'Er . . .'

'Gracie, *THINK*, did you tell them your name?'

Gracie shook her head.

'Then give me the gun . . . Gracie, give me the gun. *Please*, just give it to me, baby.'

Tears rolled down Gracie's face. 'I'm so sorry, Dar. I was only trying to help.'

Dara's heart broke for Gracie, and she spoke quickly. 'No, baby, you don't need to be sorry . . . but I need you to give me the gun, so I can put this right. *Please*.'

Dara held her hand out. After a moment's hesitation, Gracie gave her the gun.

Dara held Gracie in a long embrace, then called out to Devon.

'Devon, quickly, take her out of here . . . Take her upstairs, take her anywhere, okay.'

Once Gracie was out of the room, Dara turned to Samantha. 'I know you ain't the bad guy here. But believe me, sweetheart, if you open your mouth about what really happened here, or anything you've heard, I'll come back and find you, and I'll finish off what Gracie started.'

Just then, a police marksman trained his red dot sight through the window on Dara's forehead.

'*Put the gun down.*'

Dara immediately threw it to one side.

'*Put your hands up, and get down on your knees.*'

Dara did just that.

Within seconds, a dozen police officers rushed in, kicked her forward on to her front, pulled her arms around behind her back and handcuffed her.

Chapter One Hundred and Twenty-Seven

Dara saw Gracie first. She raised her hand and smiled.

'Gracie, hey, Gracie, how are you? Thanks for coming . . .'

Gracie didn't look well, but Dara wasn't going to say anything. Jake and Robbie had been keeping her up to date on how Gracie was really getting on.

'I'm so sorry I'm late, the traffic was terrible.' Gracie sat down on the broken blue plastic chair, opposite Dara, at the small table.

She'd lost a lot of weight in the three weeks since Dara had last seen her. Jake had said that was due to the nausea caused by the chemo she was having.

'How are you getting on, Dar? What's it like in this place?'

Dara looked around the bleak prison visiting room. The empty drink-and-snack machine over in the corner was still giving out the same strange buzzing sound as last week. There was a loud hum of noise from the kids, and the chatter of family and friends. Saturdays were always busy here. Devon and Jake had visited her last weekend, as well as Robbie. She'd been so worried about him; it had kept her awake at night. It was the first time she hadn't been there for him since they were kids, but Jake had promised to keep an eye on him for her. It was the best she could hope for.

Dara plastered a smile on her face. 'This place, God, it's a fucking ball compared to Holly Brookes. I can do it standing on my head, so you don't have to worry about me. Anyway, how are you? How's the treatment going?'

'It's okay. It's a bit brutal, but Jake and Samantha, they're looking after me brilliantly. And Devon, he's great. He's a credit to them, Dar.' Gracie's eyes filled with tears. 'You know, I can't quite believe he's my son . . . I mean, he's *their* son too, but—' Gracie stopped. She shook her head. Would she ever get used to it. 'But I'm okay, Dar, and I saw Robbie last week. We had a coffee together.'

Dara was glad. She glanced towards the miserable prison officer, who was looking the other way, then she slid her hands across the table to hold on to Gracie's. With Gracie here, she could take on the world.

'When's your plea hearing?' Gracie asked.

'Next month. The twenty-first of June, apparently. Midsummer's Day.' Dara grinned. 'You will come, won't you?'

'Of course, but . . .' Gracie was thoughtful. 'But I've been thinking about it, Dar, and I think I should tell them it was me. Let them know the truth.'

Dara was horrified. 'Keep your voice down! And no, Gracie, no bloody way, that's crazy, you can't do that.'

'It's the right thing to do. I can't have you in here, and me out there. You don't deserve this.'

'And neither do you. Are you listening to me, Gracie Perry? You keep your mouth shut.'

'But I've got nothing to lose, I'm the one who's dying, Dar—'

'Don't say that, *please* don't say that.'

'But it's true . . . and you've got your whole life ahead of you, Dar.'

'What are you talking about, Gracie?' It was Dara now who started to cry. 'You've got a chance to be with your son, to be the mother you should've always been. Gracie, you need to be with Devon for every precious moment you can.'

'But you are going to plead not guilty, aren't you?' Gracie looked afraid.

'Oh my God, of course, what do you take me for? My solicitor said the Old Bill had lost some evidence. You know, about finding my prints on the gun in the club, they've messed up, so it's looking good already.'

'What about what happened at Jake's house . . . with Samantha? No one's telling me anything, Dar.'

Once again, Dara tried to plaster on a smile. 'They're not pressing charges for the gun incident at Samantha's. She didn't give a statement, and luckily for me, it seems the gun you had, well, Jeremy is not only a boring fucker, but he's good at paperwork. It was all licensed and up to date.' She laughed, trying to make light of it all. 'So stop worrying.'

'It's hard not to.'

'Listen to me. Jake has given me the best brief, so all you need to do is concentrate on getting the treatment you need, all right?' This time, Dara was able to give Gracie a genuine smile. 'I love you, Gracie.'

'I love you too, Dar.'

'Birds of a feather . . .'

'. . . stick together.'

Chapter One Hundred and Twenty-Eight

21st June
Midsummer's Day

'. . . Ms Tailor, the court has asked you several times now. How do you plead? I need an answer, otherwise I will hold you in contempt of court.'

The judge's voice broke through Dara's memories, bringing her back into the moment. She blinked, and from the dock she looked up at Gracie. She was pale; the colour had drained from her face. But Dara was pleased to see Jake and Devon and Robbie with her. And in the row behind sat Samantha.

Once again, Dara held her Gracie's wide, frightened stare with hers. She loved her so much.

'Ms Tailor, you *need* to answer. What is your plea?'

Dara smiled at Gracie, then turned to the judge.

'Guilty.'

Gracie jumped up, screaming, 'No, Dar, no . . . *Dar, no!* Dara, what are you doing?'

Dara saw Gracie fall into Jake's arms.

'Take the defendant down,' the judge ordered. 'And silence in the gallery.'

'No . . . Dar, no!' Gracie ignored the judge and clung on to the railing, looking down at Dara.

Dara put her hands out to be cuffed by the officer. She stepped out of the dock, smiling up at Gracie.

'Gracie, it's fine,' she mouthed. 'It's all going to be fine.'

'You've got five minutes.'

Down in the holding cell, the court jailer opened the door, letting Gracie and Robbie in to see Dara. They were closely followed by Jake, Samantha and Devon.

Gracie ran up to Dara and gave her a hug.

'Dar, why did you plead guilty?' She was shaking. 'You told me it was going to be all right.'

Dara was calm. 'It *is*.'

Gracie shook her head and turned to look at the others. 'Did you know . . . did you know how she was going to plead? Robbie, did you?'

'No.' Dara lied to Gracie, but she figured some lies hurt less than the truth. 'No, it was my decision.'

'But I was the one who did it. *Me*, not you, Dar. You shouldn't be the one going to prison.'

'Gracie, don't you understand? I want you to spend the time you've got left with your son. I took him away from you once, and I'm not going to do that again.'

Gracie was panicking. 'But what about the evidence you said the police had lost? You told me they'd lost some evidence, remember?'

Dara shook her head sadly. 'That wasn't true, Gracie, but I couldn't let you go and confess. Right now, the Old Bill are happy they've got someone. There's no reason for them to look for *anyone else*. My prints were on the gun, I was at the scene, they're happy

580

with that, so let's leave it as it is. *Please*, Gracie, spend the time with your boy.'

'But I wanted to save you, Dar, not see you put in prison.'

Dara smiled, at ease with the decision she'd made. 'You did save me, Gracie. Your friendship saved me from myself.'

Dara walked up to Robbie and took his face in her hands. 'You promise to keep yourself safe?'

Tears welled up in Robbie's eyes. 'Of course . . . I love you, Dar.'

'I love you too.'

Gracie moved closer, and Dara put her arms around both of them. They clung to each other. Dara, Robbie and Gracie. The three of them together once again.

Book Six

2009

In thy face I see the map of honour, truth and loyalty.

William Shakespeare, *Henry VI*,
Act III, Scene i

Chapter One Hundred and Twenty-Nine

'Can you see it yet?'

In a smart terraced house in Leamington Spa, Becky Langtree shouted up into the loft. She'd sent her husband up there to rummage through the piles of boxes full of things they never used but might one day need. For the past twenty or more years, they'd carted dozens of boxes from one house to another.

She would've looked in the loft herself, but she didn't want to start climbing ladders at eight months pregnant, especially as she'd ballooned to the size of a small cow. And besides, her friend Yvonne had been injured in a nasty fall when she'd been painting her bathroom recently. She'd only fallen off a stepladder but had still ended up with two metal pins in her ankle. No, until the baby came, Becky decided her feet were going to be firmly on the ground.

She smiled happily, and touched her huge belly. 'What are you doing up there, Larry?'

'I'm doing what you asked me to do.'

'You sure you ain't having a sneaky fag?' Becky grinned.

She heard him laugh. He'd been trying to give up the cigarettes for a while, but she kept finding him having a sneaky puff.

'No, but that's not a bad idea,' Larry called back good-humouredly. 'Look, are you sure you need these cookbooks?'

'You know my mum loves using them.'

'Well, it's a shame they haven't done anything to improve her actual cooking.' Larry laughed again, staring at the dozens of boxes he still needed to go through. Sighing, he grabbed the top box on the largest pile, opened the lid and saw it was full of the summer sandals Becky couldn't find last year.

He pulled the next one down, blowing the dust off the top, before opening it up. It was full of sheets of coloured paper. Then he remembered: a few years ago, Becky had decided she wanted to take up origami after seeing a display at the museum. That had lasted all of a couple of months.

He put the box back and reached for the next one. He opened it and started to rummage through the contents.

He froze and stared.

'Larry, Larry, are you all right?' Becky called from the landing.

He grabbed the box, putting it under his arm, and hurried back down the ladder with it.

'What is it? What's the matter? Oh my God, don't tell me that rat's back?'

'No . . . it isn't that.' He placed the box on the floor, crouching next to it. 'Do you remember the box Jimmy's mum gave us?'

Becky felt sad to think about Mandy and her loss, but she nodded. 'Yeah, neither of us could bear to go through it, we were that gutted.'

Even now, after all these years, she remembered the pain of hearing that their mutual friend Jimmy was dead.

'Well, this is the box . . .' Larry swallowed hard. 'And do you remember, the last time he got in contact, Jimmy was all excited about having found something? He couldn't wait to tell us all about it—'

'Yeah, I do, and I remember listening to the message he left.

I thought he was a big fat liar!' She laughed warmly. 'Jimmy told so many porkies.'

Larry nodded. 'But I think, this time, he was actually telling the truth . . . Look.'

Becky watched Larry pick something out of the box.

It was a bone.

'He said they'd found a human bone . . . and I think he was right.'

Chapter One Hundred and Thirty

Chief Inspector Lewis stared at the photographs on his desk.

The net was closing in. But he wouldn't be anyone's catch.

According to Reenie's note, these were copies of the photographs she had. There was no explanation of how they had come into her possession.

He hadn't seen them before, though he recognised a lot of the men in the photos. They dated from years ago, showing Dennis when he must have been around thirty years old. He also recognised the young boy, eight years old, looking terrified. He knew who the boy was. He knew his name. And as Lewis drank back another glass of whiskey, he continued to stare at himself in the photograph. And at the little boy. Eight years old. Groomed and used by Dennis.

Getting up, he walked into the en-suite bathroom adjoining his office.

He threw the sheet over the pipe running along the ceiling. He stood on the toilet, and tightened the knot, before placing the loop over his head and around his neck.

Then he closed his eyes and stepped off the toilet.

The noose tightened around his neck.

Lewis's body twitched violently.

Then it stopped and hung lifelessly.

His eyes remained open, bulging painfully, and the tip of his tongue stuck out, dripping with blood, clamped in a steely grip between his teeth.

Chapter One Hundred and Thirty-One

Dara looked up to the sky as she walked out of the prison.

She exhaled in the fresh air. It had been two long years, though it could've been much worse. Mr Marshall had fought her corner and the murder charge had been reduced to manslaughter. She'd got five years, but with good behaviour, they'd let her out in two.

'You all right, babe?' Devon smiled at her as he greeted Dara at the gate.

She took a gulp of freedom. 'Yeah, I am. Well, I am now.' She looked towards Devon's car. 'Where's Robbie?'

There was a beat before he answered. 'No one's seen him.'

'What the hell are you talking about? How can you not have seen him? You said you were looking after him for me.'

'We have been, Dara, you know we have. But he's a grown man, and let's face it, he's an addict.'

'Don't give me that.' Prison didn't seem like it had mellowed Dara's protective streak when it came to Robbie. 'I managed to look after him for years, and still keep tabs on him,' Dara snapped. In her heart, she knew Devon was right, but the fear and worry she felt rubbed out any sort of reason.

'Like I said, he's a grown man, Dara, he does what he wants.'

'What about the club? Hasn't he been in there?'

'No, I would've known. I've been there most of this week, and

Dad was there the week before. We haven't seen him since the last time he visited you.'

'But that was *three* weeks ago.' This wasn't how Dara had pictured leaving prison.

'I know, and I've been asking around as well. And the girls have been keeping their eyes out too, especially Sharon. I'm sure it'll be fine; he's gone AWOL before, you know he has.'

Dara tried not to sound disappointed. 'But he knew I was coming out today, he knew how much I wanted to see him.'

Devon regarded her sadly. 'Dara, he ain't reliable. Call it how it is.'

She didn't want to hear it. 'Have you been to Buddy's?'

Buddy's was a crack house Robbie often frequented. Over the years, Dara had done her fair share of rescue missions, pulling Robbie out of there.

'Yeah, we have . . . Dara, I swear we've been looking.'

'*When* though? When did you go?'

'A few days ago.'

Dara stopped herself going into a rant. 'I'm sorry. I appreciate everything you've done.'

She gave him a hug and he squeezed her back lovingly.

'My pleasure, babe . . . and look, I'll help you find him.'

Dara nodded. 'Thank you . . . and thanks for picking me up today.'

Apart from Gracie, who she'd spoken to frequently, Robbie had been the first and last person on Dara's mind, every morning and every night. Two years banged up would've been the easiest twenty-four months, had she not been worried sick about him. Dara knew allowing Gracie to have time with Devon had been the right thing to do, but it had meant she couldn't be there for Robbie.

'Come on, let's go. Let's see if we can find him, shall we?' Devon winked at her, leading her to the car.

Without bothering to look back at the prison, Dara got in.

It was a couple of hours later when Dara finished checking the rooms of the third crack house she'd been in. The place was hot and squalid. A young couple lay smacked up on a dirty, blood- and shit-stained mattress on the floor. Dara had to step over a pool of vomit by the door. She pulled her top up over her nose as she passed the bathroom, trying to ignore the sight of the broken toilet covered in diarrhoea. It stank.

The usual faces were about, most of them completely out of it, but a few were coherent enough to speak. But like Devon, they hadn't seen Robbie either.

Dara walked back down the stairs. Her heart dropped as a tiny child in a soggy nappy played by its mother's side; the woman was asleep on the bare floorboards next to a burnt-out crack pipe.

Dara walked through Soho. In the distance, she saw one of the hookers Robbie sometimes hung around with, tottering somewhat unsteadily.

'Tasmin!' Dara shouted. 'Tas!'

The girl turned round. She was a teenage meth addict, and her face was covered in scabs and the lines of hard living. For a moment, Dara thought the girl was going to do a runner, but she waited for Dara to catch up with her.

'Hey, Tas, you all right?'

Chewing a piece of gum, Tasmin shrugged. Her eyes darted everywhere. Dara could see she was clucking. 'Yeah, I'm fine, what do you want? Actually, you ain't got a fiver on you, have you, Dara?'

'No, sorry.'

Tasmin sniffed. 'Suit yourself . . . Look, I have to go.' She was on a mission.

'Wait . . . Have you seen Robbie?'

'Rob?' Tasmin seemed confused. 'I'm not likely to see him, am I?'

Dara frowned. 'What do you mean?'

'He overdosed. Two weeks ago.'

Dara could hardly speak. 'Where is he? Is he in rehab?'

'No. He's dead . . .' Tasmin was matter-of-fact. 'Look, I've got to go.'

Dara could barely grasp what Tasmin had said . . . *Not Robbie. No.* That wasn't possible. She stood staring down at the pavement, her mind in freefall.

She wasn't sure how long she'd been standing there before she heard a voice behind her.

'Dara?' It was Devon. 'I've checked with Molly, she hasn't seen him . . . Wait, what's happened?'

'He's gone.' Dara couldn't look at him.

'Gone, gone where?'

It was then Dara turned to look at him. She didn't want to say the words.

When Devon saw the look in her eyes, he understood.

'Oh, holy shit, I'm so sorry . . . *Fuck*.' He was visibly upset himself.

'Take me to Gracie.'

Devon nodded.

An hour later, they pulled up on Blackshaw Road. Devon reached behind him to the back passenger seat. 'I got you the flowers you asked for.'

'Thanks, babe. I'll be back in a minute.'

593

'No worries, take as long as you want . . . And I'm so sorry about Robbie. I know it'll take time to get your head around it. But I'm here for you, we all are.'

Dara gave a small nod, took the flowers from Devon and got out of the car. She opened a metal gate and walked down the gravelled path until she came to a stop by a large oak tree.

'Hey, babe, they finally let me out. But I really needed to come and talk to you . . . Robbie's gone, Gracie, he's left me, and I don't know what to do, I don't know how to feel. I just needed him to give me a couple more weeks. Why couldn't he have waited for me?'

Dara let the tears fall, then she took a deep breath. She kissed her fingers and touched Gracie's headstone, laying the white roses – Gracie's favourite – on her grave. Gracie had wanted to be buried next to her mum and dad in Lambeth Cemetery, which Jake and Samantha had been able to arrange.

Dara looked around at the rows of graves. Gracie had been a fighter, battling to the very end, making the most of every day with Devon. The two friends had spoken most days; Dara had managed to stash a mobile phone under her mattress in her cell. The only time she hadn't spoken to Gracie was at the very end, when she'd been taken to a hospice.

Even though Dara hadn't been allowed out to see her, she'd taken solace from the knowledge that Gracie had died with her son holding her hand. Jake and Samantha had been at her bedside, and even Robbie. Life was truly a circle.

They'd let her out for Gracie's funeral, two months ago, but she'd been chained to a prison officer. This was her first time alone with Gracie.

'You look after him for me, won't you, Gracie? You look after Robbie.'

She sat down cross-legged, and read the inscription on the gravestone.

> In loving memory of
> Gracie Perry
> Friend, daughter, mother
> Safe from harm
> Sleep in eternal peace

Epilogue

Three months later

It is never too late to be what you might have been.

George Eliot

Chapter One Hundred and Thirty-Two

'. . . *Sweeping arrests have started throughout the capital, con-nected with the ongoing investigation into Holly Brookes children's home. It has been reported that hundreds of children over the course of several decades were targeted by paedophiles working at the council-run home, after authorities failed to investigate any alle-gations at the time. Police believe the ring was part of a wider network.*

Reenie Alcroft, a survivor of Holly Brookes, spoke of her relief. She said in her statement that, while nothing could give back the stolen childhoods, seeing some of the people who were involved being brought to justice was some small comfort for the victims.

Reports are coming in that eighty-five-year-old Lord Hargreaves and the Labour mayoral candidate Alan Carver are among those who have been arrested, and are currently being questioned. A spe-cial unit has been set up at Marylebone Police Station.

An excavation is ongoing at a site along the Embankment, which was formerly a children's home, after the police received a call from a member of the public, reporting the finding of a bone from a child's skeleton. The police excavation is believed to be connected with the Holly Brookes investigation . . .

Dara turned the radio off. She didn't need to listen to that. Reenie had already updated her. She'd give her a call later to find out what was happening and check she was all right. Reenie had set up a survivors' association for a lot of the kids she'd been with in Holly Brookes.

Dara sighed and turned her thoughts elsewhere, and then she smiled to herself. Devon, Jake and Samantha were due to visit next week. She was excited to show them her new home—

Her thoughts were interrupted by a loud knock on the door. Dara frowned. She wasn't expecting anyone.

Since moving into Gracie's bungalow a couple of months ago, she'd had a constant stream of visits from various neighbours, bringing her home-baked cakes and nourishing stews.

They were probably looking for gossip – eager to see if Dara really was this crazed killer they'd read about in the tabloids. Although she couldn't complain, everyone had been lovely to her, even the local vicar had knocked on the door bringing her home-made scones. It was the first time that Dara had been part of a community that truly welcomed her.

Life was quiet here, but being in Gracie's home – which she'd left to Dara in her will – was comforting. She could feel Gracie all around her. It was a happy place. Peaceful. Jeremy had even come around with his sister, Tracey, to see how she was settling in.

Dara was acutely aware that not everyone was as lucky as her. She never forgot that Holly Brookes had taken and broken so many lives. It had destroyed futures and, as Reenie had said, stolen childhoods.

There was another hard knock on the door.

'I'm coming, all right!'

She hurried along the hallway, hoping she hadn't forgotten a meeting of the Women's Institute. She gave a throaty chuckle. How had she allowed herself to be roped into the WI?

She flung open the door.

A stranger stood on the doorstep. A tall, suntanned man, with short hair and glasses.

'Dara? Dara Tailor?'

'Yeah. That's right.' She stared at him.

'Dara, it's me . . . Tommy.'

Dara felt her knees give way.

'Tommy?' It was a breathless whisper. 'Tommy? Oh my God.' She reached for her little brother's face, touching it, staring into his eyes. 'Is it really you?' Shaking, Dara wept uncontrollably.

He took her and held her in his arms.

'I'm sorry. I'm so sorry, Tommy . . . I'm so sorry I couldn't stop them.'

'Hey, it's okay, Dar, you didn't do anything wrong . . . and I'm here now.'

There were so many questions she needed to ask him, but for now, all she wanted to do was stand here forever.

Eventually, Tommy pulled away.

She looked up into his face. 'How . . . how did you find me?'

'I didn't, really. Your friend Gracie found me.' He smiled at Dara. 'She tracked me down, but I was living abroad, so I never got to meet her. But she sounded amazing . . . She asked me to give you this, the moment I saw you. She sent it to me, but she wanted me to hand it over in person.'

Tommy reached into his navy backpack, and pulled out a small package. He gave it to Dara, and she opened it on the doorstep.

It was a wooden music box and when she opened the lid, it played the tune Gracie used to sing to her. She caught her breath, and then she noticed there was a folded piece of paper inside. She took it out, handing the music box to Tommy to hold.

Trembling, she unfolded it.

The letter was in Gracie's handwriting.

601

My darling Dar,

Through the darkest times you were my light, and I know one day we'll meet again. Because of you, I laughed more and cried less. I found courage when I didn't know there was any to find.

Not only did you save me, but you saved my son and enabled me to be with him at the end. You gave me hope, you gave me love, you gave me friendship, and you gave me the most precious gift of all, you gave me your loyalty . . .

IT'S IN THE BLOOD

Discover more about The Queen of Crime . . .

MARTINA COLE's love of reading began when she was a child and she used to bunk off school to go and read in the park. Despite being expelled from school – twice – before leaving for good at 15, Martina was always writing stories, usually Mills & Boon style romances for her neighbours in exchange for cigarettes. She was in her early twenties when she started working on the manuscript of what would become her debut novel *Dangerous Lady*. But she didn't do anything with it for almost a decade.

She chose her agent for his name – Darley Anderson – and sent him the manuscript, thinking he was a woman. That was on a Friday. On Monday night, she was doing the vacuuming when she took the call: a man's voice said 'Martina Cole, you are going to be a big star'.

'MARTINA COLE, YOU ARE GOING TO BE A BIG STAR'

The rest is history: *Dangerous Lady* caused a sensation when it was published and launched one of the bestselling fiction writers of her generation. Martina Cole is now the critically acclaimed author of 26 novels, which have collectively spent over 4 years in the bestseller charts. Her books have sold over

17 million copies, making her Britain's bestselling female crime writer and *The Faithless* made her the first British female adult audience novelist to break the £50 million sales mark since Nielsen Bookscan records began. Her books have been translated into 31 languages and adapted for multiple stage plays and television series.

Martina is a passionate advocate for prisoner rehabilitation and visits prisons to give writing classes. She often quips to her classes: 'there's one thing you've got that all writers want – time' and she believes that we should 'send them out better people than when they went in'. It's therefore no surprise her books are the most requested in prison libraries, and the most stolen from bookshops!

Martina has her own film and TV production company and is keen to improve women's representation in TV, film and her books: 'I want people to remember my women'.

'I WANT PEOPLE TO REMEMBER MY WOMEN'

Her unique, powerful storytelling is acclaimed for its hard-hitting, true-to-life style – there is no one else who writes like Martina Cole.

DID YOU KNOW...

- One of Martina's most treasured possessions is a Wurlitzer jukebox from the fifties that she bought in East London. She is an avid music fan and her favourite artists include David Bowie, Jimi Hendricks and Janice Joplin. She also has a pug called Blondie!

- Martina was a punk rocker in the early seventies and loved going to gigs in Camden.

- Martina particularly likes the song 'Wish You Were Here' by Pink Floyd as it was playing in the background when she received the call about her first book deal.

- Martina still has the same agent and publisher as she did 32 years ago.

- When Martina was little, she wanted to be a librarian. As a child she absolutely loved reading – she secretly signed her mum and dad up to the library and borrowed books in their names – and even now she reads two or three books a week.

- Martina has her own library within her Tudor mansion with over 1,000 books and she likes to collect first editions of her favourites.

- Although she was expelled from her convent school for reading *The Carpetbaggers* by Harold Robbins ('They were nuns, how did they know what was in it?!'), Martina was inspired to write by her English teacher, Mrs Jones.

- Martina gets her love of books from her dad who particularly loved Greek mythology. He was a merchant seaman, away on the boats for long stretches and he'd come back for Christmas and bring the books that were big in America at the time.

- Her mum was a psychiatric nurse and had her hands full with Martina and her four siblings. Martina gets her love of film from her mum.

- Martina is a self-confessed fan of bad boys and her first boyfriend was a bank robber. He was really handsome and he had a Jag. She has been married twice but now prefers her independence, claiming 'I like a man, I just couldn't eat a whole one'.

- Roman Catholicism was important in Martina's upbringing and she has a large collection of rosaries, including one which dates back to the Middle Ages.

- As a young, single mum, Martina would sleep on the kitchen floor of her council flat so that her son could have the only bed.

- Martina is a West Ham United fan and attended the last game played at the Boleyn ground.

- Martina has a second home in Cyprus and spends several months of the year living there. She also owns bookshops there in Kakakum and Alsancak.

Bonus Content

Jacqui Rose shares her all-time favourite Martina Cole book . . .

I still remember how I felt, all those years ago, when I first read Martina Cole's *The Ladykiller*. The intimacy of her writing was so vivid and authentic, I was immediately transported to the chilling and gritty world of the Grantley Ripper, the warped serial killer who stalked the streets. Cleverly intertwined in this gripping thriller was the story of a flawed, relatable heroine, Kate Burrows. Martina took me into the heart of the families and their relationships, and I saw the world through their eyes. It was a raw, powerful and emotionally charged experience, and I'd never read anything like it before. The moment I finished *The Ladykiller*, I read it again from start to finish and, to this day, it remains one of my all-time favourite books.

Other readers will, of course, have their own favourite Martina Cole novel from her huge and exciting body of work; perhaps it is the tense and moving story of a missing child in *The Know*, or the twists and turns of *Two Women*, which explores unbreakable bonds in a dangerous and violent world, or there's *Dangerous Lady*, Martina's first book, which changed the landscape of the crime-writing world forever. With so much choice for readers these days, it's easy to forget that before Martina started writing, books like hers just didn't exist. She single-handedly created a new, gritty and powerful crime genre. A phenomenal achievement. And not only has

Martina gone on to sell millions of books and break records, but she has also inspired authors like myself to write. I can honestly say, if it wasn't for Martina, I would never have put pen to paper.

When I was reading *The Ladykiller* thirty years ago, I could never have imagined that one day I'd be collaborating with her. For me, it's what dreams are made of, and I'm honoured to have this wonderful opportunity, because there are authors, and then there is Martina Cole.

Jacqui Rose, 2024

All families have their secrets . . .

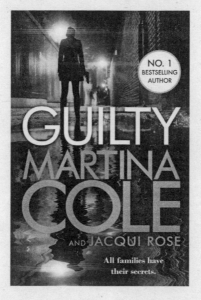

The heart-stopping new novel from Martina Cole

Coming October 2024

Available to order now

Have you read every Martina Cole book?
Time to show your loyalty . . .

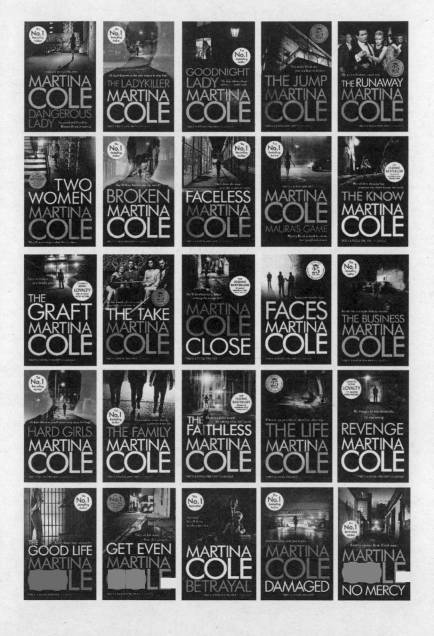

For updates, keep your
eye on Martina's Facebook page

f **/OfficialMartinaCole**

Sign up to her newsletter
for exclusive content and early access

www.martinacole.co.uk/newsletter

Explore Martina's website for more about the
Queen of Crime

www.martinacole.co.uk